THE ANATOMY OF
MURDER

Other Detection Club titles:

THE FLOATING ADMIRAL
ASK A POLICEMAN
SIX AGAINST THE YARD
THE DETECTION COLLECTION
THE SINKING ADMIRAL
THE GOLDEN AGE OF MURDER

THE ANATOMY OF MURDER

Famous crimes critically considered by members of the Detection Club

HELEN SIMPSON   JOHN RHODE
MARGARET COLE   E. R. PUNSHON
DOROTHY L. SAYERS   FRANCIS ILES
FREEMAN WILLS CROFTS

★

COLLINS
CRIME
CLUB

COLLINS CRIME CLUB
An imprint of HarperCollins*Publishers*
1 London Bridge Street
London SE1 9GF

HarperCollins*Publishers*
Macken House, 39/40 Mayor Street Upper,
Dublin 1, D01 C9W8, Ireland

www.harpercollins.co.uk

This paperback edition 2019

First published in Great Britain by
John Lane, The Bodley Head 1936

Copyright © The Detection Club 1936

ISBN 978-0-00-828319-3

Printed and bound in the UK using 100%
Renewable Electricity at CPI Group (UK) Ltd

MIX
Paper | Supporting
responsible forestry
FSC™ C007454

This book is produced from independently certified FSC™
paper to ensure responsible forest management .
For more information visit: www.harpercollins.co.uk/green

INTRODUCTION
By Martin Edwards

THE DETECTION CLUB was established in 1930 thanks to the initiative and drive of Anthony Berkeley, who wanted to create a social network of the leading detective novelists of the day. Berkeley was fascinated by criminology, as were many of his colleagues, and discussion about real life murder cases was a feature of Detection Club meetings. The prospect of playing detective themselves enthralled Club members, and they loved to discover and debate new angles on famous crimes, whether or not they had officially been "solved".

The Club funded its dinners, and the cost of renting premises at 31 Gerrard Street, Soho, through ventures such as the "round-robin" mysteries *Behind the Screen* and *The Scoop*, and the collectively produced novels *The Floating Admiral* and *Ask a Policeman*. The Club's leading lights were restless innovators in their fiction, and they liked to avoid repeating themselves. Given their shared interest in true crime (one illustration among many is the fact that the macabre Crumbles bungalow murder of 1924 provided raw material for *The Scoop*), it was almost inevitable that they should decided to put together a book of essays about intriguing cases. The highly successful result was *The Anatomy of Murder*, published in 1936.

Nobody is named as editor of the book, but it seems that Helen Simpson took on the job of liaising with the publishers and collating the essays, as well as writing one herself. The short Foreword reflects an ambitious approach characteristic of the Club's projects. The writers were not content simply to recount the facts of their cases. They aimed to add value by including new information, making use of modern investigative techniques, or by seeking to examine the psychology of the characters in the story.

In "Death of Henry Kinder", Simpson re-examined a nineteenth century case in which "the assassin had at one time some notion of dressing the part, and purchased a red Crimean shirt, on which bloodstains would not be conspicuous; but the crime itself was committed . . . in the ordinary sombre undress of a dentist." Kinder lived in Sydney, and the essay begins with a short discussion about crime in Australia. Helen de Guerry Simpson was herself born in Sydney in 1897, 32 years after Kinder met his end. Her father was a solicitor, her grandfather a French marquis, and after her parents separated, she and her mother moved to Europe. She attended Oxford University, and was a co-founder of the Oxford Women's Dramatic Society, but was sent down for breaking university rules which banned male and female students from acting together. She became a prolific author, producing poetry, plays, translations and short stories as well as novels such as *Acquittal*, and contributed dialogue to Hitchcock's film *Sabotage*. In 1927 she married fellow Australian Denis Browne, a surgeon whose uncle wrote *Robbery under Arms*, using the pen-name Rolf Boldrewood, name-checked in the first sentence of "Death of Henry Kinder".

Simpson's major contribution to detective fiction was the three books she co-wrote with Clemence Dane, also a Detection Club member. The first, *Enter Sir John*, was filmed by Alfred Hitchcock as *Murder!* Writing solo, she produced in 1931 an unusual and eccentric crime novel, *Vantage Striker* (re-titled *The Prime Minister is Dead* when published in the US), and achieved both commercial success and literary acclaim with her non-criminous novel *Boomerang* in 1932. *Sarabande for Dead Lovers* and *Under Capricorn* were filmed, the former by Ealing Studios and the latter by Hitchcock. Simpson's talents and interests were extraordinarily wide-ranging, and included riding, music, cooking and collecting antiques. She was adopted as Liberal Parliamentary candidate for the Isle of Wight in 1938, but cancer cut her life short, much to the distress of her close friend, Dorothy L. Sayers, who said, "I have never met anybody who equalled her in vivid personality and in the intense interest she brought into her contacts with people and things".

Just as an essay about a killing in the Antipodes opened the book, so "A New Zealand Tragedy" by Freeman Wills Crofts closed it. Freeman Wills Crofts (1879–1957) was an Irish-born railway engineer who beguiled a long illness by writing a detective novel. *The Cask*, which appeared in 1920, made much more of a splash than Agatha Christie's debut novel, published at about the same time, and launched a long career. Crofts' speciality was meticulous investigation, and his principal detective, Inspector French, was unequalled in the art of dismantling seemingly unbreakable alibis. Crofts' mastery of detail equipped him perfectly for the analysis of real life crime, and he took as his subject the Lakey murder case of 1933. The key elements of the story are worthy of Inspector French: "detective work of an extremely high order, involving persevering research, precise observation and deduction, magnificent team work and the use of the latest scientific methods." Crofts' concludes his account with the observation that: "Real life stories have an atmosphere of sordidness and evil which is happily absent from almost all detective novels." Suffice to say that times and tastes in fiction have changed a good deal since those words were written.

The Kinder and Lakey cases are today little discussed, but the second essay in the book—which again has a connection with Sydney— tackled a murder that ranks as a classic, and was explored in Kate Summerscale's *The Suspicions of Mr Whicher*, a best-seller which has spawned a television series. John Rhode, another good friend of Sayers, was ideally qualified to write "Constance Kent", as he had previously been responsible for *The Case of Constance Kent*, an entry in the *Famous Trials* series. Rhode's real name was Cecil John Street (1884–1965) and after a varied career encompassing distinguished service in the army, working as an electrical engineer, and writing non-fiction books about international affairs, he turned to detective fiction with aplomb, producing well in excess of one hundred novels, many of them featuring the irascible armchair detective Dr. Priestley.

Months after his book about Constance Kent appeared, Rhode received an anonymous letter from Sydney, challenging some of his statements about the case. He believed it had been written by Constance herself, but a handwriting "expert" disagreed. Not until further research took place in the Seventies was Rhode's theory vindicated. "The Sydney document" helped to shape Rhode's essay in *The Anatomy of Murder*, as he explored Constance's "elusive personality". Here he shows rather more interest in criminal psychology than he did in many of his novels, where the emphasis is on ingenious methods of murder—howdunit, rather than whydunit. Rhode donated the original letter to the Detection Club's library, although depressingly this unique item of criminal history, like the Club's Minute Book, seems to have gone astray during the Second World War, and has never turned up since.

The Constance Kent case so intrigued Sayers that she indulged in some private sleuthing of her own, annotating her copy of Rhode's book about the trial with her thoughts on aspects of the mystery. When Rhode discussed the "nerve" of the murderer, she referred back to the case that inspired *The Scoop*, pointing out that Patrick Mahon invited a woman back to the bungalow where he had killed Emily Kaye the night before, and slept with her there, with his victim's corpse in the next room.

Margaret Cole (1893–1980) tackled an equally celebrated Victorian mystery, "The Case of Adelaide Bartlett", concerning a woman whose husband died of chloroform poisoning after the couple had become involved in a *ménage-a-trois* with a vicar. The essay appeared under Margaret's name alone, although all her detective novels appeared as joint productions with her husband Douglas, better known as the left-wing economist G.D.H. Cole, and also a founder member of the Detection Club. By the mid-Thirties, Douglas was in poor health, and although he continued to write with feverish productivity, his wife came to take a much greater interest in the Detection Club than he did. Margaret was a feisty radical, whose views on politics and society were very different from Sayers—who, along with Anthony Berkeley, was the prime mover of the Club's activities—but she enjoyed the social side of their get-togethers. She also shared with Douglas a fondness and admiration for G.K. Chesterton, first President of the Detection Club, who died a few weeks before *The Anatomy of Murder* was published.

Margaret Cole's contribution to this book was her most significant venture into the field of true crime, but the Bartlett mystery has exerted a lasting appeal for detective novelists. The ingredients of sex, death and a puzzle are irresistible, and Hitchcock thought about turning the story into a film, Raymond Chandler said the events in the case were "relatively simple to tell, but completely goofy", and in 1980, one of Chesterton's successors as Club President, Julian Symons, factionalised the story in *Sweet Adelaide*, a novel offering a clever explanation of the conundrum at the heart of the case.

Ernest Robertson Punshon (1872–1956) was perhaps the least renowned contributor to *The Anatomy of Murder*, both at the time of publication and today, yet he was a talented writer who finally hit his stride in his sixties after a long literary apprenticeship. In his fifteenth novel, *Information Received*, published in 1934, he introduced the young police constable Bobby Owen, and Owen progressed up the ranks in a long series of books which often articulated distinctive and radical views on politics and society. "Business as Usual: an Impression of the Landru case" considers the criminal career of Henri Landru, a serial killer convicted of eleven murders. The essay is adorned with touches that illustrate why Sayers—a discerning but often acerbic critic—used to enthuse about his writing. An encomium from her review of *Information Received* adorned the covers of many of Punshon's later books, and although there is something of the curate's egg about Punshon's work, at his best he was, as Sayers insisted, a writer of distinction.

Sayers' interest in true crime is apparent in several of her novels, above all in *The Documents in the Case*, published in 1930, and written in collaboration with another Detection Club member, Robert Eustace. The story is influenced by the controversial case of Edith Thompson and Frederick Bywaters, lovers who were tried for the murder of Thompson's husband. Nowadays, the hanging of Edith Thompson is widely regarded as a miscarriage of justice, but Sayers lacked sympathy for Edith, and helps to explain why the characterisation in the book is not of the same high standard as the scientific concept underpinning the mystery and the epistolary style which Sayers adapted from a novelist whom she much admired, Wilkie Collins. In "The Murder of Julia Wallace", however, Sayers showed much deeper understanding of the central character in the drama, an insurance agent accused of battering his wife to death in their Liverpool home.

She argued that the mystery "provides for the detective novelist an unrivalled field for speculation." If Wallace was guilty, "then he was the classic contriver and alibi-monger that adorns the pages of a thousand mystery novels; and if he was innocent, then the real murderer was still more typically the classic villain of fiction." At a time when detective novelists, with Anthony Berkeley in the vanguard, were setting up multiple possible solutions to fictional crimes, Sayers suggested that such ingenuity was not as unrealistic as it might seem. In the Wallace case, there was "no single incident which is not susceptible of at least two interpretations, according to whether one considers that the prisoner was, in fact, an innocent man caught in a trap or a guilty man pretending to have been caught in a trap." These are compelling ingredients for a novelist, and the Wallace story has provided plot material for numerous detective novels—Sayers noted two early examples in the bibliography she appended to her essay. Two more came from the pen of the industrious Rhode: *Vegetable Duck* appeared in 1944 and *The Telephone Call* four years later. Much later, elements of the case informed P.D. James' *The Skull Beneath the Skin* and *The Murder Room*.

For Sayers, character and psychology were crucial to a proper analysis of whether or not Julia Wallace was murdered by her husband: "Though a man apparently well-balanced may give way to a sudden murderous frenzy, and may even combine that frenzy with a surprising amount of coolness and coming, it is rare for him to show no premonitory or subsequent symptoms of mental disturbance. This was one of the psychological difficulties in the way of the prosecution against Wallace. . . . The mind is indeed peculiar and the thoughts of the heart hidden. It is hopeless to explain the murder of Julia Wallace as the result of a momentary frenzy, whether Wallace was the criminal or another."

Guarded though her conclusions were, it seemed that they were vindicated by research undertaken years after her death. True crime expert Jonathan Goodman and journalist Roger Wilkes made a convincing case that one of Wallace's work colleagues committed the murder. The Wallace case has, however, never ceased to entrance crime writers. Margery Allingham wrote a short essay about the case, "The Compassionate Machine", which surfaced recently, although it was unpublished during her lifetime. Chandler considered writing about the case for the *American Weekly*; he called it "The Impossible Murder . . . the nonpareil of murder cases", but decided not to go ahead because "it has been done to a turn by Dorothy Sayers"—evidence that he read *The Anatomy of Murder*, and was impressed. He made detailed notes about the circumstances surrounding the death of Julia Wallace, and concluded that it "will always be unbeatable". As if to prove his point, during the past few years, doubts have surfaced again about Wallace's innocence, and P.D. James, a long-standing member of the Detection Club, recently contributed a thoughtful article to the *Sunday Times Magazine* which came to a very different conclusion from Sayers. The continuing swirl of speculation about Julia Wallace's murder demonstrates the lasting appeal of classic true crime cases—they are open to endless reinterpretation.

Sayers had a complicated friendship with the founder of the Detection Club, Anthony Berkeley Cox (1893–1971). He wrote most of his novels under the name Anthony Berkeley, but also earned a distinct reputation with ironic studies of criminal psychology published under the pseudonym Francis Iles, had a good deal in common with Sayers. Like her, he was talented and highly intelligent, but he was also a difficult and troubled man. At first their relations were cordial, and Sayers worked closely with Berkeley in establishing the Detection Club on a firm footing. As time passed, however, the two forceful personalities clashed more than once—not least when Berkeley complained about Sayers' delay in producing her contribution to *The Anatomy of Murder*, although this was due not to laziness on her part (far from it) but rather her relentless perfectionism.

"The Rattenbury Case" appeared under the Iles name. Perhaps this was an exercise in "branding", since his work as Iles was generally more serious and substantial than most of the books which appeared under his real name, or as by Berkeley. Under both his pen-names, he often drew on classic cases for his fiction. The death of James Maybrick in Victorian Liverpool, for instance, inspired the second Berkeley book, *The Wychford Poisoning Case*, the Armstrong and Palmer cases influenced the first two Iles books, *Malice Aforethought* and *Before the Fact*, and the Thompson-Bywaters case, which preoccupied him for years, supplied both plot elements and even the title of the third and final Iles book, *As for the Woman*.

Berkeley had long been disgusted by the hanging of Edith Thompson, and was struck by the similarities between her story and that of Alma Rattenbury. He argued—controversially, but not implausibly—that "if Mrs Thompson had not been hanged, Mrs Rattenbury surely would have been." For Berkeley, studying real life murder cases had an enduring appeal: "nothing outside fiction so effectually knocks down the front wall of a house and exposes its occupants in the details of their strange lives as does a trial for murder." His essay is, by some distance, the longest in the book. Discussing the case gave him a chance to mount a hobby horse—the hypocrisy of English society about adultery: "To say that respect cannot exist between a man and woman whose relations are legally improper is just as silly as to say that respect invariably exists between married couples."

Taken together, the stories told in *The Anatomy of Murder* represent a significant contribution to our understanding of the cases discussed, and their interest has scarcely diminished as a result of the passage of time. Many collections of essays about famous murder cases appeared during the twentieth century, but few match the quality of those in this book. The Detection Club's members were novelists first and foremost, but *The Anatomy of Murder* reveals, most pleasingly, that they possessed at least some of the detective instincts and skills of their fictional heroes and heroines.

FOREWORD

SEVEN members of the Detection Club here offer commentaries upon an equal number of murders, some famous, others unknown to the general public. In each case the writer has not been content simply to re-tell the story of the crime, but has endeavoured to throw light upon it; either by revelation of new facts, or by application of psychological tests to the mind of the criminal, or by comparison of the resources of present-day investigation with those of the past.

Sir Thomas Browne provides the writers with a common viewpoint, and the book with its motto:

> Tis not only the mischief of diseases, and the villany of poysons, that make an end of us; we vainly accuse the fury of Gunnes, and the new invention of death; it is in the power of every hand to destroy us, and we are beholding unto every one we meet, he doth not kill us.

31 GERRARD STREET,

 LONDON.

  August, 1936.

CONTENTS

PART I

DEATH OF HENRY KINDER

by Helen Simpson

DEATH OF
HENRY KINDER

CRIME in Australia: those three words start, in the mind of the reader, a train of association which runs through the gold fields of Ballarat to end in the explosive sentiment of Rolf Boldrewood's *Robbery Under Arms*. Crime in Australia puts on a red shirt, gallops gallantly, tackles its trackers in the open air. The kindly spaces of a new country afford the criminal a chance, if he escapes, to make good; finally if he should have the bad luck to encounter Sherlock Holmes during his retirement, that finely tempered instrument of justice will say: "God help us! Why does Fate play such tricks with poor helpless worms?"[1] and refrain from prosecution.

So much for the popular conception. Actually, crime in Australia follows much the same patterns as crime elsewhere. Murders are committed for the same motives, gain, elimination, and fear; and the more sensational of these are perpetrated by individuals whose surroundings would seem to guarantee their respectability.

Witness the case of that highly reputable chemist, John Tawell, of Hunter Street, Sydney, who having built a chapel for the Society of Friends, and publicly emptied six hundred gallons of rum into Sydney Harbour as an object lesson in temperance, in 1845 murdered his mistress with prussic acid and was hanged. Witness half a dozen other urban crimes, about which hangs no scent of the scrub or of saddle-leather; in particular, the murder of Henry Kinder, principal teller in the City Bank of Sydney, sufficiently well-to-do, living in a decent suburb on the North Shore of Sydney Harbour. This crime hath had elsewhere his setting; it is a domestic drama such as might have been played in any Acacia Avenue of the old world. True, the

[1] Conan Doyle: *The Boscombe Valley Mystery*.

3

assassin had at one time some notion of dressing the part, and purchased a red Crimean shirt, on which bloodstains would not be conspicuous; but the crime itself was committed, so far as can be ascertained, in the ordinary sombre undress of a dentist.

II

On October 2, 1865, the news of Henry Kinder's suicide startled his circle of respectable friends. His tendency to drink was known, but that he should have had *le vin triste* to this degree was unsuspected; the more so that he had no troubles about money, and seemed to be happy in his family life. The inexplicable suicide became a topic of conversation in Sydney. Nobody had realized that Kinder was the kind of man to drink himself into delirium or to utter violent threats against himself and his family; yet that he had done so his wife declared at the inquest, and her evidence was corroborated. The coroner directed his jury to bring in a verdict of suicide during temporary insanity, and Kinder was buried with every testimony of regret and respect. Mrs. Kinder retired to Bathurst, where she took up life again with her parents, who kept a small general shop. The talk, for a time, died down.

But not for long. The jury found that the deceased had met his death " by the discharge of a pistol with his own hand." The How, thus was answered; the Why, despite evidence of his drinking, remained mysterious. It was this last question which worked in the minds of Henry Kinder's fellow-citizens, and there were conjectures in the clubs that a certain Louis Bertrand, who had been heard making extravagant statements concerning his relations with the Kinder family, might be able to answer it. These statements the police investigated, with the result that six weeks after the inquest, on November 29th, Louis Bertrand and his wife Jane were charged before the magistrates at the Water Police Court, Sydney, with the wilful murder of Henry Kinder; Helen Mary Kinder, the dead man's widow, appearing as accessory to the fact.

4

Bertrand was brought to court from gaol, where he had been serving a sentence for using threatening language. The warrant was read to him, it seems, in his cell. "Rather a heavy charge," was his comment. The detective inquired if he should take that by way of answer. "Am I on my trial now?" the accused asked sardonically; and being told that the officer was only stating the charge, Bertrand answered emphatically: "Then my reply to it is —not guilty." This he repeated in the dock. His wife echoed him. Mrs. Kinder, brought down in custody from Bathurst to Sydney, indignantly denied any knowledge of the crime. The magistrates heard these answers, refused bail, and at the request of the police remanded the prisoners until the Monday following, December 4th.

At that hearing nothing new was revealed, except the ages of the accused; Bertrand was 25 years old, his wife 21, and Mrs. Kinder, who refused to give the year of her birth, was stated to be apparently about 30 years of age. They were remanded again until December 7th.

III

On December 7th the case for the Crown was opened by Mr. Butler; and it at once became evident that Mrs. Kinder was on her trial, not as accessory to a murder, but as an adulteress. It was "morally impossible," said counsel, to commit the other prisoners without committing her also. The evidence would consist, in the main, of admissions made by the Bertrands, with other circumstances, all of which were capable of proof. The motive was easily discoverable. Certain writings, now in the hands of the police, would afford evidence that a personal intimacy existed between Bertrand and Mrs. Kinder; and, said counsel, with the ripe conviction of all Sydney's gossips behind him, "such an intimacy could not exist without furnishing a clue to the imputed crime."

Counsel proposed to establish that there had been illicit intercourse between Louis Bertrand and Helen Kinder before the death of the latter's husband; that it had been Bertrand's design to divorce his own wife; and that Henry Kinder had been killed in order that Mrs. Kinder might be free to marry Bertrand.

Detective Richard Elliott was his first witness. This officer produced a packet containing letters found in a drawer in Bertrand's house; they were unsigned, but appeared to be in the handwriting of Mrs. Kinder. He produced a diary found in an unlocked drawer in Bertrand's bedroom. He produced a bottle labelled tincture of belladonna, and a phial labelled chloride of zinc; together with a pistol and powder flask, a box containing caps, a tomahawk, a screw such as might be used for the nipple of a pistol, a phial of white powder, unlabelled, and two books. There was a brief interlude while prisoners' counsel elicited from the detectives concerned the fact that they had not been impeded or hindered in their search; Mrs. Kinder had even asked that a certain desk, to which she could not find the key, should be broken open. She told the officer that she kept none of Mr. Bertrand's letters, but always burned them after she had read them. He found one, however, dated October 28th, signed by Bertrand. He also found, in a box which contained children's clothing, a pistol; the pistol, Mrs. Kinder told him, with which her husband had shot himself. These cross-examinations over, Mr. Butler began to read from the letters of Helen Maria Kinder.

There were nine of them; and a more curious set of documents can seldom have been produced in evidence. There is not space to quote them fully. The picture they offer is of a woman alternately cautious and abandoned. News of her three children, of churchgoing, and of the life in a small country town make up the chief of their matter, but there are outbursts which leave no doubt as to her relationship with Bertrand. It is noticeable that these grow more frequent as she becomes more bored with the life of a small country town, unfriendly to a newcomer without money, inquisitive, uncharitable, and remote from the standards of a wider world. From first to last there is no mention of her husband, and no reference which would imply that she had any knowledge of how he came by his death.

The first letter, which begins: " My dear friend," and ends: " Kindest regards to yourself and all the family, and believe me ever to remain truly yours, Ellen Kinder," is by no means compromising. Fatigue—she had had two days' coach journey, looking after her three children the while—may possibly account for the non-committal tone of it. " I do not think I was ever so tired in my life; I trust I may never again experience such utter prostration." Bathurst appeared dreadfully dull, but she would not judge hastily. In the morning she intended going to church to have a look at " the natives "—not aborigines, but such society as the town offered. This is all, except that she sends her " kind love " to Jane, Bertrand's wife.

The next letter, written just a week later, is the queerest mixture of passion and practicality.

MY DEAREST DARLING LOVE,

I have just received your dear, kind, and most welcome letter. Oh, darling, if you could but know how my heart was aching for a word of love from you. Dear, dear lover, your kind loving words seemed to have filled a void in my heart. I cannot convey to you in words the intense comfort your letter is to me. It has infused new life into my veins. . . .

I suppose you must not be ashamed of our poor home when you come up, darling, but I know that will make no difference to you. If I lived in a shanty it would be all the same, would it not? Now about your coming up, dear darling. How I should like to see your dear face, and to have a long talk with you about affairs in general. But, my own love, I fear if you were to come just now you would not find it pay you. Everything is so dull, and what I fear more is that people to whom you owe money would be down on you directly, thinking you were going to run away. Dear darling, all this advice goes sadly against the dictates of my own heart, for my spirit is fairly dying for you. A glimpse of you, oh dearest, dearest, what would I not give to be taken to your heart if only for a moment; I think it would content me.

It is no use, dear. Your love is food—nourishment to me. I cannot do without it. I tried to advise you for the best, but I cannot. I cry out in very bitterness. If I could only be near you, only see you at a distance once again, I think I could bear myself. I believe, darling, if our separation is for long, I shall go out of my mind. . . .

How is Jane? What is the matter? It is of no use to say that I am grieved at her being laid up; that would be a mere farce between you and I. As to her assertions with regard to Mr. Jackson, I shall not answer them; for if I am to be taken to task about all she may choose to say about me I shall have enough to do. . . . I know her, and you ought to by this time. If you allow everything she may say to influence you against me, I have done, but, darling, I am yours. I leave my conduct to be judged by you as you think fit. There let the matter rest. It ought never to have been broached.

Mr. Jackson, at the time this letter was written, was serving a sentence of twelve months' imprisonment for attempting to extort money from Bertrand by threats. (He had written to Bertrand saying that his association with Kinder's wife was known, and could be proved if Jackson chose to say what he knew.) He was sentenced on the day—October 23rd—that Mrs. Kinder first wrote to Bertrand from Bathurst. He was to be an important witness at the trial, and Mrs. Kinder's airy " It ought never to have been broached " covers the consciousness that she had in fact lived with Jackson as his mistress. The document ends with an account of her family's money affairs. Her father's shop did not prosper, her mother had only £50 coming in yearly from some small property in New Zealand. They were not very easily able to keep four extra persons for an indefinite time. Could Bertrand discover some opening for the family in Sydney? An hotel perhaps? "I am always well when I get a letter to strengthen me." She ends: " God bless you. Good night, darling love, and plenty kisses from your own darling Child." In the third letter, dated November 9th, she is, as ever, preoccupied equally with the future and the present. She has tried for a governess's situation, but times are bad. The clergyman has come to call. Her youngest child, Nelly, would soon be walking. She would like to get into a dressmaking business in Sydney. The thought of seeing him again sends her blood " gurgling " in her veins. " God for ever bless you and preserve you from harm, and preserve your dear children."

But Mrs. Kinder's mother was becoming suspicious, and, it would seem, not only of the relationship between her daughter and the Sydney dentist.

> She advises me to be careful what we write, as she says there are many reports with regard to us in Sydney, and that the detectives have power, and might use it if they thought to find out anything by opening our letters. I was not aware they had that power; it is only in case of there being anything suspicious with regard to people.

Mamma, in fact, read her daughter a lecture, refusing to countenance " anything wrong ". With all this, there was no question of turning away Mrs. Kinder and her children. " As far as anything in the shape of love and affectionate welcome goes, to the last crust they have I can depend." But the takings of the shop were never more than five shillings a day, and sometimes not sixpence. She could not go on being a burden; " I would rather be a common servant." Upon this situation she reflects:

> How black everything looks, Lovey, does it not? Our good fortune seems to be deserting us.

Was this a reference to the death of Kinder, an affair surely of management rather than luck? If so, it is the only reference in the letters, which run to some ten thousand words. They keep their pattern of lamentations, shrewd planning, passion, and where her family is concerned a kind of affectionate independence, together with one or two items of actual news. She had become a seamstress to help the family finances; her father was off to New Zealand again; her brother Llewellyn was staying in Bertrand's house; she was determined to come to Sydney. The last letter, dated November 21st, ends:

> When I think I shall be with you in less than a week—oh, this meeting, love, oh, I shall go mad; it is too delicious to dream of; oh, let it be in reality, darling, do, do. My feelings will burst,

9

but still, dear one, I trust you will do what is best for us in the end, I would say——

The newspaper report says: "Remainder illegible."

IV

These were the first documents read by Mr. Butler, the Crown counsel. It is odd to picture the scene. The Water Police Court is not an impressive or a roomy building. The month was December, when Sydney is beginning to feel the weight of summer. There is great humidity, heat lies upon the town like a blanket, and all the distances dance. To Bertrand, even the stuffy court must have seemed spacious compared with his cell in Darlinghurst Gaol. Mrs. Kinder, brought down from the greater heats of Bathurst, may have found the air of Sydney grateful. Only Mrs. Bertrand, poor Jane, coming to the box from her pleasant house in Wynyard Square, must have felt bitterly the confinement and the heat. Mr. Butler, who had already spoken and read for some hours, returned to the charge in the afternoon; and when the diary's handwriting had been identified by Bertrand's assistant, Alfred Burne, he began, in the passionless tones congruous with his duty, to read aloud the diary of Louis Bertrand.

October 26th. Thursday.
Lonely! Lonely! Lonely! She is gone—I am alone. Oh, my God, did I ever dream or think of such agony? I am bound to appear calm, so much the worse. I do so hate mankind. I feel as if every kindly feeling had gone with her. Ellen, dearest Ellen, I thank, I dare to thank God, for the happiness of our last few moments. Surely He could not forsake us, and yet favour us as He has done. Tears stream from my eyes, they relieve the burning anguish of my bursting heart. Oh, how shall I outlive twelve long months! Child, I love thee passionately—aye, madly. I knew not how much until thou wert gone. And yet I am calm. 'Tis the dead silence which precedes the tempest. . . .
Do not rouse the demon that I know lies dormant in me. Beware how you trifle with my love. I am no base slave to be

played with or cast off as a toy. I am terrible in my vengeance; terrible, because I call on the powers of hell to aid their master in his vengeance. God, what am I saying? Do not fear me, darling love. I would not harm thee, not thy dear self, but only sweep away as with a scimitar my enemies or those who step between my love and me. Think kindly of me—of my great failings. See what I have done for thee, for my, for our love.

Such were the first paragraphs of this document in madness. The diary was faithfully kept, reflecting Bertrand's love, his fantasies, his finances, and his health. In itself it would be enough, nowadays, to support a defence of insanity. But the magistrates of 1865 took it seriously, and Sydney shuddered as the newspapers reported it piecemeal. The journal covers only twenty-four days, from the date on which he parted from Mrs. Kinder to that on which he was summoned on the charge of writing a threatening letter to a woman, Mrs. Robertson. His triumph over Jackson makes odd reading, when it is considered that three weeks later both were serving sentences for a parallel offence.

In the train I borrowed half the *Empire*, which contained this paragraph: "Francis Arthur Jackson, convicted of sending a threatening letter to Henry L. Bertrand with the intent to extort money, sentenced to 12 months' hard labour in Parramatta Gaol." It pleased me. I am satisfied. Thus *once more* perish my enemies. He is disposed of for the present.

On the same page:

I feel that I love you as mother, sister, husband, brother, all combined. What work I have before me, God only knows, but I will call His love to help me, and strive to do right. I feel I shall. Thy dear devoted love will save me. I know it will, and we may yet be good and happy together.

An echo of the gossip which was alive concerning him may be found in the brief statement which follows: "Am doing no business whatever." He was ill, too, with some internal trouble, concerning which he makes this reflection:

I am now, by my own agonies, paying a debt to retributive justice; how and what I have made others suffer, God only knows; but if I have, I richly deserve all I now feel; and you, my love, *have you not done the same?*

'Tis strange our two natures are so much alike. I love a companion who can understand my sentiments, respond to the very beating of my heart, help me to think, to plan, and by clear judgment advise me on worldly affairs. A woman is not a toy. Women are as men make them. I have found, from experience, that half the trouble women give their husbands is caused by the husbands themselves—sometimes directly, but often from some indirect cause that might have been avoided if the man had used even moderate care in the guidance of the being sacredly entrusted to his charge. . . . One more day stolen from fate.

This was Friday, October 27th. Two days later he was up and about, spending an artistic rather than a conventional Sunday.

I awoke this morning too late for church—I did not dress or shave. I fear, my dear Nelly, that not having you to fascinate I shall become slovenly and untidy, for if I consulted my own feelings I should not dress at all.

I want fame, as well as wealth and power, and as usual little Bertrand must have his way. You know he is a spoilt child, spoilt in more ways than one. So as I was saying, I must have fame, fortune and power, as well as the most ardent, pure, passionate, and devoted love of the most fascinating, amiable and best of women that the world at present contains. There, if this is not flattery I do not know what is; but it is the truth—at least, I think it is the truth to the best of my belief, as we say in court. Oh, I must not speak of courts; we have had enough of them, at least for the present.

At this time he set to work to model two salt-cellars for the third Victorian exhibition of 1866; Fijians, " kneeling in a graceful attitude ", holding pearl shells, upon stands "emblematical of the sea shore "; the spoons to consist of paddles, " formed of some sort of shell, small of course " ; all to be cast in solid silver, frosted. " Dearest, it is for thee that I toil." He turned from this work to conversations with his sister, who recommended a divorce as being the kindest thing that he could do for poor Jane; and to his diary, intended for Ellen's reading later on, when the period of separation was over. Certain further passages of this were read with emphasis by Mr. Butler.

I should feel ashamed of my love, of what I have done for it, if it were no different from that of others. That is our only excuse, whether on earth or Heaven, for what we have accomplished. . . . Let us not be cowed or terrified at aught that besets us. I warned you what to expect, and, dearest, for the greatness of our love for one another, surely we can bear fifty times more than we have to bear. I do not fear the result. To me the end is clear and palpable, I am sure of it; I never yet failed in my life.

November 8th.

Thank God, another day gone. However will a twelvemonth pass? God only knows. My heart grows sick and faint when I look into the future. Oh, God, is this Thy retribution for our sins? Did I flatter myself that the Almighty would let me—a wretch like me—go unpunished; but I tell thee, fate, I defy thee. I feel as though my heart were rent in pieces, and then dark thoughts obtrude themselves before me, fiends rise and mock me; they point to a gate, a portal through which I feel half inclined to go; but not yet.. What would my love do without me? . . . No matter what thou hast been, my child, I hold thee as a true, virtuous wife to me, for you have been true to me, my dearest love.

Bertrand went on this day, Wednesday to see one of the directors of the City Bank, Kinder's employers, who gave him news. A temporary cross was to be put on " poor Harry's grave " in New Zealand (whence the Kinders had come to New South Wales) ; " they think that Harry did not intend to kill himself, but only to frighten his wife." When Bertrand suggested that possibly Mrs. Kinder might come to Sydney to find work, the director was evasive and recommended that " old affairs should blow over ". Next day Mrs. Kinder's father, Mr. Wood, came to see him, and they walked down together to the ferry wharf, and travelled over to the North Shore to see a mutual friend, De Fries.

I felt very strange. This is the first time I have been to the Shore since poor Harry's funeral. I am standing on the deck, my face turned towards the little house with the two chimneys, as I used to do when on wings of love I flew to my beloved. . . . How horribly jealous I was, I was mad . . . surely there can be no worse hell than our own conscience.

13

Mr. De Fries it was who gave Bertrand the first warning that all was not well, and that Sydney, unlike New Zealand, was beginning to be suspicious of Kinder's suicide. De Fries spoke reasonably ; said that he had watched the affair growing, and that he had a high regard for Jane. He told Bertrand that Mrs. Kinder cared nothing for him, that she was a calculating woman, while Jane was an affectionate and true one. He felt for Bertrand, he told him, like a brother, and exhorted him, if he cared for his happiness in this world and his welfare in the next, not to yield to temptation. The diarist listened attentively, but coming home, broke Jane's fan in a passion. That he believed, or rather, that he knew De Fries to be speaking the truth, is shown in a paragraph which ends the entry for this day :

November 12th.

Be she as wicked as Satan, as vile and wily as the serpent, I, even I, will save her, will raise her from the depth of hell. I, Ellen, even I, thy lover, wicked as I am, will be a Saviour to thee. Dear, sweet, loved Ellen, the more they oppose us the greater will be my power of resistance. Poor fools, to try and thwart my will. Indeed, if thou hast me for an enemy—I who value human life as I value weapons, to be used when required and thrown away or destroyed; some, of course, kept for future use if necessary. Beware! If I have my way in this, if I obtain this sole object of my being I feel that I shall be reclaimed; but if not, no matter from what cause, Heaven help the world, oh! I shall indeed be revenged.

Next, Mrs. Robertson, a friend to both parties, issued her warning. She advised Bertrand to have no more to do with Mrs. Kinder; and told him frankly that she would not have Ellen in her house, were she to come to Sydney. Again he listened patiently, and again there followed an outburst, a frantic act of faith.

DEAR, DEAR CHILD,

I trust that she is truly penitent for what she has done, and that with me she will be in future a truly good and virtuous woman. Why do people try to torture me thus? God knows I have misery and wretchedness enough. I am prepared for the worst and God help the world if this my forlorn hope fails. To hear her [Ellen] spoken of as bad, is sufficient to upset my intellect. · · ·

Ellen, my dear love, I must be near you. I want to look into those dear wicked eyes and I know they cannot, will not, deceive me. If I have, like others, cause to repent what I have done—I must drop this painful subject or I shall be ill—it will unman me —unfit me for the battle I am fighting. Enough excitement of mind for one day. Adieu, my thoughts. Adieu, my own Ellen.

Louis.

It is not quite the last entry, but it is the most revealing of all. The exaltation was fading; the way to happiness, which had seemed so clear and sure, was obscured. Bertrand knew that Mrs. Kinder had been the mistress of at least one of his acquaintances; that there had been other men in New Zealand he conjectured. He was tormented; the journal plainly shows him twisting away from inescapable conclusions, and so towards madness. When Mr. Butler laid down the notebook which gave such an intimate picture of Bertrand's mind, he had proved to the public's satisfaction that Bertrand had good reason to wish Kinder out of his way.

v

But Kinder met his death by the firing of a pistol close to his ear. Whose finger pulled the trigger of that pistol? Mr. Butler recalled Bertrand's assistant, Alfred Burne, who, after telling how he delivered letters from Bertrand to Mrs. Kinder, and how she had often stayed in the surgery at night, gave the following account of some remarkable expeditions:

About six weeks previous to Kinder's death he [Bertrand] asked me where I could get a boat to hire. I mentioned Buckley's among others. We went rowing the following night about 12 o'clock, to the North Shore as far as Kinder's house, opposite to the bedroom window on which the moon was shining. He said: That is his bedroom. He did not then say what was the purpose of his visit. He did not go in. He said the moon was too strong, he had come too early. . . . We went back again three nights after, taking a boat from the same place, and went up to the house. As we went over he said it was very likely that next morning Kinder would be found dead in his bed, having committed suicide, and that letters from Jackson would be found in his hand.

They arrived at Kinder's house about one in the morning. Bertrand took off his boots, gave them to Burne to hold, and climbed into the house by the dining-room window. He came back much later—Burne fell asleep meanwhile—angry because Kinder would not drink his beer, and consequently was awake. " We had drugged it," said Bertrand.

Some days, about a week later, Bertrand produced in his surgery a hatchet, and asked Burne to bore a hole in the handle so that he might tie it under his coat by a string. A young man, Ranclaud, who was staying in the house, asked what he meant to do with it. Bertrand answered abruptly, and with no care for probabilities, that he was going fishing, and went out with Burne to their hired boat. On the way, he said that Kinder had insulted him; that he was going to knock Kinder's brains out first, and then get a divorce from Mrs. Bertrand.

I remarked what object could he have in putting Mr. Kinder out of the way when Mrs. Kinder was as good as a wife to him. He said he wished to have Mrs. Kinder all to himself.

On this occasion Bertrand entered the house by the same window, but returned soon, saying that Jackson and Mrs. Kinder's brother Llewellyn were sleeping in the house, and as the boards creaked he did not think it safe.

COUNSEL: Safe to do what?
BURNE: To murder Mr. Kinder, as I understood.

A week later the expedition was repeated, but in remarkable conditions. Bertrand shaved himself at midnight; then blacked his face, donned a mask and the red Crimean shirt, topped this disguise with a slouch hat, took off his boots, drank some brandy, and set out in the boat at about 1.30 in the morning. Burne

went with him. Why he should have done so is inexplicable.
True, he was in Bertrand's employ; true, he may not have taken
seriously Bertrand's boasts and threats against Kinder. But he
was sufficiently well aware of danger when his own skin was in
question.

> On these occasions I always carried the hatchet myself; I also
> used to get him to sit in front of me in the boat for fear of acci-
> dents. I made him pull the stroke oar, while I pulled the bow oar,
> fearing that, taking me by surprise while my back was turned, he
> might throw me into the water.

That night Bertrand asked Burne to help him when he got
inside the house. If Kinder, he said, were to be killed that night,
suspicion would inevitably fall on Jackson, who was leaving
Sydney next day. The young man answered that it was all too
romantic for him, that he had no share in Mrs. Kinder and
intended to run no risk. Bertrand at this seemed to abandon his
plan, whatever it may have been, and they rowed home. This
was the last expedition in the boat.

But not the end of Bertrand's fantastic preparations. His next
act was to cut off his moustache, dress as a woman, and go with
Burne to buy two pistols at a pawnshop in Lower George Street,
then a fairly tough locality. On the day following this purchase
he acquired a sheep's head, and began to practise shooting at it
in his surgery with bullets he had made himself in a mould.
His wife and her mother ran in at the first shot, alarmed, naturally enough, by the noise and smell of smoke. This was on a
Saturday. On Monday morning Burne was told to destroy the
broken skull in the furnace, and did so. That afternoon he heard
that Kinder was dying.

At this point we get Bertrand's own version of the tragedy as
he told it to Burne on his return from Kinder's house. Kinder,
he said, had actually shot himself as the result of a practical
joke. The two men had left the house and their wives in search
of a pub and a drink. On their way back Bertrand had suggested that the women should be given a fright, and produced a

pistol, which he said had no bullet in it, but only powder and a wad. Kinder, who was drunk, agreed to put it against his head and fire; and when they came to the room where the women were, actually did so, with the result that the charge of powder drove the wad into his ear and jaw. Proof of this, said Bertrand, was that no bullet could be found.

It was a fantastic story, but Bertrand's counsel seized upon it, and later there was great argument about it and about when the doctors came upon the scene. Unfortunately, Bertrand, forgetting this sketch of a possible defence, later admitted to Burne that his wife had found a bullet, and produced from his pocket a flattened scrap of lead which he said was the bullet in question. Burne secreted one of those that had been made in the surgery to fire at the sheep's head, and gave it to the detectives; this bullet fitted the second of the pawnshop pistols.

Defence counsel could not do a great deal with Burne. They could prove him a poltroon, but by no means could they prove him a liar. The butcher who had sold the sheep's head, the pawnbroker who had sold the pistols, Buckley the boatman, Mrs. Bertrand's mother who had witnessed the pistol practice—all these in turn corroborated his story. Asked why he did not attend the inquest and there tell what he knew, he answered that he had not been subpœnaed. Asked why he had gone to the detective office afterwards with information, he gave the following answer:

It was slightly for the sake of public justice, and by way of protecting my life that I went there, the object being self-preservation in particular, the other in a slight degree.

This naïve statement virtually ended his evidence. His last admission was to the effect that he, Burne, had read part of Bertrand's diary before the detectives came; then he was told to stand down, having proved himself a useful though contemptible witness for the Crown.

VI

After certain corroborating witnesses came one Alexander Bell-house, employed in the Government Service, who had known Bertrand for some years. He repeated an extraordinary statement made to him by Bertrand a month before the trial. After a game of cards at the house in Wynyard Square, Bertrand had accompanied him to the door as he was leaving, and told him that he was responsible for the death of Kinder. " He said that he was sorry for Kinder but wanted him out of his way." He also told Bellhouse that he was a powerful mesmerist, and could do anything he liked with people. His wife knew of his attachment to Mrs. Kinder. He stated that he had put the pistol in Kinder's way, not that he had shot him. The witness was so greatly shocked by Bertrand's statement and manner that he " could not sleep that night because of it ". The impression left on his mind was that Bertrand had somehow compelled Kinder to shoot himself.

Harriet Kerr, Bertrand's sister, followed Bellhouse with an even more remarkable story.

> Early in the morning Bertrand came into my bedroom as I was washing the baby. He said, "Stay a minute, I have something to say to you." He told me to sit on the side of the bed and asked if I had read of the death of Kinder. I said I had. He paused a little, then said, "Kinder did not shoot himself. I shot him." I replied, "You must be mad to say such a thing!" He said, "No, I am not mad. I tell you I did shoot him." I said, "But how cruel of you to do so," and put my hands up to my face. He pulled them down again. I was crying, and he said, "Don't cry. I don't regret what I have done." He said when he had shot Kinder he put the pistol in his hand and a pipe in his mouth.

Three weeks later Mrs. Kerr had another talk with her brother. This time his wife was present, but asleep. " She used," said Mrs. Kerr, " to sleep a great deal. It was more like stupor." Bertrand said that he did not want to have to kill Jane, and that

a divorce would be better, if he could get up " an adultery case
with a respectable married woman ". His sister took him to task
bravely about his behaviour in general and this plan in particular.
Jane had done him no harm, she told him, and Mrs. Kinder was
a wicked woman. He knew that, he said. She was wicked
already, and he would make of her a second Lucrezia Borgia.
It was very likely, he intimated, that before his sister went to
Brisbane she would find herself attending his wife's funeral. Mrs.
Kerr went on to describe an attempt upon Jane's life. At one
o'clock in the morning there was an argument, and Bertrand,
taking up a life-preserver, threatened his wife, who cried out in
terror the strange words: " Don't kill me. You promised on your
word of honour you would not kill me." Mrs. Kerr went to
the top of the kitchen stairs and called the servant, then went up
again to the first landing, having heard the parlour door open.
Her brother was saying: " Now Jane, I want you to go into the
surgery. I want you to write on this piece of paper that you are
tired of your life." She refused, saying that he might pour poison
down her throat, but she would write nothing. He seemed to
abandon his intention, gave her a glass of brandy and water,
and sent her to bed in Mrs. Kerr's room. Poor Jane sat down
upon a chair, and there and then, to her sister-in-law's astonish-
ment, fell fast asleep.

Now comes an account of the death of Kinder. It is necessarily
second-hand; the three persons who took part in the scene were
in the dock, and so unable to give direct evidence. But Mrs.
Kerr's recollection of what she had been told was very exact,
and there is no reason to suppose that Mrs. Bertrand's story was
fabricated.

On the morning of the first Monday in October Mrs. Bertrand
was told by her husband to take the baby and accompany him
to the Kinder's house on the North Shore. It was a rainy morning, and she was reluctant that the baby should go out; however,
as always, she yielded. When they arrived at the house Bertrand
seemed more serious than usual, and more gentle with Mr.
Kinder. He walked up and down the room very fast, gloved,

and with one hand in his pocket. Jane and Mrs. Kinder were looking out of the window when they heard the report of a pistol. They turned, to see a pistol dropping from Kinder's hand as he sat in his chair, and Bertrand taking a pipe from the table which he stuck in Kinder's mouth. Mrs. Kinder ran from the room in terror; Bertrand followed, and forced her to return. He then took his wife's arm in a terrible grip, and made her face the shot man, from whose head blood was flowing. " Look at him well," said Bertrand, " I wish you to see him always before you."

Jane bathed the wound, while Mrs. Kinder and Bertrand walked up and down the verandah embracing. She found a bullet, flattened, which had dropped against the wainscot, and showed it to her husband when he next entered the room. Bertrand took it from her, saying it was just what he wanted, and she never saw it again.

But Kinder did not die of the wound in his head. A doctor was called, with whose help Jane got him to bed; she then took up her abode in the house and nursed him faithfully for four days, at the end of which time he appeared to be recovering. When she told her husband so, Bertrand in rage said that he must not live; poison should end him if a bullet could not. He made Jane " mix the poison "; and Mrs. Kinder gave it in milk to Kinder, who died soon afterwards.

This was Jane Bertrand's story of the crime. It was told to and recounted by her sister-in-law, Harriet, to whose presence in the house in Wynyard Square Jane may have owed her life.

I wished to protect Mrs. Bertrand, in fact that was what I stayed in the house for, and I must also add, I stayed partly in fear of my life. We were always in dread of our lives. He [Bertrand] did not appear to wish me out of the house, but quite the contrary. . . . I was his favourite sister, though he did not show it by his manner. He was often very eccentric. Even in gaping he would imitate the roar of a tiger and had done it in the street. . . . Bertrand often told me, at that time, that he had a great mind to murder Mrs. Bertrand and say I had done it.

VII

This evidence concerning poison was something quite unexpected by the public. The verdict at the inquest had been death by shooting, and the possibility that Kinder might have died from any other cause had not been considered. The Crown witnesses were elusive on this point. A chemist who had analysed the contents of the stomach found no traces of poison, but stated that, since certain vegetable poisons rapidly decomposed in the stomach, this analysis did not rule out the possibility that they had been employed. He was asked if aconite or belladonna came within this category of untraceable substances. (Aconite and belladonna were found in Bertrand's surgery.) He replied that they did; that one or the other might have been administered, as was asserted, on October 6th; but that now, two months later, it was a matter impossible to be proved.

The Crown accordingly let this point go, and called up the surgeons who had performed the post-mortem. They agreed as to the nature and direction of the wound. The shot had blown off the ear and broken the lower jaw; the brain itself was not touched. In short, of such a wound a man in good health and of temperate habits need not have died. But Kinder was not in good health, and he had been drinking heavily for months. He had lost a good deal of blood, and to this haemorrhage, with the shock and subsequent exhaustion, all three doctors attributed his death.

On one matter they disagreed, and here was a point eagerly caught at by the defence, since it seemed to square with what Bertrand had told Burne on the evening of the murder. Bertrand's story then was, that the whole affair was an accident, and that the pistol had been charged with powder and a wad only. No bullet had, in fact, been found in the skull by the doctors who conducted the post-mortem examination. Was it possible, asked Mr. Robberds, for the defence, that Kinder might have done as was suggested, pulled the trigger of a pistol charged but not loaded, and that the wound, which extended from the top of the ear to the lower angle of the jaw, could have been caused by gunpowder and wadding only?

Dr. Alloway, who had served in the Crimea, and had seen many gunshot wounds during his service in India as an army surgeon, gave it as his opinion that such a thing was not possible. He maintained that the external condyle of the lower jaw showed marks of having been struck by some hard substance at the point of fracture; and that wadding from a pistol could never have broken so thick a bone, no matter how great the charge of powder behind it.

Dr. Allayne did not see " anything to indicate that the injury was caused by a round substance such as a bullet ". The force of the explosion alone, he declared, was sufficient to cause such a wound—that is, if the pistol were held close to the head.

Dr. Eichler came to the conclusion that the wound had been self-inflicted, but would not give an opinion as to whether or no it was a bullet that had caused the damage to the jawbone.

If the description of the direction of the wound is correct, it is difficult to see how it could have been self-inflicted. The bullet, or wad, whichever caused the damage, had entered behind the right ear, detaching the ear itself from the scalp, and continued its course forward and downward to break the jawbone on the right side. It is quite extraordinarily difficult for a man to hold a pistol so as to inflict such a wound upon himself ; the trigger must be pulled with the thumb, and the head must be turned down and to the left at a painful angle. On the other hand, if the shot were fired by a right-handed man standing behind a seated man, the direction of the wound is easily accounted for. (According to Jane Bertrand's story, Kinder was seated, and Bertrand standing or strolling, at the time when she heard the shot fired.) There is the possibility that a suicide might point the barrel of his weapon at his jaw; but the doctors were agreed, from the evidences of powder blackening, that the missile, whatever it may have been, entered behind the ear.

It might be supposed that the case for the Crown was by

this time strong enough; but there were two more witnesses to come. Francis Arthur Jackson was brought to Sydney from Parramatta Gaol to give evidence concerning the triangular relationship between Kinder, his wife, and Bertrand. Agnes Mary Robertson, whose charge of using threatening language had brought Bertrand to Darlinghurst, appeared to testify to the dentist's frantic and unreasonable rages.

VIII

Jackson had an unsavoury story to tell. He had known the Kinders in New Zealand, where he had been intimate with the woman; this intimacy was resumed when, six months before the date of Kinder's death, he came to live in their house on the North Shore. Bertrand was a frequent and difficult visitor, who showed his feeling for Ellen Kinder very plainly, and made it clear to Jackson that he would not tolerate a rival.

During a conversation with Mrs. Kinder, as she saw Bertrand coming in she said I had better go. I said no, I thought not. I asked her when Bertrand was there which of the two men she preferred. Bertrand would not speak to me at first. . . . He asked Mrs. Kinder if she cared for him, and she bowed her head. He said he wished to remove any thought from my mind that Mrs. Kinder had cared for me from the moment she saw him.

On another occasion while I was lying in bed and he was standing at the foot of it he reiterated how very fond he was of Mrs. Kinder, that he would do anything for her, and I must not be surprised at anything I might hear after I went away. He had given me some money to go away, and said: "You would not like to be implicated in a charge for the murder of Kinder?" I said: "No, I should think it impossible." He said if I stayed in Sydney I might be implicated. I said it was impossible, and he said there were many stranger things in the country than that. He said in a year of two he would marry Mrs. Kinder. I said it was impossible, her husband being alive. He said: "All things are possible, and time will show."

Bertrand offered to pay my passage to Melbourne, and held the threat over me that if I did not go I might be implicated in Kinder's death, and remarked about the Devil having a strong will.

Jackson went to West Maitland, apparently moved by this threat. It is odd to see with what assurance Bertrand shifted about the pieces in his lunatic game, and difficult to account for their docility. Jane's submissiveness came from terror, or possibly from the administration of drugs; her stupors and dozings, which were observed not only by her sister-in-law but by visitors to the house, seem to lend colour to this explanation. She was wholly in Bertrand's power, and so maintained by his occasional and mysterious threats against the children. Not so Burne, an employee, who could leave his service when he chose; a young man with his wits about him, and over whose head Bertrand held no threat, so far as the evidence goes. And not so Jackson, another free agent.

Yet Burne did errands which he must have known were dangerous, and escorted his employer on expeditions whose confessed object was murder. Jackson, who was in a strong position to defy him, established as he was in the Kinder's house, and the lover of Mrs. Kinder; Jackson who had only to report these threats to the police to be rid of his rival; Jackson took himself out of the way obediently, and for a time held his tongue. True, he wrote a blackmailing letter later, when he learned of the coroner's verdict on Kinder; but he was not a subtle man, and there is no reason to suppose that he took himself off in order to leave Bertrand free to commit a murder from which he thus might draw some profit. Nor was it a fact that he was tired of Mrs. Kinder. He was still intent upon her, and took such steps as he might to see her alone.

> After my intimacy with Mrs. Kinder commenced I had an object in getting him [Kinder] to drink to excess. That was, to get him stupid so as to afford me opportunities for interviews or intimacy with Mrs. Kinder. The human mind is very base. I was base enough for that. By constant drinking with him I thought it would shorten his days. It would shorten anybody's days.

That Mrs. Kinder had anything to do with the murder he refused to believe. She had constantly tried to prevent Kinder from drinking in New Zealand and after they came to Sydney. She was not present at any of the conversations when Bertrand hinted that Kinder might die. She had tried to do her duty as a wife.

> I remember her saying that she would rather not have anything to do with either of us, that she intended to do her duty as a wife. At that time she requested me to leave her, and never to come near her again. Any interviews I had with her were of my own seeking. She told me she feared Bertrand. She said: "He seems to be a perfect devil," and spoke of him as being able to make her do things against her will, having a sort of clairvoyance [sic] over her, or mesmeric influence. There is nothing that I know of to incriminate her in this charge beyond intimacy with Bertrand.

He did the best he could for the accused woman, but the fact of the confessed relationship between her and Bertrand deprived his testimony of weight. A jury was not likely to be much impressed by his picture of practical Ellen Kinder as the helpless victim of a mesmerist, even though this theory found corroboration in the recollections of the witness who followed him.

So much for Jackson. Mrs. Robertson, on whose account Bertrand was undergoing imprisonment, spoke of Bertrand's mesmeric influence, which she had felt upon more than one occasion.

> When I felt a dizziness in my eyes I ran out of the room. I know he has tried to mesmerize me by following me about the house, and looking at me. He compelled me that night to kiss him in the presence of Mrs. Kinder, and made me feel very unwell. Since then I have kissed him to save his wife from violence. He said: "Do you intend to do as I bid you?" I said no. He then called his wife so that he might flog her unless I kissed him, and to save her from violence I did so.

Mrs. Robertson too had been obliged to listen to threats against Kinder, and to confidences concerning the murder. Bertrand had been at her house on Thursday, the night before Kinder died; he fell on the floor there in a kind of fit, calling: "Bring the milk and mix the poison." He declared that he must go next day and confess that it was he who fired the shot. He told a fantastic story of having bought pistols at Kinder's request, that he might fight a duel with Jackson. He maintained that it was Mrs. Kinder's suggestion that her husband should be shot while Jackson was in the house, in order that the blame might fall on him.

A chemist was recalled, there was a question or two concerning the poisons generally used in the practice of dentistry, and the case for the Crown, at this first hearing before the magistrates, closed. The magistrates refused to dismiss Mrs. Bertrand, refused bail all round, and committed all three prisoners for trial at the next sitting of the Criminal Court, to be held on Monday, December 18th.

IX

Before the prisoners came to trial, Jane Bertrand was set free. There was no evidence that she knew anything of Bertrand's preparations, and although she was, by her own confession, in the room at the time when the murder was committed, nobody could suppose that she had had any hand in it. Motive lacked wholly. She was aware of the relationship between her husband and Kinder's wife; it was not to be credited that she should connive at a crime whose sole object was to bring them together, or that she should not do all in her power to hinder a death by which, as she might have suspected, her own was foreshadowed.

Nor could a sufficient case be made out against Mrs. Kinder. Her letters, though they showed her to be infatuated with Bertrand, nowhere gave any least hint that she shared his guilt as a murderer. Bertrand's accusations against her, made to Mrs. Robertson, were unsupported; and though she showed some callousness (if Jane's account is to be believed), walking up and down with Bertrand's arm round her waist while her husband lay bleeding, and also, according to Mrs. Robertson, driving with Bertrand in a 'patent safety' hansom on the Friday that he died, there was no actual proof of her complicity. Jackson's statement—" there is nothing that I know of to incriminate her in this charge beyond intimacy with Bertrand "—eventually was echoed by the Crown.

Thus, Bertrand went into the dock of the Central Criminal Court alone.

Two new facts were brought forward at the trial, and Bertrand's counsel, Mr. Dalley, made the very most of both. It was proved that Bertrand, in the three hours which elapsed before a doctor could be found and brought to the wounded man, had staunched the bleeding and bound up Kinder's head skilfully and carefully; also that Kinder, during the days before his death, asked constantly for Bertrand, saying that he would rather have his services than those of any doctor. It was revealed, also, that Kinder supposed his wife to have shot him. Not for a moment did he behave like a suicide who has been baulked of his purpose, or like a man who knows himself to be the victim of accident; which theory the defence continued to put forward.

The Lord Chief Justice dealt with these points in his summing up. He warned the jury; told them that there could not be conceived a case which demanded a more entire absence of prejudice, if justice were to be done. After the manner of judges, even those most nearly in touch with common life, he bade the jurymen expunge from their minds all recollection of anything they might have read or heard concerning the prisoner, other than such written or spoken statements as had been offered in evidence in that court. This evidence itself, said he, they must weigh; certain parts of it, such as those which " exhibited a state of almost unparalleled wickedness ", must not be allowed undue importance. Unless they vigorously strove against preconceptions, the prisoner might be deprived of that justice to which as a citizen he was entitled. He then proceeded in these words:

Regarding him [the prisoner] as the author of the diary, and if you believe this contains the outpourings of his mind, you must not take the picture of this man's mental state as portrayed by the counsel for the defence; for there is before you, not a man, but a fiend, a monster in human shape. Against this conception you will have to struggle; for though steeped in wickedness and malignity scarcely equalled by the Tempter of mankind, the question to be decided by the evidence is, Did he murder Kinder?

Having thus made clear his own opinion of the prisoner, the Lord Chief Justice went on to consider, and dispose of, the accident theory. Supposing, said he, that Kinder did himself press the trigger of the pistol at Bertrand's suggestion; could it be denied that the object and the criminality were the same—the compassing of Kinder's death? Too many circumstances led to the belief that Bertrand wished him to die; it was difficult to assume, in face of these circumstances, that the result of Kinder pulling the trigger was both unexpected and undesired.

The staunching of the blood might be allowed to throw a favourable light upon the prisoner; on the other hand, "had he allowed the man who so wounded himself in his presence to bleed to death, he, as a dentist acquainted with the means to stop haemorrhage, might conceive that he ran some risk." The staunching of the blood, therefore, though inconsistent with the idea of guilt, was not conclusive of innocence.

The defence pleaded that only an innocent man could have prosecuted Jackson for threats which it was in Jackson's power to execute. His Honour disagreed; a man not in full possession of his senses equally might do so, or a man to whom the gratification of revenge meant more than his own safety might do so. "This point, like that of the staunching of the blood, rests on the threshold of your deliberations, and you must get rid of it before proceeding to other matters."

After dealing with the evidence of Jackson, His Honour delivered a further expression of opinion. "There is perhaps nothing so revolting in this case as the fact that this woman [Mrs. Kinder], whilst living with her husband, should be challenged to express her preference for one of two paramours in their presence."

He then passed to the diary, from which he read extracts. "Those passages in which he speaks of what the power of love can perform are pure nonsense, befitting only a madman." His Honour, in fact, laid no great stress upon the evidence offered by the diary, except in so far as it clearly depicted the state of mind of the writer, which was not that of a normal person.

In conclusion, he urged the jury to decide whether Bertrand's own confession (alleged to have been made to his sister) was to be believed, and warned them that confessions were rarely to be relied on. They must set this confession beside other circumstances offered in evidence; and only if they found that these circumstances corroborated the confession, should they allow it any weight. With the usual adjuration to allow the prisoner the benefit of any doubts they might have, His Honour dismissed the jury at one o'clock.

At two o'clock the foreman reappeared, to announce that there was no likelihood of any agreement being reached. His Honour adjourned the court for three hours. At five, and again at six, they were still undecided. An hour later they were locked up for the night. At ten next morning, after a night of argument, the position of the two opposing parties was unchanged. His Honour had no alternative; he dismissed the twelve men who had taken his warnings too closely to heart, and announced that the matter must be re-tried with another jury.

On Friday, just a week after the first trial began, proceedings were recommenced before the same judge. The evidence was heard again, summed up again, and the jury again dismissed to consider it at six in the evening. Two hours later they returned with the unanimous verdict: Guilty.

The prisoner, asked in the usual formula if he had anything to say why sentence of death should not be passed on him, uttered a long and coherent protest; his voice, the newspapers thought, "betrayed no trepidation, and perhaps only a natural weakness." This statement was so long and circumstantial that the Judge, in his final address, felt called upon to reply to it point by point. Said His Honour:

It is no infrequent thing for me to hear protestations of innocence after conviction; but I have never found it consistent with duty, truth, or the interests of society to accord them any serious consideration. Even under the gallows I have known their innocence protested by men of whose guilt I have felt as certain as of anything I have known personally myself, and whose guilt was demonstrated by evidence so clear that no human being possessed of the power of reason could doubt for an instant that the result arrived at had been right. Of course these protestations with many persons go for much, but by those with more experience, equal feeling, more responsibility, who desire to see justice and nothing more, they really pass unheeded.

You are evidently a person of great ability, acuteness, and considerable cunning, with sufficient cleverness to seize upon weak points and make them appear an excuse, which to reflecting persons could be no palliation whatsoever.

You say you are not afraid to die, and I trust you are not, but believe me that in the opinion of the majority of thinking men, wherever this evidence will go, you ought not to hope for forgiveness here.

You say you desire only to clear your character. For whose sake? For the sake of your wife and children. Can it be possible that any human being that has heard what has passed at this trial, who has read the diary, who knows your intercourse with that abandoned woman, supposes that you attempt to clear your character for the sake of your wife and children? How can you, who in the same breath utter a falsehood, be believed in this?

The jury having now pronounced their verdict, I am now at liberty to look at other matters I did not think proper to refer to before. I did not read one line of that to which I am now going to allude. I was informed that Mrs. Kinder might possibly have been tried upon evidence to be given by your wife. Upon inquiry I then made I found that she had indeed given some information that she was stated to have given to your sister in a confession, but having been permitted to see you, I believe she has receded from it.

BERTRAND: I have never seen my wife since I have been in gaol.

HIS LORDSHIP: Then it may be possible she has not receded from it. I shall feel myself called upon after your addresses to lay before the public that statement. If she was not called as a witness with the intelligence that you possess you must have known that she could not be called. She has made a statement which, unless your sister is perjured, positively confirms the verdict of the jury.

BERTRAND: My sister is perjured.

His Lordship: Then the case displays unparalleled wickedness, but this, the deepest in dye—that a sister, for no object of her own, should falsely state that your wife admitted to her that you had shot Kinder. She may have some remains of affection for your children, and even for the character of their father, but can I doubt that your sister spoke the truth when she said she heard this extraordinary statement from you?

I do not believe you are an insane man, but a perfectly sane man would never have made the declaration you have made; and I thoroughly believe your sister when she related this: "I said to his wife, Good God, has Henry really shot him"; and she answered, "Yes, he has." Her details, too, are consistent with my idea of the mode in which the deed was done.

Can anyone doubt the guilt when a man is accused by his wife and sister, and their statement sustains and accords with all the probabilities of the case? I hear your declaration with sorrow and with pain, but I place not the slightest dependence upon it.

I have a greater responsibility than the jury and I declare to you now, before God, I believe you thoroughly guilty, and I have no more doubt of it than that you are before me at this moment. When I first heard the case I did entertain doubts, and I have lain awake hours thinking over the various points involved, and determined if those doubts were not moved not to try you again. But now I have not the slightest doubt of your guilt, and I believe I can demonstrate to any man that you are guilty.

I think it utterly impossible for a rational person to believe that that man shot himself. You say he had intentions. I have had great experience in criminal trials, extending over thirty-two years, and have tried perhaps more cases than any judge in any country, and I have never known a case clearer than your own; nor have I known a single case in which a man who was really determined to kill himself talked about it to his friends. If a man talks of committing suicide, it is almost a proof that he never intends to take his life. Is there the slightest probability that without any temptation and with his pipe in his mouth—having only half an hour before been playing with his child, and just bought oysters for his wife and given them to the servant to prepare for supper—this unfortunate man should, no pistol having been seen in his possession about that time, go into the drawing-room in your presence, in the presence of your wife and his own, and commit a bungling attempt at suicide like that described by you? No person ever heard of such a thing in the annals of crime.

He might have been embarrassed and addicted to drinking.

Had he not been a drunkard his wife probably would not have been seduced by Jackson, and you would not have debauched her. If drink did not give the temptation to crime by him, it afforded opportunities for crime in others. All the records of Criminal Courts show repeated instances of crime being committed through the agency of drunkenness—the victim being a drunkard, and affording opportunities for crime against himself. I do not think Kinder was drunk on that day, but whether drunk or sober it is inconceivable that he could have intended to take his life in that bungling, stupid, incredible manner. I find you had every temptation, every motive, for destroying him. You were madly in love with this woman, with a passion eating into your vitals, and you would have committed any crime to have her as your own. Half mad I believe you to be, for you never could have talked as you did, unless there was a partial disturbance of your mind—wild, eccentric, strange, to an utterly unprecedented degree, your mind was overshadowed by the influence this unhappy woman had acquired over you.

I hear you say that at the time of writing the impassioned sentences to her, burning with love, you had no other intent than to satisfy the cravings of her romantic feelings. Why, you admit you wrote them as a deep and abandoned hypocrite. I do not believe it. I believe that, maddened by the passion of your attachment to her, you did this terrible deed, and your statements previous were to be accounted for by the idea that in saying his death was likely to occur, when it eventually took place you as his friend would not be looked on with suspicion. I do not make any excuses for Jackson; his conduct was extremely bad. But I feel some sympathy for him, believing that he spoke the truth. I think he deserves punishment, but the law was never meant for a case like his, but for persons who wrote threatening to accuse persons of crimes they never committed, I am satisfied that he believed what he said you did to him in uttering dark, mysterious, dangerous hints, and used expressions justifying him in the belief that you intended to commit the murder; and, therefore, I think the man should be pardoned. He has had sufficient punishment for writing that imprudent letter. But he did not demand money by threatening to accuse you of crime without having grounds for believing you committed it.

You allude to what you call a prejudice against you, yet you must see that it arises in an abhorrence of your proved crimes, and which is the most universal feeling of the country, and this verdict will, I believe, be received with perfect approval.

33

Nothing can pain a Judge so much as the assumption that a verdict is unjust. I believe you to be guilty, and I shall feel deeper pain than I express if I thought there were anything wrong in the verdict, because I am satisfied you will suffer death. I am sure you deserve the verdict and I am certain in my mind that it is true.

And when you talk about idle words and complain of being spoken of as a fiend, surely when one reads your journal, hears what is said by your sister, by Mrs. Robertson, by Burne, by Bellhouse, and knows why you invited this man to your house, all their testimony uniting and tending the same way, you cannot but be regarded as a fiend. You are not a human being in feeling.

I can speak of you with compassion, because I do not think that you are fully possessed of the mind that God has been pleased to give to almost all of us. On that account alone I feel some sympathy. It is distressing and sad that any father of a family, a man that might be useful in his generation, should die on the scaffold for a crime that makes human nature shudder.

The sentence is that you be taken hence to the place whence you came, and thence, on a day to be named by the Governor in Council, to the place of execution, and at that place to be hanged till your body be dead. If you are to find mercy, as I hope you will, seek it elsewhere, but from no human tribunal.

But His Honour's certainty of the prisoner's guilt, and his desire to save time, led him into an impropriety. To avoid calling again every witness who had spoken at the first trial, the Chief Justice, during the course of the second trial, read to the jury from his own notes certain items of evidence. This had been done, in fact, at the instance of the prisoner himself, who, weary with repetitions, had pleaded that His Honour should take every means to bring his ordeal soon to an end. But the Supreme Court, to which appeal was immediately made, found this a point of great significance, and the four judges' opinions were equally divided as to whether or no there had been a mistrial. It was argued for four days; the result of a similar inquiry in England, which might afford a precedent, was ascertained by letter and telegram; and as a result the Court ordered that the verdict should be vacated the record; the prisoner meanwhile being held in custody to await his third trial at the next sittings of the

Supreme Court in its criminal jurisdiction, to be held in the following May.

The Legislative Assembly of New South Wales then took up the affair. The behaviour and competence of the Chief Justice, with one of the other judges of the Supreme Court, offered matter for questions. The Government was implored, on the one hand to appeal to the Privy Council, and, alternatively, begged not to bring the judicature of the colony into disrepute by so doing. A magnificent public quarrel was blowing up, when Bertrand himself, to use one of his own phrases, cut the knot. The doctors at long last gave him a certificate of madness, and he was removed from Darlinghurst to the prison for criminal lunatics at Parramatta.

X

From the point of view of a reader of detection stories, this is an unsatisfactory crime. The murderer was insane, and the purist in these matters prefers a murderer who is *compos mentis*; the chain of logical deduction should not, he thinks, clank to a madman's fandango. It is a crime which defies all the canons. Premeditated, it yet was committed before a cloud of witness; even, one of these had been brought to the spot marked with a cross deliberately, and against her will, by the chief performer. Its object was to obtain sole possession of a woman who had already yielded to the criminal, and was, in the words of his associate, " as good as a wife to him ". It was discovered, not through any process of suspicion and inquiry, but owing to the indiscretion of the man who had actually bluffed a coroner's jury into a verdict of suicide, but who, even to save his neck, could not hold his tongue. The police had only to listen, to search, and, when they had found Bertrand's letters and diary, to present their case.

That Bertrand did kill Henry Kinder is indisputable. The amateur of crime, disgusted with the whole flamboyantly silly proceeding, finds a stimulus to curiosity at one point only. By

35

what means was Henry Kinder killed? The coroner's jury brought in a verdict of death by shooting. The post-mortem finding, death from haemorrhage and shock, was nothing more than a variation upon the jury's theme. Nor is it easy to pick out the truth from Bertrand's grimaces and boasts. Still, the puzzling facts may be compared with his fantasies to afford matter for a guess.

Kinder did not die until four days after he was wounded by the discharge of Bertrand's pistol; was, indeed, in a fair way to recover from the wound which broke his jaw and tore off most of his ear. He died suddenly, after Jane Bertrand had given him a glass of milk. This, Jane's own story, comes at second-hand; but Mrs. Robertson testified to hearing Bertrand crying out in his fit, the night before Kinder died: " Bring the milk and mix the poison." In Bertrand's possession were found two vegetable poisons, aconite and belladonna, both of a nature to defy the chemist who assisted at the investigation of Kinder's exhumed body.

To quote Dr. Ainsworth Mitchell, editor of *The Analyst*: " Medical criminals have often banked upon difficulties likely to be experienced in detecting vegetable alkaloids." The test for aconitine was not perfected until later, when Dr. Stevenson, by a series of experiments upon mice, established its presence in the body of Dr. Lamson's victim. Even so, the defence in that famous case suggested the possibility that effects attributed to aconitine might also have been caused by some substance of an alkaloidal nature formed in the decomposition of animal matter. Belladonna, more familiar nowadays under the name of its active principle, atropine, was, and is, equally as elusive. Both these poisons were (quite legitimately) in Bertrand's possession; and Bertrand was a dentist, with enough general medical knowledge to call for comment from the judge. He may be allowed, for purposes of argument, to rank as a medical criminal. It is, for the detection story reader, a problem incapable of solution; hardly a problem at all, but rather a question of looking upon this picture and on this, and making a choice of suspicions. On the one hand a man succumbs to the shock of a wound not necessarily fatal, as a result of previous known excesses in drink, by which his resistance has been weakened. " It would shorten anybody's days." On the other hand, a murderer, already over the edge of sanity, hears that the victim whose death has been for weeks the main concern of his imagination is about to recover. He has poisons at hand, and an instrument; his wife, dazed, frightened, unable to refuse to perform his will. He is aware, in some convolution of his uneasy brain, that vegetable alkaloids take a lot of tracing in a dead man's body.

Penny plain, twopence coloured. There is, and can be now no proof ; as young Osric says, nothing neither way. But to the writer, as to the reader of detection stories, the second alternative is the more acceptable of the two.

XI

The main interest of this trial, apart from those purely legal complications which eventually brought about an appeal to the Privy Council, lies in the picture it offers of a lunatic murderer going about his business unhampered by sane persons to whom he had confided his purpose. " People don't do these things," the citizens of Sydney told each other ; men capable of earning a fair living and playing a good game of cards are not to be suspected of homicidal tendencies. They took no steps, therefore, to restrain the young dentist who roared like a tiger when yawning in the street, who strolled Sydney by night dressed as a woman, vowed he could raise ghosts, and in the midst of a rubber of whist announced, with appropriate gesture, that he was the personal devil.

De Fries, Jackson, and Burne seem to have made no effort to get a doctor to Bertrand, or, when Kinder died, to inform the police of what they knew. De Fries did indeed plead with Bertrand for better treatment of his wife, and told Mrs. Robertson that he must be insane to go on as he did. But " he said it in a jocular manner." Burne, a party to all his employer's plans, buying pistols for him, rowing with him while the murderous tomahawk swung under his coat, held his tongue, would not speak until he was subpœnaed, even after Bertrand had been gaoled on another charge. He was twenty years old, and by no means unsophisticated, having played ' juvenile business ' at the Victoria Theatre before he came to the dentist as assistant. It is inconceivable that, after the first expedition in the boat, he should not have perceived Bertrand's mental condition. Having accompanied him on three of these ventures and bought the pistols, it is understandable that he should then be afraid to speak. But how came he to undertake such commissions? How came he to remain in that equivocal employment at all? Fear accounts for some part of his conduct; for the rest we must hold responsible the reluctance of the normal human being to suppose that a man with whom he is in daily contact, and from whom he takes orders, is not right in his mind.

It is evident from the behaviour of these people that in many ways Bertrand could tell a hawk from a handsaw still; he was but mad nor'-nor'-west. His journal speaks rationally of money matters, and gives a shrewd picture of Mr. Wood, Helen Kinder's shiftless father, who, having been told how matters stood between his daughter and the dentist, attempted to make capital out of his knowledge. His brutalities to poor Jane were kept secret, though he thrashed her with a whip and assaulted her with a penknife, after which last incident Jane showed her sister-in-law a pair of corsets soaked with blood. His mother-in-law, who visited the house often, was able to swear in court that he was very kind to her daughter, and by no means a man of strange manners and habits. Bellhouse, told the facts of the murder by Bertrand, casually, after a game of cards, could not make up his mind to believe that what he had heard was the truth, and lay awake all night debating the question. It would seem that in general Bertrand's manner was normal enough; so that it must have been shocking to hear him offer, over the whist-table, to raise the ghost of the man he had killed; or to look up from that most innocent of occupations, the bathing of a baby, and be told: " Kinder did not shoot himself, I shot him."

The heroine of the story, Ellen Kinder, makes no such extraordinary impression upon the mind; her behaviour rouses no question. She was a hearty, handsome, practical woman, fond of her pleasures, combining promiscuity with a genuine affection and care for her children. It is easy enough to believe that she yielded to Bertrand from fear; yet her imagination was not of a quality to tell her that the threats he was for ever making against her husband might one day come to action. The passion in her letters has in it a tang of theatre and of the expected. Perhaps this is always so; perhaps the true language of persons moved by great excitement is that of melodrama. " I had rather see you dead at my feet "; " I cannot live without seeing you "; " I shall go mad at the thought of our meeting "—all these are stock phrases which may stand for the expression of genuine as of false emotion. But the voice of the real Ellen Kinder is not to be heard in them. Rather she comes alive in such phrases as these, taken at random from her letters to her lover :

" Papa quite expects me to make a good match one of these days. I tell him I would not give thanks for the best man living, if I could make my own living."

" I feel my position very much, as I know how little we are able to afford the extra expense we must be at. If there were anything I could do to make it up I should not mind, but there is absolutely nothing. I do not know how things are to go on if it were not for the children."

" We are almost decided to take an hotel here, but on second thought I do not care much for it. I should not mind a respectable house in Sydney, but this is such a bad place. This is, oh, dreadfully matter of fact, dear dear love, but it is necessary, therefore I hope you will not mind it."

" You see, deary, an hotel is such a public affair, that my position would be noticeable directly. I should not like to be in a public, and I know that you would not like for me to be a disgrace to everyone connected with me."

" I must not forget to thank you for seeing about my business. I should like to get into a first-rate establishment for a few weeks to learn dressmaking, as a really good one would do well here. In that case, there is no place like Sydney; but, darling, I leave my-self entirely in your hands—feeling, love, you will do everything for the best."

It is not surprising after all these protestations to note that the first employment found by Mrs. Kinder after her acquittal was in an hotel. She returned to New Zealand, whence she had come three years before; a public-house keeper with some sense of the value of advertisement engaged her as barmaid, in which position she was completely successful. Almost at once, however, she married again, and, for all anyone at this date can tell, died full of years and highly respected.

PART II

CONSTANCE KENT

by John Rhode

CONSTANCE KENT

THE name of Constance Kent and the nature of the extra-ordinary crime to which she eventually confessed are familiar to almost everybody. For this reason I do not propose to give a detailed description of the crime itself. To those who wish to peruse it more fully, many sources are available.[1] My present purpose is to deal with the curious personality of the criminal herself in the light of information which has become available during the past few years.

A brief résumé of the crime may, however, be found convenient. Mr. Samuel Saville Kent had at one time been in business in the City of London. About 1834 he obtained the appointment of Sub-Inspector of Factories for the West of England, which was then the important centre of the cloth trade. In the year 1860 he was living at Road Hill House, on the border of Somerset and Wiltshire. The house stands back from the road, by which it is approached by a carriage drive. It is of a fair size, and then stood in about half an acre of ground laid out as lawn, shrubbery, kitchen-garden and flower-garden. On the right-hand side of the house, looking from the drive, was a spacious paved courtyard communicating with the kitchen and domestic offices on the one side, and on the other with the kitchen-garden. Two pairs of large and high gates opened out of the yard, one pair into a lane running parallel to the side of the house, the other into the carriage drive. Outside the latter gates and to the right of them, was a small shrubbery, concealing a detached earth-closet. At the period of the crime this closet was rarely used, the house having been fitted with inside sanitation.

On the evening of Friday, June 29, 1860, the house was occu-

---

[1] Among these I may perhaps be permitted to mention my *The Case of Constance Kent*, in the Famous Trials Series. London, Geoffrey Bles, 1928.

pied by twelve individuals. These were Mr. Kent; his second wife, who was then expecting a confinement; three daughters: Mary Ann, Elizabeth and Constance; and a son, William, of Mr. Kent's first marriage. Two daughters, Mary Amelia and Emilie, and a son, Francis Saville, of Mr. Kent's second marriage. The cook, the housemaid and the nurse, by name Elizabeth Gough. On this particular evening there was no deviation from the routine of the house. Mr. and Mrs. Kent slept in a room on the first floor. This room was in the front of the house. Separated from it by a fairly wide passage at the end of which was a dressing-room, was the nursery. In the nursery slept Elizabeth Gough and the two younger children of the second marriage: Francis Saville, aged four, and Emilie, aged two. Mary Amelia, eldest child of the second marriage, slept in the room occupied by Mr. and Mrs. Kent. The remaining rooms on the first floor were unoccupied. On the second floor the two eldest daughters of the first marriage, Mary Ann and Elizabeth, slept together in the room above that occupied by Mr. and Mrs. Kent. Constance Kent slept alone in the adjoining room, above the passage and the dressing-room. The cook and housemaid slept together in the room adjoining hers above the nursery. It is worthy of remark that the partitions between these three rooms were very thin and there is abundant evidence that sounds originating in one room could be heard in that next door. On this floor, looking out at the back of the house, was the room occupied by William Kent. Two other rooms were unoccupied.

At the usual hour, which was half-past seven, Elizabeth Gough put the youngest child Emilie to bed in the nursery. Half an hour later she put Francis Saville to bed, also in the nursery. The remainder of the family retired in rotation. Before the cook went to bed she fastened and secured the domestic offices. Similarly, before she went to bed, the housemaid fastened and secured the remainder of the ground floor, including a french window in the drawing-room which looked out towards the back of the house. The nurse went to bed a little before eleven, leaving Mr. and Mrs. Kent in the dining-room. She was some time in the nursery before she undressed, having her supper and tidying up. While she was thus occupied Mrs. Kent came into the room and looked at the children asleep in bed. Mrs. Kent then went downstairs and came up to bed a few minutes later. Until this moment the nursery door had been open in order that the nurse might hear any sound from the child who was sleeping in the Kent's room. As she went to bed, Mrs. Kent shut this door. Mr. Kent was the last to retire. He went to bed a little before midnight, having, according to his own subsequent statement, examined all the fastenings in the house.

At five o'clock the next morning the nurse awoke. She looked at Francis' cot and found that he was no longer there. This occasioned her no surprise at the time. She supposed that during the night Mrs. Kent had heard the child crying and had come in and removed him to her own room. This supposition was strengthened by the fact that the bedclothes of the cot had been neatly re-arranged. The nurse then went to sleep again.

At a quarter or twenty minutes to seven, the nurse went into Mrs. Kent's room. Supposing that Mrs. Kent had both Mary Amelia and Francis, her object was to ask for one of them so that she might dress it. She knocked twice on the door but obtained no answer, and in view of Mrs. Kent's condition thought it better to disturb her no further. However, she made another attempt at a quarter-past seven, when she found Mrs. Kent dressed in her dressing-gown. On that occasion Mrs. Kent told her that she had not seen the child. The nurse then went upstairs to the second floor to make inquiries of Mary Ann and Elizabeth. At the time of Constance Kent's appearance before the magistrates, the nurse gave the following evidence upon this point:

> Miss Constance slept in a room which is between where her two sisters sleep and where the cook and housemaid sleep. The partition between them is very thin. You can even hear a paper rustling in either room. When I went to inquire of the Misses Kent the prisoner came to the door. I observed nothing unusual in her manner at the time.[1]

[1] Quoted from a contemporary report in the *Somerset and Wilts Journal*.

45

Meanwhile the housemaid had made a significant discovery. This is best described in her own words.[1]

On Friday evening I fastened the door and shutters in the drawing-room as usual. I am positive that I did so. I have no doubt in the matter whatever. The shutters fasten with iron bars and each has two brass bolts besides. That was all made secure on Friday evening. The door has a bolt and a lock and I bolted it and turned the key of the lock, so that anyone coming from the house would have the power of unfastening the door and windows and anyone coming in from the outside must smash the windows and then would not be able to open the shutters without using a centre bit or making a hole in the shutters. On Friday evening I retired to bed about a quarter to eleven and rose about five minutes past six on Saturday morning. Mr. Kent was the last person who went to bed that evening. He is in the habit of staying till the last.

When I came down in the morning, I saw that the drawing-room door was a little open, the bolt was back and the lock turned. There was no displacement of the furniture in the room. Of the windows, the lower shutters were open, the bolts being back and the window slightly open. There was no blood, footmarks or displacement in the room.

Search within the house having proved unavailing, the alarm was given. Mr. Kent himself took horse and started for Trowbridge, some five miles away, to inform the superintendent of police. The neighbours were called in to assist the search. Two of these found the missing child. His body was in the earth-closet beside the shrubbery. The throat had been cut, almost severing the head from the body, and there was a deep wound in the breast. The body was wrapped in a bloodstained blanket which had been taken from its cot. Mr. Kent was recalled and a doctor was summoned. On his arrival he, Dr. Parsons, saw that the child had been dead at least five hours. The consensus of medical opinion subsequently agreed that death must have taken place about 1 a.m. on Saturday morning.

[1] This statement had been made at the inquest. It is quoted from the *Somerset and Wilts Journal.*

The investigation into the crime was at first carried out without the slightest attempt at method. Mr. Henry Rhodes, in his *Some Persons Unknown*[1] says:

> In this affair, the search seems to have been carried out with great negligence and indiscriminately by the police and the neighbours, while the interrogation of the members of the family left a great deal to be desired. Scientific methods, whether in the matter of taking evidence or in the discovery of clues, were not then popular.

This was no exaggeration. The local constable, though an early visitor to the scene, took no steps to preserve such clues as might exist. He seems to have departed almost immediately to inform his superiors. Meanwhile, the excited villagers took every advantage of their opportunity. To quote a contemporary account[1]:

> The house and premises were then minutely searched. Male and female searchers in the course of the day examined every individual and every room, box and water-closet about the place, emptied the earth-closet and scoured the vicinity, but without finding any knife or garment stained with blood, or any article to afford the least clue, except a piece of flannel apparently worn as a chest protector which was underneath the child's body stained with blood.

It was hardly to be expected that the zeal of these amateurs should be rewarded by success.

The inquest was held upon the following Monday. The foreman of the jury was a local parson, a close friend of Mr. Kent and his family. He seems to have done his best to shield the family from any breath of the suspicions which had already been aroused. The coroner seems to have sympathized with his attitude. No member of the family was called upon to give evidence until a protest was made by a majority of the jury. The coroner reluctantly acceded to their request. He said:

> I must say, I do not see what end will be answered by it. They will only confirm what we have already heard and say they know

[1] London, John Murray, 1931.
[2] In the *Somerset and Wilts Journal*.

no more about it. But it is the wish of the majority of the jury, it must be done.

The jury then requested that Constance and William Kent might be examined. The evidence given by Constance Kent on this occasion will be considered later. The coroner then recommended the jury to record a verdict of murder by some person or persons unknown. The majority of the jurymen were not inclined to accept this advice, but were over-ruled by their foreman. This verdict was actually returned after the inquest had lasted five hours—an hour and a half of which, it is stated, were spent by the jury in examining the body.

The next step in the investigation of the crime was an inquiry by the Trowbridge Bench, which had for its ostensible purpose the examination of witnesses. This inquiry opened on July 9th and was continued at intervals until the 27th. During this period one of the magistrates approached the Home Secretary and, as a result, Inspector Whicher, an officer of Scotland Yard, was sent to Road to assist in the investigations.

Whicher was an extremely able man. He did not arrive on the scene until a fortnight after the crime had been committed, but he set to work methodically to examine such clues as still remained. As a result he accumulated evidence which seemed to him to point to Constance Kent as the culprit. At his instance she was arrested. After being in custody for a week, she appeared before the magistrate and was triumphantly acquitted. Local opinion was not favourable to Whicher. In its eyes Constance Kent had been martyred in the cause of officialdom. Loud applause greeted the announcement of the chairman of the Bench that the prisoner should be released on her father becoming bound for her on £200, to appear when called upon.

Whicher returned to London to be overwhelmed with censure for arresting an innocent girl. But none the less he remained convinced of her guilt. On November 23rd of the same year he wrote to the Chief Superintendent of the Bristol police upon the subject. In the course of this letter he said:

Now, in my opinion, if there was ever one man to be pitied or who has been more calumniated than another, that unfortunate man is Mr. Kent. It was bad enough to have his darling child cruelly murdered, but to be branded as the murderer is far worse, and, according to the present state of public opinion, he will be so branded till the day of his death unless a confession is made by the person whom I firmly believe committed the deed. I have little doubt that the confession would have been made if Miss Constance had been remanded for another week.

The next sensation connected with the case was an extraordinary one. An unemployed mason who eventually gave his name as John Edmond Gagg, accosted a railway policeman at Wolverton station in Buckinghamshire and confessed to the crime. He was taken to Trowbridge and there examined by the magistrate. Short examination showed that never in his life had he been to Road and that he was many miles away at the commission of the crime.

The next step was the opening of an inquiry by Mr. Slack, a solicitor practising in Bath. Mr. Slack refused to divulge by which authority he acted. All he would say was that "those who instructed him had the authority by the Home Office for so doing." His inquiry opened on September 17th and, apparently as the result of it, the local police took action. Elizabeth Gough had left Mr. Kent's service by this time and had gone to her home at Isleworth. She was there arrested, brought to Trowbridge, and formally charged with the murder of Francis Saville Kent. At her appearance before the magistrate no further evidence was produced. The Bench had no option but to release her. The remarks of the chairman on this occasion are interesting:

The magistrate has determined on not committing the prisoner for trial although there was a case of grave suspicion against her, and material had been adduced which with additions might hereafter be brought to bear against her. They would bind her accordingly to appear when called on in two sureties of £50 each.

On November 3rd one of the magistrates, Mr. Saunders, opened an inquiry upon his own account. He examined a number

49

of witnesses, and in spite of, or perhaps because of, the irregularity of his proceedings he elicited certain very curious facts. For this reason the record of his proceedings is worthy of perusal in spite of its farcical nature.[1] But it led to no definite results and was finally abandoned.

Meanwhile Mr. Slack had not been idle. On November 26th an application was made by the Attorney-General at the Court of Queen's Bench before the Lord Chief Justice for a writ for a better inquest on the body of Francis Saville Kent. The Solicitor-General appeared on behalf of the writ, and Sir Fitzroy Kelly represented the coroner in opposing it. The latter gained the day. The Lord Chief Justice said that the only grounds upon which the application rested was the allegation of misconduct on the part of the coroner, in the single instance of his not accepting the offer spontaneously made by the solicitor of Mr. Kent and not examining Mr. Kent. His Lordship said he thought the coroner would have exercised the sounder discretion if he had accepted the offer, but it was not for a mere error of judgment that this court would set aside an inquisition demanded by a coroner's jury. If there had been judicial misconduct of a nature to justify the court to set aside the inquisition, it would still be a question whether that should be done and a new inquisition issued, when it was seen what the object was, viz., to examine those among whom the guilt of the crime necessarily rested, to ascertain from their separate depositions which of whom had committed the crime. That would not be a proper exercise of the jurisdiction of this court. To issue such an inquisition to obtain evidence against them for that was an object which the law would not sanction. The rule was discharged.

After this the investigation was abandoned. Mr. Kent and his family left Road Hill House and settled at Weston-super-

---

[1] A full account of Mr. Saunders' proceedings may be found in a book entitled, *The Great Crime of 1860*, published in 1861 by E. Marlborough and Co., London. The author of this book was Mr. Stapleton, a surgeon who assisted at the post-mortem on the body of the murdered child, and who was apparently on terms of intimacy with the Kent family. The book is now, unfortunately, out of print.

Mare. The contents were sold by auction, and an enormous crowd attended the sale. The object of the members of the crowd was not to bid but to inspect the earth-closet. It is recorded that

> Superintendent Foley was often requested to gratify the eager curiosity of the visitors by showing it. The spots of blood on the floor are still there, and it was strange to see young and fashionably dressed ladies seeking to learn every particular and see every spot connected with the murder.[1]

Four years later, on April 25, 1865, Constance Kent surrendered herself at Bow Street Police Court and confessed to the murder of Francis Saville Kent.

Constance Kent was the ninth child of Samuel Saville Kent's first marriage. In 1829 Mr. Kent had married Mary Ann Winder, and by her had ten children, five of whom died shortly after birth. At the date of the crime four of these children were still living, Mary Ann, Elizabeth, Constance, and William. Constance had been born at Sidmouth in February 1844. It is alleged[2] by Dr Stapleton, who subsequently became a friend of the family, that her mother had exhibited symptoms of insanity as early as 1836. According to his account, these symptoms were not very serious. He says, however, that " the early treatment of Mrs. Kent appears to have been most lamentably deficient and abortive."

Six years later, however, Mr. Kent decided to employ a capable woman to superintend the children and the household. But the fact of Mrs. Kent's insanity has been questioned. A single quotation[3] will suffice to exemplify the doubt which has been thrown upon the matter.

> Was Mrs. Kent insane? Her two eldest daughters always vehemently denied it. No act has ever been mentioned to prove

[1] *Somerset and Wilts Journal.*

[2] Stapleton, *op. cit.*

[3] This is from a remarkable document, addressed to the author shortly after the publication of his *The Case of Constance Kent*, and now deposited in the library of the Detection Club, London. It is dated February 1929, and was

it. The second governess, who was employed for the education of the two eldest daughters, arrived about the time of John's birth in 1842. She was a pretty, very capable woman. Considering Mrs. Kent's frequent confinements, also several miscarriages, and that servants took advantage of the circumstances, was it anything out of·the way that Mr. Kent was only too glad to find someone willing and able to superintend the menage? Many wives are incompetent or unwilling as housekeepers, but they are not therefore deemed insane. As Mr. Kent only ceased to live with her about two years later, did he then consider her so?

When Constance was four years old the family moved to Walton, between Clevedon and Portishead in Somersetshire. They remained here four years, and in March 1852 moved once more, this time to Baynton House, near Corsham in Wiltshire. A few weeks after this move Mrs. Kent died. In August 1853 Mr. Kent took as his second wife the governess-housekeeper, Miss Pratt. In 1855 the family moved to Road Hill House, where the four children of the second marriage were born. The second of these was Francis Saville, who was born in August 1856.

At the time of Francis' birth, Constance was twelve, and from various sources something may be gathered of her childhood. Mr. Stapleton says[1]:

For many months after her birth great apprehensions were entertained that Constance would share the fate of the four previous children of Mrs. Kent. That she struggled through the feebleness of her early infancy is chiefly due to the devotion and personal attention of Miss Pratt, by whom she was fed, nursed and waited upon for months. By degrees her bodily constitution assumed that healthy development and growth which has bestowed on her the contour and command of a powerful physique. As she grew up Constance manifested a strong, obstinate and

[1] *Op. cit.*

posted in Sydney, New South Wales. Though unsigned, it contains ample internal evidence of having been written, if not by Constance Kent herself, at least by some person having a very intimate knowledge of her childhood and history. Although anonymous, the wording of this document is sufficiently convincing to allow its quotation, not necessarily in support of facts, but as shedding light upon the strange character of Constance Kent. In subsequent notes it will be cited as the Sydney Document.

determined will, and her conduct even as a little child gave evidence of an irritable and impassioned nature.

The document already quoted[1] draws a vivid picture of the relations between Constance and Miss Pratt.

The governess had made a great pet of Constance and was very fond of her, but soon trouble began. The governess had a theory that once a child said a letter or spelt a word right it could not forget it, and she conscientiously believed that it was her duty to treat any lapse as obstinacy. The letter H gave Constance many hours of confinement in a room where she listened longingly to the music and the sights on the lawn outside. When words were to be mastered punishments became more severe. Days were spent shut up in a room with dry bread and milk and water for tea. At other times she would be stood up in a corner of the hall sobbing, "I want to be good, I do, I do," till she came to the conclusion that goodness was impossible for a child and that she could only hope to grow up quickly as grown-ups were never naughty. At times she gave way to furious fits of temper and was locked away in a distant room and sometimes in a cellar that her noise might not annoy people.

Constance did not take her punishments very seriously, but generally managed to get some amusement out of them. Once after being particularly provocative and passionate, the governess put her down in a dark wine cellar. She fell on a heap of straw and fancied herself in the dungeon of a great castle, a prisoner taken in a battle fighting for Bonnie Prince Charlie and to be taken to the block next morning. When the governess unlocked the door and told her to come up she was looking rather pleased over her fancies. The governess asked her what she was smiling about: "Oh," she said, "only the funny rats."

"What rats?" said the governess, who did not know there were any there.

"They do not hurt me. Only dance and play about."

After that, to her disappointment she was shut in the beer cellar, a light room but with a window too high to look out of. She managed to pull the spigot out of a cask of beer. After that, she was locked up in one of two spare rooms at the end of the vestibule, shut off by double doors. She liked the big room, for it had a large four-poster bed she could climb about, but the little room was dreary. The rooms had a legend attached to them and

[1] The Sydney document.

were said to be haunted on a certain date when a blue fire burned in the fireplace.

At one time at Baynton House Constance's place of punishment was in one of the empty garrets. The house was built in the shape of an E, and there was a parapet round the best part of the house. She used to climb out of the window and up the bend to the top of the roof and slide down the other side. She tied an old fur across her chest to act the monkey and call it playing Cromwell. To return she got through the window of another garret. The governess was puzzled at always finding the door unlocked with the key left in. The servants were questioned, but of course knew nothing. One day she found Constance and her brother out on the ledge, and told them not to do it as it was dangerous. Next time when she did climb out she found the window fastened. She could not climb back the way she came, but just where the parapet ended was the window of a room where the groom slept. She reached across and climbed through, and though she upset and broke a jug on the washstand, the cat got the credit for this. Afterwards, she heard that her father did not approve of the window being fastened to trap her, and said that when unruly she could be shut in the study, the room where her father wrote and kept his papers. Being on the ground floor she easily got out of the window and passed her time climbing the trees in the shrubbery, also displaying a very cruel disposition by impaling slugs and snails on sticks in trees, calling these crucifixions. The affection between Constance and the governess no longer existed.

Meanwhile, Miss Pratt's position in the household had become the subject of unfavourable comment. Mr. Kent's eldest surviving son, Edward, nine years older than Constance, seems to have been the first to express disapproval. It is reported that one morning when he was at home at Sidmouth on his holidays, he met his father coming out of the governess's room which happened to be next to his. A scene took place between father and son, as a result of which the latter was promptly sent back to school. After this Edward was very rarely at home. He took to the sea as a profession, and died at Havana of yellow fever in 1858.

At this time Constance was too young to notice anything of this. But as she grew up her childish recollections began to assume significance. She realized that there had been something mysterious about the treatment of her mother.

Why did her mother, when speaking to her, often call herself, your poor mamma, which the governess said was silly? Why was the governess taken out for drives and her mother never? Why was her father in the library with the governess while the rest of the family was with her mother? She remembered many little incidents which seemed strange. One was during a thunderstorm, when the governess acted as though she were frightened and rushed over to her father who drew her down on his knee and kissed her. The governess exclaimed: "Oh, not before the child!" Though her mother seemed to feel being placed in the background, why did she not resent it and assert herself?[1]

The relations between Mr. Kent and the governess can only be conjectural and they do not concern us directly. But in the light of subsequent events, we are bound to consider the effect of them upon a child of the passionate nature of Constance. An antagonism developed between the two, which increased after Mr. Kent's second marriage. By this time her stepmother seems to have given Constance up in despair, and made no attempt to propitiate her. In any case, Constance would have been a difficult child to propitiate if contemporary accounts of her are to be believed. On the other hand, the second Mrs. Kent seems to have shown very little sympathy with the children of the first family. These were kept under constant surveillance and their friendships very strictly regulated. On one occasion the two eldest girls made friends with the daughters of two neighbouring families, but as these families showed a reluctance to call upon the Kents, probably owing to their disapproval of Mrs. Kent, orders were issued that these friendships must cease and the prohibition was extended to the younger children.

One day when Constance and her brother were supposed to be attending to their little garden behind the shrubbery, they heard some merry laughter from the neighbouring garden. They went to the hedge and looked over longingly at the children playing with visitors. They were invited to join, but were afraid.

[1] The Sydney document.

They were seen and their disobedience punished. The little gardens were uprooted and trampled down. Constance made some futile efforts to revive hers. No pets were allowed, two little tropical birds sent by the eldest son to his sisters were confined to a cold back room and died.

There was no evidence of direct cruelty on the part of the second Mrs. Kent towards Constance. She seems to have misunderstood the child's nature and Constance, in turn, was undoubtedly resentful of authority. At school she was perpetually in trouble, mainly through the deliberate perverseness of her attitude. She became, apparently as the result of her behaviour, the odd man out of the family. She certainly seems to have been a difficult child to get on with.

We are told[1] that she did not always come home for holidays. On one occasion when she did, no one took any notice. She might just have come in from a walk. She was sitting at a window rather disconsolately when her stepmother wanted her to do some mending. She refused, and her stepmother said:

" Do you know that only for me you would have remained at school? When I said you were coming one of your sisters exclaimed : ' What, that tiresome girl! ' So you see, they do not want you."

As a result of this kind of treatment she made up her mind that she was not wanted and that everyone was against her. She formed, for a girl of her age and period, the most extraordinary resolution. This was nothing less than to dress up as a boy and run away to sea. She had acquired considerable influence over her brother, William, who was a year younger than she was. Mr. Stapleton's account[2] of her attempt to put her resolution into practice may well be quoted:

In this escapade, which was planned and executed by Constance, her younger brother William seems to have been a passive and compliant agent in his sister's hands. During the holidays, June 1856, they had been at home from school together. Their holidays had already expired, but they had been kept at home for

[1] The Sydney document.
[2] *Op. cit.*

56

a few days longer pending the return of their father from an absence on business in Devonshire. There is no evidence to show that any recent or particular fracas had happened during Mr. Kent's absence. But at all events, in the afternoon of the day before Mr. Kent's return, Constance and William were not to be found. An alarm was at once raised. Search was made but without success.

Now comes rather a curious point. Constance needed a safe hiding-place for her own purposes. The earth-closet in the shrubbery occurred to her, whether or not for the first time it is impossible to say. We may continue the story in Mr. Stapleton's own words:

After lunch on the day she left home, she went down to the closet in the shrubbery, put on some old clothes of her brother William's which she had secreted and mended, and cut off her hair, which she flung with her own clothes into the vault of the closet. She then started with her brother on a walk of ten miles to Bath, where they arrived in the evening. They went to the Greyhound Hotel where they asked for beds.

Their appearance excited the suspicions of the landlady, and they were questioned by her. Constance was very self-possessed and even insolent in her manner and language. William soon broke down and burst into tears. He was placed in bed at the inn, and as nothing could be done with Constance, the police were called in and she was given into custody for the night. She allowed herself to be separated from her brother, and was taken to the Central Police Station where she spent the night in the common detention room, maintaining the most resolute bearing and a determined silence as to her history. Early in the morning their father's servant discovered them and took them home. Upon Mr. Kent's return the same day, William at once expressed the greatest sorrow and contrition and sobbed bitterly. Constance for many days continued in solitude and gave no evidence of regret or shame at her conduct. At last she said she wished to be independent, and her object appears to have been to reach Bristol and to leave England with her brother.

That a girl of twelve should have behaved with so much resolution is almost incredible. The incident, however, is confirmed from many other sources. Constance possessed both shrewdness and determination, and was not likely to let any consideration whatever stand in her way. Shortly after this, she was sent to another school, kept by relatives of the second Mrs. Kent. It was hoped, perhaps, that they would be able to tame the intractable child. But all efforts in this direction failed. She took a delight in scandalizing her new teachers, and it would appear that after some months they refused to take charge of her any longer. Yet another attempt was made. Constance was sent as a boarder to Beckington, a village within a mile of two of the Kents' house. Here she remained off and on until shortly before the commission of the crime.

It is now time to consider the attitude adopted by Constance during the investigations which followed the crime. Her first appearance was as a witness at the inquest on July 2nd. On this occasion she is described as " a robust young lady, rather tall for her age ", and we are told " that she gave her evidence in a subdued but audible tone, without betraying any special emotion, her eyes fixed on the ground ".[1] Answering the questions of the coroner she declared that she knew nothing about this affair until her brother was found. About half-past ten on Friday night she had gone to bed and she knew nothing until after eleven o'clock. She generally slept soundly. She did not leave her bed during the night. She did not know of anyone having any spite against the boy. There had been no disagreement in the house, and she was not aware of anyone owing any grudge against the deceased. The nurse had always been kind and attentive to him. On Saturday morning she heard that he was dead. She was then getting up.

We have already seen that the news reached her through the nurse's visit to her sisters' room which was next door to her own.

The next public appearance of Constance was in the dock before the Trowbridge magistrates after her arrest by Inspector Whicher. Whicher had put into practice the principles of sound detection. He had arrived at Constance's guilt by simple deduction. How he had done so, may shortly be stated in his own words.[2]

---

[1] *Somerset and Wilts Journal.*
[2] In a letter written by him on November 23, 1860, to the Chief Superintendent of the Bristol Police.

Whoever did the deed, doubtless did it in their nightclothes. When Constance Kent went to bed that night she had three nightdresses belonging to her in the house. After the murder she had but two. What then became of the third? It was not lost in the wash as it was so craftily endeavoured to make it appear, but it was lost in some other way. Where is it, then, and what became of it?

The evidence on the subject of this nightdress must be given at some length. Sarah Cox, the housemaid, deposed as follows.[1]

I had to collect dirty linen from the room on Monday morning. That of Miss Constance is generally thrown down either in the room or on the landing, some of it on Sunday and some of it on Monday. It was so on this occasion, Monday, July 2nd. I found a nightdress of hers on the landing on Monday morning, and took it down with the rest to the lumber-room on the first floor to sort it out. I then called Miss Kent to come and put the number on the book. [This Miss Kent was Mary Ann, the eldest daughter.] I perfectly remember putting this nightdress of Miss Constance's in the basket after the murder. I left the basket in the lumber-room when I went down to the inquest about eleven o'clock with the nurse. Mr. and Mrs. Kent, the three young ladies, Master Kent, the young children, and the cook remained in the house. The baskets were covered up with the kitchen tablecloth and Mrs. Kent's dress, and the lumber-room was not locked. The laundress was to come for them about twelve or one o'clock that day. I know that I put three nightdresses into one basket and beside them Miss Elizabeth Kent made up her own bundle for herself. Miss Constance came to the door of the lumber-room after the things were in the basket, but I had not quite finished packing them. She asked me if I would look in her slip pocket and see if she had left her purse there. I looked in the basket and told her it was not there. She then asked me to go down and get her a glass of water. I did so, and she followed me to the top of the back stairs as I went out of the room. I found her there when I returned with the water, and I think I was not gone near a minute, for I went very quickly. The lumber-room is on the same floor as the nursery. She drank the water and went up the other

[1] On the occasion of Constance Kent's appearance before the magistrates on July 27, 1860. The evidence of Sarah Cox and Mrs. Holly is quoted from Appendix II of *The Great Crime of 1860*.

59

back stairs towards her own room. There was no further conversation between us. I covered down the basket and did not return to it. It was on Tuesday evening that I heard of the missing nightshirt, and I have never seen it since.

In cross-examination Sarah Cox amplified her statement:

On Saturday, June 30th, I took down a clean nightdress of Miss Constance's to be aired. I have heard that she had three altogether, but I did not know until after this. I took another clean nightdress to be aired on the following Saturday. Miss Constance's nightdresses are easily distinguishable from the other Misses Kents'. I never look over the clothes when they come from the wash. The dirty one put into the basket on the Monday after the murder, and the two I aired would make the three. I am clear that these were all Miss Constance's nightdresses. I did not observe any mark or stain upon the one that was put in the basket on the Monday, July 2nd. It appeared to have been dirtied as one would have been which had been nearly worn a week by Miss Constance.

The book in which the linen is entered is sent with clothes to the washerwoman. The clothes were entered in the book on the Monday after the murder by Miss Kent. On the Monday next after that, July 9th, the clothes were not sent to the wash in the usual way. Mrs. Holly is the name of the washerwoman to whom the clothes were sent on the Monday after the murder. The washerwoman would not have the clothes on July 9th, because there was some dispute about the nightdress. I first heard that the nightdress was missing on the Tuesday evening after the murder. A message was sent from Mrs. Holly's daughter which I received from her. She said that there were three nightdresses put down on Mrs. Kent's book and only two sent, and her mother said that it was Miss Constance's that was missing and that I must send another as the policeman had been there that day to know if she had the same number of clothes sent that week as she always had, and that her mother had told him that she had. She said that her mother said that she must have another one sent, as she was afraid that the policeman was coming again and that if one was not sent, she must go to the policeman about it.

I told her that I was sure that she had made a mistake, as I was certain that I had put three nightdresses in the basket, and that I was quite sure one of those was Miss Constance's. The clothes, including the nightdress worn by Miss Constance during the week

after the murder were not sent to the wash at all. On the following Saturday, I believe, Miss Constance borrowed a nightdress of
her sister's, there being then the two dirty ones belonging to her
in the house, which had been worn by her between June 30th and
July 7th and 14th. I am certain that I put the nightdress of Miss
Constance into the basket, but I can't swear that it went out of
the house, as I was not in the house at the time.

Mrs. Holly, the laundress, then gave evidence.

I recollect going for the clothes on the Monday after the
murder. When I got to the house I saw the cook. We went upstairs to the spare room where the clothes were generally kept.
The cook brought down one basket and I the other. I then
secured the clothes in the basket and went out and called my
daughter, Martha. The clothes were in the same state as I always
receive them. Mrs. Kent's dress was on one basket and something
else on the other. I and my daughter went straight home with
the clothes. We heard that there was a nightdress missing and
we opened the basket within five minutes after we got home and
found that one was missing. It was not our usual custom to open
the clothes so soon after receiving them. We heard a rumour
that the nightdress was missing.

Where this rumour originated is something of a mystery. The
police, as will be seen, did not visit Mrs. Holly until the Tuesday
after the murder. Superintendent Foley of Trowbridge searched
Road Hill House on the morning of Saturday, June 30th, and
requested Dr. Parsons to assist him. The latter, in his evidence
before the inquiry said:

I accompanied Mr. Foley in searching the house and went into
Miss Constance Kent's room. I examined the linen in her drawers
and the nightcap and nightgown which were on the bed. They
were all perfectly free from any stains of blood. The nightdress
was very clean, but I cannot say how long it had been worn.

It seems possible that Dr. Parsons may have been indiscreet.
Perhaps he talked about the cleanliness of the nightgown and the
obvious inference to be drawn from this. The rumour which
reached Mrs. Holly's ears can only be accounted for by some
such inference.

Mrs. Holly said that she had not seen anything of the missing nightdress. Her house and her two daughters had been searched by the police for the dress without success.

> I had the clothes home about twelve o'clock on the Monday following the murder, and in about five minutes after began to search for something that was missing. I did not say anything to the housemaid about anything being missing. I have three daughters. All three daughters were present when I examined the clothes that I brought from Mr. Kent's. I went up to get my money the next day between eleven and twelve o'clock and saw Mrs. Kent about the missing dress the same evening. I was told then that they were quite sure that Miss Constance's nightdress had been sent. The police came to my house the first time on the Tuesday evening. I am quite clear about it. Four constables came together and the parish constable as well. I was quite alarmed about it.

Mrs. Holly might well have been alarmed at such an invasion. But the police had not come to inquire about the nightdress, but to see whether Mrs. Holly could recognize the piece of flannel found with the body. Thus reassured, she decided to say nothing about the nightdress.

> I knew the nightdress was missing at the time, but I did not say anything to them—the police—about it. I told them the clothes were all right by the book. They came to me about the nightdress on the next day. I was expecting the nightdress to be sent to satisfy the book, the same as the other clothes came sometimes.

No further evidence on this subject was adduced. It seemed to Whicher that quite enough had been said to show what had actually happened. The nightdress seen by Foley and Parsons on the morning after the murder was not the one which Constance had worn the previous night. It had been taken from her chest of drawers after the commission of the crime. This, after being worn on Saturday and Sunday night, was put into the washing basket. Having dispatched the housemaid for a glass of water Constance had abstracted it from the basket to make it appear that it had been lost in the wash. The nightdress in which she had actually committed the crime had been destroyed. She would

62

thus have been found to be short of a nightdress and endeavour to account for this by making it appear that one had been lost in the wash.

The solicitor for the defence, however, contrived to push the evidence aside. He protested against the arrest of Constance on the grounds that "a paltry bedgown was missing". He then proceeded to a vicious attack upon Whicher:

And where is the evidence? The sole fact—and I am ashamed in this land of liberty and justice to refer to it—is the suspicion of Mr. Whicher, a man eager in pursuit of the murderer and anxious for the reward that has been offered. And it is upon his suspicion, unsupported by the slightest evidence whatever, that this step has been taken. The prosecution's own witnesses have cleared up the point about the bedgown, but because the washerwoman says that a certain bedgown was not sent to her, you are asked to jump to the conclusion that it was not carried away in the clothes basket.

But there can be no doubt in the mind of any person that the right number of bedgowns has been fully accounted for, and that this little peg upon which he seeks to hang this fearful crime has fallen to the ground. It rested on the evidence of the washerwoman only, and against that you have the testimony of several other witnesses. I do not wish to find fault with Mr. Whicher unnecessarily, but I think in the present instance, his professional eagerness in pursuit of the criminal has led him to take a most unprecedented course to prove a motive.[1]

Constance appears to have displayed very little concern about her arrest. Whicher's own statement[2] is evidence of her composure.

I have made an examination of the premises and I believe that the murder was committed by an inmate of the house. From many inquiries I have made and from information which I have received, I sent for Constance Kent on Monday last to her bedroom, having first previously examined her drawers and found a list of her linen, which I now produce, on which are enumerated among other articles of linen, three nightdresses as belonging to her.

[1] *Somerset and Wilts Journal.*
[2] On the occasion of his arrest of Constance Kent on July 20, 1860.

I said to her, "Is this a list of your linen?" and she replied, "Yes." I then asked, "In whose handwriting is it?" and she answered, "It is in my own writing." I said, "Here are three nightdresses. Where are they?" She replied, "I have two. The other was lost in the wash a week after the murder." She then brought the two I now produce. I also saw a nightdress and a nightcap on her bed, and said to her, "Whose are these?" She replied, "They are my sister's." The nightdresses were only soiled by being worn.

This afternoon, I again proceeded to the house and sent for the prisoner in the sitting-room. I said to her: "I am a police officer, and I hold a warrant for your apprehension, charging you with the murder of your brother, Francis Saville Kent, which I will read to you." I then read the warrant to her and she commenced crying and said, "I am innocent," which she repeated several times. I then accompanied her to her bedroom where she put on her bonnet and mantle, after which I brought her to this place. She made no further remarks to me.

On the occasion of her examination before the magistrate, we are told that "at half-past eleven, Constance Emily Kent came in, walking with a faltering step, and going up to her father gave him a trembling kiss."

Constance gave evidence before the magistrates on October 3rd, when the charge against Elizabeth was heard. On that occasion she said:

On Friday, the 29th of June, I was at home. I had been at home for about a fortnight. I had previously been to school as a boarder at Beckington. The little boy who was murdered was at home also. I last saw him in the evening when he went to bed. He was a merry, good-tempered lad, fond of romping. I was accustomed to play with him often. I had played with him that day. He appeared to be fond of me, and I was fond of him. I went to bed at about half-past ten in a room on the second floor, in a room between that of my two sisters and the two maid-servants. I remember my sister Elizabeth coming into my room that night. I went to sleep soon after that. I was nearly asleep then. I next woke at about half-past six in the morning. I did not awake in the course of the night, and I heard nothing to disturb me. I got up at half-past six. I had some time after that heard of my brother being missing.

In reply to questions by the counsel for the prosecution Constance made the following statement:

On the night of the murder she had slept in her nightdress. She had slept in that nightdress since the previous Sunday or Monday. She usually wore the same nightdress for a week and changed it on Sunday or Monday. This was the same nightdress that she had worn on Monday, Tuesday, Wednesday, Thursday and Friday. On the Saturday she had slept in the same nightdress she had worn on the previous night. She was not certain whether she had put the clean nightdress on, on the Sunday or the Monday. She did not know what had become of the nightdress of hers which was said to be missing. She had heard the prisoner go to her sisters' door on Saturday morning to ask if they had the child with them or had taken it away. She was dressing at the time. She heard Elizabeth knock at the door, and went to her own door to listen to hear what it was. Her door was quite close to her sisters'. At that time she was nearly dressed.[1]

It is, perhaps, unnecessary to recount the circumstances under which Constance actually confessed. We are told that,

she came under religious influence five years after the crime when, filled with deep sorrow and remorse, she told the clergyman of the case, that in order to free others of any suspicion cast on them it was her duty to make a public confession of her guilt. She was told she was right to obey her conscience and make any amends she could. Her life, if spared, could only be one long penance.[2]

Constance appeared before the Trowbridge Bench on April 26, 1865. A contemporary report says[3]:

She walked with a step which betrayed no emotion, but with downcast eyes and took her seat in the dock. Her conduct in the dock was at first marked by great composure. The past five years had wrought a considerable change in her appearance, she being taller and much more robust and womanly than when she was previously in this neighbourhood. Her deposition was as follows: " I wish to hand in of my own free will, a piece of paper with the

1 Following Stapleton, *op. cit.* Appendix III, reproduced from the *Bristol Daily Post.*
2 The Sydney document.
3 *Somerset and Wilts Journal.*

following written on it in my own handwriting, 'I, Constance Emily Kent, alone and unaided, did, on the night of the 29th of June, 1860, murder at Road Hill House, Wiltshire, one Francis Saville Kent. Before the deed, no one knew my intentions, nor after of my guilt. No one assisted me in the crime, nor in my evasion of discovery.' "

In reply to the chairman she replied that she had nothing further to say. The examination was adjourned and resumed on May 4th. Further evidence was taken at the conclusion of the proceedings, when Constance was asked if she desired to say anything in answer to the charge she shook her head and appeared as unmoved as during the greater part of the day. Constance appeared at the Wiltshire Assizes at Salisbury on July 21st. The proceedings were very brief. She pleaded guilty and declared that she was well aware of what the plea involved. Her counsel, Mr. Coleridge, stated that the prisoner wished to inform the court that she alone was guilty of the murder and that she wished to make her guilt known and atone for the crime with the view of clearing the character of others of any suspicion that might have been unjustly attached to them. It afforded him pleasure to have the melancholy duty of stating that there was no truth whatever in the report that the prisoner was induced to perpetrate the crime because of the harsh treatment received at the hands of her stepmother, for Miss Constance Kent had always received the most uniform kindness from that lady, and on his honour he believed it to be true.

She was sentenced to death; but, some days later, the sentence was commuted to one of penal servitude for life.

It was known that Constance had made a full confession to a Dr. Charles Bucknill, who had examined her for the purpose of ascertaining her mental condition, and to her solicitor, Mr. Rodway, in Trowbridge. It was Constance's desire that this confession should be made public, and at the end of August Dr. Bucknill published the following letter.[1]

I am requested by Miss Constance Kent to communicate the

[1] Circulated to the Press at the end of August 1865.

66

following details of her crime which she has confessed to Mr. Rodway, her solicitor, and to myself, and which she now desires to be made public.

Constance Kent first gave an account of the circumstances of her crime to Mr. Rodway, and she afterwards acknowledged to me the correctness of that account when I recapitulated it to her. The explanation of her motive she gave to me when, with the permission of the Lord Chancellor, I examined her for the purpose of ascertaining whether there were any grounds for supposing that she was labouring under mental disease. Both Mr. Rodway and I are convinced of the truthfulness and good faith of what she has said to us.

Constance Kent says that the manner in which she committed her crime was as follows:

A few days before the murder she obtained possession of a razor from a green case in her father's wardrobe and secreted it. This was the sole instrument which she used. She also secreted a candle and matches by placing them in the corner of the closet in the garden where the murder was committed. On the night of the murder she undressed herself and went to bed because she expected that her sisters would visit her room. She lay awake watching till she thought the household were all asleep, and soon after midnight she left her bedroom and went downstairs and opened the drawing-room door and window shutters.

She then went up to the nursery, withdrew the blanket from between the sheet and the counterpane and placed it on the side of the cot. She then took the child from his bed and carried him downstairs to the drawing-room. She had on her nightdress and in the drawing-room she put on her galoshes. Having the child in one arm she raised the drawing-room window with the other hand and went round the house and into the closet, the child being wrapped in the blanket and still sleeping, and while the child was in this position, she inflicted the wound in the throat. She says that she thought the blood would never come and the child was not killed, so she thrust the razor into its left side and put the body with the blanket round it into the vault. The light burnt out. The piece of flannel which she had with her was torn from an old flannel garment placed in the wastebag, and which she had taken some time before and sewed it to use for washing herself.

She went back into her bedroom, examined her dress and found only two spots of blood on it. These she washed out in the basin, and threw the water, which was but little discoloured, into the footpan in which she had washed her feet overnight. She took another of her nightdresses and got into bed. In the morning her nightdress had become dry where it had been washed. She folded it up and put it into the drawer. Her three nightdresses were examined by Mr. Foley, and she believes also by Dr. Parsons, the medical attendant of the family. She thought the bloodstains had been effectively washed out, but on holding the dress up to the light a day or two afterwards she found the stains were still visible. She secreted the dress, moving it from place to place, and eventually burned it in her own bedroom, and put the ashes or cinders into the kitchen grate. It was about five or six days after the child's death that she burnt the nightdress.

On the Saturday morning, she having cleaned the razor, she took an opportunity of replacing it unobserved in a case in the wardrobe. She abstracted the nightdress from the clothes-basket when the housemaid went to fetch a glass of water. The strange garment found in the boiler hole had no connexion whatever with these. As regards the motive of her crime, it seems that although she entertained at one time a great regard for the present Mrs. Kent, yet if any remark was at any time made which in her opinion was disparaging any member of the first family, she treasured it up and determined to revenge it. She had no ill-will against the little boy except that as one of the children of her stepmother. She declared that both her father and her stepmother had always been kind to her personally, and the following is a copy of the letter which she addressed to Mr. Rodway on this point while in prison before her trial:

DEVIZES, *May* 15*th*

Sir,—It has been stated that my feelings of revenge were excited in consequence of cruel treatment. This is entirely false. I have received the greatest kindness from both the persons accused of subjecting me to it. I have never had any ill-will towards either of them on account of their behaviour to me which has been very kind. I shall be obliged if you will make use of this statement in order that the public may be undeceived on this point.

I remain, Sir,

Yours most truly,

CONSTANCE E. KENT

She told me that when the nursemaid was accused she had fully made up her mind to confess if the nurse had been convicted, and that she had also made up her mind to commit suicide if she her-

68

self was detected. She said that she had felt herself under the influence of the devil before she committed the murder, but that she did not believe and had not believed that the devil had more to do with her crime than he had with any other wicked action. She had not said her prayers for a year before the murder and not afterwards till she came to reside at Brighton. She said that the circumstances which revived religious feelings in her mind was thinking about receiving sacrament when confirmed.

An opinion has been expressed that the peculiarities evinced by Constance Kent between the ages of twelve and seventeen may be attributed to the then transition period of her life. Moreover, the fact of her cutting off her hair and dressing herself in her brother's clothes and leaving home with the intention of going abroad, which occurred when she was only thirteen years of age, indicated a peculiarity of disposition and great determination of character which foreboded that, for good or evil, her future life would be remarkable.

This peculiar disposition which led to such singular violent resolves and actions, seems also to colour and intensify her thoughts and feelings and magnify into wrongs that were to be revenged, any little incidents or occurrences which provoked her displeasure.

Although it became my duty to advise her Counsel that she evinced no symptoms of insanity at the time of my examination, and that so far as it was possible to ascertain the state of her mind at so remote a period, there was no evidence of it at the time of the murder, I am yet of the opinion that, owing to the peculiarities of her constitution, it is probable that under prolonged solitary confinement she would become insane.

The validity of this opinion is of importance now that the sentence of death has been commuted to penal servitude for life, for no one should desire that the punishment of the criminal should be so carried out as to cause danger of a further and greater punishment not contemplated by the law.

This confession, which is undoubtedly authentic, is a most extraordinary document. The first question which arises is naturally that of motive. When he arrested Constance in 1860, Inspector Whicher realized the difficulty of proving an adequate motive for the murder. He hoped to establish this by calling a Miss Emma Moody, a school friend of Constance's. But Miss Moody's evidence was disappointing. The following is a sufficient extract:

69

I have heard her make such remarks about the child as this, that she disliked the child and pinched it, but I believe more from fun than anything else, for she was laughing at the time she said it. It was not this child more than the others. She said that she liked to tease them, this one and his younger brothers and sisters. I believe it was through jealousy and because the parents showed great partiality. I have remonstrated with her on what she said. I was walking with her one day towards Road, and I said, " Won't it be nice to go home for the holidays so soon." She said, " It may be to your home but mine's different." She also led me to infer, but I don't remember her precise words, that she did not dislike the child, but through the partiality shown by the parents the second family were much better treated than the first. I remember her saying that several times. We were talking about dress on some occasions and she said, "Mamma will not let me have anything I like, and if I said I would like a brown dress she would make me have black, and the contrary." I remember no other conversation about the deceased child. She has only slightly referred to him.

This evidence was utterly inconclusive in supplying any motive for murder. Whicher was bitterly disappointed with it. He said later:[1] " The witness, Miss Moody, in reference to animus, did not give the evidence I was given to understand she could have done."

But there is no doubt that Constance's crime was directed, not against the victim, but against her stepmother.

She vowed she would avenge her mother's wrong, if she devoted her life to it. After brooding over it for some time, she resolved that as her stepmother had robbed her mother of her father's love, she would deprive her of something she loved best. She then planned and carried out her most brutal and callous crime, one so vile and unnatural that people could not believe it possible for a young girl.[2]

This last is probably as near the truth as it is possible to get. Constance wished to be revenged on her stepmother, but not for any wrongs that she herself directly suffered. Her immature mind had brooded upon the circumstances which she had observed during her childhood, and these circumstances developed

[1] In his letter of November 23, 1860.   [2] The Sydney document.

themselves into the crime committed against her mother and the whole of the family. Her eldest brother had chosen the sea as a profession, probably because a seafaring life appealed to him. But Constance believed that he had done so merely to escape from the intrusion of Miss Pratt into the family circle. He had died abroad. To Constance this was a direct result of having been driven from home. There is plenty of evidence that the second family received preferential treatment by their parents. In Constance's eyes this was magnified into a martyrdom of the children of the first Mrs. Kent. She believed that her younger brother, William, who shared her extraordinary escapade in 1876, was not to be given a fair chance in life. This may or may not have been true at the time. Certainly Mr. Kent evinced more interest in the prospects of his younger children. Finally, there was ever present in her mind a deep resentment at the position of authority achieved by a mere governess. She was old enough, at the time of the crime, to have formed the opinion that this position had been achieved by questionable means.

In her confession she insisted that she bore no ill-will towards her stepmother. This must be interpreted to mean that she bore no ill-will on account of any personal treatment which she had received from her. The clue to the motive appears to lie in another sentence of that confession.

Although she entertained at one time a great regard for the present Mrs. Kent, yet if any remark was at any time made which in her opinion was disparaging to any member of the first family, she treasured it up and was determined to revenge it.

One may perhaps realize the cumulative effect of such a determination on a child of Constance's nature. She remembered every fancied slight. The second Mrs. Kent was not popular either with the neighbours or the servants. Constance must have heard a thousand suggestions that she was no better than she should be. Her final conclusions must have been that the household had been invaded by an immoral tyrant, who, owing to the influence she exercised over Mr. Kent, was secure from punishment. She felt this to be unjust. Punishment was deserved, and could be inflicted were anyone bold enough to assume the rôle of avenger.

Having decided that her stepmother must be punished, Constance must have reflected upon the form which the punishment should take. Punishment inflicted directly was obviously beyond her powers. But Mrs. Kent was devoted to her children, especially to the boy Francis. If anything should happen to Francis Mrs. Kent would feel the blow as acutely as though it had been directed at herself.

It does not seem to have occurred to Constance that the blow would be almost as acutely felt by her father, to whom she was apparently genuinely attached. Perhaps she believed that her father would soon recover from his sorrow at the death of his youngest son. Mr. Kent had endured such bereavements before without showing any signs of being overwhelmed by them. At the date of the crime he had already had thirteen children, and was expecting the arrival of a fourteenth. Five of these had died in their early infancy. Surely by this time such calamities must have lost their power to depress him unduly!

Constance appears to have experimented with the possibility of making away with Francis. There is very little doubt that she had determined upon the form which the punishment of Mrs. Kent was to take some time before 1860. It so happened that, one night some two years before the crime, Mrs. Kent, Constance, and the two children of the second marriage were the only occupants of the house besides the servants. Francis slept in the nursery with the nurse. During the night the nursery must have been entered, for in the morning Francis was found in his cot with the bedclothes stripped off and his bed-socks missing. It was never discovered how this happened. But Constance was believed to have been at the bottom of it and it was attributed to her well-known spirit of mischief. It was possible that she believed that the exposure of the child would cause his death. It is remarkable that this incident was not mentioned during the inquiry into the cause of the crime.

It is an axiom of criminal investigation that every confession, whether genuine or not, is open to suspicion on the grounds of detail. The criminal may be willing to confess but not, for some strange psychological reason, to reveal his methods. Constance's confession appears to be no exception to this rule. It is almost incredible that she should have committed the crime by the method to which she confessed.

It is admitted that the methods of the local police in investigating the crime were elementary in the extreme. But the following facts are incontrovertible. Dr. Parsons, as soon as he saw the body, decided that the throat must have been cut with some sharp instrument. It is true that at the inquest he declared that the wound in the breast could not have been produced by a razor. But Dr. Parsons changed his opinion so frequently that too much reliance must not be placed upon his statement. In any case, on the Saturday morning, the idea of a sharp instrument was firmly impressed upon his mind. And he succeeded in conveying this impression to Superintendent Foley.

Now Superintendent Foley, Dr. Parsons, and apparently dozens of others, searched the house from top to bottom early on Saturday morning. One may be allowed to presume that their search was directed primarily towards the discovery of a sharp instrument. Indeed, they made detailed inquiry into the knives cleaned by the garden boy that morning. But surely it must have occurred to them that there were other sharp instruments in the house. And of these sharp instruments, perhaps Mr. Kent's razors were the most obvious of all.

Yet Constance Kent in her confession says that a few days before the murder she obtained possession of a razor from a green case in her father's wardrobe and secreted it. This was the sole instrument she used. On the Saturday morning, having cleaned the razor, she took an opportunity of replacing it unobserved in the case in the wardrobe. This seems amazing. She abstracted the razor a few days before the murder. It is possible that Mr. Kent did not notice the absence of this particular razor. He may have put it aside for a time. But how could

Constance tell that he would not discover that it had not been removed from its usual place? If he had done so, she could hardly have ventured to use it subsequently. And the difficulty of replacing the razor unobserved on the Saturday morning seems almost insuperable. It is true that Mr. Kent had left the house shortly after being informed of the disappearance of his son, but almost immediately afterwards the house was invaded by a band of searchers, and Constance, self-possessed though she undoubtedly was, would hardly have faced the risk of being accosted with a razor in her hand.

On the whole it seems that her statement regarding the razor was without foundation. She declared that the razor was the sole instrument with which she had done the deed. Dr. Parsons' opinion as to the possibility of the wound in the breast having been inflicted by a razor has already been quoted. It is unnecessary to examine the medical evidence at length. But the statement of Mr. Stapleton, who was present at the post-mortem and actually assisted in it, is worthy of attention. He says:

> Upon the left side of the body below and to the outer side of the nipple, a sharp blade had been passed diagonally over the fifth rib. Severing wholly the cartilage of the sixth, partially that of the seventh rib, it had been thrust into the chest behind the membranous covering of the heart, which it had grazed without entering it. It then penetrated the diaphragm, and had grazed the stomach in a similar manner, without piercing the cavity. In its passage or during its withdrawal this blade had been violently twisted or wrenched round as was evident from the torn appearance of the muscular fibres, and the scraped irregular appearance of the exposed rib at the posterior angle of the cut and the appearance remarkably contrasted with the simple smooth surface of the other parts of its edges, and affording a reasonable inference that it was inflicted with a murderous intent and under some ferocious impulse. Very little blood had flowed from this stab, and none was found adherent to the side, nor was any coagulated upon the corresponding parts of the nightshirt. This stab injured no vital organ nor would it have caused immediate death. It would have been followed by very little bleeding, even if the heart's action and the circulation in its vessels were still going on

at the time of its infliction. Its position and appearances afford no ground for the assumption that it was done by using the knife to thrust down the body of the child into the closet.[1]

Now it will be observed that though Mr. Stapleton does not expressly say that this wound could not have been inflicted with a razor, his language is very significant. He speaks repeatedly of a stab and of a knife. It is clearly impossible to inflict a stab with an ordinary razor, and the appearance of a wound inflicted by such a weapon is very different from that inflicted by a knife. It seems unlikely that Mr. Stapleton, who was a surgeon of considerable experience, should have spoken of a stab and a knife in describing a wound inflicted by a razor.

In many other details the confession seems difficult to believe. The mystery of the nightdress is certainly explained on the line of Whicher's theory. But may not this theory, already known to Constance, have inspired her account? She states in her confession that her three nightdresses were examined by Foley, and she believed also by Dr. Parsons, the medical attendant of the family. She thought the bloodstains had been effectively washed out, but on holding the dress up to the light a day or two afterwards, she found the stains were still visible. Now the whole object of the examination of the nightdress was to discover stains. Dr. Parsons, describing the incident before the Trowbridge magistrates, said:

> I accompanied Mr. Foley in the search through the house, and in the course thereof went into Constance Kent's room. I examined her drawers and the night cap and the nightgown which were on the bed, and the whole of the bedding. The nightdress was perfectly free from any stains. The nightdress was very clean, but I could not speak as to whether it had on it the dirt resulting from a week's wear or not. There was nothing on Constance's nightdress which attracted my attention more than that it was very clean.

The attention paid to the nightdress lying on the bed, which was, of course, clean, may have distracted observation from the

[1] Stapleton, *op. cit.*

two found in the chest of drawers, but it seems incredible that though a medical man could find no bloodstains on either of the latter, they were visible to Constance a day or two afterwards. Again, Constance avers that, having found these tell-tale stains, she secreted the dress, moving it from place to place, and eventually burnt it in her own bedroom, and put the ashes of same into the kitchen grate. It was about five or six days after the child's death that she burnt the nightdress. The disappearance of a nightdress was apparently suspected from the first, since a rumour of it had reached Mrs. Holly's ears as early as the Saturday. Mrs. Holly herself confirms this disappearance. The local police were blunderingly though certainly actively looking for a nightdress. Yet Constance was able to move it about from place to place for five or six days and finally to burn it in her own bedroom. It hardly seems possible that she could have done this without arousing suspicion.

It must be admitted that queer things habitually happened at Road Hill House both before and after the murder. One of the queerest was revealed during the course of the Gilbertian inquiry held by Mr. Saunders on his own account. In the course of his examination of Police Constable Urch, the following extraordinary conversation[1] took place.

Were you present with Sergeant Watts in Road Hill House when he found a certain thing?—Yes; I was

What was it?—Some woman's nightshift.

Where did Sergeant Watts find the article?—In the boiler hole.

Where was the boiler?—In the first kitchen going in, sir.

Was there anyone present? Was it at the entrance of the boiler hole or pushed far up?—It was in, sir, as if to light the fire.

Was it dry or was it wet?—It was dry, sir, but very dirty.

What do you mean by dirty?—I mean as if it had been worn a long time.

What was the dirt upon it?—It had some blood about it.

Was it much blood or little? A large quantity or a small quantity?—There were several places with blood upon them.

Did they appear to have been there for some time?—Well, sir,

[1] Quoted from Stapleton, *op. cit*. Appendix IV.

I did not touch it myself. Sergeant Watts unfolded it, looked at it, and carried it to the coach-house.

Were there any initials on the shift?—I do not know, sir; I did not see any.

Was it a coarse article or a fine article of dress—such as servants wear or more like what young ladies wear?—I should think, sir, it was one of the servants.

Was it the size for a full-grown servant or a young woman—a full-grown woman servant or a nursegirl?—It was not a large one. We remarked two or three others there, but it was a small one.

It transpired that the shift had been given to Foley, who apparently suppressed it. He certainly never informed Whicher of the discovery. It may be urged with some truth that this is more incredible than anything in Constance's confession. A crime is committed under circumstances which make the discovery of a bloodstained nightdress indispensable. Something of the kind is actually found on the night after the murder. Yet a responsible officer of police is so satisfied that the shift could have no connexion with the crime that the existence of it is never mentioned. It is impossible to ignore the possibility that this bloodstained shift was actually the nightdress worn by Constance during the commission of the crime. How and when she conveyed it to the boiler hole is not apparent. But she may have done so immediately after returning to the house from the earth-closet. The evidence that either Foley or Dr. Parsons saw three nightdresses belonging to her on Saturday morning is not conclusive. Constance, in her confession, denies that the shift had any connexion with the deed. But, as has already been pointed out, too much reliance must not be placed upon the details of this confession.

The route taken by her when carrying the child from the nursery to the earth-closet has been questioned. And yet, in this particular, the confession is probably correct. It was certainly not the shortest route she could have taken, but any alternative route had its disadvantages. The most obvious way to reach the earth-closet from the house was to leave the house by the back door and cross the yard. But the watchdog was at large in the yard. He might have barked and raised the alarm. Actually there is evidence of a kind that the dog did bark that night. An anonymous policeman is said to have declared that about one o'clock on the night of the murder, the house dog barked as he passed the house. Again:

> Two men, one of them named Joe Moon, were on the night of the murder working in a neighbouring quarry or limekiln. Very early in the morning they heard the house dog barking loudly, and remarked one to the other, " There must be something wrong at Mr. Kent's. The dog is barking so." [1]

Constance may therefore have actually passed through the yard. The next most direct route would be through the front door, and so to the earth-closet, without passing through the yard at all. Why the window of the drawing-room should have been taken as the means of exit from the house it is difficult to say. This window was situated at almost the farthest point of the house from the closet, and its use involved a journey round two sides of the house and, incidentally, a passage under the windows of the room in which Mr. and Mrs. Kent were sleeping. It was, in fact, the most roundabout route which could have been chosen.

So much for the confession and for the very curious problems to which it gives rise. But it must not be forgotten that the evidence of Constance's guilt rests entirely upon this confession. Her trial at the Assizes took no more than a few minutes. She pleaded guilty and her counsel then made a short statement. This concluded the proceedings, and the judge sentenced her to death. Very general regret was expressed at the time that no trial had taken place. Had Constance pleaded not guilty, much that remains unexplained might have been revealed. It was said at the time,[2] apparently with authority, that thirty-five witnesses would have been called, and that their united statements would have presented the case against the prisoner in a manner which would have left no reasonable doubt of her guilt quite irrespective

[1] From an article in the *Somerset and Wilts Journal*.
[2] In an article in the *Daily Telegraph*.

of her confession. The point is, that these thirty-five witnesses must have been available in 1860. It is extremely improbable that they could have given any fresh evidence five years after the crime had been committed.

The temptation to speculate as to what would have happened had not the investigations into the crime been so hopelessly bungled is almost irresistible. The proceedings at the inquest were farcical. The one aim of the coroner and of the foreman of the jury seems to have been to exonerate the members of the family. They could not believe that persons of their station in life could have committed such a crime. Much the same reluctance even to consider their guilt seems to have inspired the local police. They acted from the first upon this theory. No member of the family could possibly have committed the crime. Therefore the criminal must be sought among the servants, or some intruder from outside must be imagined.

Inspector Whicher was the first to tackle the case scientifically. That he failed to establish his case is by no means to his discredit. It must be remembered that he did not arrive on the scene until a fortnight after the crime, by which time several important clues had undoubtedly been destroyed. He was also an object of local jealousy. Nobody concerned, from Superintendent Foley to the parish constable, had the slightest intention of allowing a stranger to succeed where they had failed if they could possibly help it. They withheld information from him, and there is reason to suppose that they even deliberately misled him. Scotland Yard was in those days a comparatively recent institution and had not yet gained the confidence either of the county constabularies or of the public.

A leading authority upon criminal investigation[1] has said:

> The scene of the crime must be inspected both in its general aspect and in detail, and must be considered as far as possible in relation to the facts. The time allotted to this close examination is far from being lost and the results compensate largely for the apparent delay. After this, the investigating officer must find out

[1] Dr. Hans Gross, *Criminal Investigation*. London. Sweet and Maxwell.

the persons best able to give information about the case, which will enable him to become at least approximately acquainted with the circumstances. Habit, above all, helps the investigating officer in examining people with a view to obtaining this preliminary information. He learns little by little not to waste time over details, while forgetting nothing of importance.

Had Whicher been summoned, and had he arrived on the scene on Saturday following the crime, would he have been able to reach success upon these lines?

He would, at all events, have been confronted with a mass of conflicting evidence. Even the medical evidence was apparently unreliable. At the time of the inquest Dr. Parsons stated that he was of the opinion that death had not been due to suffocation, that the child had not been even partially suffocated at the time the fatal wound was inflicted. This opinion was upheld both by Mr. Stapleton and by the coroner, himself a surgeon. By 1865, however, Mr. Stapleton had changed his mind. In the course of his evidence before the Trowbridge Bench, he said:

> In my opinion, the incision in the throat was the immediate cause of death, but the appearance of the place where the body was found was such as to induce me to suppose that the throat was not cut there, or that the circulation of the child was in a great degree stopped by suffocation before it was done.

Any sort of attempt to establish motive would have been hopeless. We have already seen how Miss Moody's evidence disappointed Whicher's expectations. Had Mr. Stapleton in his capacity as friend of the family been consulted, his statement would have been verbose and unsatisfactory.

> As she grew up, Constance manifested a strong, obstinate, and determined will, and her conduct, even as a little child, gave evidences of an irritable and impassioned nature. Whether the governess possessed that experience and tact and moral weight which fitted her for the responsible and arduous duties she had undertaken, whether in the delicate and unusual position in which she consented to remain in Mr. Kent's family, she taught her heart to lavish on that child the unceasing and considerate care, and motherly tenderness and patience, which its more than

orphanage required, these are questions to which her memory and conscience only can reply. It is not expressed or intimated by those who observed her conduct, and must have watched and criticized it too, that she was either unfaithful or unequal to this difficult and trying task.... That Constance was ever treated with cruelty by her stepmother is emphatically denied even by her own sisters. Amongst our social evils, troublesome children and indiscreet, impatient parents are not uncommon, nor are they incurable, and these details can assume importance in this family only in consequence of the events which have since transpired and which have originated the presumption, perhaps neither correct nor warrantable, of the child's irritation and dislike of a relation which had been imposed upon it, and against which other resistance was impossible.[1]

Whicher would have immediately arrived at the conclusion that some person sleeping in the house on that night had committed the crime. Had he been called to the scene at once he would have been able to interview all these people before their minds had become distracted by a flood of rumour and gossip. He would have inquired into the history and habits of each of them, and would very soon have come to the conclusion that Constance was an abnormal child. The motive of the crime, though inexplicable to the normal mind, would then have transpired.

Whicher would probably have been able to elucidate the exact truth about the nightdresses. Had it been Whicher, instead of Foley and Parsons, who examined the house on the Saturday morning, the very obvious clues which then existed would not have escaped his attention. He would not have mistaken a roughly washed and dried nightdress for a clean one. And he most certainly would not have rested until he had satisfied himself about all the sharp weapons to be found in the house. Whether or not he would have succeeded in breaking down the resistance of the one person who must have guessed the secret from the first is very doubtful. It is impossible to believe that Mr. Kent can have had any doubts as to the identity of the culprit. He was aware of the peculiarity of Constance's nature, and he had

[1] Stapleton, *op. cit.*

plenty of experience of her erratic behaviour. By a process of elimination alone he must have come to the conviction of his daughter's guilt. By his silence, he placed himself in a terrible position. From the date of the crime until Constance's confession, he was very widely suspected of having been guilty of the murder of his son. He found himself between the horns of an awful dilemma. He must either endure the obloquy to which a suspected murderer is subject, or he must divulge his own suspicions, and so bring about the arrest, and most probably the conviction, of his daughter.

It may perhaps be permissible to speculate as to Constance's character. Of her appearance there is no reliable record. We are told that " no likeness or description of Constance is accurate." She always, as much as possible, concealed her features and slipped out of sight if strangers came near. In a contemporary report of her appearance at the Assizes, it is stated that " she is an exceedingly plain-looking young person, and totally unlike the photographs which are sold as portraits of her. She has a broad, full and uninteresting face which wears more an expression of stupid dullness than intelligence." We can only suppose that her expression on this occasion belied her. Stupid dullness is certainly not a characteristic of her crime and of her subsequent conduct. She contrived, in spite of Whicher's suspicions, to create an impression of her innocence and to secure public sympathy. On the other hand, her undoubted intelligence is not that associated with the criminal type. Constance was not by any means a born criminal. Her crime was not committed upon personal grounds. No doubt, she had by slow degrees convinced herself that she was the individual appointed by Providence as the avenger of wrongs. She wished to punish her stepmother and she certainly hit upon the most effective means of doing so. It will be argued that she showed disregard of human life and that therefore she must have had criminal instincts. But it is more probable that she believed that she was offering a sacrifice rather than committing a murder. A sacrifice to her mother's memory and for the fancied wrongs of her children.

Abraham would have sacrificed his son in the interests of his own welfare had not the angel of the Lord restrained him. No such divine interference manifested itself in favour of Constance's victim. She may have interpreted this as a sign of approval on the part of Providence at whose behest she believed herself to be acting. It is probable that she never gave a thought to the consequences which must inevitably follow her deed. She probably believed that the murderer of the child would remain undiscovered and that the deed itself would soon be forgotten. She could not have anticipated the storm of abuse and suspicion which would burst on the whole family.

She seems to have foreseen that such a callous and brutal murder would not be attributed to a girl of sixteen. She was undoubtedly sufficiently intelligent to count upon this. Contrition she certainly never felt until she eventually confessed under the influence of religious emotion. And, even then, the whole of her confession seems to suggest the absence of true contrition. She confessed, not to save her own soul, but to remove the load of suspicion from others. It is possible that the original idea of justification never left her till very much later.

It is possible that, in a sense, the crime saved her character. Before it there is ample evidence that she was a wayward, passionate girl. She showed little or no consideration for others and she would probably have developed into a selfish, headstrong woman. After the crime, her character seems to have changed entirely.

It was obviously impossible for the Kent family to remain at Road Hill House. They went for a short time to Weston-super-Mare, but found themselves still too near the scene of the tragedy. From Weston-super-Mare, they removed to Wales, but Constance did not accompany them. This is surely evidence that Mr. Kent at least was fully cognisant of the secret. Constance left England and stayed for a couple of years at a convent in France. Not, to be noted, as an inmate, but as a pupil. In 1863 she came back to England, where she stayed as a visitor in a religious house at Brighton. From all that can be gleaned of her life during this period, it was seen that this seclusion was in accordance with her own wishes. Her rebellious nature seems to have entirely changed and to have been replaced by an intense desire to live under some sort of discipline. We may conjecture that the latter was an illustration of her true nature. Her turbulent childhood may have been merely the reaction to Mrs. Kent's injudicious treatment.

After her reprieve Constance remained in prison until 1885. Various glimpses of her during that period remain, but unfortunately most of them are mutually contradictory. A single instance will serve to show how contradictory are these glimpses. Major Arthur Griffiths, in *Secrets of the Prison House*, says:

> Constance Kent, whom I remember at Millbank, was first employed in the laundry and afterwards as a nurse in the Infirmary. A small, mouse-like little creature, with much of the promptitude of the mouse or the lizard's surprise in disappearing when alarmed. The approach of any strange or unknown face whom she feared might come to spy her out and stare, constituted a real alarm for Constance Kent. No doubt there were features in her face which the criminal anthropologist would have seized as suggesting an instinctive criminality. High cheek-bones, a lowering overhanging brow and deep-set small eyes. But yet her manner was prepossessing and her intelligence was of a high order.

A correspondent who acted for a time as chaplain of Fulham Convict Prison, informed the author that he remembers Constance being confined there. It was his duty to visit her and read her letters at a time when she was pleading for her release. He also says that he does not at all agree with Major Griffiths' description of her. On the other hand, we are told[1] that Major Griffiths' description of her is about nearest to the truth. Her best points were a fresh complexion and a quantity of golden brown hair. On one point all accounts of her prison life are, however, agreed. She was docile and uncomplaining. She was for a time confined in Portland Prison, where she executed a series of mosaics. These are still to be seen in the Chapel of St. Peter's and have been much admired.

---

[1] The Sydney document.

After her release she disappeared from view. The legend that she married a clergyman is entirely without foundation, as are many of the legends connected with her and with her family. The anonymous correspondent so frequently quoted, says: "After her release she changed her name and went overseas and, single-handed, fought her way to a good position, and made a home for herself, where she was well-liked and respected before she died."

Constance remains, in spite of all research, an elusive personality. That she escaped detection is probably her greatest claim to fame. But the science of detection was then in its infancy, and local prejudice was in her favour. Mr. and Mrs. Kent had for long been unpopular with their neighbours. The crime, it was argued, could not have been committed by a mere girl, and it was unlikely that it had been committed by Mrs. Kent. Mr. Kent's unpopularity made of him a scapegoat welcome to local opinion. Who but a strong and determined man could have committed such a crime? The motives attributed to him are too scandalous to be worthy of repetition. Whicher probably made insufficient allowance for local prejudice and acted too hastily. The evidence which he was able to produce was inconclusive. He did not hope for an immediate conviction of Constance, but for a remand. He was of the opinion that had she remained in custody she would have confessed. This opinion was possibly optimistic. Constance knew that public sympathy was on her side. Unless Whicher had been able to obtain conclusive evidence in the matter of the nightdresses, unless he had been able to produce the weapon with which the crime was committed, Constance would probably have remained obdurate. And in that case, as she knew well enough, her release could only be a matter of time. She had already shown that she possessed sufficient obstinacy and firmness of will to put up with any amount of temporary inconvenience.

But the remand was not granted and Whicher had to admit failure. Her counsel's speech on her behalf was frankly an appeal to sentiment. He adopted a tone of virtuous indignation. There was not a tittle of evidence against her, not one word on which the finger of infamy could be pointed against her. Although a most atrocious murder had been committed, it had been followed by a judicious murder no less atrocious. If the murderer were never discovered, it would never be forgotten that this young lady had been dragged like a common felon to Devizes Gaol. That fact alone was quite sufficient to ensure the sympathy of every man in the country and the kingdom. The steps which had been taken must blast her hopes and prospects for life. He besought the magistrates immediately to liberate the young lady and to restore her to her friends and her home.

The fact that this speech was greeted with applause is indicative of the difficulties with which Whicher had to contend.

But though Whicher failed, the reasons for his failure have already been pointed out. The Road Hill murder teaches a lesson which even in these days is apt to be overlooked. It is essential that, immediately after the discovery of a crime, the services of an experienced investigating officer should be secured. Where the scene of the crime is a large town, there is usually no difficulty about this. But in country districts the local police, however efficient they may be, have not as a rule the necessary experience. In spite of this they are sometimes loth to enlist the aid of Scotland Yard. The perils of such a course are accurately exemplified in the case of Constance Kent.

PART III

THE CASE OF ADELAIDE BARTLETT

by Margaret Cole

THE CASE OF
ADELAIDE BARTLETT

THIS is the story of Adelaide Bartlett, who stood her trial in the winter of 1885–6 for the death of her husband, Edwin Bartlett, after the coroner's inquest had resulted in a verdict of wilful murder. At the trial she had been acquitted, though the Judge's summing-up was distinctly unfavourable, and if a verdict of Not Proven had been possible under the English Law, that is the verdict that would have been given. When the verdict was announced there was " immense cheering " in court, which caused Mr. Justice Wills to exclaim : " This conduct is an outrage." One may, however, perhaps conclude that the British public, or some section of it, thought at the time that she ought not to have been hanged.

This trial is, I think, one of the most interesting of British criminal trials, first, because the tale is not a tale of horror or brutality. None of the people concerned, however odd, or, if you like, however foolish they may have been, were monsters ; they were not even trying to be unkind to one another. Indeed, it would rather appear that they were all trying to be as nice as possible under rather difficult circumstances. No one ever heard the Barletts disagree, and the first angry word was spoken after Edwin's death, when that somewhat feeble creature, the Reverend George Dyson, was endeavouring to ensure his own escape. The second reason is that it shows up the law's limitations in certain quite definite ways. It is very clear that, if you are going to get into trouble with the law, it does not pay to be odd, particularly if your oddity is in any way connected with your sexual or matrimonial relations.

Edwin Bartlett was undoubtedly an odd man, with uncommon (though by no means unheard-of) ideas on a good many subjects ; and Adelaide Bartlett, his wife, who was much less odd, was very nearly hanged because in the year 1885 she had in her possession a book which discussed birth-control, and, what was more, had actually lent it to a gentleman friend.

Said the Judge: "Gentlemen, I cannot—sitting here—I cannot have such garbage passed under my eyes, and then allow it to go forth that an English judge concurs in the view that it is a specimen of pure and healthy literature." Ugh! Ugh! Ugh! Later, in his summing-up, his horror—the horror of the law at anything at all unusual, anything out of its ken—led him into the definite but not uncommon injustice of denying that the oddity existed at all. Said he: "It looks . . . as though we had two persons to deal with abundantly vulgar and commonplace in their habits and ways of life." But nobody who has read the evidence—and presumably the learned Judge had at least listened to it—can have any doubt that whatever Edwin Bartlett was, he was not commonplace. The Judge's remark was just a piece of gross prejudice, and if the prosecution could have suggested any really plausible way in which Adelaide Bartlett could have got a large quantity of chloroform into her husband's stomach, it would probably have succeeded in hanging her.

The trial also shows the curious and innate inability of the law to distinguish between types of untrue statement. The law assumes that people in giving evidence either speak the truth or tell lies, and further, that speaking the truth is quite easy. Either you do or you don't, and there's an end of it. It follows, first, that if two or more people lie confidently and cannot be proved to be lying, the law is more likely to accept their statements as facts than those of one person whose evidence cannot be corroborated; and, secondly, that if a witness finds the truth difficult to explain, as every practical person knows that it very often is, and hesitates, qualifies, and appears to contradict himself, the law is very ready to brand that person as a liar, or, at the least, as "a very unsatisfactory witness". In this story, the unfortunate Dr. Leach, who seems to have been really doing his best to explain the curious circumstances of the Bartlett household, was heavily bullied by counsel and sat upon by the Judge at every turn. This sort of nursery mentality: " Now, Tommy, you can just give me a plain answer, yes or no, without any of your naughty quibbling. Did you and Harry spill that ink, or did you not? " " Well, nurse, you see, we didn't exactly *spill* it——" " None of your ' didn't exactlys '—into the corner with you ! "—this sort of thing makes one wonder at times whether there is any real connexion between law and justice.

Finally, the law is even behind the nursery in that it does not appear to know, what every intelligent nurse or mother knows, that there is an enormous difference between lying in the strict sense and telling fairy-stories, between saying, " No, I did *not* take the plums," when you did, and saying, " Mother, I saw a whale in the pond this morning," or even, " Mother, I stayed awake for hours and hours last night." Everybody of any experience knows that there are many people who remain for the whole of their lives so much under the influence of their own emotional states that they are quite incapable of distinguishing between objective and subjective truth, so that their statements at different times flatly and perplexingly contradict one another. They are not lying in any sense that they would recognize to be lying; it is simply that their impression of what is happening or has happened has changed without their knowing it. And it is again clear, to any person of experience reading the Bartlett case, that there was a great deal of ' subjective evidence ' about, which was given upon oath and believed by the witnesses, but which might or might not correspond to the facts. But the court, being the law, was unable to recognize this subjective evidence for what it was. It had either to accept it and make the best sense it could of the result, or, if it discovered that at some point it conflicted with some known fact, to call the witness a liar. For instance, Adelaide Bartlett told Dr. Leach that she was married at sixteen. She was not ; she was nearly twenty. Therefore Adelaide Bartlett was a liar. But surely it was clear that she was not lying ; she felt as though she had been married at sixteen, and, as the story went, she really might have been. That is not the way in which to get at the truth of facts which depend so largely on states of emotion.

But it is time to turn to the facts themselves, as they were brought out in court. It is necessary to be like Dr. Leach, and to add this qualification, because there are certainly many gaps missing which must be filled by conjecture. In particular, we have to do without the voice of Edwin Bartlett, who was in fact the centre of the picture. It is very unfortunate that Edwin did not keep a diary. He was exactly the sort of man who ought to have kept a diary, and if he had, how useful it would have been!

The story begins, then, with Edwin Bartlett, grocer, marrying Adelaide de la Tremouille, spinster, aged 19, in 1875. Adelaide came from Orléans; nothing is known about her parentage, though it has been suggested that she was illegitimate and had English blood. Edwin possessed a father and at least two brothers, and a grocery business in Herne Hill, which was about to become mildly prosperous; at least, at the time of his death, ten years later, he and his partner were the owners of half a dozen grocers' shops.

Nothing, again, is known of Edwin's courtship; but almost immediately two unusual features appear. For his first act after marriage was to send his nineteen-year-old wife to school for a couple of years; it was not until 1877 that she came to live with him. Why he did this we do not know; presumably he wanted her to be better educated, as he seems to have been a man who had a great admiration for the sort of cheap learning that can be easily displayed. There have been other and more distinguished men who set seriously about the business of educating their wives, notably the estimable Thomas Day; but few of them began so late in the subject's life.

Anyhow, in 1877, Adelaide, now, we trust, sufficiently educated, came to Herne Hill and began to live with her husband. It should be mentioned that her dowry, whatever it was, seems to have been usefully employed in her husband's business; it is less clear to what purpose, if any, her education was utilized. According to herself, she was exhibited at intervals to entertain her husband's business friends—for some time she had no friends at all of her own.

The Bartletts were, to all appearances, happy. But almost

directly Edwin's mother died and his father came to live with them at Herne Hill. Old Mr. Bartlett, who was by now almost entirely dependent on his son, was undoubtedly a nasty old gentleman. He disliked and quarrelled with his daughter-in-law from the first; when Edwin fell ill he immediately suggested there was something wrong about it; when Edwin died he was prompt to indicate that his wife must have murdered him; and when he was put in the witness-box he did his best to blacken Adelaide's character, though he was a trifle hampered by the existence of a document, signed by himself some years previously, which declared that all the accusations he had made were false. Edwin now being dead, he naturally stated that the document was signed under duress, and that every word he had said was true; but that was the sort of lie with which the law is capable of dealing.

The only fact of any importance which emerged from all this was that in 1878 or 1879 Adelaide ran away for a time. Nobody really knows where she ran to, or why; the most obvious probability is that she was 'fed up' with her father-in-law and possibly a bit bored.

In 1881 Adelaide was confined. The labour was very difficult, and the child was stillborn. Edwin, who appears not to have liked doctors much until he was ill himself, would not have a doctor called until it was too late; and, whether or not Adelaide could have had another child, they did not make the experiment. The nurse who attended her was called Annie Walker. She seems to have been a pleasant and intelligent woman, and Adelaide, who it will be remembered, had at that time no woman friend, confided in her to some extent. But, as far as Annie Walker's recollections went, the confidences did not amount to much. Mrs. Bartlett said " her husband did not appreciate her work, and she worked beautifully." I should think most midwives have in their time listened to hundreds of similar confidences.

In 1881, also, Edwin fell ill. This is a very interesting fact, and I could wish that more information was available about it. He is said to have had a nervous breakdown, caused by laying a floor, which is surely a very odd cause for a nervous breakdown. One could understand it better if he had strained his back or burst a blood-vessel; but no, he only had a nervous breakdown, necessitating a sea-voyage, and one is well enough acquainted with a certain type of mind to wonder whether it was not Adelaide's illness rather than the floor-laying which made Edwin feel that he must be ill himself and so secure a little sympathy and attention. However, this possibility interested nobody at the time, so we must leave it at that.

Thereafter the story proceeds uneventfully until the year of Edwin's illness and death. The Bartletts moved twice, becoming, one presumes, a little bit better off as time went on. They made acquaintance, at some time or other, with a couple called Matthews, who remained the only friends they had—though there is no evidence to show that they were ever really intimate. During the years between 1881 and 1885 Edwin, it would seem, got more and more wrapped up in his work, or, at any rate, said he did. "It was work, work, work with him all the time," old Mr. Bartlett exclaimed petulantly; and when, at some time in the latter year the Bartletts took a holiday at Dover, Edwin used frequently to catch a train at 3 a.m. in order to get up to business in town, where he sometimes stayed until eight in the evening. That in itself, one would think, would be more liable to lead to a nervous breakdown than any amount of floor-laying. However, in the meantime, he had found, or thought he had, a sufficient means of keeping his young wife from fretting.

For in the early months of 1885 the Bartletts had made the acquaintance of the Reverend George Dyson, who was then a Wesleyan minister at Putney. He was comparatively young, only 27 at the date of the trial, and from the first both the Bartletts were all over him. The principal reason for this seems to have been that he was better educated even than Adelaide after her husband had done all he could for her, and, furthermore, if one can say so without being unduly offensive, that his cultural goods were all in the shop window. There is not a particle of evidence that the Reverend George Dyson was really a person of deep or wide attainment. The poem which he wrote to Adelaide, and

94

went to almost indecent lengths to recover, has for its final verse:

> Who is it that hath burst the door,
> Enclosed the heart that shut before,
> And set her queen-like on its throne,
> And made its homage all her own?
> My Birdie——

and there is no reason to suppose that the rest of the poem was any better. On literary grounds, if no other, it was possibly wise to suppress it. But to say this is not to deny in the least that George Dyson may have been of great value, at any rate in the opening stages of their acquaintance, to the Bartlett pair. Everyone is perfectly familiar with the phenomenon of the person with a small amount of culture acting as guide, philosopher and friend to those who have less (much like last term's new boy smoothing the path of this term's new boy), and it is priggish to deny its value.

At any rate, Edwin Bartlett had no doubts at all. He jumped at George Dyson as a means of keeping Adelaide happy and occupied while he was away on business. Nor does that fact, fortunately for Adelaide, rest upon the evidence of either herself or George Dyson alone. From the attitude which both the prosecution and the Judge took up, it seems pretty clear that without outside confirmation they would have dismissed such a story, having already caught out both Dyson and Adelaide in misstatements of fact; but there was a letter in existence in Edwin's own handwriting which put the matter beyond all doubt. Here is the letter. It was written in September 1885, while the Bartletts were staying at Dover.

14 ST. JAMES STREET,
DOVER.
Monday.

DEAR GEORGE,

Permit me to say I feel great pleasure in thus addressing you for the first time. To me it is a privilege that I am allowed to feel towards you as a brother, and I hope our friendship may ripen as time goes on, without anything to mar its brightness. Would that I could find words to express my thankfulness to you for the very loving letter you sent to Adelaide to-day. It would have done anybody good to see her overflowing with joy as she read it whilst walking along the street, and afterwards as she read it to me. I felt my heart going out to you. I long to tell you how proud I feel at the thought I would soon be able to clasp the hand of the man who from his heart could pen such noble thoughts. Who can help loving him? I felt that I must say two words, ' Thank you ', and my desire to do so is my excuse for troubling you with this. Looking towards the future with joyfulness, I am,

Yours affectionately,
EDWIN.

Now it is quite idle to pretend, as the learned Judge tried to pretend in his summing-up, having by then, as we observed, decided that he was dealing only with "vulgar commonplace people", that there is nothing remarkable in this letter "beyond a little tendency towards over-sentimentality". The over-sentimentality is there all right; some might even suggest that what Edwin Bartlett did to his new friend in the ministry was to slobber over him. But it is certainly not the letter of what the law considers an ordinary man. Ordinary men, the ordinary men whom the law knows and whom the members of the jury are considered to resemble, do not feel thankful to see their wives overflowing with joy as they read other men's letters; they are more apt to scowl and frown. But Edwin Bartlett overflowed with joy, and when he was absent encouraged the Reverend George Dyson to spend a considerable amount of time with Adelaide. While they lived at Merton Dyson came nearly every day to see her, often staying on after Edwin had returned from business. When they were on holiday at Dover he ran down more than once to call on them, and when they moved to Pimlico Edwin presented him with a season ticket in order to facilitate his visits, since the young Wesleyan minister, like most other young Wesleyan ministers, had very little money of his own. In fact, without taking into account the evidence of anyone whose credibility in the eyes of the law was doubtful, it may safely be said that Edwin Bartlett shoved his wife, if not exactly into the arms, at least into terms of affectionate friendship with George Dyson. It must be observed also, however, that he did not shove her, nor did she enter upon anything which in police-courts would be called 'intimacy'. If there had been any evidence at all to show that George Dyson was Adelaide's lover in a police-court sense, we may be certain that the prosecution would have dragged it out. The best that they could find was that Dyson had kissed her, both in and out of her husband's presence, that she had been sitting on the floor with her head against his knee, and that upon one occasion the long lace curtains, which in the best Victorian fashion covered the sitting-room windows, were noticed by a servant to be pinned together. As, however, the door was not locked upon that or any other occasion, it cannot be supposed that there was any great attempt at concealment.

Finally, Edwin, as far as we know, continued to love and trust both the other members of the triangle until the end of his days. We must, of course, in fairness remember that, as I said earlier, we have not access to Edwin's private thoughts; but at least he uttered no derogatory word to anyone else. And in September 1885 he went off to his place of business and there altered his will, leaving Adelaide free to marry again without losing his money, and naming Dyson his executor. This does not prove, as Adelaide at one time suggested, that Edwin was contemplating his own speedy death; but it does surely show that he was contemplating that the close connexion between Dyson and his wife should continue whatever happened to him; and he can hardly have failed to think of the possibility that if he died the other two might marry.

Here, then, you have these three people, in October and November 1885, living on what were undoubtedly queer terms. They would be queer terms nowadays; they were queerer in 1885, though it should be remembered that oddity is not an invention of the post-War period, nor confined to the intelligentsia. Possibly grocers ought not to presume to have curious views on society; but sometimes they have.

Anyhow, these three oddities seems to have been happy enough, and for the moment we might take a look at them and their characters before things went wrong. We know least of Edwin, because he never appears before us in person; but we can get an idea of him—a man of forty, very much devoted to work, with hardly any outside recreations and no friends other than business acquaintances, except George Dyson: a dutiful son, to the extent that he kept his unpleasant old father and saw to it that he did not want, but not so dutiful as to support him against his wife: and undoubtedly an earnest and affectionate, if not a very amusing or sensitive husband. He does not, as I have said, seem to have had any outside amusements to speak of; but he had some intellectual interests, and liked to discuss, both with George Dyson and with others, questions such as mesmerism and the relations of the sexes.

Old Mr. Bartlett, who would have cut his tongue out sooner than invent anything favourable to Adelaide, recollected him saying that a man ought to have two wives, one to take out and one to do the work, and Dr. Leach and George Dyson both deposed to curious conversations they had with him. He told Dr. Leach at one time that he was being mesmerized by a friend from a distance, and with Dyson he discussed whether polygamy was permitted by the Bible. Both Dyson and Leach, who were the only men with whom he was on terms of intimacy, were much impressed, in a way which they found difficult to explain to the Judge, who continually and peevishly called for 'facts', with the abnormality of Edwin's views on matters which were not matters of business; and the doctor went so far as to wonder whether his patient was not suffering from delusions. Dr. Leach, it should be emphasized, was quite new to the situation, for he was only called in at the time of Edwin's last illness. It would seem as though Edwin had a mind that was interested in unorthodox ideas, but lacked both the educational training or the natural common sense that would have enabled him to judge among them. There are plenty of people of this type in the world; they are apt to be found among the ardent supporters of new religions, 'new' political parties and 'new' economics. Edwin, however, spent too much time on his business to be able to do more than talk about his views in private.

George Dyson's character came out quite clearly at the inquest and trial—much more clearly than he could at all have relished. He was a weak, sloppy-minded young fellow with a certain amount of looks, manners, and cheap culture, whose head had been turned by the admiration of those two who were his seniors. It may well be that this was the first occasion upon which such admiration had come his way, for he was not, according to the *Daily Telegraph*, a very good preacher; and if he had been passionately devoted to his own calling it is strange that he was able to give up so much time to educating Adelaide Bartlett. He certainly enjoyed thoroughly being guide, philosopher, and friend to the couple, and until the catastrophe seems to have been amiable enough, if a little lacking in strength and character. According to his own story, he told Edwin at the time of the making of the will, that he was getting too fond of Adelaide, and suggested that he should discontinue seeing her. To this Edwin replied, in effect, " What are you fussing about ? " and he made no further move. It would have demanded a greater effort than he was capable of to put an end to this pleasant, flattering, rather sentimental way of life; and it was not until the rude breath of publicity showed what the law would be likely to think of his conduct that he rushed to the opposite extreme, as is the way with the weak when stricken by panic. From that time, as we shall see, the Reverend George Dyson ceased to be either guide, philosopher, or friend to his former admirer.

Last, we come to the accused herself—Adelaide Bartlett, who is in some ways the most interesting of the three. Adelaide's photograph, taken at the age of thirty, shows a vigorous, dark young woman, with cropped curling hair, thick eyebrows, wide, dark eyes, and a full mouth—certainly a face of vigour and character. She was strong and healthy, having quite got over the illness which resulted from her pregnancy, fond of children, though she had none, and dogs, and enjoyed vigorous exercise. We are told that she was hot-tempered, and her face would bear out that possibility, though the only real evidence of it is that she quarrelled with her father-in-law and lost her temper with Dyson at a time when his pusillanimity must have been almost unendurable. She did not, apparently, lose her temper with Edwin during all the period of his illness, though that involved her in constant watching and in the performance of a large number of unpleasant duties. She was certainly a person of strong character and lively emotions, though not passionate in the erotic sense—at least, if she was, as Freudians may assert, her passions were assuredly not awakened. Whatever the truth about her marital relations with her husband, they were not passionate, and her relations with Dyson could hardly even have been termed philanderous. The other important fact about her is that she was practically friendless and occupationless, that this strong affectionate nature had until the arrival of Dyson nothing to expend itself on except a husband who was continually at work. If she had had any sort of job, or even a woman friend with whom she could spend time and talk over her life, in all probability this history would never have needed to be written. As things were, she was almost bound to get bored and fidgety without perhaps knowing why. We know that once in the early days she became so exasperated that she left her husband's house. We do not know how their relations stood at the beginning of 1885; but it is at least conjecturable that Adelaide, after ten years of married life and no present or likely outlet for her energies, was beginning to become 'edgy' and unreasonable, and that Edwin jumped at the friendship of George Dyson as a means of making his wife a useful companion without being a nuisance to him. His whole attitude, in spite of his undoubted affection, bears a certain resemblance to that of a man towards a pet dog which he has bought when young, trained carefully and taught to do tricks, and is prepared to treat kindly and play with when he has time. If the pet dog develops a personality of its own and becomes discontented, the pleasure in its possession becomes much less. The arrival of George Dyson may very well have seemed to Edwin as a godsend to enable his pet dog to be kept happy and amused, and to prevent it from resenting his long absences from home and his lack of adequate interest in the pet dog's own avocations. Such an attitude may be unusual, but it is hardly incredible.

Whatever the truth, right through the autumn of 1885 the parties were happy enough. Edwin had signed his new will, which must greatly have pleased Adelaide, since under the old will she stood to be disinherited if she married again after his death, and was known to have resented this long before she met Dyson. (Even the Judge admitted that he saw nothing discreditable to her in that; and fortunately that particular form of tyranny seems to be now on the wane, though one of the strongest of the minor arguments for the doing away with inheritance is the great opportunity it gives to nasty old men and nasty old women for prolonging their nastinesses beyond the grave.)

The Bartletts left Dover and moved into lodgings in Claverton Street, Pimlico, in a house kept by one Frederick Doggett, who was also Registrar of Births, Marriages, and Deaths for the district; and asked as soon as possible to be provided with separate beds. (It was not unheard of, the Judge admitted, even in 1885, for married couples possessed of sufficient means to prefer not to occupy the same bed.) George Dyson was given a season ticket from Putney to Waterloo in order to enable him to continue his ministrations, and all seemed to be going well. But on December 8th Edwin Bartlett felt so ill at his work that he went home early; and from that time the troubles began. He never recovered from that illness, though he had ups and downs, and it continued till his sudden death some time in the night of New Year's Eve.

It was a most peculiar illness. Its cause was never diagnosed—it would almost seem, from the evidence, as though nobody ever asked about the cause; but its symptoms, as related by Dr. Leach, present a remarkable combination. Its chief characteristic, I venture to suggest after carefully reading all the evidence, was morbid hysteria, and I shall revert later to possible explanations of its inception. I do not mean to imply that there was nothing physically wrong with Edwin; obviously there was; but several of the symptoms, such as sleeplessness, were of a kind which hysteria would increase, and there is abundant evidence of despair, depression, curious fancies, and a desire to be fussed and made much of, continuing throughout its course. He liked to have his wife, for example, in constant attendance on him all the time; all through his illness she never undressed or went to bed herself, but slept in a chair at the foot of his bed, *holding his foot,* which seemed in some way to soothe him to sleep. On one occasion he told Dr. Leach that he had risen from his bed and stood for two hours over his sleeping wife drawing vital mesmeric force from her. Neither Dr. Leach nor Adelaide believed this statement, but that it should have been made shows the mental condition of the man. Dr. Leach, at all events, thought that the trouble lay in the mind as much as in the body, and half-way through the course of the illness was trying to persuade his patient to pull himself together and go for a holiday. " I wanted him to go to Torquay alone," he told the court. " He was practically a hysterical patient, and his wife petted him very much." Certainly Dr. Leach did not think that Edwin Bartlett's sufferings, however much they distressed him and exhausted his wife, were likely to end in death.

Whether they were or were not exaggerated by hysteria, Edwin's symptoms were unpleasant enough, as a bare recital will show. It was on December 8th that he went home ill from his office, and two days later, on the 10th, as he seemed really in a bad way, Adelaide sent for Dr. Alfred Leach, who lived just round the corner. Neither of the Bartletts had ever met Dr. Leach before; he was sent for because he happened to be the nearest doctor available. He came, and found Edwin suffering from vomiting, diarrhœa, severe pain in the side, hæmorrhage, nervous exhaustion, and sleeplessness. Naturally, with all these unpleasant conditions pursuing him, he was in a very low and gloomy condition; and he had a further symptom which perplexed Dr. Leach considerably. On looking into his mouth Dr. Leach saw a blue line around his gums, and formed the firm opinion that he was suffering from mercurial poisoning. He was so much impressed by this that he made an excuse to send Mrs. Bartlett out of the room, and then asked Edwin whether the presence of mercury was to be accounted for in the ordinary way —i.e. in plain language, whether he had been suffering from syphilis and had taken mercury as a remedy.

Edwin replied that he had not, and there were no signs of syphilis found in him either then or afterwards. As to the presence of mercury, he explained it by saying that he had taken a 'large pill' out of a drawer and eaten it. He could not remember whence or how he had procured this pill; and Dr. Leach, not unnaturally, seems to have formed the opinion that a man who could tell him such a story was either lying or incredibly foolish. However, he proceeded to treat him as best he could. He gave him bismuth, cinchona, and nux vomica, and a mouthwash of chlorate of potash and lemon syrup, as his mouth was in a very unpleasant condition. Edwin, however, continued ill, and on the next day Dr. Leach added to his prescription bicarbonate of soda, bromide of ammonium and tincture of chloroform. Three days later, on the 14th, he had an opium pill for his sleeplessness, and a different mouth lotion, and on the following day a preparation of gentian and nux vomica.

Still he remained ill, and when Dr. Leach visited him on the 16th he found him suffering, in addition to his other woes, from flatulence and great pain in the tongue and teeth. At this time the doctor examined his patient's mouth more closely—as he might well have done before—and found that his teeth were in a very bad condition. This was not surprising, for ten or eleven years previously Edwin Bartlett had had from a dentist a form of treatment which must, one hopes, have been unusual even sixty years ago. He had had most of his teeth sawn off, and artificial teeth put in to replace them, without the roots and stumps of the old teeth being removed. Old Mr. Bartlett, who provided the information about this operation, explained that the sawing-off was necessary "because his teeth were all stuck together". It was "a most exceptional treatment", as the Judge commented. Naturally, after this lapse of time, the roots and gums were in "a most horrible condition", and Dr. Leach promptly sent for a dentist called Roberts, who on the 16th took out two of the stumps, on the 17th about eleven, on the 21st four, and one more on the 31st. Mr. Roberts also, on the occasion of his first visit, confirmed Dr. Leach by finding traces of mercurial poisoning.

After the 17th Dr. Leach expected his patient to improve rapidly, though he continued to prescribe a variegated series of medicines for him. On the 18th he gave him a strong dose of Epsom salts and some bromide of ammonia with chloral hydrate; on the 19th and 20th he gave him more chloral hydrate and morphia, with on the latter day some bromide as well; and on the 22nd another mouthwash. Nevertheless, he thought his patient better and was beginning to urge him to get up and go out into the air. But Edwin Bartlett did not agree that he was better; he would not go out, and he became very distressed, not to say tearful, at the thought of the doctor's ceasing to call on him. On the 19th a curious incident occurred. Edwin Bartlett asked Dr. Leach to get a second opinion. Not, he explained, because he felt any lack of confidence, but because "some people"—which could only have meant his father—were making unpleasant remarks about his wife's nursing. Dr. Leach called a Dr. Dudley, who came and concurred in the treatment.

Well, by the 21st Dr. Leach thought that there was nothing medically the matter with his patient and that "what would have done him good would have been to have sent him on a sea-trip, with no one to nurse him and hold his toe and that sort of nonsense." One may guess, in fact, that Dr. Leach was by this time wondering whether he would not soon have Adelaide as well on his hands as a patient. The toe-holding and "that sort of nonsense" had now gone on for nearly a fortnight, quite long enough to shake the endurance of one not used to the strain of sick nursing.

But Edwin Bartlett never went on his sea-trip. Perhaps he was not quite as recovered as Dr. Leach rather impatiently surmised; at any rate he succeeded, on the 23rd, in passing a lumbricoid worm, and this upset him considerably. In Dr. Leach's words, "that threw everything back again". It is certainly distressing to discover that one is suffering from worms; but only a very nervous patient would leap, as Edwin Bartlett did, to the conviction that there were worms wriggling up his throat. After his death the doctors, at Dr. Leach's request, searched his body carefully for worms, but there was never a trace of any but the one that appeared on the 23rd.

But that one was an undeniable worm, and had to be treated. So on the 26th, having on the previous day tried a new tonic containing phosphate of strychnine, he was given a vermifuge, composed of santonine, sulphate of soda and Urwick's extract; and in order that he might not be too uncomfortable he was told to expel it with a draught of sulphate of magnesium and tincture of jalap. This he took, and followed it up on his own responsibility with two globules of croton oil. Now croton oil is a very strong purge. Attendants in badly run lunatic asylums have frequently got into trouble for using croton oil to keep their patients weak and pliant; and one would accordingly have had expected it to have at any rate some effect on Edwin Bartlett. But not a bit—this remarkable patient only observed that it gave him a warm, comfortable feeling; and though Dr. Leach fed him on hot tea and coffee and applied galvanism to his abdomen, still nothing happened. Then Dr. Leach gave up in despair; but it would seem, notwithstanding his fears, that Edwin was able to absorb worm-powders easily into his system, for after this his health began to improve again, and on the 30th Dr. Leach again suggested discontinuing his attendance. Mrs. Bartlett begged him not to, "because it makes him so distressed"; and to this entreaty he agreed, and, further, made arrangements for Edwin to have yet another tooth taken out on the following day. By this time he had begun to suspect that Edwin was suffering from incipient necrosis of the jaw.

So we come to the last day of Edwin Bartlett's life—a day on which, although he had a tooth out under gas, he appeared to be in better spirits than he had been for some time. Not only was he in better spirits; he had also managed to acquire a fairly tolerable appetite, for, in spite of his encounter with the dentist, he succeeded in putting away oysters, jugged hare, bread and butter, cake, mango chutney, and more oysters. He told his landlady, after the jugged hare, that he could eat three such dinners every day; and almost his last recorded utterance registered his intention of getting up an hour earlier at the thought of having a large haddock for breakfast.

At four in the morning of New Year's Day Mr. Doggett was woken by Adelaide Bartlett, who told him that her husband was dead. He came up, found Edwin dead in bed, and the fire burning brightly, as though it had recently been mended. (I have mentioned this point because it received great stress from the prosecution, though how putting more coal on the fire could prove Adelaide Bartlett a murderess, I confess I am unable to understand. If she woke up, as she said, and found Edwin's foot cold in her hands, surely to mend the fire would be a very natural action. Everyone is not necessarily dead who has cold feet; they may even, perhaps, be suffering from cold, if the fire has died down.)

Dr. Leach was summoned, and confirmed the death, feeling very puzzled. At the earliest possible opportunity, Adelaide sent off telegrams to old Mr. Bartlett, Mr. Matthews, and Mr. Baxter, the dead man's partner—not, it should be observed, to George Dyson. Mr. Bartlett, when he came, was obviously bristling with suspicions. He smelt his dead son's lips for signs of prussic acid poisoning, declared that there was something wrong about the death and that the police must be sent for, and began feeling in the pocket's of Adelaide's cloak to see if she had hidden anything there. He also kissed her, which even the Judge felt was going rather far.

The upshot was that it was felt that there must be a post-mortem —a decision in which Adelaide eagerly concurred—and an inquest. A police officer arrived to search the rooms, but his search was rather perfunctory, and he might have missed quite a number of things.

The post-mortem was held on January 2nd, and, greatly to Dr.

Leach's surprise, though no definite conclusions were reached, it was found that some of the organs smelt strongly of chloroform. Subsequent analysis established that Edwin had died of chloroform poisoning in the stomach. Dr. Leach promptly communicated this fact to Adelaide, expecting that it would set her mind at rest; but, again to his surprise—throughout these events, poor Dr. Leach was continually being surprised—he found that he had caused her considerable distress. The post-mortem had already caused even more distress to the Reverend George Dyson, as will shortly appear.

Where had the chloroform come from? There was no chloroform to be seen, though Dr. Leach looked around for it, and among all his variegated drugging of Edwin, his doctor had never prescribed pure chloroform. The explanation, at the coroner's court, which was held early in February, was provided by George Dyson.

George Dyson told the court that on December 27th Mrs. Bartlett had privately asked him to buy her some chloroform in order that she might use it to quieten her husband, who in the course of his illness suffered from violent internal paroxysms. She added that, as she would have to administer the chloroform by sprinkling it upon a handkerchief which she would wave in front of his face, and as chloroform was extremely volatile, she would have to have a fairly large quantity of the drug. When Dyson asked why she could not get it through the doctor, she replied that the doctor would not believe that she was "skilled in the administration of chloroform".

Whether he believed this tale or not—we must, I think, in view of his evident anxiety to save his skin, believe that it was substantially the tale which he was told—Dyson was sufficiently under the influence of the stronger character to do as he was asked. He bought the chloroform, in four separate purchases, lying as to the reason for which it was wanted, but making no other attempt to cover his actions; and on the 29th, having emptied his four bottles into one, handed the big bottle to Adelaide. That bottle was never seen again. The police officer who searched the room failed to find it; old Mr. Bartlett is our witness that it was not concealed in Adelaide's cloak. Adelaide herself said that at a later stage she threw it, empty, into a pond; but nobody found it.

Not unnaturally, when Dyson heard on January 2nd that the dead man's organs had smelt of chloroform, he was horribly frightened. On the next morning he threw away his little bottles on Wimbledon Common, where one of them was subsequently found by the police. At the earliest possible opportunity he tackled Adelaide and asked her what she had done with the chloroform. She replied: "Oh, damn the chloroform!" and stamped her foot at him. Nevertheless he remained agitated, and on other occasions cross-questioned her in no friendly manner. He cried out: "I am a ruined man!" and consulted a friend, who wisely counselled him to wait until the results of the analysis were known, and not go wildly dashing off to the police. Neither this counsel nor his running round in circles availed him much, for at the inquest the jury which returned a verdict against Adelaide Bartlett found that the Reverend George Dyson had been an accessory after the fact. When the trial came on, however, it was observed that the Crown had decided not to proceed against him, but to use him as a witness. It was suggested that this was fortunate for Adelaide, since it enabled her counsel to cross-examine him; it should, however, be remarked that the Crown advisers presumably knew what they were about, and valued the testimony that they could get by allowing Dyson to give evidence.

The explanation—if there be an explanation—of the whole tragedy falls into two parts: the administration of the poison, and the condition of things which led up to it. Sir Edward Clarke, who defended Adelaide, decided—quite rightly, as he was dealing with the law—that the former aspect, which to my mind is far the less interesting, was the one on which to concentrate; and, accordingly, much time was spent in disputing how the chloroform could have got into Edwin Bartlett's stomach.

There was, of course, more than one way in which this might have happened. The prosecution, rather unfortunately for themselves, based their case throughout on the theory that Adelaide

Bartlett killed her husband by first stupefying him as he slept and then pouring the rest of the poison down his throat; and Sir Edward Clarke, who had given much more study to the scientific side of the problem than had his Crown opponent, had no difficulty at all in showing that such an operation would have been one of extraordinary subtlety, and would have needed either remarkable skill or remarkable good fortune to enable it to be successfully performed. The prosecution tried to make much of the fact that in the house there was a copy of a work of reference, Squire's *Companion to the British Pharmacopœia*, which appeared to open naturally at the pages dealing with chloroform. They suggested that it was from this book that Adelaide derived the knowledge which enabled her to commit her crime; but Sir Edward Clarke observed that even if she had studied it with all care, all that she would have found out was that chloroform was volatile—which would not have helped her much.

I do not propose to follow in detail all the lengthy evidence which was given by the medical witnesses. The net effect was that, while the doctors were not prepared to swear that it would be impossible to commit murder by these means, they all thought it was highly unlikely. There appeared to have been only one authentic case in the whole course of medical history of the successful chloroforming of a patient during sleep—and he was a boy of sixteen, and not a grown man in a nervous and hysterical condition. It was this great improbability that saved Adelaide Bartlett; if the prosecution could have thought in time of any more plausible way in which she could have administered the poison she would certainly have been convicted.

If that hypothesis were ruled out as too difficult, there were various others. There was accident—but that also was highly unlikely. Liquid chloroform burns and causes violent pain; if Edwin had drunk liquid chloroform in mistake for something else he would certainly not have died without mentioning the fact. The theory that the defence in its closing speech put up was that Edwin Bartlett committed suicide, that in despair of enjoying life again he turned his face to the wall and drank off the chloroform.

This theory, like the suggestion subsequently published by Dr. Leach, that he drank the poison to annoy his wife, and accidentally drank too much, involves consideration of the relationship of the Bartletts, and must for the moment be deferred.

Finally, the last speech of the advocate for the Crown hinted that there was another means by which murder might have been committed. Suppose that Adelaide Bartlett, whose care and scrupulousness as a nurse her husband had never had any reason to doubt, had handed him the chloroform to drink, suggesting, perhaps, that it was a new medicine guaranteed to make him sleep. Would he not have taken it from her hand, and might he not have swallowed it down before he realized that he was drinking poison? The Judge, in his summing-up, ruled this explanation out of order. It had not been made in time and according to the proper forms, and therefore, by the rules of the law game, the jury must not pay any attention to it. So they did not; but if the learned Attorney-General had realized rather earlier that his first hypothesis was going to fall down on him, things might not have gone so well for his prisoner. The law is a curious beast; it is not really interested to find out what did happen, or why, but whether a theory put forward by one party to the dispute can or cannot be proved according to the rules.

Leaving for the moment the question how the chloroform got into Edwin Bartlett, let us consider for a while how it came to be in his room at all. We know the actual physical means by which it got there; it was bought at four separate shops by George Dyson and given to Adelaide Bartlett at her request. But for what purpose did she want it?

Here we come on to more difficult ground. We do not know from Adelaide herself why she wanted it, for did she not give evidence, on the advice of her lawyers, either at the inquest or at the trial. We have to rely upon stories told by Dyson and by Dr. Leach, both of whom the Judge thought highly unreliable witnesses, and we have the further difficulty that the stories themselves, as far as they concern the relations between the Bartletts, come under the heading of 'subjective truth', that is, we may believe that they adequately represent the emotional situation without necessarily being correct in all details.

Adelaide, on January 26th, after the analysis had shown death to be due to chloroform poisoning, came to Dr. Leach, and told him in confidence, as her private physician, what must have been almost the full history of her married life. She began by saying that she was married at sixteen. This was one of the details that was certainly not true, though she seems to have been so undeveloped at the time of her marriage that she may very well have felt like sixteen, even though she was three years older. But, she said, her husband had always had peculiar ideas about marriage, and when they married it was on the understanding that there should be no intercourse between them. This rule was kept, even after she returned from her convent school to live in her husband's house, and was only broken once, when she petitioned to be allowed to have a child. But the child died, as we know; and after that they resumed their platonic relations, sharing the same bed for years, but without being lovers. They always got on very well, she said, except on one occasion, when they quarrelled about old Mr. Bartlett's treatment of her: it was then that she ran away.

But during the last few months of his life, she said, and after they had become so friendly with George Dyson, Edwin's nature seemed to change, and he wanted to lay claim to the rights which he had had for ten years but never exercised. She resisted; she told him that "he had practically made her over to George Dyson", and that it was not fair now, suddenly, to demand to be her husband in the full sense. As to what the phrase quoted meant, or meant to Adelaide, we are rather in the dark. Dr. Leach does not seem to have pressed for an explanation; nor did the court. It did not mean that Dyson was her lover, for he was not. The only direct light that is thrown upon it is Bartlett's will naming Dyson as executor, and a conversation which Dyson had with him some time in October concerning Adelaide, in the course of which Dyson said to him, "If ever she comes under my care I shall have to teach her differently," or some such words. Dyson made it quite clear that in his opinion Edwin certainly intended his friend and his wife to come together after his death, even if he did not say so definitely. Of course, that is not quite the same thing as "making her over" during his lifetime; but it is not so far off.

At all events Adelaide did not at all want to live with Edwin as his wife, and did her best to make that plain. The decision to take separate beds on the move to Claverton Street fits in obviously with this part of her story. But Edwin was not moved by her objections. The more ill he got the more he seemed to want to make love to her, and this at a time when she was becoming exhausted and worn by sick-nursing. So at last she conceived a plan to stupefy him when he began to make these advances, by soaking a handkerchief in chloroform and waving it in his face; and for this purpose she got Dyson to buy her some chloroform, giving him another reason for wanting it, as she was too shy to give him the real one. Dr. Leach, to whom she poured all this out on January 26th, remarked that if she had tried the experiment, she would probably have upset the bottle and chloroformed them both.

But she never tried it. The bottle worried her, she said, lying there in her drawer, and on New Year's Eve, when Edwin was lying in his bed, she made confession. She told him all about it, and gave him the bottle, which was corked but not full. "He was not cross; we talked amicably and seriously, and he turned round on his side and pretended to go to sleep, or to sulk, or something of that sort." (It was this part of her story which caused the defence to suggest that Edwin might have killed himself.) Then she left him with the bottle beside him, changed her clothes, and composed herself to sleep at the foot of the bed. She heard him snoring violently, but took no notice; and when she woke at four in the morning, he was dead. She could not say whether any chloroform had disappeared from the bottle; but she took it and hid it somewhere, and at a later date threw it into Peckham Rye Pond. It was not found there; but neither was it found anywhere else.

Now, what is one to make of all this? Mr. Justice Wills

thought it a farrago of indecent nonsense, and Dr. Leach a fool for believing any of it, as he obviously did. But is it really so incredible? Plenty more people, even in 1885, had curious lives than ever came into court.

It is pretty certain that Edwin and Adelaide Bartlett married upon platonic terms, that, whether or no the statement about their never having lived together as man and wife was strictly accurate—it all depends exactly what you mean or exactly what Adelaide meant by 'living together'—their mode of life had very little in it that was sexual, and that this mode of life suited Edwin excellently until two or three months before his death. Adelaide was inclined to be bored; psycho-analysts will no doubt say that the boredom was due purely to the lack of a full sex life. But if it was, she certainly did not know it, and she was quite happy again when George Dyson turned up. She did not want to sleep with him. I myself think that, like a good many women, she did not want to sleep with anybody; quite possibly the episode of the baby that died had given her a horror of the whole thing. But she did very much enjoy being petted and made a fuss of, and to have a little superior culture offered her. Edwin, until about October, also approved of the arrangement very well. He liked to have Adelaide kept amused and happy while he was away, by a young man for whom he had conceived a great and almost embarrassing admiration, who regarded him with friendship and affection, and was always ready to discuss and to offer advice. It seems fairly clear, whatever the Judge thought about it, that he did contemplate George and Adelaide marrying if he should die.

But during the last months of his life something changed in Edwin Bartlett. It is difficult to be sure what that was or why it happened; but there are various points to be noted. In the first place, he was just over forty, an age when men are notoriously apt to suffer sex-changes, if only temporarily. Mostly, men go off the rails; Edwin seems to have gone *on* the rails, though with no less unfortunate effects. Secondly, he was definitely overworking; his body, therefore, was ripe for a breakdown of some sort

113

as soon as his mind would concede it, and his old teeth had probably been poisoning him for some time. So, I suggest, he began to feel sorry for himself, and probably also to feel, at the back of his mind, that Adelaide was getting rather too much interested in the playmate he had found her, and that master was getting a little bit pushed out. At any rate, the whole course of his illness suggests an attempt to get into the middle of the picture, and to keep his wife busy about him. He wants her to be with him all the time, to hold his toe, and generally feed him with her own vitality. Sometimes he'll feel better, sometimes worse; but all the time he is in such a mental state as to demand her continual attention.

Then, on top of all this, he wants to possess her as he has never possessed her before. The Judge found it quite incredible that this desire should have come upon him while he was ill. I do not find it so. In the first place, sexual desire is not in the least incompatible with a certain amount of bodily discomfort, and he was not at any time really disablingly ill. He had not, for instance, a high fever. Secondly, I submit that there are one or two facts, which were not all disclosed at the trial, which suggest that Adelaide's disclosures to Dr Leach did not cover the whole facts of her husband's life. After his death, there were found, not in a box or anywhere like that, but in his trouser pocket, a number of French letters. This is fact number one. Fact number two is that he undoubtedly suggested more than once that a man ought to be allowed two wives—one for companionship, and one, as it were, for use. Adelaide, we know, was the companion. And fact number three is that both Dr. Leach and the dentist, at the beginning of his last illness, found him suffering from mercurial poisoning— and he gave no credible explanation of how the mercury could have got inside him. Do not these three facts require some explanation? And is it not at least a possible explanation that Edwin Bartlett, through the ten years of his married life, was platonic with his wife while finding natural satisfaction elsewhere, that in the October or November he got a nasty fright which caused him to forswear outside amusements, and that thenceforward he was intending to take Adelaide for use as well as companionship? That suggestion would remove some of the learned Judge's difficulties.

I do not suggest that Adelaide would have been aware of his previous habits or of the reason for the change. Whether she was or was not, I find no difficulty in understanding that the change was extremely distasteful to her. As I have said, she did not want to sleep with anybody, and Edwin, in his condition at the time, can hardly have been an attractive lover. Besides, she was extremely tired, probably near hysteria herself, and certainly in no condition to deal with a sudden new strain. For Adelaide, as I read her, was a person of courage and vitality, but inclined to be impatient and not very good at standing strains. She had been doing an altogether ridiculous amount of nursing, and she was the kind of person who, being in excellent health, light-heartedly undertakes a long, exhausting and unpleasant job without in the least realizing the extent to which it can fray one's nerves. That is the type which, without warning, suddenly cracks—and she had nobody to help her. She did not have the 'time off' which any professional nurse would have had; she had no intimate women friends, and it was not possible, even under the circumstances, for her to discuss this particular problem with Dyson—not that it was likely to help her much if she had; for if ever there was a broken reed it was that young Wesleyan minister. Even her doctor was a stranger, and her husband's father an enemy.

So she bought the chloroform, and I think it quite likely that the reason she gave to Dr. Leach was a true reason, and that she had some sort of vague idea that she might be able to choke Edwin off if he became too affectionate. I think it is certainly more probable than that she intended to pour it down his throat. Beyond that we do not know. Her account of her last conversation with Edwin may have been true. He may have subsequently, in a fit of despair—possibly a fit of indigestion, which he well deserved—have drunk off the poison, or he may have swallowed it, intending to get a little more attention. Both these explanations involve some difficulties; both suggest that the final conversation, whatever it may have been about, was not really amicable.

And it is very difficult to believe that, in either event, Edwin died without making a sound that would disturb his wife.

It may be that her control, in the middle of the night, suddenly broke and that she persuaded him either to drink the chloroform or to allow himself to be stupefied so that she could pour it down. If that was so, the real breaking-point came, I suggest, when Dr. Leach informed her that he was practically recovered and was suffering from nothing but hysteria. For hysteria is neither fatal nor easily cured, and the prospect of Edwin living with her another thirty years or so, off and on, in that condition might well have seemed too appalling to face. If, after spending a day eating heartily and appearing better, he developed another attack of melancholia and affection late at night, one can see that it might have been the last straw, and that she might have taken one of those insane decisions which strong characters, strained too hard and left too much to their own resources, do sometimes come to in the middle of the night. Luckily, they do not often have the means of action ready to hand. Adelaide Bartlett had.

This much is clear. She knew, or half knew, even before the post-mortem, that the bottle of chloroform had something to do with her husband's death. If she did not kill him, she felt herself guilty of some neglect or other—perhaps she had simply resolved to go to sleep and take no notice of any noise he made; she must have been sleepy enough. If she did kill him, she did not properly realize it. She had only, as it were, emotionally willed his death, and had not taken in that her pipe dream was a reality. Hence her clamour for a post-mortem and her rage at Dyson's fears. It must have been a sudden, half-insane impulse. But if the jury had been allowed to consider the possibility of her having poisoned Edwin with his own partial co-operation, she would never have gone free—because she was odd, and because she had a book on birth-control. So possibly, though by curious ways, justice was in the end served.

PART IV

AN IMPRESSION OF THE LANDRU CASE

by E. R. Punshon

BUSINESS AS USUAL

AN IMPRESSION OF THE LANDRU CASE

I

THE MURDERER AS MAN OF AFFAIRS

DURING that four-year feast of horror and of terror we remember as the war, there were few phrases aroused an indignation more general than the recommendation of a certain German diplomat that neutral ships engaged in trade with the Allies should be 'sunk without trace'. About such total disappearance indeed there is always a quality both of mystery and dread that seems to affect the mind to a peculiar degree. The chances of fate we are all aware that we must reckon with. Death itself all know, and know that all must face in time; its portals may be awful, but they are familiar, and from the familiar there has always been taken away something at least of the terrible.

But when what happens is simply that our place and habitation knows us no longer, when we are not and none can tell why, when no spot of earth can be pointed to as our last resting-place, when the veil of the unknown covers all with such obscurity that even the actual fact of death can only be surmised, not proved, then indeed in such a fate there is felt to be an element of terror unique in its own degree of poignancy, when to the mystery of death is added the mystery of the unknown.

Thus in this story of events that passed not so many years ago, the mystery of complete and utter disappearance which befell in the midst of a great and crowded city, a long succession of eleven people—ten women and a boy—seems to set the tale quite apart in the sad category of crime. Others have killed as remorselessly, others have claimed as many victims or more, only Henri Désiré Landru succeeded in concealing so completely the fate of his victims, that concerning it nothing can be declared with certainty. Indeed, it is not too much to say that, in each case considered apart and by itself, conviction would have been impossible. No jury could have been asked to bring in a verdict of guilty had each case stood alone. No proof existed that the supposed victims were even dead, nothing to show they had not simply gone about their business, as Landru protested that they had, and were not, as his advocate suggested, quietly living somewhere or another ignorant even of the accusation brought against their supposed murderer and, therefore, not coming forward to show themselves and prove his innocence.

But if in logic it is impossible to add eleven probabilities together to make one certainty; if, in law, case ' A ' should always be considered without reference to case ' B '; life, even in France, is more than either logic or law. Of late years, too, scientists have made us aware of what they call ' statistical laws ', telling us that, for example, if the table we were sitting at vanished at some moment from our ken, that would be no miracle but merely the result of a quite conceivable accident, that of all the violently circulating molecules composing the table chancing to find themselves all in one spot at one moment. But that is as unlikely as that all the inhabitants of London should chance to decide to take a walk down Fleet Street at the same hour of the same afternoon, even though such a decision is quite conceivable of each one of them taken separately. So, though in each case of these disappearances wherein Landru stands convicted, absolute proof is lacking, yet when with a monotonous and dreadful regularity it is shown that he was the last person with whom the missing individual was seen and after that was seen no more, then it may be claimed there is achieved that complete certainty which is above all proof, since proof must always rest upon premise that must in its turn be proved, and so on, indefinitely.

Of the eleven people whose strange fate it was thus to be, as it were, annihilated, there is not much to be said, for they were all of them just those who form the vast majority of mankind—the *tout le monde* in French, the ' Everyman ' or rather ' Everywoman' in English, the neighbours, fellow-citizens, the casual passers-by with whom we all rub shoulders as we go to and fro about our daily business. None of them could have dreamed, busy as they were with their own concerns, so trivial to the rest of us, so significant and important to themselves, that the Fates had flung for them dice marked with a doom so dreadfully unknown.

For the most part they were middle-aged women, widows or elderly spinsters, though one was a lad of eighteen or twenty, and another, seen hovering for a moment on the outskirts of the tragedy before it engulfed her too, was a young girl. She was an orphan apparently. She seems to have had not a friend or a relative in the world, she had no money, she had nothing to attract attention in looks or talent or education, nothing to suggest the strange doom awaiting her. She seemed inevitably destined for the quiet, laborious life of the average working girl, possibly with marriage in the future or some small, modest niche in the world she would be able to make or find for herself. We have the merest glimpse of her, gathering flowers, enjoying the fresh country air at Gambais, near the Forest of Rambouillet, chattering with her 'uncle', as she called Landru, using his pet name in talking to him, and then passing into the unknown, no more to be seen or heard of, leaving us to guess in vain why or how.

Surely the very extremity of wantonness to take a child as harmless, as indifferent, as a mouse behind the skirting-board, and ere yet her life had well begun involve her in so dark and strange a tragedy.

It is in 1915 that the story begins, so far at least as is known, though prologues as yet unheard of there may well have been. They were days when the world, in its madness, was tearing itself to pieces, when the foolish mumbling of the guns could be plainly heard in quiet weather on the Surrey downs, and yet when, as it is a little hard to remember, the business of daily life had still to go on as usual, when buying and selling, eating and drinking, rising up in the morning and lying down at night had still to continue.

'Business as usual' had indeed come into its own; unhappy phrase invented at the beginning of the war by those who imagined that war was still conducted under the limited liability act; then becoming a term of reproach for failure to understand that when the house burned nothing mattered but extinguishing the flames; then coming back into a tacit acceptance, as it was realized that even in the midst of terrors hitherto undreamed of the daily trivialities still kept their place, and that each morning tea and toast still bulked as largely in the daily economy as tidings of defeat and victory and lists of casualties whole columns long.

'Business as usual', then, and no one pursued this ideal more thoroughly than Henri Désiré Landru, going briskly, methodically, industriously about his business, though indeed what that business was none of those dreamed who sat by him in train or tram, passed him in the street, bargained with him for the purchase of the certainly rather peculiar odds and ends, the bits of furniture, and so on, he had at times to dispose of. Occasionally, too, smart and confident, he would step into a bank or a broker's office with government bonds or share certificates he had to dispose of, formerly the property of a Madame This or That, widow or spinster, as the case might be, and now recently come into his possession.

And always he had his note-book ready to hand, so that everything might be jotted down and nothing forgotten or overlooked. A man indeed who understood routine and made of it murder's accepted servant, a man to whom method and routine were necessary since, in addition to his chief business of assassination, he had so many other things to think of, a man to whom method was so much a habit that, though one might think the exact hour of a murder was not easily forgotten on the one hand, or on the other hand its record either prudent or important, was yet obliged to jot it down, day, hour, and minute all carefully recorded in that same note-book with all the other details of daily engagements and expenses—so much for a bus fare, this hour for meeting a friend to drink with him a glass of wine, or a cup of coffee, for Landru was a sober man; that hour for the completion of the latest murder!

No wonder that to all who came in contact with him he seemed the very type of the busy, careful, efficient man of affairs, smiling and cheerful, his pleasant, gentle manner covering a keen business sense.

" I know well how to claim my commission," he said of himself later on.

A man diligent in his affairs shall stand before kings; there is Scriptural authority for believing, and for Henri Désiré Landru, whose diligence none could doubt, the promise was destined to prove as true as might be in a republic, for if he never came to stand before kings, at any rate, presently, he was to stand up in a court!

In general, his chief dealings were in furniture, but he traded in motors also, and indeed in anything that presented itself for sale or purchase. He was tenant, too, of a small garage, and as befitted a methodical man of business, he was always punctual in paying his rent and other charges—in fact all through his queer history of fraud and murder there is no suggestion that he ever failed to meet his daily obligations. What he owed he paid, even to the final payment one morning in a Versailles square. Probably to his precise and punctual mind a debt was a worry, but a swindle or a murder merely a business transaction, popular prejudice made it necessary to carry out in private. He owned, too, a kind of light lorry he used for conveying recent acquisitions to this garage, where presently an unsympathetic police, rummaging and searching, were to find such things as the false hair of women, who, according to Landru, had parted from him to go travelling in foreign countries; the identity papers of little servant girls who, according to Landru, had left him to seek for fresh posts they would have no chance of obtaining without those papers; the cherished trifles, china ornaments, and so on, elderly widows had clung to all their lives till now when, according to Landru, they had confided them to him before departing about their business; small pieces of family jewellery that had been the pride of equally elderly spinsters and their proof of social standing, but that now, too, had found their way to the garage where was stored this strange collection, almost every item once the property of a woman who once had known Landru and now was known to none.

In fact it seems as if about this time any insertion in a Paris newspaper of what in France is called a *petite annonce*, in England a ' small classified ', offering furniture for sale, would be apt to bring the pleasant, smiling, soft-spoken, confidence-creating Landru to the door, ready to make an offer all the more liberal, since his intention was to pay otherwise than in cash.

And how could the anxious, slightly flustered, slightly worried middle-aged woman, anxious to secure for her possessions the best price possible—how could she dream that the step upon her stairs of this prospective purchaser was the step of Death in Mystery, that when she opened the door to his soft knock, it was that soon she might pass through that open door to a doom none would ever know?

Fantastic such an idea would have seemed and yet so it was to be, not once alone, but time after time, one after another in the most tragic, singular procession surely the world has ever seen—this long line of drab, work-worn, middle-aged, quiet, saving women passing from the warm security of the little homes they had made for themselves to an enigmatic fate a whole world would presently discuss and all the skill and effort of the police of France fail to elucidate.

The beginning indeed is clear enough. The start of the affair can easily be reconstructed, from imagination only, it is true, since no record is there to be consulted, but on a foundation of reasonable, almost certain conjecture, so that the picture forms itself as plainly as though before an eye-witness.

Nearly always the start is the *petite annonce*. Sometimes it is one that Landru, always a great patron of the *petite annonce*, inserts, offering to buy furniture. Occasionally it is an announcement of furniture that for some reason some woman wishes to dispose of. Or it takes the form of a matrimonial advertisement, couched in the queer abbreviated form the economical French love to employ, with Landru in the character of the business man possessing a small capital and seeking wife and partner with savings to match his own.

One can so easily imagine the hesitations and the doubts with which the insertion or the reading of these advertisements would be accompanied, how carefully they would be considered, how prudently the final decision would be arrived at, that at any rate there could be no harm in finding out what this unknown monsieur had to say for himself or what price he would be prepared to offer for whatever was to be sold.

Writing materials are sought, therefore; a letter composed with care and difficulty, for one does not write a letter every day, it is dropped into the post, there is an answer, and the Angel of Death comes leading to the door that gentle, quiet-spoken Landru, in whom one has confidence from the start, so favourable is the instant impression that he makes.

Only the very faintest knowledge of the psychology of the average lower middle-class Frenchwoman is needed to understand with what suspicion and hostility the advent of this potential buyer had been awaited. One had been prepared for all, one had expected every effort to beat down prices to the lowest possible figure. Instead, here was this polite, smiling, gentle man, *un vrai monsieur*, so liberal in his views, willing to offer a price better than could have been dreamed of, and above all much more interested apparently in oneself than in one's possessions.

As the presiding magistrate remarked to Landru later on : " It seems it was your habit to enter as a client, to emerge as a *fiancé*."

The tale he told no doubt varied in every instance. As the flood of refugees poured into Paris from the invaded regions, he became one of them. He had enormous claims against the State for his factory in Lille occupied by the Germans. Or he had rendered immense services to the State, for which he was to be rewarded by an appointment as consul in Australia. Or else it was Brazil, where the future domicile was to be established, and as it was obviously impossible to think of taking one's furniture to Brazil or Australia, it had better be sold and Landru could obtain the best possible price. Sometimes the stories were not so precise, no doubt Landru doled them out according to the probable credulity of the listener. Inquiries about consular appointments in Australia or commercial enterprises in Brazil can be made in the appropriate quarters. Questions may even be asked about factories said to have flourished in the invaded districts, and though the solitary and ill-educated women whom Landru sought out were credulous enough, yet even they might still have friends to make awkward inquiries. But in war time important secret service rendered to the State is a safe card to play, and Landru appears to have employed it more than once. Even so, doubts seem to have been aroused occasionally, and ' Mr. Mystery ' was the name given him by the acquaintance of at least one of his victims, though whether the name was bestowed in admiration or in suspicion, or perhaps in a mingling of both, does not seem too clear.

The details, then, would vary with the circumstances. No exact information is to be obtained, except in each case from what the concierge remembered of confidences made to her, for it is noticeable that all these women led such lonely lives, with relatives so few or so distant, that it was only to the concierge they were able to gossip about the charming gentleman who had so unexpectedly come into their lives, of his attentions and unfailing kindness, his courtesy, and the happy prospects opening out before them. In one or two cases when friends might have wondered why Madame So-and-So had cut herself off from them so entirely, Landru took pains to send a box of chocolates as a parting present, or flowers—he had always a weakness for flowers—that had come ostensibly all the way from Nice, where it was to be assumed the lady was happily and comfortably installed in her new life. Impossible to suppose that harm had come to one who took the trouble to send such lovely flowers in such profusion all the way from the South of France.

But if the details varied, the end was the same. A little trip to the country would be proposed, a pleasant excursion, such as town-dwellers love all the world over, and Parisians perhaps more than most. There was a little villa at Vernouillet, small and pleasant town in the valley of the Seine. Later it was another small villa, the Villa Tric, as it was called from the landlord's name, in the lonely village of Gambais, on the outskirts of the forest of Rambouillet, not very far from where in that same forest every morning a fleet of lorries from Paris deposits fresh tons of the refuse of the great city in enormous pits and disused quarries that exist there, and that the authorities have adopted this method of filling in.

A careful and far-seeing man like Landru, so cautious and so calculating, may possibly have noticed this, have watched with interest in the early morning that long line of lorries issuing fully laden from Paris and returning empty, and have perceived that from this public enterprise some private profit might be drawn.

At any rate it was in Gambais that the idyll, begun when a prospective purchaser of furniture called in answer to an advertisement at a small Paris flat, would presently draw to its conclusion.

One morning Landru and Madame—there are ten names that can be filled in at choice—would set out, Landru, one is sure, as smiling and attentive and polite as ever, and Madame—take which name you prefer from the list—one can well imagine, in high spirits at the prospects of this country jaunt with the *vrai monsieur* who had power to depict their joint future in such glowing colours and who, for proof of his position in the world, was able to boast of the reality of the favourite dream of the Parisian —a little villa in the country.

She would be quite content to wait while he left her for a moment to buy their tickets and presently he would return still smiling and attentive as ever, with the tickets, one single and one return.

A thoughtful man, it is to be noted, and one with an eye to detail. Why go to the unnecessary expense of buying a return ticket for one who would not return?

Carefully he would enter the details in his note-book, jotting down exactly how much for the single ticket, how much for the return, while no doubt Madame looked on admiringly, and with true French love of thrift thought how fortunate she was to have found a man who knew so well how to look after his sous.

Here, for instance, are the items of the expenses for one such day copied directly from his note-book, his careful note-book, for April 4, 1918:

						Fr.
Garage voiture ...	...	...	...	...	...	1.00
Figues 1.80 + .45 rembourse de valise		...		...	...	2.25
Voiture, Invalides, 3.00, billets, 3.10 & 4.95				...	...	11.05
1 pneumatique à 7h. 0.40 ...		...	...	...	...	.40
Diligence ...	...	...	...	...	...	2.40

The price for a single ticket from Paris to the nearest station to the village of Gambais—a diligence running between the station and the village—being at that time three francs ten, or a return ticket four francs ninety-five.

Grotesquely, and a little horribly, reminiscent, is it not, of the old legendary tag of duelling days: " Pistols for two ; coffee for one " ?

And there the story ends so far as any facts are known. It was a Madame Pascal to whom these special entries referred. She had been a dressmaker, earning a comfortable, if modest living. On that morning of April 4, 1918, Landru called at her small flat, and with him she left for the country trip they had planned together. At the railway station he bought, as duly entered in his note-book, one single ticket and one return. Since then, since that hour when she left her flat with Landru, the man whose ' charming courtesy ', whose ' perfect breeding ' she had so often praised to friends, she has never more been seen, nor has any recognizable trace of her been found. That April 4th she stepped out of the ranks of the living to be no more heard of, and the next day, April 5th, Landru, content and tranquil, returned alone to Paris, having first in his careful, precise, business-like manner jotted down in his note-book the small expenses of the previous day such items as the purchase of a cup of coffee, a roll, tobacco, and so on. Also there is noted in larger, clearer figures, at the top of the page for that day the hour of five-fifteen in the evening, though with no indication of what event it was he considered interesting enough to record in this manner.

Within a week, having entered into possession of Madame Pascal's flat, he had sold her furniture and her personal belongings, and so was her tale done, till it began to be retold again in a court-room at Versailles.

Yet how within that brief space of time between, say, a quarter-past five in the evening and Landru's presentation at the station for Gambais of the return ticket to Paris with which he had so thoughtfully provided himself, did he manage and contrive so successfully to dispose of Madame Pascal's body that no trace remained, no sign of struggle, no bloodstains to be found, no cry heard, nothing?

A busy and efficient man this Henri Désiré Landru seems to have been, that much praise at least he has fairly earned.

II

THE MURDERER DOMESTIC

At this time Landru, born in 1869, and therefore in middle age, was a man to all appearance *rangé*, as the French say. His parents seem to have been, to quote the story books, " poor but honest ". The father is described as a *mécanicien*, a rather vague term that might cover any occupation from that of driving an express on one of the railways to casual stoking in the boiler-house of any factory. Probably the civil state of Landru senior was more akin to the latter occupation than to the former. Nothing is recorded to his discredit and, indeed, nothing to remark on his life save his method of quitting it, for he committed suicide in the Bois de Boulogne in 1912. It is no doubt far-fetched to suggest that the motive for this suicide may have been his realization of the kind of monster he had brought into the world. His wife in the usual thrifty French fashion helped the family income by doing needlework. So far as is known there is nothing in the family history to suggest any taint of degeneracy or disease. In his childhood, too,

Landru appears to have made a good impression. He became a choir boy which certainly would not have happened had anything serious been known to his discredit, and his taste for music he retained to the end—indeed, when he was not murdering, music and flowers had always their appeal for him. He even went on to take ' minor orders ' as a sub-deacon, so that his general conduct must certainly have been regarded as exemplary by the authorities of the church he attended. At this time he was in fact, as the presiding magistrate at his trial remarked, *un peu de l'église*, the suggestion being that it was to this early association with the Church that he owed the peculiar suavity of his manner, the ingratiating, confidence-creating way he undoubtedly had. But one is inclined to suspect that presiding magistrate of being something of an ' anti-clerical ' in French politics, and of meaning to hint that it was from the Church Landru had learned how to impose upon credulous and foolish women. Rather one may suspect it was that smooth tongue of his which had enabled him to impose upon his ecclesiastical superiors and to hide from them his real disposition.

In various offices where he worked as a boy his conduct was still satisfactory, and when in due time he was called up for military service his army record remains good. He left at the expiration of his time with non-commissioned rank, and only then does he seem to have drifted in some way or another into the ranks of petty crime. Motors attracted him. He had again a certain skill as a mechanic—he claimed credit for one or two small inventions—and some offence connected with the buying or selling of a motor lorry earned him a sentence of three years. Soon after his release the police were looking for him again, but he managed to evade their attentions successfully. During his three years in prison his mother had died, and some time or another he had married. Apparently he was a good and kind husband, and no woman with whom he came in contact had ever a word of complaint to make against him—till at least in a moment of incredulous amazement they understood too late, and probably too briefly to understand in full; for surely one so efficient and painstaking as Landru, however he gave death, must have given it easily and swiftly.

To the credit of the French police, once they were convinced that Landru's wife had never had the least suspicion of the nature of his peculiar activities, they took care that neither she nor her children should be referred to. In the long trial once only something is said of " a good and simple woman who knew nothing of these things", and Landru himself does not omit to point out that he is admitted to have been a good husband and father. The French newspapers, too, either because they are so much less enterprising than our own or because they have more respect for the decencies of private life, make no reference to her. It is true that, owing to his unfortunate misunderstandings with the police, Landru was unable to live at home with his family, but he seems always to have kept in touch with them; and when, after one of his successful business transactions, he had to take over possession of furniture recently belonging to a woman now understood to be happily travelling in England or resident in Nice or somewhere else where furniture in a Paris apartment was no longer of value to her, then it was his son, a lad of sixteen or seventeen, whom he called upon to help convey it to the garage, where in due time so many oddities were to be poked out by interfering police officers.

There is an odd little scene recorded when at the Gambais villa this lad is seen in the garden picking flowers he explains he means to give to his mother; and Landru looks on approvingly, remarking that one cannot take too many pains to show attention to one's mother. He failed, however, to explain to the woman who was with him at the time—the one woman who visited Gambais and lived to tell the tale—that this mother was in fact his own wife and the boy his eldest son. But one cannot go into every detail, and the boy himself seems to have preserved an equally discreet silence, never forgetting the character of ' apprentice ' assigned to him.

It is odd to notice, though, how all through this strange, dark tale of murder, ruthless and repeated and so callously efficient, there runs perpetually this motive of flowers and of music.

About Landru's personal appearance there does not seem to have been much to account for that success he had with the women whose complete confidence he won time and again. He is described as small, slight, insignificant; probably he owed his easy triumphs to his caressing, insinuating manner and his persuasive tongue, the tongue of the readiest liar, one imagines, that hell ever spawned.

Photographs show him as the almost comically typical representative of what the French call the *petit bourgeois*. It may be that the very ordinariness of his appearance helped to create that confidence he seems to have won so easily. Who could imagine that a man who looked so exactly like everyone else could be in fact so strangely, so dreadfully different? An old man could not have won such personal success, a young man might have been regarded with more suspicion, but why mistrust this plain, sober, tranquil, gentle-spoken man of middle age, whose middle-class respectability proclaimed itself aloud to all the world, who differed from the thousand like him only in being so much more polite, so extremely punctilious and well bred. Nor is there any Frenchwoman, whatever her station, but attaches importance to politeness and good breeding. No wonder Landru attracts, when in him good breeding is so ingrained that presently, on a bleak February dawn, when he has business in a Versailles square with, as the bitter Parisian jest ran at the time, the only 'widow' he had not known how to cheat, he refuses to recognize one of the officials whose duty it is to see that business well and truly carried out, until proper introductions have been effected!

Let the reader put the question to himself. Could he find it credible that the next typical clerk or shopman he sees hurrying to or from the city in the rush hours, bowler hat, umbrella, attaché case, season ticket, morning or evening paper under one arm, could he believe that man was a murderer not once but a dozen times, a murderer, too, so skilful and efficient that, grimmest of magicians, he could make the body of his victim vanish 'without trace'?

Always it is a part of the peculiar horror of this tale that makes it outstanding in the record of human wickedness, that everything is so drab, so ordinary, so commonplace, so ' everydayish ' to quote the French expression. The actors in it are all the least conspicuous of folk, types of the everyday citizen whose ordinary destiny would be to slip unnoticed from undistinguished cradle by an uneventful and laborious life to one more grave in a crowded city cemetery—the Mr. and Mrs. Zero of our civilization, the tiniest of cogs in the revolving wheels that make society go round. All through the tale runs this ' dailiness of daily life ' till at the end, abruptly and without warning, leaps up mystery and horror unparalleled.

When the amazing record of his crimes became known, people began to talk of the hypnotic power of Landru's eyes. They seem to have been small and bright under bushy eyebrows, and he had a way of gazing into the distance as though his immediate surroundings were unworthy of his attention. Whether this was unconscious or a deliberate pose on his part remains doubtful, but it was certainly effective in impressing all who came in contact with him with a certain quality in him of a proud and aloof tranquillity—and a proud and aloof tranquillity is not exactly what one expects in a man accused of nearly a dozen murders. The murderer ferocious, the murderer brutal, greedy, frenzied, passionate, we can understand, but not the murderer tranquil and gentle, the murderer who seems as if he might turn from the corpse of his victim to give the cat a saucer of milk or to chat over the fence with a neighbour about the garden flowers.

Talk about hypnotic power may, however, be dismissed as a discovery after the event. Possibly, too, the sketches made in court give a better idea of Landru's personality than the exact and precise photographs that misrepresent the more because they misrepresent nothing. In the sketches one seems to get a glimpse of a certain demoniac power the man's deeds show that he possessed, however well he kept it hidden in common life. There is one drawing, too, that shows him bending forward a little, his eloquent hands held out, his attitude full of an eager sincerity, truth almost visibly oozing from him as he stands there in the

Versailles court-room before his judges, and lies and lies and lies again with such conviction he almost turns the false into the true.

The sketches, too, seem to show that the facial angle is bad; though the presence of a heavy, close-growing beard makes the point a little difficult to decide with certainty. But the backward slope of the head is clearly marked, and is suggestive. Clearly marked, too, is the breadth of the head above the ear—an indication of the intellectual powers the man certainly possessed, in spite of the efforts of a famous English journalist to write him down a fool. A fool he certainly was not, except in that high sense in which all sin is the supreme folly.

To give an instance of the clear insight that was at times in the man, however clouded by vanity and greed, it may be pointed out that the reason he gave for offering better prices for the furniture he was bargaining to acquire (thus by so unexpected a liberality earning the confidence of the gratified seller) was that after the war there was likely to be a great scarcity of manufactured goods, so that anyone with a store laid up would be able to sell at a big profit.

The reflection seems obvious to-day, commonplace indeed. To have entertained it, however, at that time—while the war still raged—is proof of exceptional insight. Some of those to whom that same insight came were led by it to fortune. One remembers, for instance, how the British Government offered for sale by public contract some enormous collection or another of textiles manufactured for war use, and how there was at first considerable hesitation to buy. When at last one speculator plucked up courage and ventured the purchase, he was able to sell again retail at a profit that made him a millionaire in a month or two.

So might it easily have been with Landru, since he was of those who had acumen enough to realize the famine of the world for those commodities of which the war had so long deprived it. Had Landru but followed the gleam thus vouchsafed him he might well, with his talent for buying and selling and his passion for method and precision, have acquired prosperity and wealth and all the honour and renown that wealth brings with it. Instead he chose another path, possibly arguing that since public slaughter had become the business of all the world, a little private slaughter might be permitted to the individual.

A very noticeable feature of his physical make-up was his baldness. It seems to have struck the imagination of the Parisian public, perhaps because there is something respectable, almost avuncular about baldness; one finds it difficult to imagine a bald Don Juan, to conceive a bald Lothario making a conquest of two hundred and eighty-three women—for that is the incredible and altogether preposterous number of the women that the careful investigation of the Paris police established as the count of his finacées. Though one may be permitted to doubt whether in all those cases actual *fiançailles* had been announced, for in France the *fiançailles* is a serious and public affair. But still, in this incredible business one may believe anything—even two hundred and eighty-three fiancées. Perhaps, like Clive, Landru stood amazed at his own moderation when he reflected that out of them all he had contented himself with murdering only ten—at least that is all the prosecution brought forward, with one boy thrown in as if for makeweight.

If, however, Landru had lost his hair Nature had compensated him with the gift of a magnificent and luxurious beard. To-day beards are out of fashion; but in France, at that time, they still had their admirers, and Landru's appears to have played its part in the success of its owner's numerous courtships. Maybe it was gratitude for this assistance that made him show concern for it at the last and emulate Sir Thomas More in expressing a solicitude for its safety from the touch of steel. No doubt a beard may be regarded as a symbol of respectability, and we can no more imagine Don Juan bearded than bald. All that there is of middle-age responsibility, of middle-class respectability, may be looked on as embodied in the beard; the beard that, so to speak, waved Landru on through his two hundred and eighty-three successive conquests.

In every description of him there are two points that continually emerge, that are always commented on. The first is the unstudied composure of the man, the quiet and slightly distant courtesy in which he never failed. There was about him a kind of haughty indifference that seemed to lift him above the fret and fuss of everyday experience, even when that everyday experience was trial for his life. The second detail that is commonly re-marked upon is the long slenderness of his nervous fingers, elo-quent and caressing—and something more as well. Easy to picture them caressing with tender gentleness an infatuated woman, stroking a tired forehead, stroking more softly still the worn cheeks, stealing down as gentle as silk to twine themselves about the throat till all at once they tighten, all in an instant turning into so fierce, so murderous, so effective a grip, the victim would scarcely have time to recognize the change from the pretence of love to the reality of death.

Of Landru, in his domestic capacity, we have perhaps the most intimate picture ever presented of the murderer at home. Charles Peace, too, seems to have had a pleasant domestic side to his character and a taste for music as marked as Landru's—there seems no record that Peace shared Landru's passion for flowers—but no such picture of Peace in his fireside slippers is extant as that provided of Landru in a little pamphlet sold at the time on the streets of Paris and written by a Mlle Fernande Segret, she who enjoys the unique experience of being the only woman who visited the Gambais villa in Landru's company and came away again alive.

" *Voilà mon petit Paradis*," said he the first time he took her there, though one may justifiably complain that *petit Paradis* is hardly a well-chosen term for this private slaughter-house, this secluded shambles whereto, as to the lion's den in the story, so many footsteps led but none returned.

One wonders why he spared her. It cannot have been because she had no money. One of his assassinations brought him no more than two francs, which seems poor pay for what must really be a troublesome and tedious job—even for an expert—hardly enough, indeed, to cover the ' overhead '. Was he really fond of her? It hardly seems likely that he could be fond of anyone, but then with Landru anything is possible. He may merely have felt that there was no hurry, or more likely she owed her safety to the fact that she was in more intimate relations with her family, and a disappearance too abrupt might have set them worrying for details of her fate. Most of his other victims, it will be remembered, were solitary folk, with few friends or relatives and none likely to make prompt inquiry.

At the trial Mlle Segret described herself as *artiste lyrique*, though she omitted to supply details of her professional engagements and qualifications. At the time she met Landru she was working as an assistant in a shop, and she gives a long description of the classic ' pick up ', how in a tram one day she and a companion observed a fellow-passenger—male—looking at them ; how when they alighted he alighted too ; how he spoke to them and was duly and properly snubbed ; how nevertheless he persisted, warning them gravely of the dangers young women encountered who went alone about the streets of Paris ; how gradually his persistence and more especially his courtesy and air of breeding— *un vrai monsieur* always, it will be noticed—impressed her, till finally he is permitted to call at her home.

There, too, the impression he makes is favourable. It always was. He proposes marriage—by this time, with his score approaching the fourth hundred, he must have been acquiring a certain facility in this—he is accepted and he proves himself the ideal lover. His betrothed grows almost lyrical, *artiste lyrique* in fact, as she describes his courteous attentions—the *petits soins*— his kindness and his thoughtfulness, the presents he makes her. A veritable bower of flowers she describes his room, on one occasion when she and her mother—for the proprieties must be observed—go there to dine with him. And then his intellectual tastes ! Among novelists his favourite author was Balzac ; his favourite bedside book *Le Disciple*, by Paul Bourget. How many happy hours they spent together, reading these and other classics of French literature ! In poetry his taste was equally refined, and he would often recite with admirable effect the verses of de Musset, Lamartine, and others of similar standing. In music he certainly preferred the lighter, gayer tunes to more severe compositions, but he had merely contempt for the music-hall; childish, he found it, and void of intellectual interest.

Altogether an admirable picture, and this idyllic courtship took its pleasant intellectual course with only two drawbacks; one, Landru's habit of vanishing now and again, presumably when it was time for another murder to be committed, wherefrom he would return to his flowers, his books and music, his pleasantly intellectual intercourse with his betrothed, all the grave and sober routine of his well-regulated life.

Once he rebuked a certain too great liking for the theatre he seems to have detected in Mlle Segret, with the remark that one could well give up visiting the theatre when life itself presented to the onlooker so rich a feast of comedy. It was at any rate a comedy that he was doing his best to turn into a tragedy.

The second drawback was that the promised marriage seemed a long time in getting itself celebrated. Not that Landru, to whom plausible excuse was as natural as breathing, lacked good and plentiful explanations. In his usual character of refugee from the invaded districts he had no papers, and in France there is little one can do, and nothing official, without papers. But official arrangements had been made to meet the case of those refugees who had lost these necessary documents, and finally Mlle Segret and her mother (who appears to have had her suspicions) went to visit the mayor of the particular town in which, for them, Landru had situated that prosperous factory of his prewar days. Alas! the mayor had never heard either of Landru or his factory. But Landru, though a little hurt at this display of a certain lack of confidence, had his explanation ready. The mayor, an old friend, had been so worried by innumerable inquiries that finally he had adopted the expedient of denying everybody and everything!

As explanation, it cannot be counted among Landru's happiest efforts. Still, it served its purpose, and presently (the question of marriage slipping into the background) Mlle Segret is seen established as Landru's 'companion' as she discreetly expresses it. As pseudo-husband he proved as kind, thoughtful, attentive, as he had been as suitor, and proudly she records that when she went with him to visit friends she would receive many congratulations on her alliance with a man so gay, so charming, always the life and soul of the party, so evidently superior in intellect and breeding.

Once or twice again he took her to the Gambais villa and still, unlike all his other feminine companions, she had the luck to return alive. The way in which the villagers stared at him and her worried her a little, but he explained carelessly that country people were always like that, they always stared at every visitor from Paris—and then he would resume humming his favourite tune: *Adieu, notre petite table.* Mlle Segret does not seem to have cared much for the Gambais villa. She found it of a " comfort only relative." In her character of good housewife she discovered that the bedding was apt to grow damp during their absences. But she seems never to have noticed anything suspicious, and such cooking as was necessary she carried out on the kitchen stove with no thought that it had ever been put to uses quite other than domestic.

She was always willing enough to return to their cosy Paris flat, where life passed so pleasantly, and the only drawback those mysterious absences that Landru still indulged in and from which he would return more smiling, more amiable, more courteous than ever—and also more plentifully supplied with money; often, for example, with a government bond or two for sale, recently transferred to him by the elderly widow or spinster to whom it had originally belonged and concerning whose present whereabouts her former neighbours were idly wondering.

But presently the secret of these absences was explained; presumably Mlle Segret's curiosity was becoming so strong that something had to be done to satisfy it. So one day Landru confessed to her that he was in police employ, there were at times errands of special importance which he had to undertake at the request of the police authorities. He made the confession —the word is used advisedly—with considerable reluctance, for in France the 'flic' enjoys no such respect and confidence as we in England accord to those who defend society against its lawless enemies. He would give it up as soon as he possibly could, he promised, and indeed of promises his stock was always inexhaustible; and meanwhile here was the explanation of his sudden and mysterious absences.

In the intervals of these absences he was busy with all sorts and kinds of projects. But here Mlle Segret interposes an acute psychological observation. Never, she says, did she see him work with perseverance; never could he keep his mind fixed for long on any one project. For a hall-mark of the criminal mind is this incapacity for steady application. Steady and regular employ is abhorrent to it, the result of an inherent weakness of the will unable to remain for long faithful to one idea. Again and again in criminological studies one comes across this weakness of willpower that Landru's 'companion' notes when she records his failure to keep constant to any one of his numerous designs.

None the less his affairs seemed prosperous enough, and one day in the Rue de Rivoli they observed and jointly admired a dinner service, richly gilt and of an exquisite pattern. It was a fine sunny spring morning, they were both in happy mood; Landru because his affairs were going so well, Mlle Segret because a day or two before he had promised her a speedy wedding.

Was it a promise that he meant to perform? Legally, it was impossible, since he had already wife and family. One wonders if perhaps that offer was but the first step towards another trip to Gambais, for which this time of the two railway tickets purchased one would have been a single only!

Impossible to say, for as it happened a relative of one of the women who had made one of those trips to Gambais, for which one ticket had needed to be a single only, was also enjoying a stroll in the sunshine that fine April morning. While Landru and his companion were consulting over the purchase of that dinner service which would be such an addition to their home, this relative of the vanished woman was in his turn watching them. When they made up their minds to effect the purchase and entered the shop, he entered close behind. He heard the bargaining, he heard Landru explaining that he had not enough money in his pocket to pay on the spot the full amount required. But he would pay a hundred francs on account and the rest on delivery. The shopkeeper was more than willing. And monsieur's address? Landru gave it, the shopkeeper noted it down, repeating it aloud to make sure he had it correct. Landru confirmed it as correct, and pleased and excited as children with their new purchase he and Mlle Segret went off home to be ready to receive it, while that other customer, whom they had hardly noticed, hurried round to the police to tell them he had found at last the mysterious individual in whose company his aunt had last been seen before her sudden, complete, and inexplicable disappearance.

Early next morning, about seven—Landru, industrious man, had already been out, probably to his garage, and had just returned for the continental breakfast of coffee and a roll—two veritable *agents de la Sûreté* knocked at his door. When he understood their errand, though surely he must have known this was the end, must have felt the chill of death strike into his soul, he showed only his presently familiar attitude of a proud and tranquil indifference. " What! Arrest me in my own home ! " he exclaimed, scandalized at this departure from his own high standard of breeding and correctitude. But that indeed was the purpose of his visitors and one they proceeded forthwith to carry out. Mlle Segret expressed her natural dismay and earned a rebuke from Landru.

" Don't trouble your head about all this," he commanded. " It will be easily arranged."

But the arrangement was not to be so easy as all that, though the long battle that Landru was now to fight against all the forces of the law is as remarkable as any recorded in the legal history of any country.

As for Mlle Segret, she was destined to see him only twice more: once, that same evening, when, his first interrogation over, she was allowed to say him farewell, and he with a touch of sentiment whispered to her the words of his favourite tune,

"*Adieu! notre petite table*"; and once more in the Versailles court when she appeared there to give some not very important evidence, and it was observed that he was as tranquilly indifferent to her as he was to all the long line of witnesses who bored him with their dull and interminable testimony.

III

THE MURDERER AS CAPTAIN OF HIS SOUL

It was in April 1919 when this arrest was carried out, and the relaxation of the pressure of the war—that war of which Landru had once scandalized the Segret family by remarking it was ending too soon for him—permitted the police to give the affair more attention than might have otherwise been possible.

There had been, it was noticed at the time, a touch of quite incredulous horror in the voice of that first examining magistrate when he told Landru he was accused of no less than " four assassinations! " The tale was not to stop there. Poking about in the garage Landru used as a kind of warehouse, the police found the oddest things. A bunch of false hair, for example, presently identified as having belonged to Mme Buisson. Now where was Mme Buisson for whom indeed her family had been searching for some time? And then the papers of identity of that young servant girl, Andrée Babelay, who in the morning of her life had come in contact with Landru, is for a moment seen laughing and chatting with him and calling him by his pet name, and then is no more heard of. If she was still in life, why had she parted with these papers without which indeed no French citizen is officially alive at all? How, for instance, without them could she have obtained the new situation Landru explained she had left him to secure?

Inconceivably, grotesquely, incredibly, the number mounted, and further back into the past extended the police inquiries. Back through the long years of the war they traced Landru's peculiar activities, finally ending their researches just before its outbreak, in the summer of 1914, when Landru had smiled his way into the friendship and the confidence of a Madame Cuchet, a widow who possessed a son of eighteen and certain property. They lived together, widow, son, and Landru, at the Vernouillet villa; and there, after a time, Landru continued to live alone. Madame and her son, he explained, had gone to England for reasons that might be guessed, since at that time many widows with only sons were torn between the claims of patriotism and those of maternal affection but that he, Landru, would never betray, since whatever the reason was it had been given to him in confidence.

The investigation continued, and gradually Paris and the world began to hear rumours of this incredible re-incarnation of the Bluebeard of the nursery tales. When it became known that Landru had made conquest of nearly three hundred feminine hearts, Paris fairly gasped, and could not even resist a certain feeling of bewildered admiration. A man with close on three hundred fiancées—' formidable '. The thing seemed to pass into the fantastic, the unreal, it took on the quality of some fairy-tale of the heroic age when everything was on a larger scale than in cramped modern days! The horror and the tragedy and the mystery of the fate of all these unlucky women grew half forgotten, while Landru's bald head shone through a score of music-hall sketches, his beard wagged on every cabaret stage, the two hundred and eighty-three fiancées became the staple fare of every jester and comedian avid of easy applause, till there was hardly a theatre audience but was ready to rock with laughter at the mere mention of the number—two hundred and eighty and three! It seemed as if to so incredible a horror laughter had become the only possible reaction.

Then, too, it began to be known that the police were not finding Landru an easy person to deal with. Confronted with a mass of overwhelming evidence, he admitted nothing, he had an explanation for all—or else the noblest, most chivalrous of motives for offering none. One had to be careful, too; all the niceties had to be observed. If his spectacles were mislaid, for instance, the whole investigation had to be suspended till they were found again. Any new magistrate or police officer coming into the affair had to be duly presented to Landru and their credentials shown or he would have nothing to do with them. Never, in fact, was there such a stickler for etiquette, never a man more ready to stand upon every formality—and never once did he weaken, hesitate, alter in any way his attitude of imperturbable and tranquil indifference, as of one for whom all these things had but a passing and temporary interest.

And let it be remembered that in France such investigations are not carried out with any such scrupulous consideration for the convenience and the rights and the susceptibilities of the suspected person as must be shown in England. In France the sole object is to get at the truth, and to that aim all else is subordinated. In England also the object is to get at the truth, but often, as it seems, on condition that nothing must be said or done to hurt the feelings of the accused. In France there are no judge's rules that the police are expected to be governed by under penalty of being held up to universal execration for the practice of brutal and unfair methods. No French police officer giving evidence risks being asked in horror-stricken tones by defending counsel: " Were you not endeavouring to induce the prisoner to confess? " And if a confession is produced in France it is assumed to be true, in England the assumption appears to be that it must be proof of innocence, since no one would confess except under the pressure of a brutal and unscrupulous police, to which again only the innocent could succumb!

From April 1919 till November 1921 the investigation continued, while Paris giggled over the incredible tale, and Landru, imperturbable and tranquil as ever, submitted to innumerable confrontations, questionings, reconstructions, without for one moment weakening or faltering or varying his perpetual response: " You bring these accusations against me? Well, it is your business to prove them. Do so."

It was a task that was not showing itself so easy. Ample, overwhelming evidence there was that all these women had last been seen in Landru's company and then never seen again. But there the proof ended abruptly. Landru's simple explanation was that they had gone about their own affairs. He had had certain purely business transactions with them, conducted no doubt in a pleasant, social manner. Even in business one had to respect the courtesies. But, the business concluded, they had parted with mutual esteem, and he knew nothing of what had happened to them afterwards. Why should he? Was every business man to be responsible for the future of every client he dealt with?

So it went on all through the two and a half long years of the investigation, and not all the efforts of the most skilled, the most experienced police officers in Paris could draw from Landru any single admission. They took him to the villa at Vernouillet, to the Gambais villa he had once so inappropriately described as his '*petit Paradis*'; they showed him carcasses of sheep being consumed in that stove in the kitchen he had been careful, they reminded him, to have installed when he first rented the villa, and he still looked on with his air of mild and tranquil interest. They pointed out that his consumption of fuel had been large, and he explained that those dishonest neighbours of his had taken advantage of his absences in Paris to raid his store of coal. Only once did he make an admission that seems a little enlightening. One of his victims had had two pet dogs, and there was proof that, after she had vanished from the Villa Tric, her two dogs were still there. How had he disposed of them, then? It was a point that might be of interest. At last he explained. He had strangled them.

" It is the gentlest and easiest of deaths," he added, and only in the silence that followed, only when he saw how those to whom he had spoken were looking at him did he appear to realize that in that sentence might be found a significance of its own.

Finally, he was brought before a jury in a little court-room at Versailles, and '*tout Paris*' flocked to hear the trial of this man who had become something of a legend. Every woman with a new hat or frock to show took it to Versailles to display; no actress with a flair for publicity could afford to be seen elsewhere while the court was sitting; no man of the world but quickly lost his reputation if he could not recount the latest Landru story.

For Landru did not disappoint. To the end he preserved his ready tongue, his quick wit, his impressive air of tranquil disdain for all this fuss; his open, and not unrighteous, contempt, for the horde of gaping, scrambling spectators; his dignified assumption of complete innocence; above all, his attitude that if the prosecution alleged these things against him then it was their business to produce proof of what they said. Negligently he would drop hints from time to time that his innocence would be established, the prosecution for ever confounded, when two or three of his pretended victims would appear in court alive and well as was altogether likely to happen, Landru promised, in a day or two, though indeed, in fact, it has not happened yet.

There appeared in the witness box a long line of witnesses and each day the court was littered with the strangest collection of bits of furniture, old clothing, cheap furs, and so on and so on, melancholy relics that drew from one witness a cry of real emotion.

" If my sister were alive," she exclaimed, " never would she have parted with these things of hers she was always so proud of and always took such care of."

It was perhaps the nearest the prosecution ever got to establishing that main fact they had to establish, and whereof they never succeeded in producing strict legal proof—evidence, that is, of the actual death of any single one of all those whose names figured on the long *acte d'accusation*. Evidence in plenty that each one had last been seen in Landru's company, evidence as much as could be wished that afterwards no friend or relative had had any further news, that promises to write had not been fulfilled, that their possessions, their property, their most intimate belongings had passed into Landru's hands, but of how, if he had murdered, those murders had been carried out, of how afterwards the bodies had been disposed of; on those points the prosecution had frankly to avow there was nothing to be said with certainty.

In the courtyard of the Gambais villa, it is true, a few handfuls of charred bones and a collection of human teeth had been found. But then close by was the Gambais cemetery with an ossuary full of human bones that all the children of the village had access to. And it was proved, too, that the key of the villa had for some time been in the care of a man of deficient intelligence. Who could tell what tricks might have been played by that disordered intelligence, by the malice or mistaken zeal of neighbours, by the mischief of children, or even by the police themselves? How tempting to throw down a few burnt bones to provide the evidence admittedly lacking!

True, again, there were various witnesses to depose that thick fumes of smoke and even gleams of fire, had been seen coming from the chimney of the Villa Tric, busy as any factory. The gleams of fire had been seen, according to the evidence, on a dark night. Easy enough at once to turn up the records and prove that particular night was particularly clear. Another witness spoke of a smell of burnt flesh, and the court was visibly affected till Landru woke from his usual haughty and tranquil indifference. Ah, yes, he remembered. It was one day when some cutlets were being cooked for dinner and by inexcusable neglect they had been burnt to a cinder. No doubt—with a courteous inclination of the head towards the witness—that was the occasion to which madame referred.

Then again, one police officer bicycling very early in the morning in the district on some errand connected with the case, had observed with interest that long line of lorries which every morning brought thousands of tons of refuse from Paris to dump in old quarries and disused gravel pits in the Rambouillet forest. He had imagined that Landru, too, that busy and observant man, might one morning have watched this daily procession. Not difficult perhaps if one had burnt a body in a stove to heap together the remains, the unconsumed portions, the ashes in general, in a convenient parcel and deposit them at night, where in the morning they would be buried for ever under fresh tons of Paris refuse from all the dustbins of the multitudinous city.

He had put the theory before his superiors and they had listened and been interested. But where was your proof? If that had been Landru's method, no one had seen him about his black business in the black night, nor could it be hoped that after months and even years of the deposit of so many tons of refuse, the secret they hid, if indeed they hid it, could be discovered.

Landru had been also, it was proved, a frequent purchaser of saws, and saws may be used for other things than those small carpentering jobs and alterations he had undoubtedly carried out. But then again what proof is there in that? At the end all that could be shown as possible relics of ten women and a boy was just a few scraps of burnt bones and a collection of human teeth. For the rest, nothing but idle conjecture and the aloof and patient smile of Landru.

Yet the imagination boggles a little at this picture of the man carrying out his murders, dissecting and burning to ashes the body with such neat dexterity, disposing of those ashes with equal efficiency, and then returning to Paris, courteous, smiling, pleasant as ever, probably humming his favourite tune, *Adieu, notre petite table*, and resuming there his sober, respectable, well-ordered life with its flowers, its music, its poetic recitations and literary discussions.

Nor was the prosecution more successful in establishing the method. There was no trace or spot of blood to be found any-where, no sign of any struggle. Poison? Yes, there was a book treating of poison in his possession, but nothing to show that Landru had ever purchased anything of the sort. One remembers, though, those long and slender fingers of his, and that remark he once dropped that strangling is the gentlest of deaths. It is also, as every doctor knows, a method of inflicting death in which an extraordinary degree of perfection can be attained.

So the long duel went on, with Landru never at a loss and seldom disappointing an audience that had come to expect his epigrams, and was indeed ready, such was now his reputation, to laugh at them before they were well uttered, just as to-day Mr. Bernard Shaw has only to rise from his place to have his audience already on the giggle. Not that Landru always encouraged laughter. Temperamental as any other spoilt favourite of the public, sometimes he would turn on his audience and rend it with contempt and scorn.

"There is nothing to laugh at, I defend my life," he flashed out once when there was too much laughter in court.

Some of his replies, too, are undeniably effective.

"How could I foresee," he demands, when urged to explain some of the entries in that curious note-book of his, "that one day I should be asked to remember such trifling details?"

"My accounts were not kept with a view to satisfying a police inquiry," he protests on another occasion; and when pressed to say why he had not offered to the examining magistrate a specially ingenious explanation he had just produced, he has his reply ready: "Oh, he and I, we were not on very good terms," he explains.

Occasionally, too, he does not hesitate to rebuke his judges when they fall short of his own high standard of breeding. The presiding judge had chanced to mention that one of the vanished women had given her age as 39, though in reality it was 44. Landru is shocked.

"Ah, monsieur le juge," he says, "I should never have told that."

Now and then his patience wears a little thin.

"Every time you find a figure in my note-book, you call it an assassination," he cries, and when told that his explanations are not simple, he answered: "You mean you do not take them simply."

Always he keeps in his replies to that high standard of courtesy, that innate breeding, which had so struck all these women who unfortunately were not in court to bear testimony to its charm. Again and again he is pressed to explain why, as his note-book entries show, when he took them to Gambais he bought always one single ticket and one return.

"I could hardly buy a return ticket for a lady," he answers at last with a deprecatory movement of the hand.

Obviously a man of breeding could not suggest to a lady that her sojourn was to be limited by anything but her own will.

And his possession of the most personal, private effects he explains in the same way:

"Madame did not wish that things like that should be seen by third persons," he explains with a delicate hint of rebuke to these coarse-minded lawyers and police who had been pulling them about and peering at them and examining them with little thought of the rules of good breeding.

"Ah, Monsieur le Président, we seek the truth together," he assures that gentleman on one occasion; and later he rebukes him gently: "Do not let us try to find a tragedy everywhere," he urges; and another time he says loftily that his private life concerns neither the public nor the law.

So it continues all through the three long weeks of his trial, while the world waited for the verdict and all Paris fought for a seat at what had become something like a public entertainment. Once indeed the crush became so great that Landru was moved to offer his own place to anyone who cared to occupy it. On an outburst of temper occurring between some of the lawyers in the case, one of those professional disputes that are almost a matter of etiquette and custom, and on one of them threatening to retire, Landru is openly sympathetic.

"I also I could wish to retire from the case," he observes.

All through these lighter interludes, however, he clung to his main point. He was not there to prove anything. The prosecution accused him of certain things, and it was their business to prove what they advanced. For himself, he knew nothing about the ladies mentioned, who had presumably gone about their business. On certain points his tongue was sealed—to him private life was sacred. On other points he could say nothing for he did not remember the exact details, and he would suggest nothing that he could not prove. Once indeed his feelings overcame him, and he exclaimed:

"I am deeply hurt that I am not believed."

His composure never leaves him. All through the long ordeal

of the three weeks' trial he shows himself as much the master of himself, the captain of his soul, as in the still longer, still more trying ordeal of those thirty months when day by day he was being questioned, and day by day being faced with new facts, new details, new demands for fresh explanations, days when he had to fight alone against all the resources of trained, expert, experienced officers of police.

Whence then did this man draw his unconquerable firmness? The inspiration of the hero and the martyr one can understand, but this strangler of women, this multiple assassin, this huckster of stolen furniture, this unimaginable liar, whence his? Is it that the Creator has stamped the human soul so greatly with His own impress that never is it wholly lost? How poor and thin before such a spectacle do those theories seem that would proclaim man the creature of his endocrine glands. Is it then the secretions of the glands that can make of the same man a strangler of helpless, solitary women and gift him with a soul of rocklike fortitude?

But the end had come now, and on November 30, 1921, the jury return a verdict of guilty, adding, somewhat surprisingly, a recommendation to mercy that, equally surprisingly, the relatives of the murdered women sign as well. In fact, everyone seems to have signed except Landru himself, who refused with his usual aloof and cold indifference.

EPILOGUE

But before there is enacted the final scene, Landru had one more card to play, and apparently he played it for pure love of the game since he must have known by now there was no trick left that it could take.

A few hours before his execution, when it was perfectly certain there would be no reprieve, he asked for paper and pen and composed a long letter to Monsieur Godefroy, the, as we should say, leading counsel for the prosecution. It is nearly two thousand words in length, say a newspaper column and a half. The handwriting is clear, neat and regular, there are few corrections, there is no sign of mental agitation, it is written with a facility that would do credit to a practised journalist and a sense of drama a novelist might be proud of.

The purport is to describe the trial in terms of a long duel between a consciously innocent Landru and a prosecuting counsel in whose mind Landru depicts a constant struggle between an original conviction of the prisoner's guilt and a tumult of growing doubt. He draws a contrast between his powerful adversary, the trained experienced lawyer with all the resources of the State behind him, and the writer of the letter, solitary, alone, a prisoner, kept in ignorance of all. With extraordinary skill Landru paints the surprise, the doubt, the hesitation he persists he saw invading the lawyer's mind, the effort to expel them, their return again and again, stronger than ever, while all the time Landru himself, superior and pitying, follows with a detached interest the course of this inner battle. In spite of the indifference and detachment Landru had assumed in court, he must have watched the opposing lawyers with the closest attention, for he can reproduce their gestures, remember their expressions, and always put on each his own interpretation of an increasing and troubled sense of his innocence that they, on their side, were trying to suppress. He reminds M. Godefroy of little discrepancies in the evidence and pretends to have noted how they brought him an increasing disquiet. Towards the end of the letter he draws a poetic picture of that *petit Paradis* at Gambais he knows M. Godefroy has visited, and asks him, with a passing reference to Werther, if a place so lovely could possibly have been the scene of such crimes as the prosecution have imagined? The lawyer is supposed to have felt this, and impatient with himself and his growing doubts, to have decided to end it, crying loudly but in ill-assured tones: " No pity, strike without fear."

The letter is as incredible a production as is everything else connected with this case. Remember that the thing was written by a man undoubtedly guilty of eleven sordid and brutal murders, and now on the very eve of paying the last penalty. It concludes with the assurance that the writer would die innocent and tranquil, and he hopes, but evidently with little confidence, that M. Godefroy may be able to say the same when his time comes.

A few hours after the completion of this extraordinary epistle the writer is dead, and of his execution there is one detail that may be noted. So thin, so worn, so frail had he become that when he was thrown on the plank of the guillotine his weight was too small to set in action automatically the knife, as should have been the case. The executioner had himself to release it before it would fall.

There is proof there that though his mind had remained firm and calm and tranquil to the end, his body had felt the strain. But he retained his courtesy and his sense of breeding to the end. Almost his last words were an apology to the priest on duty for not attending mass because, he said, speaking of his guards and executioners, he would be sorry " to keep these gentlemen waiting "

PART V

THE MURDER OF JULIA WALLACE

by Dorothy L. Sayers

THE MURDER OF
JULIA WALLACE

The question is not: Who did this crime? The question is: Did the prisoner do it?—or rather, to put it more accurately: Is it proved to your reasonable satisfaction and beyond all reasonable doubt that the prisoner did it? It is a fallacy to say: "If the prisoner did not do it, who did?" It is a fallacy to look at it and say: "It is very difficult to think the prisoner did not do it"; and it may be equally difficult to think the prisoner did do it.... Can you say, taking all this evidence as a whole ... that you are satisfied beyond reasonable doubt that it was the hand of the prisoner, and no other hand that murdered this woman? If you are not so satisfied ... if it is not established to your reasonable satisfaction as a matter of evidence, as a matter of fact, of legal evidence and legal proof, then it is your duty to find the prisoner not guilty.—*Mr. Justice Wright's summing-up in the trial of William Herbert Wallace.*

WHEN a crime has been committed, the facts may be examined from three different points of view, very carefully distinguished by the learned Judge whose words I have just quoted. The people ask at once: "Who did it?" The law never has to ask this question; it waits until the people, through their representatives, the police, have produced a tentative answer by accusing a suspect, and it then asks one question only: "Did the prisoner do it?"—which is not at all the same thing. The detective novelist, a special sort of person among the people, also asks: "Who did it?" And his professional bias also prompts him to add, and to press with peculiar interest, that further question of which the law can take no cognisance: "If the prisoner did not do it, who did?"

The people, guided by instinct and communal experience, are naturally inclined to favour the most simple and obvious explanation of the facts; also it is a relief to their minds if they can believe that the right person has been accused, convicted and put out of the way; they prefer, therefore, on the whole, that the accused person should be convicted. The detective novelist, as a class, hankers after complication and ingenuity, and is disposed to reject the obvious and acquit the accused, if possible. It is the business also of the law to acquit the accused, if possible; and having done this, the law makes an end of the matter. But the detective novelist is uneasy until he has gone further and found some new and satisfying explanation of the problem.

The case of the Wallace murder shows law and people strangely and interestingly at odds, and provides for the detective novelist an unrivalled field for speculation. William Herbert Wallace was convicted by the people and acquitted by the law; and whether he was guilty or innocent the story is of a sort that (one would think) could only have been put together by the perverted ingenuity of a detective novelist. For if he was guilty, then he was the classic contriver and alibi-monger that adorns the pages of a thousand mystery novels; and if he was innocent, then the real murderer was still more typically the classic villain of fiction. And, since law and people pronounced opposing judgments, any explanation that the novelist can suggest will have the professional merit of flouting opinion and avoiding the obvious.

As in every criminal case that comes to trial, the available facts are only such as were openly produced in court. This restricted material is that upon which people, law and novelist alike have to work. The police, indeed, and the solicitors for the defence, may have had other material at their disposal; but since they did not produce it we may suppose that it was not helpful to them; and the law had to base its decision upon the evidence given at the trial. For the purpose of this article I propose, therefore, to use only the published evidence, so as to place law, people and novelist all in the same position. This is the more easy and suitable since there was, throughout the trial, remarkably little conflict of evidence. With a few trifling exceptions the facts were admitted by both sides; the only difficulty was how to interpret them. It will be seen that there is, from first to last, no single incident which is not susceptible of at least two interpretations, according to whether one considers that the prisoner was, in fact, an innocent man caught in a trap or a guilty man pretending to have been caught in a trap. Nowhere shall we find that 'master-clue' beloved of the detective novelist, which can only lead in one direction. The problem of the Wallace murder had no key-move and ended, in fact, in stalemate.

Nothing could be more respectable, more harmless, more remote from savage violence, than the antecedents of the man who in 1931 was accused of brutally beating out his wife's brains with a poker. Born in 1878, in the Lake District, William Herbert Wallace was apprenticed to the drapery trade. At the age of twenty-three (driven, according to his own statement, by a romantic *Wanderlust*) he sailed for India to take up a post as salesman in Calcutta. Here he fell seriously ill, and, after a period of employment as advertising manager in the less trying climate of Shanghai, was forced for his health's sake to return to England. He obtained a situation in Manchester, where he interested himself in politics and was appointed Liberal Agent for the Ripon Division of the West Riding. While visiting Harrogate, in 1911, he made the acquaintance of his future wife, and on March 24, 1913, he married her. When the war put an end to his political work, he obtained employment as a district agent for the Prudential Assurance Company, and moved with his wife to Liverpool. Here they rented a small, two-storeyed house, No. 29 Wolverton Street, in the suburb of Anfield, and here they lived for sixteen uneventful years, in what seemed to be, in the words of a witness, "the best relations possible".

It is, of course, always difficult to be certain how far an appearance of married harmony may not conceal elements of disruption. Unless the parties attract the notice of neighbours or servants by the throwing of crockery, by loud and abusive language, by open infidelities or by open complaints, a great deal of quiet mutual irritation may go on without anybody's being much the wiser. The Wallaces had no children, kept no servant but a charwoman who came in once a week, and saw but few friends; so that, if indeed they had any disagreements, they were better placed than many people for keeping their troubles to themselves. A caustic judge once expressed the opinion that, in the case of a married couple, there was no need to look for the motive for murder, since marriage was a motive in itself ; while a cynic once argued upon the same lines to the present writer that, who but the husband *could* want to get rid of the wife? Since nobody else could be shown to have any motive for murdering Mrs. Wallace, the murderer *must* be the husband, since after all he *was* her husband, and so had his motive ready made. After his release, Wallace wrote:

> Our days and months and years were filled with complete enjoyment, placid, perhaps, but with all the happiness of quietude and mutual interest and affection. Neither of us cared very much for entertaining other people or for being entertained; we were sufficient in ourselves.

It is in that very self-sufficiency, that intimate companionship extending over days and months and years, that some writers have discovered the hidden motive for the crime: they were too close to one another, the monotony was unendurable, the husband's nerves gave way under the silent strain and he killed his wife because he was bored with her. If there had been open quarrels, that fact would have told against the husband; equally, the fact that there were no such quarrels may be held to tell against him also. Where human nature is concerned, there can never be any certainty; it all depends on the way you look at these things.

And yet it is exceedingly rare, when a husband and wife are at odds, that nobody at all should have any knowledge of their difficulties. One might think that, at some time or other during those sixteen years, the self-control of a hopelessly irritated husband would have given way. It is quite certain that, had there been any evidence at all of domestic trouble, the prosecution would have produced it, for the sheer absence of any comprehensible motive was the weakest point in their case against Wallace. There was, at any rate, no 'eternal triangle'—no other woman and no other man; if there had been any such persons it is almost inconceivable that the researches of the police could have failed to unearth them. Nor could Wallace have had any financial motive for murdering his wife, since, though she was insured for a small sum, his accounts were in perfect order and he had a sufficient balance in the bank. We may weave what fancies we like about the situation; the *fact* remains that no evidence of motive was ever put forward for the murder of Julia Wallace by her husband or anybody else.

What evidence can we, *in fact*, produce about the relations between the Wallaces?

There is, first of all, the undisputed fact that they lived together for nearly eighteen years and had no children. What conclusion we ought to draw from this circumstance we do not know, for nothing was ever said about it. Had their married relations always been normal? We do not know; at any rate, no evidence was brought to the contrary. Did Wallace, perhaps, blame his wife for their childlessness and determine to put her out of the way so that he might marry someone else before it was too late? It is a possibility; he was in no position to get a divorce, and the scandal of an irregular relation with another partner would no doubt have prejudiced him in his employment. We can only say that the prosecution made no suggestion of any such motive. Or did Mrs. Wallace perhaps lay the blame on her husband and drive him to murderous fury by taunts and insults? There was a case in the last century—closely parallel in some respects to the Wallace case—in which that situation does seem to have occurred; but here, there is again no evidence. Neither William nor Julia Wallace was of strong physique, and their means, though sufficient, were not ample; they may have been incapable of having children, or they may, for reasons of health or finance, have agreed to remain childless; we do not know—all is conjecture.

In the absence of a family, what were their common interests? Here we can draw upon the evidence of the witnesses, on the evidence of Wallace himself at the time of the trial and after, and on the evidence of Wallace's diaries—of which those portions at any rate which were written before the murder may be supposed to be fairly reliable.

In Wallace, then, we have one of those mild dabblers in science and philosophy common among self-educated men of a speculative turn of mind. A witness for the prosecution described him, aptly enough, as " a man who is intellectual, and varied in his habits of study, and that sort of thing ". It was, indeed, exactly that sort of thing. He " looked at all things with the eyes of a naturalist " ; he read and noted in his journal the newest theories about atomic physics ; he made amateur chemical experiments in a back bedroom, which he had fitted up as a laboratory ; he strove to model his behaviour upon the stoic precepts of Marcus Aurelius ; he was interested in music, and at the age of fifty ' took up ' the violin (in half a dozen lessons from a friend) ; and he was a keen and skilful chess-player. Witnesses spoke of him as " a placid man ", " scrupulously honest ", " an absolute gentleman in every respect " ; one feels that he was perhaps a little fussy, a little pedantic, a little too fond of improving himself and other people, and something perhaps of an old maid married.

His wife Julia was, in his own words, " an excellent pianist, no mean artist in water-colour, a fluent French scholar, and of a cultured literary taste ". She was dark and small, not very robust, but apparently capable of doing the greater part of the work of their little six-roomed house. One gathers that they enjoyed country rambles and excursions together (he, the naturalist, and she, the artist) ; that in the evenings they sometimes went out together to a play or cinema, or enjoyed a musical evening at home (she, the pianist and he, the fiddler) in the front sitting-room that was otherwise only used for ' company '. True, Julia failed to appreciate the " inner significance and real meaning " of *The Master Builder*, and her husband thought this strange ; but she evidently did her best to share his interests.

> When she was with me [he wrote after the trial] her passion for novelty and discovery gave me countless hours of joy in explaining, as far as I could, the great riddles of the universe. . . .

As I passed from practical to theoretical science my wife tried hard to keep pace with me in the newer problems of physics. . . . The hours and hours we spent together examining specimens under the microscope.

The perfect wife, surely, and model womanly woman! Only one phrase in the diary may perhaps reveal the more trying side of womanliness:

Nothing can ever bring her back, and however much I want her, or however much I miss her loving smiles and aimless chatter . . .

Was that aimless chatter perhaps less lovable in reality than in retrospect? But probably the plainest expression of the feeling between them is to be found in Wallace's sober entry for March 25, 1929, nearly two years before the murder:

Julia reminds me to-day it was fifteen years ago yesterday since we were married. Well, I don't think either of us regrets the step. We seem to have pulled well together, and I think we both get as much pleasure and contentment out of life as most people . . .

One feels, perhaps, that here the pupil of the stoics is controlling the pen more firmly than on some other occasions; but it is scarcely the expression of a man driven to madness by disillusionment and exasperation.

And now, having made ourselves acquainted with the principal characters, we come to the strange plot of the melodrama.

The only time I left my wife alone in our little home [wrote Wallace in a published article] was to visit the Chess Club at the City Café, to deliver my lectures [on chemistry] at the Technical College, or to attend to my insurance business. On all other occasions my wife was my inseparable companion.

Monday was one of the days on which the Liverpool Central Chess Club held its regular meetings, and accordingly, on the night of Monday, January 19, 1931, Wallace left his inseparable companion at about a quarter-past seven, in order to attend the meeting and take part in a championship competition in which his name was down to play that evening. At about 7.20

the telephone rang in the café and was answered by the waitress, who then called Mr. Beattie, the captain of the Chess Club, to come and take the message. The caller, who spoke in "a strong, rather gruff voice", asked whether Mr. Wallace was in the club. Mr. Beattie said no, he was not, but would be there presently; would the caller ring up again. The caller said, "No, I am too busy; I have got my girl's twenty-first birthday on, and I want to see Mr. Wallace on a matter of business; it is something in the nature of his business." Mr. Beattie then offered to take a message, and the caller said he wanted Wallace to come and see him the following evening at 7.30, giving his name as "R. M. Qualtrough," and his address as "25 Menlove Gardens East, Mossley Hill."

Half an hour or so later, that is, at about a quarter to eight, Mr. Beattie saw that Wallace had come into the café and started a game of chess with a man called McCartney. "Oh, Wallace," said Mr. Beattie, "I have a message for you." "Oh, who from?" said Wallace. "From a man named Qualtrough," replied Mr. Beattie. "Qualtrough, Qualtrough," repeated Wallace. "Who is Qualtrough?" Mr. Beattie said, "Well, if you don't know, I don't," and gave the message. Wallace again said, "I don't know the chap. Where is Menlove Gardens East?" Mr. Beattie did not know, nor did another member of the club whom they consulted, but they all agreed that it was probably to be found in the same district as Menlove Avenue. Having noted down the name and address in his diary, Wallace went on to finish and win his game of chess. Nothing further seems to have been said about the mysterious message until Wallace was going home, accompanied by two other members of the club. He then asked, "Qualtrough? Have you heard of that name before?" His friend said he had only heard of one person of that name, and they then discussed the best way of getting to Menlove Gardens. Wallace said he was not sure whether he would go at all, but if he did, he would take the tram to Menlove Avenue. So ended the first act of the tragedy.

Now, whatever else is uncertain about the Wallace case, one

thing is abundantly clear: that, whoever sent the telephone message from "Qualtrough", it was not a genuine message but the first deliberate step towards the commission of a crime. At the trial, Wallace was accused of having sent the message himself, by way of establishing an alibi for the Tuesday evening; he himself maintained that it was sent by an enemy, so as to lure him away from home. Any argument directed to prove or disprove the genuineness of the message is beside the point: there never was an R. M. Qualtrough; there never was a Menlove Gardens East; there never was any genuine insurance business to be transacted. Whoever sent the message was the murderer; all we have to inquire is, was "Qualtrough" Wallace, or was he somebody else?

The first interesting fact is that the message was sent from a telephone kiosk about four hundred yards from Wallace's own house, and sent at exactly the time that Wallace was due to pass that kiosk on his way to the Central Café. Counsel for the prosecution made great play with this fact.

> Assuming he [Wallace] left the house on this three minutes journey at 7.15, he could easily have been in the box by 7.18; but by a singular coincidence the man who wanted him, Qualtrough, was in that telephone box at the identical time at which Mr. Wallace might have been there, and, by another singular coincidence, was trying to ring up Mr. Wallace. . . . It was a box that he [Wallace] has used. . . . The man in the box telephoned through to the Central Café. Nobody but Wallace knew that Wallace was going to be at the café; no one. . . . The man rings up, and . . . assuming that it was the prisoner . . . no doubt disguising his voice. . . . He is asked if he will ring up later. . . . He says "No." . . . If it was Wallace, obviously he would say he could not ring up later, because he would not be there. If the man had important business, and he wanted to speak to a man he did not know, do you not think he would then want to ring up later? And remember, when he was ringing up he was four hundred yards only from the house of Mr. Wallace, and it is perfectly clear that he did not call there, and he did not leave any note there. What he did do, was to telephone up to a place where he could not know he [Wallace] was going to be—it is

common ground that the man who rang up . . . was planning the murder. . . . You would have thought he would be certain to see that his message . . . would get home. . . . He does nothing of the sort. . . . He never inquires afterwards whether Wallace came there and got his message, but he leaves the whole thing in the air.

Now this argument is curiously contradictory. At one point, counsel asks, " If the man had important business, would he not have done so-and-so ? " But in the next breath he admits that the man had no important business, except crime ; therefore it is clear that whatever his actions might be, they could not be such as one would expect of an innocent man making a business appointment. The question that counsel was really trying to ask was not : " Can we now believe the message genuine ? " but : " Could Wallace at that time have innocently believed the message genuine ? " But let us examine the whole business of the telephone call carefully, point by point ; for it is the very centre of the problem.

First of all : Is it true that nobody but Wallace could possibly have known that he was going to the City Café on January 19th ? It is not true. Wallace was scheduled to play a championship game that night, and the list of fixtures was openly displayed in the café where anybody might see it. The meetings of the chess club always began at about the same time—roughly 7.45. Wallace was a fairly regular attendant, and we know that he was definitely expected on the Monday, because Mr. Beattie said as much to " Qualtrough ". Therefore, any frequenter of the café might reasonably have looked to find him there.

Secondly : Where was the famous telephone kiosk, and what was it like ? The Wallaces' house was one of a row, all having their front doors upon Wolverton Street and their back doors upon a lane running roughly parallel to the street. At a point some four hundred yards from No. 29 street and lane converged, and at this strategic point stood the kiosk—a dim little erection, lit only by the reflected rays of a street-lamp. Whether Wallace left his house by the front or the back door, he was bound to pass the kiosk on the way to the Central Café. Equally, anybody who wanted to know whether he was going to the Central Café that night had only to stand at the corner of the two streets and see whether he passed the kiosk. Thus counsel's "coincidence" turns out to be no coincidence at all, for if "Qualtrough" was not Wallace, then he must have been watching in or near the kiosk to make sure that Wallace went to the café, and, having made sure, he telephoned.

Is there anything that might indicate whether "Qualtrough" was Wallace or somebody else? There is the curious evidence of the girl at the telephone exchange. She was spoken to by the caller, who said: "Operator, I have pressed button A, but have not had my correspondent yet." She then connected him and thought no more about it. Now, counsel drew attention to the fact that Wallace often spoke from that call-box; he should, therefore, have known how to use it. But the whole point of button A's existence is that you should *not* press button A *until* you have heard your "correspondent" speak. Either, then, "Qualtrough" was unfamiliar with a public call-box, or he was too much agitated to remember the procedure. Whoever he was, he may well have been agitated: but the more usual mistake with button A is to forget to press it at all. The point is a trifling one; but, such as it is, it tells, perhaps, slightly in Wallace's favour.

Now comes the question why "Qualtrough" rang up when he did. If he was Wallace, then 7.18 was obviously the only time at which he could ring up. If not, then why did he not wait till Wallace had reached the café, or deliver a note or message at the house? There can be only one answer to this: that his face, voice and handwriting were known to the Wallaces and that he did not dare to risk recognition. Still less could he ring again later in the evening. The voice might have been disguised; Mr. Beattie said that at the time it did not seem to him to be anything but a natural one, and that it "would be a great stretch of imagination" to say that it was anything like Wallace's. But supposing it was not Wallace, how could "Qualtrough" venture, in his own voice or a disguised one, on a prolonged conversation with

Wallace? He would have had to answer every kind of inconvenient question: details about himself, details about "Menlove Gardens East", details about the mysterious "business", and he would have had to be an uncommonly skilful liar to get through without letting Wallace smell a rat. The tale of the birthday party was a little fishy; but the vague message sent through Mr. Beattie had its merits, for it held out a bait of indeterminate size and splendour.

> Seeing the name and the daughter coming of age had been suggested [said Wallace in court] I considered it might result in a policy of something like £100 endowment, or something of that nature. I did not expect it would be less than that.

To a man in Wallace's position, that would have been business worth getting. Besides, if the name was not to be found in the directory, or the address was discovered to be non-existent, how easy to suppose that Mr. Beattie had heard wrongly or noted the details carelessly.

All through this case one has to remember that Wallace lived in a small way and worked for very small profits. Nobody is more pertinacious than your small insurance agent. He will go miles to secure a few shillings. He would not be disconcerted by failing to find "R. M. Qualtrough" in a list of householders; the man might be a lodger, a domestic servant, a newcomer to the district. Wallace said afterwards that he had not thought to look up the address in the directory; but in any case, new streets and houses were being run up all over the place at a great rate, and it might have been one of those. It was nearly as certain as death and taxation that Wallace would never rest content till he had investigated the whole matter personally and on the spot.

And finally, did "Qualtrough" take no steps to ascertain that his message had "gone home"? We cannot say that. He had only to follow Wallace to the café. Whoever he was, he must have been a habitué of the place to have known of Wallace's engagement to play there that night. It is possible that he actually arrived in time to hear the message delivered. Once we admit that he must have known Wallace and the café, all the rest follows. Any explanation that fits Wallace as the murderer also fits any murderer we may like to postulate.

The stage being now set, the curtain goes up on Act II. It is preceded by a curious little interlude. At 3.30 on the following afternoon, James Edward Rothwell, a police constable, was bicycling along a street called Maiden Lane, and saw Wallace walking on the pavement.

> He was dressed in a tweed suit and a light fawn raincoat. His face was haggard and drawn, and he seemed very distressed. He was dabbing his eye with his coat-sleeve, and he appeared to me as if he had been crying.

It was suggested to P.C. Rothwell that Wallace's eyes might have been merely watering from the cold, but the constable stuck to his opinion. On the other hand, we have the evidence of three women upon whom Wallace called between 3.30 and 5.45 to collect their insurance, that he seemed " calm " and " just as usual ", that he cracked jokes with one and enjoyed a cup of tea with another. Whether the constable or the ladies were the better qualified to detect signs of emotion in an insurance agent is a question. Women are said to be observant by nature, and policemen should be observant by profession. The one certain fact is that, on that morning and afternoon of Tuesday, January 29th, Wallace transacted all his business in his ordinary accurate manner.

He stopped collecting, by his own account, at a few minutes to six and then went home for his tea. And it is now that we come to the one serious conflict of evidence in the whole case. Some time between 6.30 and 6.45 the milk-boy called with the milk; Mrs. Wallace took it in, and that is the last occasion on which she was seen alive by any disinterested person. The milk-boy, Alan Croxton Close, was 14 years old, and in his evidence he said he knew he delivered the milk at 6.30, because when he passed Holy Trinity Church it was 6.25, and it took him five minutes to get from there to 29 Wolverton Street.

On the other hand, Allison Wildman, aged 16, who was delivering a newspaper at No. 27, next door, said she got there at 6.43, and that when she had delivered her paper and gone, Close was still standing at the door of No. 29. She, too, relied on Holy Trinity Church clock. Moreover, she was seen by some boys leaving Wolverton Street some minutes after 6.40. Further doubt was thrown on Close's evidence by a number of other little boys who maintained that on the day after the murder he had told them, "I saw Mrs. Wallace at a quarter to seven"; and it was rather suggested that young Close had altered his opinion to fit the police case against Wallace. It is a close thing—a matter of five or eight minutes—the kind of point on which nobody but the characters in a detective novel can reasonably be expected to be accurate; its importance (just as in a detective story) lies in the fact that, if Mrs. Wallace was alive at 6.45 it was almost impossible that Wallace could have murdered her; for at 7.10 at the very latest he was changing trams at the junction of Smithdown Road and Lodge Lane, a good twenty minutes' ride from his home. To commit the murder between 6.30 and 6.50 would have been pretty quick work; to commit it between 6.45 and 6.50 would have been something like a conjuring trick.

Wallace stated that he left the house that evening by the back door. This, he explained, was his usual custom in the early part of the evening.

> If I was going out after six, and I knew I was going to be out an hour or two, I might go out by the back door and ask my wife to come down and bolt it after me, and on my return come in by the front door, because I would have my key.

This seems reasonable; we get the picture of the front door with its patent lock and the backyard door with its builder's lock and iron bolts, which (and this must be borne in mind) the householder would *expect* to find bolted against him on his return. Mrs. Wallace, on this occasion, accompanied her husband—or so he said—by way of the back as far as the backyard gate and there he left her, with instructions to bolt the door after him.

Now, if "Qualtrough" was lurking about the telephone kiosk at ten minutes to seven on that dark January night, what might he have seen? In the light of the adjacent street-lamp he would have seen Wallace's slight figure, dressed, not in the fawn rain-coat (for the weather had cleared), but in an overcoat, come briskly up from the back lane towards the tramway stop. That would have been his cue that the coast was clear at No. 29, and that his dupe was out of the way for a good hour at least. Now would be his moment for going to the house. If, by any chance, Mrs. Wallace had somebody with her, he could still make some excuse and withdraw; but if she was alone, the path to crime lay open.

Nobody (except the not impossible "Qualtrough") seems to have seen Wallace at this stage of his journey. He is next heard of some time between 7.6 and 7.10, at the tram-junction at Smithdown Road, asking the conductor, one Thomas Charles Phillips, whether the tram went from there to Menlove Gardens East. Phillips replied, " No, you can get on No. 5, 5A, 5W or a No. 7 car." There was nothing in this to suggest to Wallace that Menlove Gardens East might not exist, so he got on, observing that he was a stranger in the district and had important business at Menlove Gardens East. Later, while paying his fare, he re-minded the conductor that he wanted to be put off at Menlove Gardens East, and a little later mentioned his destination for the third time and was told to change at Penny Lane. When they got there, Phillips shouted " Menlove Gardens, change here," and saw his fussy passenger sprinting to catch the No. 7 car, which went to Calderstone. The time was then 7.15.

On the Calderstone car, Wallace again anxiously asked the conductor to put him off at Menlove Gardens East. Accordingly, he was put off at Menlove Gardens West, the conductor saying to him, " You will probably find Menlove Gardens East in that direction." Wallace replied, "Thank you; I am a complete stranger round here."

Now, it was said afterwards that these persistent inquiries and repeated asseverations that he was a stranger in the district and had important business there, were unnatural, and showed that Wallace was eager to impress his personality upon the tram-conductors in order to establish his alibi. This may be so—though, if fussy inquiries and irrelevant personal confidences are a proof of criminal intent, then the proportion of criminals engaged daily in establishing alibis on public vehicles must be a shockingly high one.

It is interesting that he did not succeed in impressing himself upon the conductor of the first tram—the one nearest home. The early part of the alibi is obviously the most important; did he, being guilty, think it dangerous to attract attention to himself at that stage in the proceedings? Or did he, being innocent, make no inquiry, merely because he knew the way as far as Smithdown Road? We may note at this point that Wallace appears never to have tried to establish an alibi in the strict sense of the word. He never suggested, for instance, that he was already out of the house by the time the milk-boy came. A villain in a book would, one feels, not have neglected this important point; but the argument cuts both ways, since a definite statement about times may be challenged; a mere vagueness leaves the onus of proof upon the prosecution.

Next comes the evidence of Sydney Herbert Green, a clerk, who found Wallace wandering about Menlove Gardens West and looking in vain for Menlove Gardens East. Green informed him that there was no such place. Wallace then said he would try 25 Menlove Gardens West. This he did, asking the wife of the occupier whether anybody called " Qualtrough " lived there. She said no, and he went away.

Then came a complication which was very damaging to Wallace, for when he had inspected Menlove Gardens North and South he roamed along Menlove Avenue and then found himself (by his own account unexpectedly) in a road which he did know. Between Menlove Avenue and Allerton Road runs Green Lane, and in Green Lane lived a Mr. Crewe, who was a superintendent of the Prudential Assurance Company and whom Wallace had visited on five occasions to take violin lessons. This, said the prosecution, proved that Wallace was lying when he said he did not know the district. Mr. Crewe said in cross-examination that the violin lessons had been given two years ago and always on winter evenings after dark. There are, of course, some people who, after passing half a dozen times along a tram-route by night are familiar with every crossing and turning to left and right of the route, and who never visit a house without making themselves acquainted with all the surrounding streets. Others (of whom the present writer is one) allow themselves to be carted incuriously from point to point, remaining in the end as ignorant of the general topography of the district as when they started. Wallace, if one may trust to his evidence, was of the latter sort. " How used you to go to Woolton Woods with your wife? "—" I probably inquired of some driver of a car, which car would take us there and got on that car." A statement which, if untrue, was well invented to square with his known behaviour on the night of the crime. As for knowing the lay-out of Menlove Gardens, Mr. Crewe, who had lived just round the corner for three and a half years, said definitely in evidence that, previously to the trial, he himself had not had any idea whether there was a Menlove Gardens East or not.

At any rate, suggested counsel, when Wallace found himself in Green Lane, why did he not call at Mr. Crewe's house and ask his assistance in finding " Qualtrough's " address? Wallace replied that he did; he knocked at the door but could get no answer. Mr. Crewe was, in fact, out that night; so that the statement was not capable of disproof.

Having failed here, Wallace met a policeman and again inquired for Menlove Gardens East. The constable said, categorically, that there was no such place: there was Menlove Gardens, North, South and West, and Menlove Avenue, but no Menlove Gardens East. He suggested that Wallace should try 25 Menlove Avenue (which he pointed out); Wallace thanked him and then asked where he could find a directory. The constable said he could see one at the newsagent's in Allerton Road, or at the police station or post office. Wallace then explained, " I am an insurance agent looking for a Mr. Qualtrough who rang up the club and left a message for me with my colleague to ring up [? visit] Mr. Qualtrough at 25 Menlove Gardens East." Whether this outburst of confidence was a necessary part of alibi-faking, or was merely the ordinary citizen's apologetic anxiety to justify his existence in the eyes of the police, is again a matter of interpretation. Wallace then said, " It is not 8 o'clock yet ? " and the constable agreed that it was only a quarter to. The alibi again? or only a reasonable desire to know whether the newspaper shop would still be open? However that may be, it is in the shop that we next find Wallace at 8.10, searching the directory for Menlove Gardens East. In the meantime, he had apparently been looking for the post office, but could not find it. He hunted the directory for some time, and then said, " Do you know what I am looking for ? " The manageress said (not unnaturally) that she did not, he then told her that he was looking for 25 Menlove Gardens East. She then assured him that there was no such place. Curiously enough, he does not seem to have mentioned the name of Qualtrough in the shop; he said that he looked for the name in the book and could not find it; and by this time he was probably convinced that, whoever Qualtrough was, he was not a householder.

It was now about 8.20, and according to Wallace himself, he was beginning to get a little alarmed. If he was innocent, this was perhaps not unnatural. There did seem to be something rather queer about " Qualtrough ", and he could not but remember that there had been one or two recent burglaries in the neighbourhood of Wolverton Street, and that it was a well-known trick of burglars to lure away householders with bogus telephone messages. Further, this was a Tuesday night—the night when, as a rule, he had a good deal of the insurance money in the house. So, giving up the vain search for Qualtrough, he walked to the nearest tram-stop to begin the journey home.

In the meantime, Mr. John Sharpe Johnston, an engineer, who lived next door to the Wallaces at 31 Wolverton Street, was getting ready to go out with his wife for the evening. The two families had been neighbours for the last ten years, and knew one another, in Mrs. Johnston's own words, "as neighbours". There seems to have been no very great intimacy. In all those years Mrs. Johnston had been into No. 29 "about three times", and then only into the front sitting-room. On all three occasions Wallace had been absent, so that Mrs. Johnston had never seen the Wallaces together in their own home; nor, evidently, had the two women been accustomed to run in and out of each other's back kitchens in the informal way that neighbours sometimes fall into. Mr. Johnston had, indeed, seen the Wallaces together from time to time, and thought them "a very loving couple, very affectionate"; but he cannot have known them very well, for he had never heard Mrs. Wallace's Christian name—or, if he had, not often enough to remember what it was. Of one thing, however, the Johnstons were quite certain : they had never heard any quarrelling going on next door, though, since the houses shared a party-wall, they would have been likely to hear anything exciting that there was to be heard.

A little before 8.45 on the Tuesday evening, the Johnstons heard somebody knocking, as it might be with the fist or palm of the hand, at the Wallaces' back door. This was nothing unusual, so they paid no particular attention to it. On going out, by way of the back door, into the entry that runs parallel to Wolverton Street, they met Wallace, just coming down at an ordinary walking pace from the Breck Road end of the entry towards his own back door. To Mrs. Johnston's polite "Good evening, Mr. Wallace," he replied only with the question, "Have you heard anything unusual to-night?" Mrs. Johnston said, in some surprise, "No—why? What has happened?" To which Wallace replied: "I have been round to the front door and also to the back, and they are both fastened against me."

It is at this point that the detective-story writer becomes exasperated with the published accounts of the case. To him the exact mechanism of locks and bolts is meat and drink, and in writing his books he makes his witnesses offer precise information on the subject, illustrating his points, if necessary, with neat diagrams. Now, in the Wallace case, we are concerned with no less than three doors and their fastenings, all of which are of the utmost importance; yet, of these, one lock only seems to have been brought into court, and of that there is no published description, while the witnesses are maddening vague in their evidence, so that it is often difficult to say whether by "lock" they mean a mortice-lock or a safety-lock, or even the mechanism of the door *handle*; whether by "bolt" they mean an iron bolt, or the catch of a safety-lock; and even whether by "back door" they mean the kitchen door or the yard door leading to the entry. By careful piecing together of the various statements, we may, however, come to the following conclusions.

1. The front door was the one by which Wallace was accustomed to let himself in with his own key on returning home at night. From the data furnished in evidence, it seems likely that the lock was an automatic lock, though not of the "Yale" type; but it is clear that no key can have been left in it on the inside, as this would prevent its being opened by another key from without. It may even have been a small mortice-lock, which Wallace would lock after him, removing and carrying away the key. This door also had a bolt, which is not described. It may have been a safety-catch or a small and easily sliding bolt immediately beneath the lock-plate. If it was a stiff, heavy or double bolt, then one suggestion that was made becomes quite incredible, as will be seen. It is really extraordinary that so few details should have been reported about this bolt.

2. The back *kitchen* door seems to have had a handle, a bolt or bolts, and possibly also a lock. The mechanism of the handle seems to have been stiff and faulty.

3. The back *yard* door had apparently a latch and a bolt. It is not perfectly clear from the evidence whether it was this door or the back kitchen door which Wallace expected his wife to have bolted after him when he left; he apparently contradicted himself a little about this, but no energetic effort seems to have been made to clear the matter up.

In any case, when Wallace told the Johnstons that both doors were fastened against him, they were "all standing in the entry before the door into the entry had been opened". As to what followed, let us look first at Mr. Johnston's evidence as given at the trial:

> What did you say to him then?—I suggested that he tried the door again, as if it was the back door, and if he could not open it, I would get the key of my back door and try.

[By a process of deduction, we may see what Mr. Johnston had in his mind. Here was no question of a Yale lock, for which another person's key would be useless; and it would be equally useless to try to open an ordinary lock from outside if the key had been left in the lock *inside*. Therefore, he must have thought that Mrs. Wallace had gone out by the back and taken the key with her.]

> When you said, "Try again" and you would see, what did he do?—He went up to the door.

[Apparently the back door of the house; see later.]

> Did Mr. Wallace say anything when he went in, or when he went up the yard?—When he got to the door, he called out, "It opens now."

[Mrs. Johnston's evidence here interestingly supplements her husband's. She remembered that Wallace, as he crossed the yard, looked back over his shoulder and said: " She (meaning his wife) will not have gone out; she has such a bad cold." Here we have then, Wallace answering, and rebutting, Mr. Johnston's unspoken assumption in the matter of the key.]

> Were you able to hear, from where you were, whether he tried with his key or anything?—No, he did not seem to try the key; he seemed to turn the knob in the usual way.—And said, "It opens now?"—Yes.

> MR. JUSTICE WRIGHT: Could you see?—Yes; I could see him at the door, my lord.

To supplement this, we have Wallace's own statement made at the police station.

> I . . . then pulled out my key and went to open the front door and found it secure and could not open it with my key. I then went round to the back. The door leading from the entry to the back yard was closed, but not bolted. I went to the back door of the house and I was unable to get in. I do not know if the door was bolted or not; it sticks sometimes, but I think the door was bolted, though I am not sure. . . . I tried my key in the front door again and found the lock did not work properly.

Putting these two statements together, it is clear that Wallace meant it to be understood that he had tried first the front door, then the back door *of the house*, and then the front door again, and that he was coming round to the back for the second time when he met the Johnstons in the entry. It is perhaps a little surprising to find Mr. Johnston asserting that their conversation took place " before the door into the entry had been opened ". Did Wallace, then, carefully shut it behind him after his first fruitless attempt on the back door of the house? Unless the door had a spring, and shut to of itself, he must have done; and this does not look very much like agitation of mind. A similar unnecessary carefulness proved the downfall, under cross-examination, of Fox the matricide. Curiously enough, nothing seems to have been made of this point by the prosecution.

Now, with regard to the back door of the house: nobody, except Mr. Johnston when he offered the help of his own key, seems to have suggested that it was locked at any time. Wallace said he thought at first that it was bolted, and subsequently came to the conclusion that the handle was merely stiff. At any rate, he eventually got in without using any key. And at this point we may take the evidence given subsequently by a locksmith.

> Witness produced another lock which he said was from the back kitchen door and found to be rusty. When the knob was turned, with difficulty, the spring bolt remained inside the lock and the knob returned to its former position.

The mention of the "knob" seems to show definitely that the reference is not to the lock, but to the latching mechanism operated by the door handle. This evidence gives support to the theory that Wallace, when he first tried the door, was misled by its stiffness into supposing it to be bolted when, as a matter of fact, the latch had merely stuck.

We shall have to come back later to this question about the locks. We will take up the story at the point where Wallace opened the door, as described by Mr. Johnston, and went in, leaving his neighbours in the yard. They do not seem to have noticed any light in the back kitchen (Wallace said that there was a gas-jet, reduced to a very feeble glimmer, over the sink); upstairs, however, the windows of the "middle bedroom" where the Wallaces slept, and of the "back room" which Wallace used as a workshop, were dimly lit, as though the gas had been left on, but turned down low.

After Wallace entered the house the Johnstons heard him call out twice, and shortly afterwards they saw first the light in the middle bedroom turned up full and then a match struck in "the small room at the top of the stairs". In "about a minute and a half" Wallace came hurrying out, saying to them: "Come and see; she has been killed." His manner, observed Mr. Johnston, who was a witness commendably free from any tendency to exaggerated language, "seemed a bit excited". Mrs. Johnston said he spoke "in a distressed tone, his words were very hurried, you know"—by which, as she explained, she meant "agitated".

At this news they all went into the house. Wallace led them through the back kitchen and the main kitchen, where he had already lit the gas, and into the front sitting-room, where a dreadful sight awaited them. The body of Mrs. Wallace lay stretched upon the hearth-rug, her feet near the gas-fire and her head towards the door. Her skull had been brutally battered in with such force as to scatter her brains about the floor, and her blood was splashed all around—on the carpet, on the arm-chair by the fireplace, on the violin-case lying on the seat of the chair, and on the wall behind. Mrs. Johnston cried out, "Oh, you poor darling!" and felt the dead woman's hand. It is not recorded what either of the two men said; but Mr. Johnston reported that Wallace appeared, all the time, "as though he was suffering from a shock. He was quiet, walking round; he did not shout, or anything like that."

There was plenty of light to see the grisly state of things, because, when Wallace had first gone into the house he had lit the gas in the sitting-room. He was cross-examined over and over again about his movements, and nothing could be clearer, or one might think, more natural, than the account he gave. He said that, after passing through the back kitchen, he opened the door into the main kitchen, which was where he would have expected to find his wife, if she was still sitting up. It was dark, and he lit the gas (which was sensible of him if he wanted to see where he was going), and then, matchbox in hand, he went straight upstairs to see if his wife was in the bedroom, calling to her as he went. Here he turned up the light, and, finding the room empty, searched the other rooms on that floor with the aid of his matches, and then came down again to try the front sitting-room —the last place where she might be expected to be, but the only other room in the house.

> The door was closed to, and I pushed it a little open, and then I struck a match in quite the ordinary way, that I probably did every night I went into the room in the dark. I held it up, and as I held it up I could see my wife was lying there on the floor.
>
> You told the officer that you thought she was in a fit?—That was my first impression, but it only lasted possibly a fraction of a second, because I stooped down, with the same match, and I could see there was evidence of signs of a disturbance and blood, and I saw that she had been hit.
>
> Did you light the light?—Yes, I did.
>
> Which light?—The one on the right-hand side near the window.
>
> Why did you light that one?—It is the one we always use.

Now, the questions asked by the prosecution about this were

directed to two points. First: Why, unless he knew beforehand that he was going to find a body on the floor, did he strike a match on the sitting-room threshold at all? He could have seen his way into the room quite well by reflected light from the kitchen. And secondly: Why did he walk round the body to light the farther of the two gas-jets, instead of the one nearest to him?

Now these, one would say, were the sort of questions that could only occur to a man who had never in his life had anything to do with gas. It is absolutely automatic with anyone who lives in a house with gas-lighting, to strike the match *at the threshold*, if he thinks he may have occasion to light the gas; so much so, that the present writer, for some time after making the change-over from gas to electricity, could seldom enter a room at night without first striking a match in the doorway or, at least, making a tentative gesture towards the pocket that held the matchbox. Equally automatic would be the action of lighting the accustomed gas-jet; since a jet that is seldom used may easily turn out to have a clogged burner or a broken mantle, and the realization of this, though quite subconscious, is enough to inhibit entirely any recourse to that jet in an emergency.

Having lit the gas, felt his wife's hand and looked at her injuries, Wallace, as he said, saw that she was quite dead, and at once rushed out and called his friends. It is difficult to see what else he could have done; and all this part of the story seems perfectly consistent with his innocence.

Seeing that poor Mrs. Wallace was past all help, they all three went back into the kitchen, and there Wallace drew their attention to the lid of a cabinet, which appeared to have been wrenched off and was lying on the floor. Then he reached up to a shelf and took down a cash-box. Mr. Johnston asked whether anything was missing. Wallace said he thought about £4 had gone, though he could not be certain until he looked through his books.

This business of the cash-box is rather mysterious. It was presumably examined for finger-prints, but no evidence about this seems to have been given.[1] Wallace's prints would have been on it in any case, since he handled it to take it down; if there were others, we hear nothing of them. It was said, "Why, if an outside murderer had stolen the money, should he have so carefully replaced the box on the shelf?" It might, with equal force, have been asked why, if Wallace wanted to pretend that the murderer had been there, did *he* put it back? Common sense would have suggested that he should produce the appearance of as much disorder as possible. Like almost everything else in this extraordinary case the question cuts two ways. Then, how did it happen that there had been so little money in the box? Wallace's accounts were gone into very carefully at the trial, and everything he then said was found to be correct. On an ordinary Tuesday he would have had about £30 or £40 of the company's in his possession, ready for paying in on the Wednesday, which was the regular accounting day; on one Tuesday in each month he might have as much as £80 or £100, or even more. On this particular Tuesday, however, he had less than usual, first, because he had been laid up with influenza on the Saturday and had not made his round; secondly, because out of the £14 or so he had collected on the Monday and Tuesday (his other regular collecting-days) he had paid away about £10 10s. 0d., in sick benefit; thus leaving about £4. Let us see which way this evidence tells.

1. Supposing that there was an outside murderer, why did he not come on the Monday night, when he knew that Wallace was safely occupied with his chess-match?—Answer: Because his intention was to steal the insurance money, and what he wanted was to get Wallace out of the way on the *Tuesday* night, when a bigger sum would have been collected.

2. If the intention was to steal, why did not the thief select some night when both Wallace and his wife were out of the house?—Answer: Because (as Wallace said in evidence) when they were both out of the house they always took any of the company's money with them for greater safety.

---

[1] The point was put to Detective-Sergeant Bailey in cross-examination, but he replied vaguely, and the matter was apparently never cleared up.

3. But how could an outside murderer have known this?—Answer: If there was an outside murderer, he was obviously somebody well acquainted with Wallace and his habits, as is clear from other considerations mentioned earlier.

4. If Wallace himself was the murderer, would he not also select the Tuesday night, in order to suggest that the murderer was a thief in search of the insurance money?—Certainly he would.

5. In that case, since he *did* know and was probably the only person who *could* know that there would be less money that week than usual, why did he not postpone the crime to a day when he could stage a really impressive robbery?—This question is difficult to answer; unless, of course, Wallace had some idea that he might be called upon to make good the loss; in which case his failure to collect on the Saturday might all be part of the plan.

It should be said at once that there was never any suggestion that Wallace himself committed the crime for money: his accounts were all in order; there was only the £4 of insurance money; no private liabilities were disclosed; his wife was insured for the trifling sum of £20, and, though she had £90 in the savings-bank, Wallace's own bank balance was £152—ample for any emergency.

After looking at the cash-box Mr. Johnston suggested that Wallace should go and see if anything had been taken from upstairs. Wallace went up and come down almost at once, saying: "There is £5 in a jar they have not taken."

Mr. Johnston then went out for the police, and Mrs. Johnston went back with Wallace into the blood-bespattered sitting-room. Here, he stooped over his wife, and said, "They have finished her; look at the brains." Mrs. Johnston, not unnaturally, seems to have preferred not to look at any such thing; instead, she gazed round the room and said, "What ever have they used?"

Wallace made no suggestion about this; he got up and came round to the other side of the body and then said, "Why, what ever was she doing with her mackintosh, and my mackintosh?"

Mrs. Johnston then saw that there was a mackintosh lying, as she expressed it, "roughed up" and almost hidden under the body. (Later, a policeman with a gift for description said it was "as though it had been put in this position round the shoulder, and tucked in by the side, as though the body was a living person and you were trying to make it comfortable.") Mrs. Johnston was not quite sure whether Wallace had said "her" or "a" mackintosh; she was, however, quite positive that he ended his sentence by identifying the mackintosh as his own. Abandoning the problem of how the garment came there, the two of them then went into the kitchen. The fire was nearly out—"just a few live embers"—and Mrs. Johnston, "feeling that she must do something", relit it, with Wallace's assistance. Then, while they waited together in the kitchen, Wallace, who till then had been "quite collected", twice broke down and sobbed for a moment, with his head in his hands.

Now Mrs. Johnston offers us a little more evidence about the front door:

> A little later there was a knock at the door, I understand?—Yes.
> Did you try to open the door?—Yes.
> Were you able to?—No; it is a different lock to mine, and I think I was agitated, and I drew back and let Mr. Wallace open it.
> Do you know whether or not the door was bolted?—I do not.
> If he [Wallace] says he undid the bolt, you would not contradict him, would you?—I do not know whether he did, but I cannot remember that.

Nothing here is said about the necessity of a key to open the door from the inside: Mrs. Johnston merely attributes her failure to agitation and the fact that the lock was of another pattern from her own. Nor does it seem likely that she could have failed to notice the drawing of a heavy bolt or of a double bolt. The door, at any rate, was opened to admit a policeman; and he said that he did not hear any bolt withdrawn.

To this policeman, by name Frederick Robert Williams, Wallace said: "Something terrible has happened, officer." The policeman came in, examined the body, and then heard Wallace's account of his efforts to enter the house, at the front, at the back, at the front again—" this time I found the door was bolted " —again at the back—" this time I found it would open." Both then, and later, at the trial, Wallace asserted quite definitely and positively that the front door was actually bolted when he let P.C. Williams in, and this is one of the most extraordinary points about the case. If Wallace was innocent, then it is difficult to see why the real murderer or anybody else should have bolted the door; if he was guilty, then, by sticking to the tale of the bolted door (which rested on no evidence but his own), he probably did more damage to his own case than by any other thing he said.

Leaving the matter of the bolts for a moment, let us accompany P.C. Williams on his tour of the house. Omitting the questions of examining counsel, his story ran more or less like this:

In the middle bedroom the gas-jet was lit; accused said he changed in this room before going out and left the light burning. On the mantelpiece I noticed an ornament from which five or six £1 notes were protruding. Accused partly extracted the notes, and said, " Here is some money which has not been touched." I requested him to put the ornament and notes back, which he did.

P.C. Williams should have spoken sooner; a smear of blood was subsequently found on one of the notes, but by that time it was impossible to say that it had not got there from Wallace's hands after his examination of the corpse.

I approached a curtained recess to the right of the fireplace. Accused said, " My wife's clothes are there, they have not been touched." I looked in, and apparently they were undisturbed. In the back room which has been converted into a laboratory, accused said, " Everything seems all right here ". In the bathroom there was a small light; accused said, " We usually have a light here."

So far, everything seemed to square with Wallace's story. Next comes a very curious little circumstance, which squares with no imaginable theory of the crime.

> We went into the front bedroom. It was in a state of disorder; the bed-clothes were half on the bed and half on the floor; there were a couple of pillows lying near the fireplace; there was a dressing-table in the room, containing drawers and a mirror, and also a wardrobe; the drawers of the dressing-table were shut and the drawers of the wardrobe were shut.

On the subject of the front bedroom, the published evidence is more vague and unsatisfactory even than it is about the locks. Counsel for the defence seems to have asked the prisoner:

> It is said that the bed in the front bedroom was somehow disarranged, and there were some of your wife's hats on it?—Yes.

[This is all we ever hear about the hats.]

> Do you know anything about that?—I do not think I had been in that room for probably a fortnight before the 20th or the 19th January.

Here the detective-story writer (and, one would think, everybody else) would ask instantly: Did your wife often go into the room? Were there sheets on the bed? If so, were you, or was your wife proposing to sleep there on the night of the 20th? Why? Did you always occupy the same room as your wife, and if not, why not? According to Wallace, his wife's bedroom "would look down on the yard" (i.e. she slept in the "middle bedroom"), and, since he himself changed his clothes in that room, the presumption is that he occupied it with her; but the position is never made clear. If the room was merely a spare room, then, one asks: What is the meaning of the disorder? Would an outside thief and murderer overlook the occupied bedroom with its five £1 notes on the mantelpiece, and make straight for the spare room? And why should he there confine himself to ransacking the bed, either omitting to open any drawers and cupboards, or else carefully shutting them all up after him? And if the murderer was Wallace, trying to present a convincing picture of a search for valuables, then why did he stage it, so absurdly, in this room rather than in the other?

It seems highly probable that the disorder in the front room had nothing to do with the murder; there is, however, a curious and interesting parallel in the case of the Gilchrist murder (Edinburgh, 1909). Here, the murderer, after battering his victim to death, made straight, not for the old lady's own bedroom where she kept her jewels in the wardrobe, but for the spare bedroom, where, disregarding various articles of value upon the dressing-table, he broke open a box containing papers. In this case, however, the murderer is known to have been interrupted in the middle of his activities, and it has been suggested that some paper, and no ordinary valuable, was the real object of his search. Our detective novelist might play with two theories in this connection: (1) The rather melodramatic one that the murderer of Julia Wallace was in search of something that he had cause to believe might be found secreted under the spare room mattress; or (2), the idea that Wallace, in staging his murder, deliberately modelled his effects upon the Gilchrist case; this might explain his curious insistence in the matter of the bolted front door, and his subsequent statement that he at first believed the murderer to be still in the house.

Having searched the bedrooms, they went downstairs again. In the kitchen Wallace showed P.C. Williams the cabinet and the cash-box, and also picked up a lady's handbag from a chair, saying that it belonged to his wife. It contained a £1 note and some small change. They were then joined in the sitting-room by Police Sergeant Breslin, in whose presence Williams observed: "That looks like a mackintosh." Wallace, who was standing in the doorway, said, "Yes, it is an old one of mine," and, glancing out into the hall, added, "it usually hangs here." It was not until past 10 o'clock that the mackintosh was closely examined. By that time Superintendent Moore had arrived, and he, after hearing Wallace's story and examining the rooms and doors of the house, again asked Wallace whose the mackintosh was. This time Wallace seemed to hesitate in his answer, and the Superintendent pulled the mackintosh out, saying, "Take it up and let's have a look at it. It's a gent's mackintosh." Wallace said, "If there are two patches on the inside it is mine," and, finding the patches, continued in the same breath, "It is mine." A great deal was made, later, of this brief hesitation; it appears, however, quite natural that, seeing the importance the police were inclined to attach to the mackintosh, Wallace should have thought it well to verify, by proof, his first general impression that the garment was his.

When the mackintosh was pulled out it was found to be heavily spattered with blood on the right side, both inside and out. Also —which was more remarkable—it was very much burnt, and part of Mrs. Wallace's skirt was burnt also. Yet the gas-fire before which she lay was not alight when the body was found. Two theories were advanced to account for the burning. One was that the murderer (in that case Wallace) had tried to destroy the mackintosh by burning it at the gas-fire and had accidentally burnt Mrs. Wallace's skirt in the process; the other, that the fire had been alight when the murder was committed, that Mrs. Wallace had fallen against it and set her skirt alight, and that either she was wearing the mackintosh at the time, or that the murderer had been wearing it and had burnt it in stooping to turn out the gas.

In the same way, two theories were advanced to account for the blood. Mrs. Wallace (who had a cold) might have slipped the mackintosh loosely about her shoulders for warmth, let the murderer in at the door, stooped down to light the gas fire and been struck down with the mackintosh still about her; or else, the murderer might himself have put on the mackintosh to protect himself from bloodstains.

One thing seemed fairly clear: unless the murderer had had some sort of protection he must have been heavily spattered and stained with blood. Now, throughout the house, there were no signs of bloodstains (except, of course, in the sitting-room), other than the smear on the £1 note in the bedroom and a small clot on the lavatory pan in the bathroom, which, it was admitted, might have been dropped there by one of the numerous police-men [1] who were roaming about the place all night. There were no damp towels in the bathroom and no appearance that anybody had recently taken a bath. Nor was any blood found on Wallace, nor on any clothes belonging to him.

Next comes the question of the weapon. The charwoman, Sarah Jane Draper, gave evidence that since her last visit on January 7th two objects had disappeared from the house: the kitchen poker and an iron bar that was usually kept in the sitting-room for cleaning under the gas fire. Search was made for these all about the house and yard and in every conceivable place, including the drains, along the tram route between Wolverton Street and Menlove Gardens where they or one of them might have been thrown away; but neither of them was ever found. Nor was any suggestion ever put forward why two weapons should have been used or why either of them should have been removed (unless, indeed, on the general principle of "making it more difficult"). For consider: whoever did the murder, it was to his advantage to leave the weapon in the house. There are only three reasons for getting rid of a weapon: (1) To conceal the fact that a murder has been committed at all; in this case no attempt was made to pretend that the death was suicide or accident. (2) To prevent identification by finger-prints; in this case finger-prints could easily have been wiped off. (3) To destroy a ready means of identification, as, for instance, where the murderer uses his own pistol or walking-stick; in this case the weapon was identified only with the house itself, and if the murderer came from outside, the use of a weapon identified with the house would assist him in throwing the blame on Wallace, whereas, if Wallace himself was the murderer, by far the readiest way of fixing suspicion upon himself was to use a weapon belong-ing to the house *and remove it*, since its removal created a strong

[1] These included a constable, a police-sergeant, a detective-sergeant, a de-tective-inspector and a detective-superintendent. Novelists who restrict their commission of inquiry to a " man from the Yard " and a gifted amateur are letting themselves off too easily. But it is hard work inventing names and characteristics for so many different policemen.

presumption that no weapon had been brought from outside. Whichever way one looks at it, the carrying away of the weapon (still more, two weapons) was an idiotic and entirely unnecessary error, involving the risk of discovery. Still, somebody made that error and took that risk, and since it could benefit nobody it gives us no help in solving the mystery. It seems likely that the weapon actually used was the iron bar; the poker, if it was not used to break open the cabinet, may have been lost on some other occasion, or Mrs. Draper have merely imagined the loss of a poker.

The body itself was examined by various medical witnesses, who, as usual, differed a good deal about the probable time of death. Professor MacFall, called by the prosecution, judged, from the fact that *rigor mortis* was present in the neck and upper part of the right arm when he saw the corpse at ten o'clock, that death had taken place " four hours or more " before his arrival. Since Mrs. Wallace had been seen alive by the milk-boy certainly not *earlier* than 6.30, this witness *must* have been at least half an hour out in his calculations. Dr. Pierce, also a witness for the prosecution, agreed with him in giving " about six o'clock " as the probable time of death. Prosecuting counsel at this point supplied the world with an admirable example of the folly of not letting well alone :

> You say about six o'clock. What limit on either side would you give?—I would give two hours' limit on either side.
> Mr. Justice Wright (*pouncing on this admission of human fallibility*): It might have been between four and eight?—Yes, my lord.
> Counsel (*making the best of it*): Would you say that death could not possibly have occurred after eight o'clock?—I would say definitely it could not have occurred after eight o'clock.
> Cross-examining Counsel (*consolidating his advantage, after ascertaining that witness had omitted to apply all the tests he might have applied*): When you say you think it was six o'clock, it might have been four o'clock in the afternoon or might have been eight o'clock?—And there were other factors as well.
> So it follows she might have met her death at any hour within this time that night?—Yes.

From all this the detective novelist may well conclude that he ought not to allow his medical men to be too dogmatic in deducing the exact time of death from the appearance of the body. In fact, in the words of Professor Dible, F.R.C.S., who was called for the defence, "it is an enormously difficult subject, full of pitfalls". Nothing, in fact, emerged at the trial except that it was probable, on the whole, that Mrs. Wallace was murdered round about the time that Wallace left the house. This is exactly what one would expect. If Wallace did it, the only possible time was between about 6.30 and about 6.50; if anybody else did it, he would no doubt have entered the house as early as possible after Wallace's departure, so as to give himself an ample margin for retreat.

To go back to the night of the murder: Superintendent Moore, who came on the scene at 10.5, carefully examined all the doors and windows of the house, and found no signs that anyone had broken in. Having borrowed Wallace's latchkey and tried it in the front door, he found that, though it would open the door with a little trouble, the lock was defective. Wallace, when told, said, "It was not like that this morning"—though, actually, it turned out that the lock must have been out of order for some time. Wallace's first account was that the first time he tried the front door lock the key would not turn and that the second time he became convinced that the door was bolted. Superintendent Moore's account was that the key had a tendency to slip round in the lock, and "that if the key was turned beyond a certain point it would re-lock the door". At one point Wallace adopted Superintendent Moore's explanation, and was much criticized because this did not agree with his earlier account of the matter.

It seems quite possible that both Wallace's accounts were perfectly honest. When he first arrived at the house the key may have stuck in the defective lock as he said. The second time it may have turned too far, as it did with Superintendent Moore, and re-locked the door. Wallace, in the flustered state of his mind, finding that, though the key turned, the door would not open, may have jumped to the conclusion that the bolt had been shot between his two attempts. As to his saying, " it was not like that this morning ", that may amount to no more than any man's natural reluctance to admit that he can have made a conspicuous ass of himself. It is curious that he did not, apparently, on that night, inform Superintendent Moore that the door had been actually bolted when he opened it to admit P.C. Williams.

Apparently, however, he had told P.C. Williams and he may well have thought this enough. At the trial he said, wearily, that he really could not remember what he *had* said to the Superintendent. After all, when one has had to tell the same story half a dozen times in one night, and innumerable times since then, it may be difficult to remember exactly to which policeman one told what details of it.

We may bring down the curtain upon the third act of the tragedy by quoting two little word-pictures of Wallace's demeanour on that memorable night. Professor MacFall said :

> I was very struck with it, it was abnormal. He was too quiet, too collected, for a person whose wife had been killed in that way that he described. He was not nearly so affected as I was myself. . . . I think he was smoking cigarettes most of the time. Whilst I was in the room, examining the body and the blood, he came in smoking a cigarette, and he leaned over in front of the sideboard and flicked the ash into a bowl upon the sideboard. It struck me at the time as being unnatural.

Detective Inspector Herbert Gold, who arrived on the scene at 10.30, agreed that Wallace was " cool and calm ".

> When I first went into the house on the night of the murder, he was sitting in the kitchen. In fact, he had the cat on his knee and was stroking the cat, and he did not look to me like a man who had just battered his wife to death.

Wallace's own comment, in an article written after the trial, was :

For forty years I had drilled myself in iron control and prided myself on never displaying an emotion outwardly in public. I trained myself to be a stoic. My griefs and joys can be as intense as those of any man, but the rule of my life has always been to give them expression only in privacy. Stoicism is so little practised to-day that when seen it is called callousness.

The Emperor Marcus Aurelius is, it would seem, not the wisest counsellor for those who may have to make their appearance before a British jury.

At about four or five o'clock on the Wednesday morning, Wallace was allowed to leave the house to sleep—supposing he could sleep—at his sister-in-law's. During twelve hours of the next day he was detained at the police station, making a statement and answering questions about his movements on the Monday and Tuesday evenings. In particular, he was told that the fateful telephone call had been put in from a call-box in the Anfield district near his own home.

The consequence of this was that on January 22nd, happening to meet Mr. Beattie, Wallace questioned him very closely about the exact time of the call, adding, most unfortunately for himself : " I have just left the police; they have cleared me."

This conversation was reported back to the police, who, of course, pounced on it like tigers. Why should Wallace be so much interested in the time? Why should he announce that he was " cleared " when nobody, so far, had suggested that he was suspected? As to the first, Wallace replied: " I had an idea; we all have ideas; it was indiscreet of me."

Asked at the trial to amplify this cryptic remark, he explained that by this time he had realized he might be suspected and thought that, if he could ascertain from Mr. Beattie that the call had been put through at seven, whereas he himself did not leave his house till 7.15, it would be a complete proof of his innocence. Thinking it over, he saw that for him, a suspected person, to be seen talking to a witness in the case, was an indiscretion. Yes; but *why* should he imagine himself suspected? To which

Wallace replied that if his conversation with Mr. Beattie had been reported he must have been followed and watched, and that this showed clearly that he *was* suspected, a fact which he realized at the time. Looking at it from the purely common-sense point of view, one must confess that Wallace would have been a fool indeed *not* to realize that, in a case where a married woman is murdered, the husband is always the first person to be suspected. It was in fact admitted by the police witnesses at the trial that, between the time of the murder and of the arrest, Wallace had to be given police protection while he was collecting his insurance money because the people in the district were hostile to him. Some further light may be thrown on his statement, " I had ideas; we all have ideas," by the fact that on that same January 22nd he mentioned the name of a certain man, known to him and his wife and connected with the Prudential, who was the object of his own suspicions. This person turned out to have an alibi, and nothing, of course, was said about him at the trial; but it is quite likely that he may have had something to do with Wallace's indiscreet " ideas ". On the same occasion, Wallace mentioned the name of another possible suspect, and, after his death in 1933, papers were found among his belongings in which he named the murderer. Nothing, however, was discovered that definitely pointed to the guilt of anyone else, so on February 2nd Wallace was arrested and charged, and on March 4th, at the conclusion of the police court inquiry, was sent up for trial at Liverpool Assizes.

It is not neccesary to go through the trial[1] itself, since most of the important points in the evidence have already been discussed. We may, however, spend a little time in examining the theory of the prosecution as it eventually took shape in court.

The theory was that Wallace, having prepared his alibi the evening before, suggested to his wife after tea that they should

---

[1] April 22, 1931, before Mr. Justice Wright; for the Crown, Mr. E. G. Hemmerde, K.C., Recorder of Liverpool, and Mr. Leslie Walsh; for the defence, Mr. Roland Oliver, K.C., and Mr. S. Scholefield Allen.

have one of their customary violin practices in the front room. While she went to light the gas fire and get the music ready Wallace went upstairs and stripped himself naked, so that his clothes should not be stained with blood. He then slipped on the mackintosh, came down, and, catching his wife just as she was stooping to light the fire, struck her dead with repeated blows from the iron bar, with which he had already armed himself. Then, wiping his bare feet on the hearth rug, and perhaps making a hasty attempt to burn the incriminating mackintosh at the gas fire, he went upstairs, dressed, disarranged the front room and broke open the cabinet in the kitchen and then hurried out to catch his tram and establish his alibi, taking (for some reason or other) the bloodstained weapon with him.

As regards this part of the theory, several criticisms may occur to us. To commit a murder naked is no new idea; the thing was done by Courvoisier, who murdered Lord William Russell in 1840, and it was suspected in the case of Lizzie Borden, tried for murdering her father and stepmother in Fall River, Massachusetts, in 1892. But the mackintosh complicates the matter. It can scarcely be supposed to have been slipped on in order to take Mrs. Wallace more effectively by surprise; even if the poor woman had been given a preliminary warning by the startling apparition of a naked husband on the threshold, the smallness of the room would have enabled him to spring upon her before she could escape or call for assistance. The only conceivable justification for the mackintosh would be a curious prudery. That is not impossible. In the lower middle class there is no doubt many a man who would not—literally to save his life—appear mother-naked before his wife, even if he knew for certain that that astonishing sight was the last sight she was doomed ever to see in the world. Yet it seems strange that a murderer who had shown so much foresight in preparing the alibi should have allowed such a consideration to influence him. As for the suggested attempt to burn the mackintosh, a moment's thought would suggest that the proper place for that was not the gas-fire in the sitting-room, but the coal fire in the kitchen, which, at 6.30, when they had just finished tea, must have been burning cheerfully. It was stated in evidence that the mackintosh was of a material that would burn easily; an hour in the kitchen grate would probably have destroyed all but the buckle and buttons, which might easily have escaped search or identification. It is most unlikely that the burning of the mackintosh was anything but accidental, whoever committed the murder.

The second point is, of course, the witlessness of the disturbance created in the front room and elsewhere. Anybody wishing to suggest that a thief had gone upstairs would have removed the £1 notes from the middle bedroom and flung open the drawers and wardrobe as though in search for money.

The third unsatisfactory point is the time factor. It is astonishing what can be done in twenty minutes, which was the longest time possible that Wallace can have had at his disposal. Still, he must, at any rate, have washed his face, hands and feet, and that so carefully as to leave no smear of blood anywhere in the bathroom, dressed from top to toe, broken open the cabinet and rifled the cash-box and administered (again without leaving a trace) as much rough cleaning to the iron bar as would enable him to carry it away without staining anything it touched. The thorough removal of bloodstains is no very quick or easy matter, as anybody knows well who has tried to clean up the mess produced by a cut finger.

The other part of the theory brings us back to the vexed question of the locked doors. The theory was that Wallace, in order to get witnesses to his discovery of the body, pretended that he could not get in, when, in fact, he could have done so. We may, I think, dismiss any suggestion that he had in fact entered the house before encountering the Johnstons. What they heard and saw agreed very well with the estimated time of his arrival home and his account of his own actions. They heard him knocking, as he said, at the back door and, a few minutes later, met him coming down from the end of the entry as though, in the interval, he had been round to the front. If he was the murderer he would probably not risk making an actual entry, which might be observed by someone living in the street, if he was going to deny it afterwards.

Let us assume that Wallace is guilty and is endeavouring to present a picture of a murder committed by a third party. It is going to be a ticklish business—more ticklish than it appears at first sight. The proper handling of bolts and locks has in all likelihood planted more grey hairs in the heads of detective novelists and other planners of perfect murders than any other branch of this amiable study. Let us see how it must have presented itself to him—remembering that his meeting with the Johnstons was entirely fortuitous, and could not have entered into his calculations one way or the other.

First, then, the simplest way to suggest an intruder from without is, obviously, to follow the excellent example set by the wicked Elders who accused Susannah. They, it will be remembered, "opened the garden doors" and subsequently testified that an apocryphal young man had been in the garden "and opened the doors and leaped out". So, the apocryphal murderer must be supposed to have left the house by some means or other, and the most natural thing would be to make it appear that he escaped either by the front, leaving the door on the automatic lock, or by the back, leaving the door latched, or—more picturesquely—wide open as though in rapid flight. But alas! Where a murderer could get out Wallace could get in, and this would mean "discovering" the body without any witness to support him. He must, therefore, find "both doors locked against him". But he cannot *really* find them so, for two reasons: (1) because he is not skilled as the murderers of fiction in shooting inside bolts from the outside by means of strings and other gadgets, and (2) because, if he did, then by hypothesis the murderer would be still inside the house when Wallace arrived with his witnesses, and it would be exceedingly difficult to fake the hasty departure of a non-existent murderer after the door was opened. He must, then, only *pretend* to be unable to get in, and *pretend* to suppose that the murderer might be still in the house. As a matter of fact, he did say all allong that his first thought was that the murderer was still there, but that he abandoned that theory when they got in and found the house empty. Now, it is at this point that the emergence of the Johnstons from their back door must have upset the plans of a guilty Wallace most horribly. But for them he might have pretended that his knocking at the back door had disturbed the murderer, who must have then opened the kitchen door and fled while Wallace was trying the front for the second time. With the Johnstons there to see and hear anybody escaping, he could not very well put up that story.

Supposing the Johnstons had not come out, could the story have held water? The detective of fiction would say no; and for this reason: A cautious medical witness, inspecting a corpse at 9 o'clock, may find it difficult to say precisely whether the person was killed within two hours either way of 6 o'clock. But he will have no hesitation in saying whether or not death took place within the last quarter of an hour or so. "I would say definitely," said Dr. Pierce, "it could not have occurred after 8 o'clock." That being so, how could the murderer be supposed to have been occupying the time between the murder and Wallace's return? To explain such unaccountable lingering on the scene of the crime, one would have to present the picture of a thorough ransacking of the house from top to bottom; and this, as we know, was not done. But a consideration of this kind would probably not have occurred to Wallace beforehand, or perhaps to anybody except a detective novelist.

But, as things turned out, there the Johnstons were: and now what was Wallace to do about the front door? Was he still to insist that it had been bolted, put it on the bolt (if this had not been already done), and draw the Johnstons' attention to the bolt? This he certainly did not do, and it is odd that it does not seem to have occurred, either to him or to Mrs. Johnston, to verify that matter of the front door bolt while they were waiting for the police. If, on the other hand, Wallace, thinking his story over, had decided to leave the question of the bolt in a decent obscurity, it is odd that he should have persisted at the trial in asserting that it *was* bolted, when, in the meantime, the police themselves had offered him a perfectly good explanation for his inability to make the door open. Perhaps he felt that, having once told P.C. Williams the door was bolted, he had better stick to his story. Perhaps, when all is said and done, it really was bolted and he was telling the truth. The more we examine the question the more complicated it becomes, especially when we are left in such doubt as to the exact machinery of the lock.

Then again, if Wallace, having come back in the ordinary way and been unable to get in at the front, had gone round to the back and found the door locked, this ought not to have surprised or alarmed him. In the ordinary way it would be locked, since Mrs. Wallace would expect him to enter by the front. His story was that he was both surprised and alarmed. Why? Because of the queerness of the telephone call and the fact that he could see no light in the front kitchen. But if the curtains of the front kitchen window were drawn he could not have seen a light in any case, so why the alarm? To this he replied that by looking sideways at the back kitchen window one could have seen the light shining through from the front kitchen. Not if the door between the two kitchens was shut? Well, no. This did not seem satisfactory. If he thought his wife was upstairs, why did he not shout to her instead of knocking gently? Wallace replied simply that he did not think of it. If he had been trying to give the impression that the noise he made had scared the murderer away, one would rather expect him to make as much hullabaloo as possible. On the other hand, too much hullabaloo might have brought out the neighbours. The neighbours did, in point of fact, come out for another reason.

That Wallace's mind was confused, both at the time and after, about the locked doors is evident. He said, for instance, that when he could get in by neither door, he at first thought his wife might have slipped out to the post. This is inconsistent with the statement that he thought a man was in the house, but is not in itself unreasonable, and is supported by his remark to the Johnstons as he crossed the yard. He might, in that case, having tried and failed at the front door and got no answer at the back, have thought that Mrs. Wallace had "slipped out" the back way, locking the back door after her and taking the key. If so, it would naturally be useless to shout at her bedroom window, and he would go round and make another attempt on the front door while waiting for her return. And it was possibly then that he first became really disturbed in his mind. It is not easy to remember the exact sequence of one's actions or thoughts in a moment of agitation. His own phrase, used in the course of cross-examination, probably corresponds with the feelings of the normal person in such a situation: "I was both uneasy and not uneasy, if you follow me." One has often felt like that: vaguely worried yet able to present one's self with a number of possible explanations, inconsistent with one another, but all quite credible separately.

And, of course, the fact remains that both those locks *were* defective, and had been so for a long time. Whether Wallace, knowing this, used the circumstance deliberately to throw an atmosphere of confusion about the whole case, or whether he was genuinely mistaken in supposing both or either of the doors to be fastened, it seems now impossible to say. It is pretty certain that he did not himself deliberately damage either of the locks in advance in order to support his story.

Now let us take the other side of the question. Suppose Wallace was innocent, how did the murderer get in? The answer was suggested by the defence. He presented himself at the front door and was let in by Mrs. Wallace, saying that he wanted to leave a note for Wallace or wait for his return. She had thrown Wallace's mackintosh over her shoulders before opening the front door (we know she had a slight cold at the time). She took the murderer into the front parlour (the usual place for receiving guests and strangers) and was there struck down. Her skirt caught fire. The murderer extinguished the flames with the bloodstained mackintosh, turned out fire and gas-light, bolted both doors in order to have notice of Wallace's return (?), washed his hands in the back kitchen (?), rifled the cash-box and cabinet, and departed, leaving the back door latched (and the front door still bolted?) and carrying the iron bar with him (!)

There are, of course, difficulties about this too. We know that there were several people, including the two men suspected by Wallace, whom Mrs. Wallace would readily have let in if they had called. She would also, if Wallace had told her (as he said he did) about the message from "Qualtrough", have let in anyone giving that name. Whoever the caller was, he was probably known to Mrs. Wallace, so that she had to be murdered lest she should identify him later. Would not the intending murderer in that case have brought his own weapon with him? We do not know that he did not. We have no evidence that the iron bar was the weapon used. We know only that it disappeared. An outside murderer might, seeing it handy, have used it in preference to his own or, more subtly, having used his own, he might have removed the iron bar for the express purpose of incriminating Wallace. In fact, the only thoroughly satisfactory reason anybody could possibly have for taking it away would be that it was clean and, therefore, if left behind, could *not* incriminate Wallace. But one cannot expect (outside a detective novel) a thoroughly satisfactory reason for any person's actions.

An explanation of the iron bar's disappearance is offered by Miss Winifred Duke in her novel, *Skin for Skin*, which presents a reconstruction of the crime on the hypothesis that Wallace was the murderer. She makes him conceal the bar in his umbrella and drop it down a drain at the far end of his tram journey, in the neighbourhood of Menlove Gardens. The only reply that can be made to this is that the police said they had searched "everywhere", and they can scarcely have omitted to search the Menlove Gardens district. Wallace could scarcely have carried it very far afield, for his time-table leaves no room for such an excursion. If the bar had been found in the neighbourhood, it would have certainly incriminated Wallace. Since it was never found it incriminates nobody, and such witness as it bears is slightly in Wallace's favour. Its chief function is to darken counsel. Indeed, the iron bar has bothered everybody who has attempted to deal critically with the case.

Our alternative theory does indeed leave us with a blood-stained murderer obliged to clean himself and escape. But whereas Wallace had twenty minutes only in which to do everything and then travel by tram, the "other man" had getting on for two hours and might then remove himself inconspicuously on foot (possibly to a bicycle, or a car parked somewhere handy). He had more time for cleaning, and he need not appear so scrupulously clean.

Further, we are not obliged to suppose that the outside murderer went upstairs at all. The £1 notes would then be left unappropriated because he never went near them, and the bath-room clean and dry because he did not wash himself there. As for the front bedroom, the likeliest explanation of all is that the murderer never went there and had nothing to do with it. His ring at the door may have disturbed Mrs. Wallace when she was engaged in turning over the bedding for some domestic purpose of her own. Perhaps she had piled the bed-clothes and pillows on the foot of the bed, and they fell off, as they usually do in such circumstances. The appearance of the room, as described, is more suggestive of some such household accident than of a search by a thief.

The trial itself occupied four days. Wallace himself made a very good witness—too good, perhaps, for a jury. He was, as ever, "cool and collected", and there is no kind of prisoner a jury dislikes so much, except, indeed, a hot and agitated one. But he impressed the judge. "When reference is made to discrepancies in his statement," said Mr. Justice Wright summing up, "I cannot help thinking it is wonderful how his statements are as lucid and consistent as they have been." Counsel for the prosecution, though as usual conspicuously fair in the general treatment of the case, perhaps helped a little to confuse the issues by arguing, from time to time, as though the defence was that "Qualtrough's" call was a genuine business inquiry, which it could not on any hypothesis have been; while Mr. Roland Oliver, in endeavouring to cast contempt upon the theory of the prosecution, asked the prisoner, absurdly enough, " Were you accustomed to play the violin naked in a mackintosh?" which again confused the issue. The defence also attacked the police vigorously for not having called the newspaper girl and the little boys who supported her testimony, going so far as to accuse them of deliberately suppressing evidence in order to give colour to their case. This may have prejudiced the jury, who commonly do not care to hear the police attacked, though the judge, while deprecating the attack, said he thought the police had committed an error of judgment. There was probably also a certain amount of prejudice arising from the evidence that had already come out in the magistrate's court, and from the general tendency to suspect married persons of murdering one another. But the chief difficulty in the way of the defence was the difficulty with which we started out: that the common man, however well he knows that his duty is to ask, " Did this man do it?" will insist on asking instead, " Who could have done it, if not this man?" It is perfectly evident, in the judge's summing-up, that he was aware of this difficulty. He summed up dead in the prisoner's favour, and again and again repeated his caution that the verdict must be given according to the evidence.

Members of the jury, you, I believe, are living more or less in this neighbourhood: I come here as a stranger . . . you must approach this matter without any preconceived notions at all. Your business here is to listen to the evidence, and to consider the evidence and nothing else. A man cannot be convicted of any crime, least of all murder, merely on probabilities . . . if you have other possibilities, a jury would not, and I believe ought not to, come to the conclusion that the charge is established. . . . The question is not: Who did this crime? The question is: Did the prisoner do it? . . . It is not a question of determining who or what sort of person other than the prisoner did the crime or could have done the crime; it is a question whether it is brought home to the prisoner, and whether it is brought home by the evidence. If every matter relied on as circumstantial is equally or substantially consistent both with the guilt or innocence of the prisoner, the multiplication of those instances may not take you any further in coming to a conclusion of guilt. . . . In conclusion I will only remind you what the question you have to determine is. The question is: Can you have any doubt that the prisoner did it? You may think: "Well, some one did it." . . . Can you say it was absolutely impossible that there was no such person [as an unknown murderer]? . . . Can you say . . . that you are satisfied beyond reasonable doubt that it was the hand of the prisoner, and no other hand, that murdered this woman? If you are not so satisfied, if it is not proved, whatever your feelings may be . . . then it is your duty to find the prisoner not guilty.

The jury, after an hour's retirement, found the prisoner guilty.

The prisoner, being asked if he had anything to say, briefly replied: " I am not guilty. I don't want to say anything else."

In passing sentence, the judge, whose summing-up had been a most brilliant exposition of the inconclusive nature of the evidence, pointedly omitted the customary expression of agreement with the verdict.

It is said that, when the verdict was announced, a gasp of surprise went round the court. On the general public, if not on the jury, the summing-up had produced a deep impression.

Nor, whatever rumours may have been going about beforehand in the neighbourhood of Wolverton Street, was the main body of Liverpudlians at all happy about the conviction. Their extreme uneasiness led to one result which was logical enough, no doubt, but highly unusual in this Christian country: a special Service of Intercession was held in Liverpool Cathedral that God might guide the Court of Criminal Appeal to a right decision when the case of Wallace came before it.

The answer to prayer might be considered spectacular. On May 19th, the Lords of Appeal, after a two days' hearing quashed the conviction on the ground that the evidence was insufficient to support the verdict; this being the first time in English legal history that a conviction for murder had been set aside on those grounds. The phrasing of the judgment is exceedingly cautious, but, in the words of the learned barrister to whom we owe the best and fullest study of this extraordinary case:

> The fact that the Court of Criminal Appeal decided to quash the conviction shows how strong must have been the views of the judges that the verdict was not merely against the weight of evidence, but that it was unreasonable.

Judges in this country are, indeed, exceedingly jealous of any interference with the powers and privileges of a jury, and will in general always uphold its verdict unless they see very strong reason to the contrary.

The judgments of God, unlike those of earthly judges, are, however, inscrutable. Any writer of fiction rash enough to embellish his *dénouement* with an incident so unlikely as a public appeal to Divine Justice must interpret the answer according to his own theological fancy. If he believes that the All-Just and All-Merciful declared for the innocent through the mouths of the Lords of Appeal, the facts will support that theory; but if he believes that the world is ruled by an ingenious sadist, eager to wring the last ounce of suffering out of an offending creature, he may point out that Wallace was preserved only to suffer two years of complicated mental torture and to die at length by a far crueller death than the hangman's rope. Like every other piece of testimony in the Wallace case, the evidence may be interpreted both ways.

The Prudential Assurance Company, who had behaved throughout in a very friendly way to Wallace, expressed their full belief in his innocence by at once taking him back and giving him a new job in their employment. It was, however, impossible for him to continue with his work as a collector on account of the suspicion which still clung about him. He was, in fact, obliged to leave Liverpool and retire to a cottage in Cheshire. The diary which he kept for a year after his release contains many references to the rebuffs he received from his former acquaintances, together with expressions of his love for his wife which have every appearance of being genuine. He seems to have spent his spare time pottering about his garden and equipping his home with little ingenious household gadgets, and trying every means to fight off the appalling loneliness of spirit which threatened to overcome him. "What I fear most is the long nights." "I seem to miss her more and more, and cannot drive the thought of her cruel end out of my mind." "There are now several daffodils in bloom, and lots of tulips coming along. How delighted dear Julia would have been, and I can only too sadly picture how lovingly she would have tended the garden."

On September 14, 1931, occurs a remarkable passage:

> Just as I was going to dinner —— stopped me, and said he wanted to talk to me for a few minutes. It was a desperately awkward position. Eventually I decided not to hear what he had to say. I told him I would talk to him some day and give him something to think about. He must realize that I suspect him of the terrible crime. I fear I let him see clearly what I thought, and it may unfortunately put him on his guard. I wonder if it is any good putting a private detective on to his track in the hope of something coming to light. I am more than half persuaded to try it.

Other allusions to the same person are made from time to time. Are we to believe them sincere? Or must we suppose that all this was part of some strange elaborate scheme for bamboozling the world through the medium of a private diary, which there was no reason to suppose that anyone was likely to see but Wallace himself? That he should have made this kind of accusation (as he did) in newspaper articles proves nothing; but the diary (which is far more restrained and convincing in style than the statements published over his signature) is another matter. One can only say that, if he was a guilty man, he kept up the pretence of innocence to himself with an extraordinary assiduity and appearance of sincerity.

On February 26, 1933, Wallace died of cancer of the kidneys. It is, of course, well known that disease affecting those organs produces very remarkable and deleterious changes in a person's character; but whether the trouble had already begun in 1931, and if so, whether it could have resulted in so strange a madness, with such a combination of cunning and bestial ferocity as the murderer of Julia Wallace displayed, is a matter for physicians to judge. So far as can be seen, Wallace showed no signs of mental or spiritual deterioration either before or after the crime.

It is interesting to compare the case of Wallace with that of the unfortunate clergyman, the Rev. J. S. Watson, who in 1869 murdered his wife under rather similar circumstances. Here, again, it was the case of a childless couple who had married for love and lived peaceably together for many years. The husband, a man of mild behaviour and considerable literary ability, suddenly seized the opportunity one afternoon, when the servant was out of the house, to batter his wife to death with exactly the same uncontrolled brutality as was used on Mrs. Wallace. But here the resemblance ends. Poor Mr. Watson had for some time shown symptoms of melancholia and disturbance of mind; the wife was known to drink; there had been quarrels; and the husband, though at first he denied his guilt, soon after made an attempt at suicide and confessed the crime; nor, though he at first made some blundering efforts to cover up his tracks, did Watson contrive anything remotely approaching the elaborate ingenuity of the "Qualtrough" alibi. The superficial resemblances only serve to emphasize the fundamental disparity between the two cases.

Though a man apparently well-balanced may give way to a sudden murderous frenzy, and may even combine that frenzy with a surprising amount of coolness and cunning, it is rare for him to show *no* premonitory or subsequent symptoms of mental disturbance. This was one of the psychological difficulties in the way of the prosecution against Wallace. Dr. MacFall gave it as his opinion that the brutality of the murder was a sign of frenzy. He was asked:

> So, if this is the work of a maniac, and Wallace is a sane man, he did not do it?—He may be sane now.

> If he has been sane all his life, and is sane now, it would be some momentary frenzy?—The mind is very peculiar.

> The fact that a man has been sane fifty-two years, and has been sane while in custody for the last three months, would rather tend to prove that he has always been sane?—Not necessarily.... We know very little about the private lives of persons or their thoughts.

The mind is indeed peculiar and the thoughts of the heart hidden. It is hopeless to explain the murder of Julia Wallace as the result of a momentary frenzy, whether Wallace was the criminal or another. The crime was carefully prepared in cold blood; the extraordinary ferocity of the actual assault was probably due less to frenzied savagery than to sudden alarm at the actual moment of the murder. It has, over and over again, come as a shocking surprise to murderers that their victims took so long to die and make such a mess about it; they have struck repeated blows, to make sure, confessing afterwards, "I thought she would never die"; "Who could have thought that the old man had so much blood in him?"

Before leaving the case for the consideration of those who may like to make of it a "tale for a chimney-corner", two small points ought perhaps to be mentioned. One is the statement made by a young woman at the trial that on the night of the murder she saw Wallace at about 8.40 at night "talking to a man" at the bottom of the entry to Richmond Park, near Breck Road. She did not know Wallace at all well, and he himself denied the whole episode. In all probability she was quite mistaken, nor could anything very much be made out of the story either by the prosecution or the defence; it is mentioned here only for completeness and for the sake of any suggestion it may offer for the novelist's ingenuity to work upon. The only practical step that was taken about it seems to have been that the police made an especially careful search of the waste ground in and about Richmond Park in the hope of finding the iron bar; but without success.

The second point concerns the choice of the name "Qualtrough". This name is extremely common in the Isle of Man, and should also, therefore, be pretty familiar to Liverpudlians. It might therefore seem a suspicious circumstance that Wallace should have professed never to have heard it before, but that it was apparently unknown also to Mr. Beattie, and that among Wallace's other acquaintances at the chess club only one said he had "heard it once before". Now, if one is preparing to give a false name, one will, as a rule, give a name that is exceedingly common, such as Brown or Smith, or one that is subconsciously already in one's mind for some reason or another. Since, to Manxmen, the name "Qualtrough" is apparently as familiar as "Smith" to an Englishman, it might seem reasonable to look for a murderer who either came from Man, or frequently went there for reasons of business or pleasure. On the other hand, if it could be shown that Wallace (either through the books of the Prudential or in some other connexion) had recently had the name brought to his notice, then that fact would strengthen suspicion against him, particularly in view of his categorical statement that he had never heard it before. It is a little curious that if the name was exceedingly well known in that part of Liverpool, no one should have drawn attention to the fact in evidence. The detective writer ought not, I think, to neglect that line of investigation.

There, then, the story remains, a mystery as insoluble as when the Court of Appeal decided that there was no evidence upon which to come to a conclusion. "We are not," said the Lord Chief Justice, "concerned here with suspicion, however grave, or with theories, however ingenious." But the detective novelist does, and must, concern himself with ingenious theories, and here is a case ready made for him, in which scarcely any "theory, however ingenious" could very well come amiss. It is interesting that the story should already have been handled twice by writers of fiction, and both times from the point of view that Wallace may have been guilty. Mr. George Goodchild and Mr. C. E. Bechhofer Roberts in *The Jury Disagree* have used the case only as a basis on which to erect a story which includes fresh incidents and complications not forming part of the actual evidence, and have given it a 'key-incident' solution in the recognized 'detective' manner. Miss Winifred Duke, in *Skin for Skin*, has followed the facts with scrupulous exactness, concerning herself almost exclusively with the psychological problem of how Wallace might have come to do it (if he did do it) and what effect it had upon him.

With both novels, the criminal's motive may be summed-up in the cynical words of *Marriage à la Mode*:

PALAMEDE: O, now I have found it! you dislike her for no other reason but that she's your wife.

RHODOPHIL: And is not that enough?

It remains for some other writer, who does not find it "enough", or who is convinced by his study of the case that Wallace was telling the truth, or who merely prefers the more out-of-the-way solution to the more obvious one, to tell the story again, identifying "Qualtrough" with that to us unknown man whom Wallace himself named as the murderer.

BIBLIOGRAPHY

Books Dealing with the Case Itself

The Trial of William Herbert Wallace, edited with an Introduction by W. F. Wyndham-Brown, Barrister-at-Law of the Middle Temple and of the Northern Circuit. London: Victor Gollancz, 1933.

This is the fullest account of the case available in book form. I am indebted to it for the greater part of the evidence at the trial, for the judgment on Appeal, and for the quotations taken from Wallace's diary.

Six Trials, by Winifred Duke. London: Victor Gollancz, 1934.

A clear summary of the case in brief compass, under the title: "The Perfect Murder"

Newspaper Reports

The following may be consulted under the dates of the inquest, magistrates' inquiry, trial and appeal:

Liverpool Post and Mercury; Liverpool Daily Echo; Liverpool Weekly Post.

Fiction Based on the Case

The Jury Disagree, by George Goodchild and C. E. Bechhofer Roberts ("Ephesian"). London: Jarrolds, 1934.

Skin for Skin, by Winifred Duke. London: Victor Gollancz, 1935.

PART VI

THE RATTENBURY CASE

by Francis Iles

DEDICATED TO

WILLIAM ROUGHEAD, Esq., W.S.

MAESTRO OF CRIMINOLOGICAL ESSAYISTS

THE RATTENBURY CASE

IT was the women of England who hanged Mrs. Edith
Thompson: or so, at any rate, it has been said.

"Away with this vamp!" they are reputed to have cried in
their hearts. "Away with this wrecker of the sacred Home,
which is our chief means of livelihood! Away with this blot
upon our profession of Wife! We will teach all such that they
had better be content with their allowance of one man apiece,
or it will be the worse for them. Away, above all, with this
stealer of young men, when young men are so scarce! To our
daughters we owe it no less than to ourselves, and therefore we
cry 'Away with her!'"

If this be true, the women of England acted only as their
instincts bade them. When society is threatened, it will coalesce
in one mass to crush the menace. Proust (was it Proust?) has
said that in such a case society will open its ranks to include many
whom normally it is unwilling to receive. In this instance many
strange shoulders must have rubbed together; for in their determination to destroy anything that is out of pattern, women are
more united and at the same time more ruthless than men. Moreover, here it was the institution of the Home itself that was
threatened; and when that happens it is the women, not the men,
who rush as one person, as if in mere self-preservation, to the
defence.

However, if it was the women of England who hanged Mrs.
Thompson, against all reason and all justice, then it was equally
due to the women of England that Mrs. Rattenbury was saved
from the gallows; for if Mrs. Thompson had not been hanged,
Mrs. Rattenbury surely would have been.

It is impossible to avoid comparing these two cases; for not
only the cases themselves but the characters of the two women
concerned had so many points in common. The factors that are
common to both cases are obvious: the points of character

scarcely less so. Both women possessed that strange force and power of impressing the other sex, which derives from an ego-centric neuroticism in the female. (In the male it is interesting to note the reverse is usually the case : women are more difficult to bamboozle in this particular respect—though to make up for that they are a great deal easier in other and no less fatal respects.)

Both, again, were highly-strung, excitable, and at times hysterical ; both were inevitably wrapped up in themselves and their own affairs. But whereas Mrs. Rattenbury's vices were of the usual, ordinary kind which in a higher stratum of society are taken for granted, or even admired, Mrs. Thompson was Woman Herself : essential Woman, raised to a super-normal degree. (That if anything was what frightened the women of England about her. Every feminine attribute which they saw and admired in themselves, they had to recognize in Mrs. Thompson developed to a pitch far beyond their own ; in every department of their sex they were outclassed. Perhaps it was not only the women of England who were frightened, after all.)

But if the characters of these two women are comparable in some degree, the two young men whom they officially ' led astray ' were quite dissimilar.

Bywaters was, fundamentally, a decent lad ; and it is an irony that it was his very decency which led him to murder. Dismissing the theory that his murder was committed on the spur of a momentary intolerable impulse (and anyone who has seen the knife which Bywaters carried with him that night will have difficulty in maintaining this theory : it was not the kind of knife which would sit comfortably in the pocket of even a ship's steward), one may yet believe that he had had almost to drive himself to murder, as a point of honour. For a decent man, when he feels his passion for a woman waning, will go to much greater lengths on her behalf than when his love was at its height, with some obscure idea of proving to himself as well as to her that he would not be such a cad as to fall out of love with her. A man less punctilious will not feel this impulse.

So it may have been with Bywaters; but so it certainly was not with Stoner.

For Stoner there is not very much to be said, though there is a little. His motive was, in all probability, mainly a sordid one, though we shall see that to some extent it may have been mixed. As to his character, the evidence of a relative at his trial that Stoner was " a good, honest lad and the best boy he had ever seen in his life" may be excused as an exaggeration due to *ex parte* prejudice. Stoner may not have been the worst lad in the world, but he certainly possessed his share of unpleasing points.

The Rattenburys were both Canadian by birth. Francis Mawson Rattenbury, sixty-seven years old at the time of the crime, was a retired architect. By a previous marriage he had two sons, now adult. Mrs. Rattenbury was a good-looking woman of thirty-eight. She had been married twice before. Her first husband was killed in the war; from the second she was divorced. By the latter she had a son aged thirteen who was away at school in March 1935. Mr. and Mrs. Rattenbury had a joint son, John, six years old at that date. Since his birth Mrs. Rattenbury had, in the useful phrase, not 'lived with' her husband.

In 1935 the Rattenburys were living at the Villa Madeira, Manor Road, Bournemouth, a stuffy little house which was definitely below the standard of life to which their income entitled them. It is not possible to say exactly how much that income was; but Mrs. Rattenbury in her evidence accounted for at least £1,000 a year which passed through her own hands, so that it is not unreasonable to suppose that the total income must have been anything from £1,500 to £2,000 a year.

Mr. Rattenbury himself, though not an impossible person, seems not to have been a very lovable one. He was close with money, and his wife had to lie to him freely in order to obtain the sums she wanted; though it is quite possible that she wanted too much, and wanted it for purposes of which few husbands could approve. His temper was uncertain, and there was a fair amount of bickering and quarrels. Mr. Rattenbury also talked a great deal about committing suicide; but one evening when his wife, bored by mere talk, challenged him to proceed to action in the matter, Mr. Rattenbury evidently saw the error of his words, for he blacked her eye for her. With pardonable exasperation Mrs. Rattenbury retaliated by biting the arm that struck her, and thought so highly of her black eye that she called in her doctor at midnight to attend to it and kept it in bed for three days.

The doctor's opinion, as expressed later, was that Mr. Rattenbury was "a very charming, quiet man", and it must therefore have been something of a surprise to him to see the havoc this charming, quiet man had wrought. However, he refrained, with or without an effort, from asking any questions as to what might have made the quiet charm temporarily slip, and proceeded to dress Mrs. Rattenbury's wounds. After that he gave her a quarter of a grain of morphia to quieten her (one may imagine that she needed quietening), and then went downstairs to remonstrate with the forceful sexagenarian. It appeared, however, that Mr. Rattenbury had gone back on his blow, for he had left the house still threatening suicide. The doctor, who seems to have revised his optimistic opinion of Mr. Rattenbury by this time, thought seriously enough of the incident to inform the police. (It may be worth mentioning that the quarter-grain of morphia gave Mrs. Rattenbury eight hours' sound sleep, and that when the doctor saw her the next morning she was peaceful and calm: one of those small points, so insignificant at the time, which assume an unexpected importance later.)

It is upon little snapshots such as this that an appreciation must always be based of the everyday life in a household to which murder comes later, usually as a quite unexpected visitor; but it must not be forgotten that such snapshots show the high lights only. Eyes were not being blacked in the Villa Madeira every day.

It was almost every other day, however, that the doctor was being called in. Between March 1934 and February 1935 he saw Mrs. Rattenbury at least seventy times, with fees amounting to over fifty guineas. In his evidence the doctor was a little cautious about the reasons for these visits, and many of them appear to have followed a summons due to excitability, temperament, or any other upsetting cause. Mrs. Rattenbury's motto, in fact, seems to have been: when in a tantrum, send for the doctor. She had, however, been genuinely suffering from pulmonary tuberculosis since 1932, and in that year she was sent to a nursing-home for a fortnight's observation.

This doctor was not only Mrs. Rattenbury's medical attendant for two and a half years but something of a family friend, and his is the only outside evidence we have of the conditions and temperaments at the Villa Madeira. It is interesting, therefore, to learn that Mr. Rattenbury had mentioned many times to the doctor his wish to commit suicide; so that it seems established that this "very charming, quiet man" had a definitely morbid streak in him—except, no doubt, late at night, as we shall see.

Concerning Mrs. Rattenbury the doctor sounds a little careful. His description of her temperament as 'uneven' strikes one as a kindly understatement, and under pressure he amended this to 'excitable'; and he attributed her sudden fits of excitement sometimes to too much alcohol and sometimes "if there were any upset or she was cross".

"So when she was cross or there was an upset, she sent for you, did she?" asked counsel; and the doctor agreed that "if it was necessary" she did so. This seems a perfect little picture of an excitable, rather silly woman, and it fits nicely with Miss Riggs' equally graphic remark that Mrs. Rattenbury "ran about a good deal".

However, reading between the lines of the doctor's evidence, one gathers the impression that in spite of her tantrums he liked Mrs. Rattenbury as a person, and he emphasized her devotion to her children, particularly to little John.

On the whole, however, notwithstanding a very infrequent black eye and a less infrequent tantrum or two, the relations of Mr. and Mrs. Rattenbury at this time (1934) were not unfriendly; and when asked at her trial if her married life had been happy, Mrs. Rattenbury threw out her hand and said simply: " Like that ". At the same time she admitted frankly that she had not loved her husband and, if he had wanted his rights as a husband in March 1935, she would not have been willing to give them to him. Taking it by and large, then, married life at the Villa Madeira up till 1935 must have been, below the surface, much the same as married life in any other British villa where a lady with a temperament was living with a husband old enough to be her father.

That surface was, however, definitely different.

For one thing, the Rattenburys kept a chef, a figure that must be rare in the smaller villas of Britain. (There was no chef employed after Stoner was engaged; and one of the minor mysteries about this strange household is: Who did the cooking? Presumably Miss Irene Riggs, along with all the rest of the work of the house; but this seems a curious descent from the glory of a chef.) Another point of difference between the Villa Madeira and other villas was the amount of drink consumed.

Perhaps we begin to see here why the Rattenburys' standard of living was not up to their income. There may have been method in Mr. Rattenbury's meanness. What they saved on the rent they could spend on drink. Both Mr. and Mrs. Rattenbury had a weakness for the bottle.

Mrs. Rattenbury's preference was for cocktails and wine; and it is depressing, but at the same time illuminating, to learn that the cocktails consumed at the Villa Madeira were bought ready-made. Anyone who has sampled the usual ready-made cocktail, consisting of almost undiluted Italian vermouth, will understand why this information should be depressing. Its illumination lies in showing that Mrs. Rattenbury evidently drank cocktails for the sake of drinking cocktails and not for any finer points, such as flavour. We have no information about the wine that was drunk at the Villa Madeira, and possibly we are spared some rather hideous knowledge.

Mrs. Rattenbury did not drink steadily, but in bouts. In her own somewhat peculiar words: " My life with Mr. Rattenbury was so what you call monotonous that at times I used to take too many cocktails to bring up one's spirits—take them to excess." Mr. Rattenbury, on the other hand, stuck to whisky, and appears to have drunk it in doses as regular as they were large. " He always was jolly, late at night," said his wife of him in her evidence, and this almost casual remark is interesting. To keep up the practice over years of becoming ' jolly ' every night will need larger and larger quantities of whisky. By the time one is sixty-seven it will need a very large amount indeed. One may safely say, therefore, that Mr. Rattenbury was an exceptionally heavy drinker.

Besides Mr. and Mrs. Rattenbury and their small son, the only other occupant of the household in 1934 was Miss Irene Riggs, the ' maid-companion '—or perhaps it should be ' companion-help '. Miss Riggs in any case was not quite in the position of a servant. She was on terms of intimate friendship with Mrs. Rattenbury, who called her ' darling ', and she found the household an ' extremely pleasant ' one.

Miss Riggs did, however, consider its atmosphere " just a little unusual ", though she did not find it strange that Mrs. Rattenbury should have the habit of patrolling the garden late at night in her pyjamas, or stay up all night long playing the piano or the gramophone. And here Miss Riggs artlessly voiced a profound truth of human nature. Had she from the fastness of her own bed heard Mrs. Rattenbury making this music downstairs in the sitting-room all night long, Miss Riggs would doubtless have thought it very queer indeed; but, in fact, she found it quite normal and ordinary, " because I used to be with her ". It is always the things that other people do which are queer, never the things one does oneself.

It is necessary to keep this truth constantly in the mind for a proper understanding of the protagonist here (the court regarded Mrs. Rattenbury as the protagonist in this domestic drama, although it was not her hand which wielded the mallet, and we may as well accept the court's ruling). We may find the things that Mrs. Rattenbury did very strange and queer. To Mrs. Rattenbury herself they would appear not merely ordinary but inevitable, simply because it was she who was doing them.

Mrs. Rattenbury was a woman of some small culture—though some of her turns of phrase were a little odd. At any rate she had had a musical education of a sort, and between bouts she used to compose songs, with which under the pseudonym of ' Lozanne' she had had a certain success. She was also probably ' artistic', if one could be sure what that horrible word exactly means.

This, then, was the household which George Percy Stoner entered in September 1934; ignorant then, no doubt, of the terms upon which he was doing so.

Now habits, good or bad, must not be confused with character. They are not always even a reflection of character any more than accomplishments are. Bad habits, in fine, do not necessarily mean a bad character.

Mrs. Rattenbury had one or two unfortunate habits, just as she had two or three unfortunate characteristics. Her mode of life, which she herself, of course, found perfectly normal, caused a British judge and jury subsequently to shudder. She, undoubtedly, was what the British lower middle-class would call a ' bad' woman. And calling her this, they would, in the usual wholesale way, deny her any redeeming qualities at all.

And no doubt so far as the petty vices go, the little vices of the body, we may all join in righteous condemnation of Mrs. Rattenbury. We may hold up pious hands of horror that a woman could drink too many cocktails, seduce a possibly innocent lad, smoke too many cigarettes, and all the rest of it. But these things are not the worst in the world. The personal vices, which leave any other individual untouched, are only minor ones; it is those which involve hurt, spiritual or physical, to another person that are the important ones. It may be argued, as indeed it was in court, that Mrs. Rattenbury by becoming his mistress caused definite hurt to Stoner, and we shall consider this question later. Here it is enough to say that, even if this is true, the damage done was completely unconscious; and that does make a difference.

For without in any way defending or excusing this woman and her foolishness, one must in honesty say that in the greater vices, the mean vices of the spirit, she seems to have been completely lacking. She was, on the contrary, in this respect rather fine: impulsively generous on the whole; and allowing for her temperament, unselfish; truthful; so far as one can judge, honest; and certainly kind-hearted. To sand the sugar, to overwork an underpaid apprentice, to lend money on oppressive terms, to bully the weak, to terrify the timid, to cheat one's neighbour within the law: all these things are worse than drinking too many cocktails—worse even than hiring a young lout to satisfy the urgings of an over-ardent nature. So let the many citizens of credit and blameless renown, who habitually indulge these spiritual vices, think twice before they condemn the merely physical ones. (But, of course, they will not think even once.)

After all, everyone who came into contact with Mrs. Rattenbury seems to have liked her at once, and gone on liking her; and that is not only sound evidence of character but a thing that few of us can say of ourselves.

Above all, let those frigid souls who, having only feeble ones of their own, consider that all sexual promptings are a matter of deliberate choice by a vicious nature, or at least are subject to easy control, try to realize that all people are not like themselves. This is the official attitude towards all questions of sex in our Criminal Courts, and it is a regrettable one.

For it was this unkindness of Nature which was to prove fatal to Mrs. Rattenbury, and this almost alone. And it must be admitted that here Mrs. Rattenbury had bad luck. Even in a country notorious for its female frigidity, there are plenty of exceptions; but warm blood brings few of its possessors to the dock on a charge of murder.

For Mrs. Rattenbury was, to put it at its lowest, a highly-sexed woman. She was also an attractive one, and she was married to an elderly and possibly impotent husband. For six years she and her husband had occupied separate rooms. The situation must have been irksome to her. So after bearing it as long as she could, she followed the example of her betters and advertised for a chauffeur. It may be taken for granted that she looked over the applicants with a more than usually critical eye.

The successful candidate for this dual post was George Percy Stoner, a youth of seventeen and a half, lustier than he looked, the son of a bricklayer. Whether or no Stoner intentionally deceived Mrs. Rattenbury about his age, she certainly did not realize when she engaged him that he was so young. However that may be, in September 1934 young Stoner entered on his nominal duties as chauffeur, which consisted chiefly in driving the small boy to and from school every day, at a salary of £1 a week. On November 22nd he embarked on his real job, and became Mrs. Rattenbury's lover, at no official increase in salary. Whatever his capabilities in the former rôle, there is reason to believe than in the latter he was more than satisfactory.

Stoner was a lad whose physical properties as an adult outstripped his mental ones. As a child he had been backward in everything. He could not walk until he was three; he was anything but brilliant at his lessons, and indeed had very little schooling; his health was indifferent. As a boy he had few friends, and those younger than himself. It is significant that, at his trial, the only evidence of character called on his behalf was that of close relations, which has little value. However, it was plain that in his post at the Villa Madeira he worked hard at his new duties; for his parents noticed that by Christmas he had become much paler, his eyes sunken and his face drawn.

At first Stoner continued to sleep at home and presented himself for duty by day only. Mrs. Rattenbury would occasionally accompany John in the car to school, and there were other expeditions in these early days, including a trip to Oxford, where they stayed the night. On this occasion, however, Mrs. Rattenbury took Miss Riggs with them, as chaperon. It was the last pleasure-trip that was to come the way of poor Miss Riggs who, in the pre-Stoner period, had usually shared Mrs. Rattenbury's jaunts to London and elsewhere.

With tolerable swiftness the relations between Mrs. Rattenbury and her young chauffeur became more friendly. It is always surprising to realize, in retrospect, how short was the period during which an important development occurred, when its progress at the time seemed so leisurely and gradual. These two must have seemed to themselves quite old friends when, early in November, Stoner confided to Mrs. Rattenbury that there was something queer about his brain for which he had to take a mysterious medicine. The nature of the medicine he refused to divulge.

Here Stoner seems to have been taking a leaf out of Mrs. Rattenbury's own book. It is a symptom of the kind of temperament and mentality with which Mrs. Rattenbury was afflicted, that the chief topic of conversation on the part of the victims is themselves: their feelings, their sufferings and, by obvious implication, their own singular importance. Evidently Stoner felt that the boot should not be confined to one foot. He could play that game too.

He succeeded to a degree that must have gratified him. Mrs. Rattenbury was duly alarmed, and questioned him closely. Under the interrogation he still refused to say what it was that he was taking for this curious malady, but assured his employer that whatever it might be he was taking it only two or three times a year and would soon have to take it no more, for the malady would in time be outgrown. This rather tame development of a promising piece of bluff may have been due to an inkling that part of Mrs. Rattenbury's alarm was not on Stoner's behalf at all but on that of little John, who was being driven to school daily by a self-confessedly queer brain, and that if he overplayed his hand he might lose his job. If so, Stoner had suspected rightly. Mrs. Rattenbury was not yet such a fool as she became later. She did, in fact, continue after this revelation to watch Stoner with some anxiety for a week or two, until reassured that, whatever this unnamed malady might be, it did not appear to be making her employee in any way abnormal.

There is a cunning about this piece of strategic counterbluff which arouses the admiration. It may have been an unconscious lesson that Stoner had learned, but it turned the tables so completely. No doubt it was prompted by Mrs. Rattenbury's notorious horror of drugs; and if so, calculated or instinctive, it was a move which could not have been bettered. Nothing was more likely to engage Mrs. Rattenbury's shuddering interest and goodwill. There was, of course, not a word of truth in it; and it is therefore all the more amusing to note that it was this inspired invention on Stoner's part that became the groundwork on which his entire defence at the trial was subsequently based.

On November 22nd, as we have seen, Mrs. Rattenbury became Stoner's mistress. The details attending this important and fatal event in the lives of both participants are unfortunately not known to us. The usual and easy view is that wicked Mrs. Rattenbury, a woman of thirty-eight, deliberately seduced the young and innocent lad of seventeen and a half. Perhaps she did. Without doubt she had intended this *dénouement* from the first. On the other hand, perhaps not so much seduction was required. And we have no evidence that Stoner, even at seventeen and a half, was innocent. The chances, for one reason and another, are probably against it. And even if he had been inexperienced, he was a lad of strong passions, too; and it is quite on the cards that, even while Mrs. Rattenbury was considering how to bring the event about, Stoner, too, was wondering whether *he* might not be able to seduce this charming lady who was plainly so much interested in him already.

There is no question of defending or condemning this event, nor does it matter to this account whether it was, absolutely, a good or a bad thing. The important question is not what we think about it, but what the two people concerned thought. To arrive at that we must get away from the atmosphere of the courts, with their necessarily conventional outlook and their complete disregard of human nature and of the difference between human beings. The court held, as it was almost bound to hold, that Mrs. Rattenbury wickedly seduced Stoner, knowing it to be an evil

226

action. The truth probably lies in Mrs. Rattenbury's reply to the direct question of whether it was she who had taken the initiative: " No, I think it was mutual." Certainly Mrs. Rattenbury (whether through moral deficiency or any other cause, does not matter) had no idea that she was doing a deliberately wicked thing. Equally certainly, neither she nor Stoner would have thought that it was anything to make such a fuss about. No doubt this was very reprehensible of both of them, but that is how things are in the event.

After the liaison had been consummated, then, a bedroom was put at Stoner's disposal at the Villa Madeira. He left his home and in future occupied either this bedroom or Mrs. Rattenbury's from night to night as was the more convenient. Mr. Rattenbury, it may be said, slept downstairs.

Mr. Rattenbury, indeed, who could not have been ignorant of this arrangement, appears to have regarded it with equanimity. Two years earlier he had told his wife to lead her own life, and shortly after Stoner had moved into the house Mrs. Rattenbury informed her husband that she had taken him at his word. Mr. Rattenbury's reaction to this engaging frankness is not recorded, but it seems that only one person viewed the situation with disfavour. Miss Riggs, the close friend and confidante of Mrs. Rattenbury for the last four years, could naturally not feel enthusiastic about being supplanted.

Mrs. Rattenbury now had things as she wanted them; and if she had kept both her head and a firm hand on the situation, the secrets of the Villa Madeira would never have found their way into gleeful print. But she did not. She committed the mistake, fatal in her case, of falling in love with Stoner.

The fatal element was Mrs. Rattenbury's generosity. In a material way she could express her affection only by showering gifts upon its object; and upon Stoner she now proceeded to shower ten-pound notes, silk pyjamas, gold watches, and anything else for which he expressed a wish. For a young man of Stoner's upbringing and incomplete mental development this was the worst possible treatment. Such unwonted lavishness undoubtedly went to his head.

It must be emphasized, however, that even so, the situation as between Mrs. Rattenbury and Stoner was, during this incubation period from November to March, no unique one. It is not even so very unusual. Certainly there was nothing to show that, in this particular instance, it was brewing up for murder.

January 1935 seems to have been a more or less peaceful month in the Rattenbury home, so far as peace ever could attend that storm-centre, its mistress; at all events, we hear of no particular upsets. Stoner was being taken more and more into the confidence of Mrs. Rattenbury, and he now cashed all her cheques for her. At the same time he was gaining influence over her. At his request she gave up her cocktails altogether (surely the measure of a great love); and his now increasing jealousy, though it irked her at times, must on the whole have delighted her.

In February the drug *motif* crops up again.

Mrs. Rattenbury and Stoner had their quarrels. As early as January Stoner had been heard to threaten Mrs. Rattenbury's life, though this threat was not taken very seriously by anyone. In February, however, a more serious quarrel occurred. Between eleven and twelve o'clock one night Miss Riggs, from her bedroom, heard it begin in Mrs. Rattenbury's room, continue along the passage, and progress into Stoner's bedroom. Thinking it more serious than usual, Miss Riggs got up to investigate. She found the combatants in a clinch, Stoner having obtained a ' firm hold ' of Mrs. Rattenbury, who was ' rather scared '. Miss Riggs separated them.

The cause of this quarrel is not given, but from its date and the direction of its progress one may guess that it had something to do with the efforts that Mrs. Rattenbury was making at this time to break the connexion between herself and Stoner on account of the disparity in their ages. This break Stoner violently opposed. The re-introduction of the drug theme here was probably made by Stoner as a further weapon to support his case, by way of an appeal *ad misericordiam* to reinforce the appeal *ad cor*.

In any case Stoner told Mrs. Rattenbury one morning that he had to go up to London that day to obtain a further supply of his mysterious drug, and his manner was extremely agitated.

Once again the effect of this communication on Mrs. Rattenbury was all that Stoner could have hoped. Her agitation instantly rivalled his own, and she begged him not to go. Stoner, however, was the adamant young drug-fiend and went, leaving his mistress almost in hysterics. As usual when upset, Mrs. Rattenbury at once telephoned for her doctor.

On this occasion, however, she had a good excuse for doing so, for she told the doctor all about Stoner's distressing story and implored his help. The doctor promised to have a talk with Stoner.

The talk took place the next day, and Stoner admitted readily enough that it was cocaine that he was taking: he had found some lying about in the house and sampled it and it had given him a pleasant sensation. The doctor accepted this story, warned Stoner about the drug, and offered to help him if he wished to give it up. It is a pity that the doctor did not question Stoner a little more closely on this occasion, for it might have saved a lot of wasted time at the trial had he done so. He might, for instance, have learned that Stoner considered cocaine to be a brown powder with black spots and that one can take a heaped-up teaspoonful of it containing thirty-six grains with not even any unpleasant after-effects, though the average fatal dose is fifteen grains. The doctor, however, confined himself, in reporting the interview to Mrs. Rattenbury, to warning her with professionally impersonal caution that " if you want to stop someone taking cocaine you would not give them more money than you could help."

Stoner must have come away from that interview tolerably cock-a-hoop. He knew very little about cocaine, but he had nevertheless taken the doctor in; and with instinctive cunning he had said that he had been unable to obtain any in London on the previous day, and so had run no risk of being asked to show a sample of the noxious stuff he was taking. And though

Stoner did not know it, the foundations of his subsequent defence had now been cemented.

(It may be as well to say here that Stoner never did take cocaine, or any similar drug. The reliable medical evidence at the trial definitely disproved that Stoner could have been a cocaine-addict, and Mr. Justice Humphreys made his opinion on the point quite clear in his summing-up. The whole story must have been made up by Stoner simply to impress Mrs. Rattenbury. What he was taking was an aphrodisiac.)

From February the chain of significant events links up to Tuesday, March 19th. On that day Mrs. Rattenbury took Stoner with her on a jaunt to London. It is not too much to say that it was to this visit to London that Mr. Rattenbury's murder was directly due.

Mrs. Rattenbury and Stoner stayed, as brother and sister, at a good hotel. Mrs. Rattenbury signed the register as "Mrs. Rattenbury and brother"; when the clerk asked her to fill in the name of her brother, she wrote what he took to be "George Stone". March 19th was spent chiefly in shopping for Stoner. Purchases made at Harrods' included two pairs of shoes and trees, three pairs of men's *crêpe de Chine* pyjamas at 60s. a pair, shirts, ties, silk and linen handkerchiefs, socks, gloves, underwear, a grey suit, a blue suit, and a mackintosh. In fact Stoner did pretty well. On the same day Stoner bought Mrs. Rattenbury a present of a diamond ring for £15 10s., in Bond Street. But as Mrs. Rattenbury had given him £20 for the purpose, Stoner did not do badly out of this either.

That seems to have concluded the shopping, and the next days were spent in sight-seeing, cinemas, theatres, and restaurants in the usual way. These four days of luxury, in the company of a woman who was ready to gratify every whim, completed Stoner's moral disintegration.

Mrs. Rattenbury had obtained the money for this jaunt by telling her husband that she had to go to London for an operation. It was her custom to tell some lie of this kind regularly every June and December in order to squeeze something extra out of her husband over and above her regular housekeeping and personal allowance of £600 a year; and she must have been a good liar, because she usually managed to raise another £150 or more on each of these occasions. This time she must have managed things exceptionally well, for not only was the dividend an interim one but it was much larger than usual; for Mr. Rattenbury, rendered soft no doubt by pity that his wife should have to undergo yet another operation (she had had one or two recently), parted with no less than £250.

Mrs. Rattenbury must not only have told her story well; she must have chosen her time with equal care. It is a little surprising to find a man reputedly mean handing out a sum of this size, until one remembers that in the evenings Mr. Rattenbury was ' jolly'. Perhaps Mrs. Rattenbury selected an evening when Mr. Rattenbury was even ' jollier' than usual; for when she turned up again, hale and whole, four days later, nothing appears to have been said about the singular speed of this operation and the patient's recovery from it. One may assume that Mr. Rattenbury, in the extremes of his jollity, had forgotten all about it. That he might equally well have forgotten about the cheque, and that it might be very much to Mrs. Rattenbury's advantage that he should never remember, is a possible, if perhaps somewhat academic point in favour of premeditation which does not seem to have been made by the prosecution at the trial. In any case, within forty-eight hours Mr. Rattenbury was to have no chance of remembering any inconsistencies of this sort.

Stoner and Mrs. Rattenbury returned to the Villa Madeira at half-past ten on Friday evening, March 22nd. Mr. Rattenbury was in bed, jolly, and asked no questions.

On the Saturday morning Mrs. Rattenbury went with Stoner in the car to collect her small son from school, as he was to come home for the week-end. (He was a day-boy when Stoner was first engaged, but we hear of him now as a boarder.) In the afternoon Stoner drove Mrs. Rattenbury and the little boy over to watch Mrs. Rattenbury's elder son playing football at his school. Mr. Rattenbury stayed at home. The evening passed quietly, with Mr. and Mrs. Rattenbury playing cards together; "just the same as any other night", except that it happened to be Mr. Rattenbury's last on earth.

On Sunday Mr. Rattenbury was depressed. He was interested financially in a block of flats that was being built at Southampton, and the investment was worrying him. To cheer him up Mrs. Rattenbury took him for a drive in the morning and was particularly nice to him, but Mr. Rattenbury's gloom remained. After lunch Mr. Rattenbury went to sleep, and Mrs. Rattenbury played with John: "the usual Sunday afternoon". The three of them had tea in Mrs. Rattenbury's bedroom. Miss Riggs was out for the afternoon and evening, and Stoner brought up the tea, as apparently was not unusual.

The door of the bedroom was normally ajar, with a clothes-basket to wedge it open. Shortly after Stoner had brought the tea somebody, probably the little boy, moved the basket and the door remained shut for a time.

After tea the trio moved down to the drawing-room, little John was in and out, and Mr. Rattenbury was engaged with a book. Some mystery was made about this book at the trial, and Mrs. Rattenbury's *résumé* of its story was as follows: " The person in the book said he had lived too long and, before he became doddering, as far as I can understand, he finished himself." This project appealed to Mr. Rattenbury in his present state of gloom. He read passages with approval to his wife from time to time and repeated his admiration of anyone who could commit suicide in such circumstances. Mr. Rattenbury became more and more depressed.

Again Mrs. Rattenbury tried to cheer him up, and suggested a visit to Bridport for both of them on the next day. Mr. Rattenbury assented to this. His partner in the flat-building proposition lived there, and Mr. Rattenbury thought it might be possible to make some more favourable financial adjustment. Mrs. Rattenbury telephoned at once to Bridport and arranged for herself and her husband to stay the following night with their friend.

The telephone was in Mr. Rattenbury's bedroom, which was next door to the drawing-room.

While Mrs. Rattenbury was still telephoning, Stoner came into the room. He was very angry and he had in his hand what Mrs. Rattenbury thought was a revolver but which proved to be a toy pistol. As this is the crucial point in the case, it will perhaps be better to give what followed in Mrs. Rattenbury's own words, from her examination-in-chief at the trial:

What did Stoner say he would do to you?—He said he would kill me if I went to Bridport.

Could you go on talking there without being overheard by your husband?—Yes, we could have done, because Mr. Rattenbury did not really take very much notice. We went into the dining-room to continue the conversation. Stoner still had the revolver. He accused me of living with Mr. Rattenbury that afternoon with the bedroom door closed.

What did you say to him?—I told him I had not. I told him not to make an ass of himself.

What did he then say?—He told me I must never have the bedroom door closed again, and that if I went to Bridport he would not drive. He was very annoyed at me going to Bridport. We had rather an unpleasant time about it. Afterwards I thought it was all right.

Did he give any reasons why you were not to go to Bridport?—He did not want me to be with Mr. Rattenbury. He was very jealous of Mr. Rattenbury—unnecessarily so. He thought I would have to share the same bedroom. I assured him I would have a separate bedroom.

What effect did that seem to have on him?—I thought it was all right, but I suppose he could not have taken it seriously. He could not have believed me.

MR. JUSTICE HUMPHREYS: But he seemed to have believed you and to be all right?—Yes.

This artless passage sheds a remarkable light on the relations in this strange household, with a middle-aged woman receiving orders, threats and reproaches from her young servant and the sexagenarian husband " not really taking very much notice " as he meditated on suicide in the adjoining room.

Mrs. Rattenbury was not asked anything about her own feelings regarding this almost demented jealousy of Stoner's, but it is not difficult to imagine that it was not altogether displeasing to her.

In any case she disregarded it, for she returned to the drawing-room and talked to her husband "about how nice it was that we were going to Bridport the next day. I tried to make him jolly."

Later Mrs. Rattenbury put John to bed, and then played cards with her husband in the drawing-room. "He seemed quite jolly then."

There was a little dog called Diana in the house, and it was Mrs. Rattenbury's practice to put her out into the garden each night through the French windows in the drawing-room, Mr. Rattenbury letting her in five minutes later. (This seems to show that Mr. Rattenbury, although ' jolly ' every night, was not helpless.) On this particular night she put the dog out as usual and closed the windows, after which she kissed Mr. Rattenbury good-night, saying: "Good night, darling." "I always kissed him good-night," she remarked in her evidence.

She went upstairs to the bathroom and then to her bedroom, where the little boy, too, was now asleep. In the bedroom she found the dog. Since the afternoon Mrs. Rattenbury had been wearing pyjamas, with her own underclothes underneath. She now undressed and resumed the pyjamas, did a little packing in preparation for the visit to Bridport, and got into bed. Expecting Stoner, she did not go to sleep but got out of bed from time to time as she thought of something else to put into her suit-case.

At a few minutes past ten Miss Riggs returned to the house. As she came in she saw Stoner hanging over the banisters, looking down into the hall. He told her that he was seeing if the lights were out. This seems to have given Miss Riggs an uneasy feeling, and hearing what she thought to be unusual breathing, she went to investigate. She switched on the light in Mr. Rattenbury's bedroom with the "premonition that something was wrong", but seeing that he was not in bed thought he might be asleep in his chair in the drawing-room and did not wish to disturb him there. Her premonition now allayed, Miss Riggs went upstairs.

Shortly after she had got into bed Mrs. Rattenbury came into her room and talked to her for ten minutes or so about the expedition to Bridport on the following day. Mrs. Rattenbury seemed a little excited over the trip in her usual way, but not unduly so, and apart from this there was nothing abnormal in her manner. Having discussed the preparations with Miss Riggs, Mrs. Rattenbury returned to bed.

As to what happened next, in Mrs. Rattenbury's bedroom, we have only Mrs. Rattenbury's word for it; and in view of the very different statements which Mrs. Rattenbury herself made later, and which were of course given great prominence in the press, there is every excuse for caution. Nevertheless, Mrs. Rattenbury impressed everyone who heard her at her trial as an exceptionally truthful witness, telling the truth even when it was against herself, and the version she then gave is probably the correct one. At any rate it tallies with other evidence, and is perfectly reasonable.

According to Mrs. Rattenbury, then, Stoner came into her bedroom shortly after she had returned from Miss Riggs. He was in his pyjamas and got into bed with her. He seemed agitated, and Mrs. Rattenbury asked him what the matter was. Stoner replied that he was in trouble but could not tell her what it was. On Mrs. Rattenbury insisting, Stoner said that she would not be able to bear it. Mrs. Rattenbury, thinking that the trouble had to do with some private affair of Stoner's outside the household, answered that she was strong enough to bear anything. Stoner then told her that she was not going to Bridport the next day, because he had hurt Mr. Rattenbury. He added that he had hit Mr. Rattenbury over the head with a mallet and hidden the mallet out of doors.

At first Mrs. Rattenbury did not understand what Stoner meant, until she heard Mr. Rattenbury groan in the room below. It was, as she described it later, " a jolly good groan ". Hearing it, Mrs. Rattenbury jumped out of bed and ran downstairs. Miss Riggs, in her own bedroom, heard her go.

235

This is Mrs. Rattenbury's own description of what followed:

> I found Mr. Rattenbury sitting in that chair. I tried to rub his hands. They were cold. I tried to take his pulse, and shook him to make him speak. I did not call for help right away. I tried to make him speak first. Then I saw this blood, and went around the table. I trod on his false teeth. That made me hysterical and I yelled. I took a drink of whisky to save myself being sick, and yelled for Irene. I drank some whisky neat. I tried to become senseless, to blot out the picture.

From that point Mrs. Rattenbury's memory afterwards failed, perhaps conveniently. She remembered being sick after her whisky, and putting a towel round her husband's head, but nothing more. She did not remember even sending for the doctor.

Mrs. Rattenbury estimated that it was three minutes after she got downstairs before she called for Miss Riggs. Miss Riggs jumped up at once and hurried downstairs. She found Mrs. Rattenbury in the drawing-room in her pyjamas, her feet bare. Mr. Rattenbury was sitting in his armchair, unconscious, and Miss Riggs noticed that he had what appeared to be a black eye. Mrs. Rattenbury was in a state of hysterical terror: a changed woman from the wildly excited conversationalist of ten minutes before. She was talking incoherently to her husband, and Miss Riggs could distinguish no words but " Oh, poor ' Rats ', what has happened? " The scene Miss Riggs described later as ' dreadful '.

Seeing Miss Riggs, Mrs. Rattenbury told her to telephone for the doctor. Miss Riggs did so, and Mrs. Rattenbury added that Stoner was to hurry off in the car to see if the doctor could be brought a little more quickly. Miss Riggs therefore called Stoner down. Mrs. Rattenbury was still somewhat hysterical, and kept calling out in agitated impatience: " Hurry, hurry! Can't somebody do something? " Before going off in the car, Stoner helped the two women carry Mr. Rattenbury into his adjoining bedroom and put him on the bed.

The prosecution made a point at the trial that Mrs. Rattenbury called Miss Riggs downstairs and not Stoner, " the man whom, in the circumstances, you might have supposed she would have called if it were nothing more than a case of illness". This, however, seems a point of doubtful value. The moment of confrontation with a corpse or near-corpse is of great importance in determining the amount of pre-knowledge on the part of a suspect. Mrs. Rattenbury seems to have acted in a perfectly natural way, as if she had suddenly received a great shock and not merely the minor shock of seeing in its actuality the grim scene she expected. And in the case of such a shock it was surely more natural for her to summon first the reliable friend of many years standing than the young partner of her passions. It is a sign of the weakness of the subsequent case against Mrs. Rattenbury that it should have been felt necessary to emphasize such insignificant matters.

While waiting for the doctor Mrs. Rattenbury filled up the time by roaming the house and continuously drinking whisky-and-soda. At her instructions Miss Riggs cleared up most of the blood in the drawing-room; she also tried to wash Mr. Rattenbury's coat and waistcoat in the bathroom. Mrs. Rattenbury insisted on her doing this, because she did not wish the little boy to be upset by the sight of the blood the next morning. There was, in consequence, little blood about when the doctor arrived, and Miss Riggs' statement, therefore, becomes all the more important, that when she first reached the drawing-room she noticed that the blood lying around was not fresh but already thick and congealed. This, at any rate, shows that Mrs. Rattenbury could not have committed the murder herself just before Miss Riggs' arrival; and in view of the complete lack of material evidence concerning the actual commission of the crime, any fact which proves anything at all in this case is welcome.

When the doctor arrived he found the door of the house open, and walked in. Mrs. Rattenbury met him with wild excitement, still in her pyjamas, with bare feet, a glass of whisky in her hand, and the doctor thought that she was already a little intoxicated. She took him into the bedroom, where Mr. Rattenbury was lying partially dressed on the bed with a bloodstained towel round his head. The doctor noticed that Mr. Rattenbury's breathing was laboured, and asked what had happened. Mrs. Rattenbury replied: " Look at him! Look at the blood! Somebody has tried to finish him."

The doctor, seeing that the case was a surgical one, telephoned for Mr. Rooke, a Boscombe surgeon. While they were waiting for the latter's arrival Mrs. Rattenbury told the doctor how happy her husband had been at the prospect of the trip to Bridport on the following day, and how he had read to her a passage in a book about suicide. She tried to show the doctor the book, which was on the piano, but the doctor told her he had no time to bother with it. Mrs. Rattenbury also told the doctor that she had gone to bed and been aroused by a cry or a noise of some sort, had gone downstairs, and had found her husband in his chair with a pool of blood on the carpet.

It will be noticed that in this, the first of the many statements she made, Mrs. Rattenbury is (*a*) shielding Stoner, (*b*) introducing the suicide suggestion, (*c*) leaving the way open to an assault by a stranger. At her trial the impression was, of course, conveyed that all this was done deliberately, in pursuance of a pre-arranged plan, and hysteria is not at this point admitted. That is only recognized when Mrs. Rattenbury goes on later to accuse herself, the suggestion being that she then, in hysterical frenzy, threw away all her carefully-planned defences and screamed out the truth.

To understand the real situation is, however, not difficult. Assuming that Mrs. Rattenbury's version of what happened upstairs is correct, she knew from the beginning that it was Stoner who had done this to her husband. That her husband should have been attacked by a stranger would, of course, have provoked a *crise des nerfs* in this highly-strung woman; but it would not, I think, have produced such extreme reactions as Mrs. Rattenbury did, in fact, display. It was the knowledge that Stoner's hand was responsible for the attack that upset her even more than the attack itself. This particularly accounts for her efforts to drug her mind with whisky. It was not as she said the ' picture ' that she wished to 'blot out' but the instinctively unwelcome knowledge of the artist's identity.

To shield Stoner was therefore her first aim, conscious or unconscious; and to do this she was ready to throw out any suggestion, however absurd, that jumped into her mind. This, combined with alcohol, is the only way to account for so preposterous a theory as that Mr. Rattenbury committed suicide by striking himself repeatedly on the head with a mallet. (In the early newspaper accounts of the case, prominence was given to an alleged statement of Mrs. Rattenbury's: "He did it himself. He did it with a mallet." This statement, if it was ever made at all, was not adduced in evidence at the trial.)

When Mr. Rooke arrived he was able to make only a cursory examination of Mr. Rattenbury; he found it impossible to make a thorough one both on account of the blood and of the disturbance to which he was subjected. Mrs. Rattenbury was pressing her attentions on her husband to such an extent as to impede the surgeon in his work; she was trying to remove his shirt and calling for scissors with which to do so, and making remarks which appeared to Mr. Rooke incoherent. He tried to persuade her to keep away from the bed without success, and seeing that she was in an abnormal state Mr. Rooke considered that the only thing was to have Mr. Rattenbury removed to a nursing-home.

This was accordingly done, and on a further examination there it was found that the bone on the left side of Mr. Rattenbury's head had been driven into the brain. Three blows appeared to have been dealt him. The first, in Mr. Rooke's opinion, was a blow above the ear, delivered probably from behind. This would have the effect of making Mr. Rattenbury crumple up in a forward direction. Two further blows were then struck as he was toppling over.

When the doctors had made these discoveries, it became plain that the question of accident could be dismissed and that Mr. Rattenbury was suffering from applied violence. In consequence, the doctor, who had hitherto been considering the possibility that

Mr. Rattenbury might have had a fall and hit his head against a piece of furniture, telephoned his information to the police.

From this point the sequence of events, as it was disjointedly presented in court, becomes somewhat confused; but disentangling the story as best one may, I think the following account is tolerably accurate.

The first policeman to arrive at the Villa Madeira was P.C. Bagwell. To him Mrs. Rattenbury, now thoroughly drunk, said:

> I was playing cards with my husband until nine o'clock. Then I went to my bedroom. At about 10.30 I heard a yell and came downstairs into the drawing-room. I saw my husband sitting in the armchair and sent for Dr. O'Donnell.

This is a fairly coherent statement, for " the accused then said ". It must, however, be remembered, both in regard to this and still more to later statements of Mrs. Rattenbury's as reported officially, that these police versions of remarks made by suspected persons are often extremely misleading on three counts. In the first place, the context of circumstances is omitted, and these are in the highest degree important; in the second, only the words used by the suspect are written down, and not anything said by the policeman; thirdly, intervals of time are not noted, so that remarks are often made to appear consecutive, which were, in fact, not so. One must therefore remember the conditions at the Villa Madeira at this time, with Mrs. Rattenbury tolerably drunk and half the time incoherent in her speech, playing the radio-gramophone, and, no doubt, screaming disjointed replies to the policeman's questions, interrupting Miss Riggs and with Miss Riggs interrupting her, while the policeman wrote down in his note-book what he saw and what he heard, perhaps even being shaken and jogged by Mrs. Rattenbury while he was doing so.

P.C. Bagwell was followed by Inspector Mills. It was now past midnight, and the atmosphere in the little drawing-room instead of growing calmer was becoming still more hectic. To the Inspector Mrs. Rattenbury explained how, on hearing groans, she had come downstairs and found her husband in the chair with the blood flowing from his head. In answer to a question of the Inspector's, she also told him that the French windows, which at this time were open, had been shut and locked when she first came downstairs. Inspector Mills, of course, realized that this meant that no one could have come in from outside, struck the blows, and escaped the same way; in other words, the assailant must probably be some member of the household.

Inspector Mills then went off to have a look round, and Mrs. Rattenbury was left alone with P.C. Bagwell, to whom she is alleged to have made the following ' statement ':

> I know who did it. [Here the constable cautioned her.] I did it with a mallet. It is hidden. Rats has lived too long. No, my lover did it. I will give you £10. No, I won't bribe you.

This is obviously no statement, but a series of disconnected remarks, some of them no doubt made in reply to questions. However, the importance of these wild words is that the mallet is now mentioned for the first time, and for the first time Mrs. Rattenbury is accusing herself.

What followed after this is not quite clear; but in spite of Mrs. Rattenbury's incriminating words, both the policemen seem to have withdrawn from the house, Inspector Mills to go to the nursing-home for a word with the doctors, and P.C. Bagwell for another and more modest reason. For Mrs. Rattenbury, it seems, was now pressing her attentions upon him to an embarassing degree. She was, in fact, trying to kiss him; and the constable was not willing to be kissed. He therefore withdrew, telling Miss Riggs that he was going to fetch another police-officer, presumably to protect him.

Mrs. Rattenbury and Miss Riggs were now left alone in the house. Stoner was still waiting in the car outside the nursing-home, where Inspector Mills saw him, apparently peacefully asleep.

All this time Mrs. Rattenbury had been drinking at intervals, and according to her own account she was not used to whisky. In any case she was now very drunk indeed; so drunk that she took it very hard to be deprived of her policeman. She tried to get out of the house after him, rushing from one door to another. Miss Riggs had, however, locked them all and taken out the keys. This extraordinary tragi-farce receives its final touch in an answer made by Miss Riggs in her evidence at the trial. When asked how she managed to detain Mrs. Rattenbury in the house during this period and keep her from pursuit of the fleeing policeman, Miss Riggs replied simply: " I was sitting on her in the dining-room."

Inspector Mills also seems to have been a little apprehensive of this wild woman. " I have been to Manor Road," he told the doctor, at the nursing-home, " but that woman is drunk."

Later, P.C. Bagwell arrived with his bodyguard, all of whom at once began to ask Mrs. Rattenbury questions. Presumably, however, they did not get much out of her, for, according to Miss Riggs, " at times you could make out what she was saying, but at others you could not ".

Inspector Mills returned to the villa at about 3.30 a.m. He told Mrs. Rattenbury that her husband's condition was a critical one, and she replied: " Will this be against me? " The Inspector cautioned her, and Mrs. Rattenbury then made another ' statement ':

> I did it. He gave me the book. He has lived too long. He said, " Dear, dear." I will tell you in the morning where the mallet is. Have you told the coroner yet? I shall make a better job of it next time. Irene does not know. I made a proper muddle of it. I thought I was strong enough.

Fortunately, we have a picture of the conditions under which this ' statement ' was made, for the doctor arrived back from the nursing-home at about this time, driven by Stoner, and this is his description of the scene that met him:

> I found Mrs. Rattenbury intoxicated and excited. The radio-gramophone was playing and there were four police officers in the house, and she was running about among them from room to room. I tried to explain to her her husband's condition, but she could not take it in. I thought the only thing to do was to stop the exhibition I saw by giving her morphia.

As soon as she saw him Mrs. Rattenbury rushed towards the

doctor, who took her upstairs and administered to her the large but justifiable dose of half a grain of morphia hypodermically in the arm. Mrs. Rattenbury, however, was not to be quietened so easily. Before the morphia could take effect she was downstairs again making another wild 'statement'.

In this instance we have two witnesses to what was said, and a comparison of their evidence is not uninstructive. According to Inspector Mills:

> Mrs. Rattenbury came downstairs and said, "I know who did it—his son." I asked her how old the son was, and she replied, "Thirty-two, but he is not here." Dr. O'Donnell came into the room and said, "I have given her morphia. I don't think she is fit to make a statement."

And according to the doctor :

> I went downstairs and saw Miss Riggs and Stoner to see if I could find out anything. When I returned to the sitting-room about five minutes later I found Mrs. Rattenbury was there. Inspector Mills was in the room, and he asked her, "Do you suspect anybody?" Her reply was, "Yes." "Whom do you suspect?" the officer asked, and she said, "I think his son did it." Inspector Mills asked Mrs. Rattenbury, "What age is his son?" Her reply was, "Thirty-six." The Inspector asked, "Where is his son?" and she said, "I don't know." I asked Inspector Mills if he had cautioned the lady, and his reply was "No." I then said, "Look at her condition. She is full of whisky and I have just given her a large dose of morphia. She is not fit to make a statement to you or anybody else."

It will be noticed that the Inspector's version, while not exactly inaccurate, is nevertheless somewhat selective as well as condensed. The doctor's is not only more vivid, but conveys far more correctly what really occurred. The apparent and silly non-sequitur "thirty-two, but he is not here", from the Inspector's note-book, is typical, as is the implication that Mrs. Rattenbury volunteered the first sentence of this 'statement'. From the doctor's evidence we see that the latter was not made on the speaker's own initiative but was in reply to a question, and there was no non-sequitur at all.

After this Mrs. Rattenbury really was got to bed, though not without difficulty, and the doctor, having supervised this operation, left the house. It must by now have been after 4 a.m.

During nearly all this time, ever since he had been sent to bring the doctor, Stoner had been outside the house. He had no idea that Mrs. Rattenbury had been making ' statements ', and he had had no chance of consulting with her, nor indeed did he appear to want one. After Mrs. Rattenbury had gone to bed, Stoner appears to have "walked about the house", but no one enlightened him as to anything Mrs. Rattenbury had said. Inspector Mills asked him once if he had seen a mallet anywhere, and Stoner replied that he had not; if he wondered how the Inspector could know anything about a mallet, he kept his curiosity to himself.

In spite of the morphia Mrs. Rattenbury was not to be allowed much sleep. Not in bed till four o'clock or thereabouts, she was being badgered again shortly after six. At that time Detective-Inspector Carter, a recent arrival on the scene, and Miss Riggs went up to her bedroom, taking coffee with them with which to pull Mrs. Rattenbury together. They seem to have got some of the coffee down her, but according to Miss Riggs Mrs. Rattenbury was unable to hold the cup and could drink only "after a fashion". She was, however, sufficiently roused to cause this entry in the Detective-Inspector's note-book, dated 6.10 a.m.:

> I picked up the mallet and he dared me to hit him. He said, "You have not guts enough to do it." I hit him and hid the mallet. He is not dead, is he? Are you the coroner?

The officer decided, however, that Mrs. Rattenbury was "not normal", and these remarks of hers were in consequence not put in as evidence at the trial. Not, however, that anything was lost by the omission, for Mrs. Rattenbury's next ' statement ' repeated them word for word, with the omission only of the last question.

Mrs. Rattenbury may not have been normal at this early hour, nevertheless she was ordered, or persuaded, or permitted out of bed a few minutes later, and sent to have a bath. According to Detective-Inspector Carter she was anxious to get up, and for a time he would not allow her to do so; according to counsel for the defence, the Detective-Inspector insisted on feeding her coffee and sending her to have a bath in order to create the semblance of her being in a reasonable condition for the taking of a statement. The onlooker must choose which version is more likely to be the correct one; though it is possible to say that even a person as highly strung as Mrs. Rattenbury would have difficulty in throwing off the effects of a half-grain of morphia after barely two hours' sleep.

After her bath Mrs. Rattenbury seems to have held a kind of police-reception in her bedroom, willy or nilly. In any case, Miss Riggs is reported to have said something to this effect: "Give the woman a chance; she can't get dressed with three police-officers in the room." To this plea, however, Detective-Inspector Carter must have turned a literally deaf ear, for he could not afterwards remember ever having heard it. However, when a police-matron arrived the officers left the room. That an official eye had at this stage to be kept on Mrs. Rattenbury is, of course, undeniable; but three pairs of official eyes was, perhaps, overdoing it. Possibly, however, the distressing experience of P.C. Bagwell was still in the minds of these officers, and they were clinging together by way of mutual protection.

During the small hours, investigations by the police had not been unfruitful, and in the garden there had been found a mallet to which human hairs and a piece of skin were still adhering.

While waiting for Mrs. Rattenbury to get dressed, under the supervision of the police-matron, Detective-Inspector Carter took the following statement from Stoner at 7.30 a.m.:

I retired to my bedroom at about 8.5 p.m. on Sunday, March 24th, leaving Mr. and Mrs. Rattenbury and the boy John in the drawing-room. About 10.30 I was aroused by Mrs. Rattenbury shouting to me to come down. I came down into the drawing-room and saw Mr. Rattenbury sitting in the armchair with blood running from his head. Mrs. Rattenbury was crying and screaming and said to me, "Help me to get 'Rats' to bed. He has been hurt." I then took the car and went to Dr. O'Donnell's house. He had left before I got there. When I returned, on the instructions of Mrs. Rattenbury I cleaned the blood from the floor. Mrs. Rattenbury was sober, and as far as I know she had not been drinking. When I went to bed she was in a normal condition.

I have never seen a mallet on the premises. Until I was aroused I heard no sound of a quarrel or any noise of any kind. Since September 1934 I have been employed by Mr. and Mrs. Rattenbury. They have been on the best of terms. I said to her, "How did this happen?" She said, "I do not know." Mr. Rattenbury was fully dressed in the armchair and Mrs. Rattenbury was dressed in pyjamas and had bare feet.

This ' statement ' bears unmistakable signs of having been obtained by question and answer, and the prompting behind it shows clearly through. There is, of course, no objection at all to a police-officer obtaining his information this way and then summarizing it. The objection is to calling the result a ' statement '. It is not. The term ' statement ' should be limited to a spontaneous production on the part of the stater, in his own words and without promptings or suggestions. To call a mere summary of interrogation a ' statement ' is to destroy the importance of the genuine article.

It will be noticed from this ' statement ' that Stoner seems, at this stage, to have no story ready to account for the attack on Mr. Rattenbury. Had he had one in his mind, he would surely have put it forward during this interrogation. It is, of course, possible that he did so, and that Detective-Inspector Carter, having already made up his mind that Mrs. Rattenbury was the guilty person (and, indeed, at this point with every justification), did not think it worth including in the summary; and if this is the case, it is a pity. There is no reason at all for assuming that this is what happened, though we do know that police-officers are occasionally inclined to be a little too selective as to what they include in these summaries. The point is, however, not a negligible one, and it would be interesting to have this possible doubt cleared up. The degree of premeditation in Mr. Rattenbury's murder is difficult to assess, and any fact which has some bearing on this question deserves scrutiny. In the same way, any evidence as to Stoner's intelligence, or lack of it, is important. If, nine hours after the crime, Stoner had not produced some story to explain Mr. Rattenbury's death without incriminating either himself or Mrs. Rattenbury, this is a large point against pre-meditation as well as a tolerable proof of stupidity. (Or, if premeditation had nevertheless existed, the proof is that of an almost incredible degree of stupidity.) If, on the other hand, some such story was hinted at, even if not developed, it would be extremely interesting to know what it was. Lastly, if Stoner suggested no theory, not so much through inability to invent one as on account of mental inertia, and was merely standing by in masterly inactivity, waiting to see what might develop and under the impression that there was no incriminating evidence against either himself or Mrs. Rattenbury (and this is perhaps the most likely explanation), then he was an exceedingly stupid young man. And I think Stoner must have been an exceedingly stupid young man.

At 8.15 Mrs. Rattenbury was dressed and ready, and Detective-Inspector Carter again attended her in her bedroom. To him she now appeared to be perfectly normal and no longer under the in-fluence of drugs. From other evidence, however, it appears that with the Detective-Inspector the wish was father to the self-deception. At the trial Mrs. Rattenbury's counsel naturally sug-gested that it was unfair to question her in this state. But was it? The Detective-Inspector had every reason, at this stage, to believe that it was she who had made the attack on her husband, and he wanted the truth. It may well have seemed to him that he had a better chance of getting it, in the case of a woman of Mrs. Rattenbury's temperament, when she had not too many of her rather volatile wits about her. If that was his hope, it was not to be fulfilled.

In any case, at 8.15 Detective-Inspector Carter first cautioned her and then charged her with doing grievous bodily harm with intent to murder. (At this time, of course, Mr. Rattenbury was still alive.) Mrs. Rattenbury thereupon made a 'statement', which of all the 'statements' connected with this case looks most like a genuine one:

About 9 p.m. on March 24 I was playing cards with my husband when he dared me to kill him, as he wanted to die. I picked up a mallet and he then said, " You have not guts enough to do it." I then hit him with the mallet. I hid the mallet outside the house. I would have shot him if I had had a gun.

According to Detective-Inspector Carter, Mrs. Rattenbury appeared to understand what she was saying and doing, and before signing the statement she read it aloud quite clearly.

Mrs. Rattenbury was then escorted out of the house. In the hall were Stoner and Miss Riggs. Mrs. Rattenbury said to them : " Don't make fools of yourselves." Stoner replied : " You have got yourself into this mess by talking too much." This remark seems to have a touch of asperity, and no doubt Stoner felt that he had reason for annoyance.

After this somewhat dramatic encounter Mrs. Rattenbury was taken to Bournemouth Police Station, where she was charged. In reply she said : " That's right. I did it deliberately, and I would do it again."

What was Stoner doing, to allow his mistress to be arrested like this under his very nose ? What was Mrs. Rattenbury doing, confessing to the murder in this exceedingly unnatural and almost studiedly callous way ?

As to the first question, counsel for the prosecution answered it in his own way. He suggested that the two sentences exchanged in the hall between Mrs. Rattenbury and Stoner, combined with Stoner's willingness to see Mrs. Rattenbury arrested, indicated a conspiracy to murder between the two of them ; for in that case it would be merely bad luck should one be taken, with no moral obligation on the other to come forward too. This is a perfectly sound argument, and the words used in the hall are quite capable of bearing this construction. On the other hand, there is an equally good argument against conspiracy even at this stage, and that is the absence of any common story between the two. Surely if they had planned the murder between them, almost one of the first things they would decide would be the story they were to tell the police. Even if Stoner was stupid enough to omit this, Mrs.

Rattenbury certainly was not. (Curiously, Mrs. Rattenbury's counsel does not seem to have used exactly this argument. His point against conspiracy was the absence from Mrs. Rattenbury's first two statements of any alibis, mutual or otherwise, for herself and, presumably, Stoner.)

Perhaps it is not difficult to realize why Stoner stood by and watched Mrs. Rattenbury being carried off. We must put ourselves in his place. He was very young, and Mrs. Rattenbury must always have seemed to him the person on whom to rely— which is not by any means the same thing as believing that he was as much under her domination as all sides at the trial seemed to agree. He must have been expecting her to get him somehow out of the mess. Perhaps he did not believe that she could be in any serious danger. He had not heard her charged. And to speak just then was so very final. It could do no harm to wait. And mingled with all this there was probably that curious annoyance which we sometimes feel when someone of whom we are fond is hurt or made unhappy : a selfish annoyance, coming from resentment that our own feelings should be lacerated, too, on account of our very fondness. A tinge of that might well have decided Stoner, dithering as he must have been, whether to speak or not.

As for Mrs. Rattenbury, she had no such hesitations. She had confessed, without any word as to a conspiracy, in order to save Stoner. There can be no other possible reason, except that she was speaking the truth ; and she is entitled to full credit for what she did, because she certainly was not speaking the truth. It may well be, however, that she felt a big share of responsibility for what had happened to her husband, without which she would hardly have undertaken the full consequences. In any case, and even discounting the hazy hang-over from the morphia, Mrs. Rattenbury did a plucky thing, entirely in accordance with the public-school code.

With regard to this hang-over it is worth noting that, when her own doctor saw Mrs. Rattenbury at the police-station, he found her still so much under the influence of the morphia that she appeared dazed and was swaying and unable to walk without support. The prison doctor also found the effects persisting for another two days. Besides invalidating the statements she made on the morning of March 25th, this also conclusively shows that Mrs. Rattenbury could not have been a drug-fiend as well as a drinker, as the prosecution rather unnecessarily suggested later.

Just before the police-officer took her away from the house Mrs. Rattenbury whispered to Miss Riggs: " Tell Stoner he must give me the mallet." The significance of this is obvious. Miss Riggs duly passed on the message, but Stoner did not have a chance to answer because Miss Riggs herself added: " But I see the police have got it."

Mrs. Rattenbury now passes out of the picture, and we have a curious situation at the Villa Madeira, where Miss Riggs now knows perfectly well who killed Mr. Rattenbury, but apparently does nothing about it, and Stoner knows she knows. Stoner indeed went so far as to say to Miss Riggs, soon after Mrs. Rattenbury had been taken away: " I suppose you know who did it." According to Miss Riggs herself, she made no reply to this, and nothing further was said. Presumably, however, the two eyed each other at intervals in what used to be known as an old-fashioned way.

In this remarkable state of neutrality Miss Riggs and Stoner seem to have lived at the Villa Madeira for three days, with an occasional exchange to keep up the tension. On one occasion, for instance, Miss Riggs asked Stoner if there would be his finger-prints on the mallet, to which Stoner replied with complete frankness: " No, I wore gloves." If this is correctly reported, it is by far the most important statement that Stoner made.

Then, on the Tuesday, Miss Riggs asked Stoner, almost casually, why he had done it. Stoner answered because he had seen Mr. Rattenbury with Mrs. Rattenbury in the afternoon. (When Miss Riggs testified to this reply, the judge asked her, not without reason, whether Stoner was sober when he made it. Miss Riggs affirmed that he was perfectly sober. The mystery must therefore remain.)

On this day, too, Miss Riggs drove with Stoner to Wimborne,

for some reason unnamed, and on the way back Stoner pointed to a house where an ex-policeman lived, and said that the occupant could bear him out that he was out that way at about 8.30 on the Sunday evening. This remark, brought out in Miss Riggs' examination-in-chief, was not followed up at the trial, and its significance is not apparent, except that it contradicts Stoner's first statement to Detective-Inspector Carter that he went up to his bedroom that evening at 8.15.

On the Wednesday evening Stoner was a little drunk, and appeared upset too. He called to Miss Riggs to come to him in his bedroom, as he wanted to speak to her " on her own ". Upon Miss Riggs complying, Stoner confided to her that Mrs. Rattenbury was in gaol and it was he who had put her there; and he was going up to see her and give himself up. No doubt Miss Riggs approved of this course for reasons of her own as well as for the sake of justice; for Stoner's admissions during these days had put her, strictly speaking, in the position of an accessory after the fact. Miss Riggs must have appreciated this, for in the end she gave the police the information which it was her duty to pass on to them.

On this day Mrs. Rattenbury wrote to Stoner from prison:

> I must see you, darling. Please write to me. This is the third letter I have written. Hope you receive this. I hardly know how to write now. Let me know how 'Rats' is getting on. No more now. God bless you. My love be with you always.
>
> LOZANNE
>
> Have you talked with Dr. O'D. about how 'Rats' is? Goodness, there is so much I want to know! Please ask Irene to give you a few bobbing pins for my hair. I think they will be allowed.

On Thursday morning Miss Riggs woke at 6.30 and heard Stoner already getting up. He left the house at 6.50, came back about ten minutes later, and then left again. Later in the day—where, when, or in what circumstances we are not told—he was arrested by Detective-Inspector Carter and taken to Bournemouth Police Station. When charged, he replied, " I understand." There is no information as to whether Stoner's arrest was unexpected by himself or whether he gave himself up; but if the former, we may at any rate give him credit for the right intention. Stoner may not have been a pleasing character, but he had at any rate this elementary decency once he realized that Mrs. Rattenbury's position really was a serious one.

On this day Mr. Rattenbury died, at the nursing-home, without having recovered consciousness. It was therefore with his murder that Stoner was charged.

The next day, in the detention-room of the Bournemouth police-court, Stoner remarked to the constable on duty: "Do you know Mrs. Rattenbury had nothing to do with this affair?"

The constable cautioned him, but Stoner went on:

> When I did the job I believe he was asleep. I hit him and then went upstairs and told Mrs. Rattenbury. She rushed down then. You see, I watched through the french window and saw her kiss him good night—then leave the room. I waited, and then crept in through the french window, which was unlocked. I think he must have been asleep when I hit him. Still, it ain't much use saying anything. I don't suppose they will let her out yet. You know, there should be a doctor with her when they tell her I'm arrested, because she will go out of her mind.

This statement seems spontaneous, and its interest needs no underlining. In view of what was suggested later, however, it is worth noting here that this statement is important not only for what it includes but for what it omits. There is, for instance, no hint that Stoner had been inhaling cocaine on the Sunday evening.

Mrs. Rattenbury had appeared first before the magistrates on March 25th, and been remanded. When she appeared again, with Stoner, on April 3rd, she was charged with murder, jointly with Stoner. The case opened on April 11th, and continued from week to week in the usual way.

In the meantime the inquest on Mr. Rattenbury had been opened on April 2nd, for formal evidence of death only. The police surgeon gave evidence that the cause of death was laceration of and haemorrhage into the brain and into the skull, as a result of a compound fracture produced by injuries. The coroner pressed him to add that the injury was produced by a blow, but the surgeon very properly refused. The inquest was then adjourned till June 27th. By that date the trial was over, and a non-committal verdict was returned to the effect that the damage as detailed by the police surgeon had been produced by " a violent injury ".

On April 18th Mrs. Rattenbury wrote a letter to Miss Riggs containing the following passages :

Oh, Lord! To-morrow Good Friday and I dare not think of the children. I have been pretending I have not any here. If one thought for five minutes they would go mad. Good Friday will be like Sunday here. Of all the days in the week, Sunday is the worst.

I have to control my mind like the devil not to think of little John. Yes, take him out on Sundays, darling. C. was awfully pleased to hear from you. My M. not doing anything. Can you? Messages of love are not much use to me now, I want your help. . . . However, I feel awfully sad being separated in such a ghastly way from everything that one loves. S.'s feelings must take some weighing up, but he will be the same and not allow himself to think.

Should think his remorse at what he has brought upon my head, the children, etc.—smashed life—would drive him a raving lunatic. Frightful responsibility to hold in one person's hands. God deliver me from such a hellish responsibility. I cannot have courage enough to bear that pain. My own is more than enough in a hundred lifetimes as it is.

At times have found my feelings very hard and bitter. Oh, my God, appallingly so, but have managed to drown these feelings and get one's heart soft again. Darling, God bless you; bless us all and get us out of this nightmare. My love to your M. and F. My love be with you always.

LOZANNE

Those interested in human problems may speculate why Mrs. Rattenbury should have signed this letter to Miss Riggs " Lozanne ", a name which had never been used between them before.

The magistrates having duly committed both Mrs. Rattenbury

and Stoner, and the grand jury having returned a true bill, their joint trial began at the Old Bailey on Monday, May 27th, only just over two months from the date of the murder. Queues waited hours for the opening of the court, and unemployed men offered to sell their places for large sums.

Mr. Justice Humphreys was on the bench, and Mr. R. P. Croom-Johnson, K.C., M.P., led for the prosecution, assisted by Mr. Anthony Hawke. For Mrs. Rattenbury were Mr. T. J. O'Connor, K.C., and the Hon. E. E. Montague. Mr. J. D. Casswell, fresh from a successful appeal for murder before the House of Lords, appeared for Stoner. Both prisoners are reported as pleading not guilty in " faint but firm voices ".

While the jury were being sworn Mr. Casswell made an application that the accused should be tried separately, and on the direction of the judge the jury left the box while the case was argued. Mr. Casswell quoted the letter written by Mrs. Rattenbury to Miss Riggs on April 18th and submitted that it showed a distinct intention to throw responsibility on the other prisoner. Mr. Justice Humphreys held that there was no ground for directing that there should be separate trials. Mr. Croom-Johnson accordingly opened the case for the prosecution.

He outlined the relations between Mrs. Rattenbury and Stoner, gave a short account of the events which took place on the night of March 24th, and produced the fatal mallet, suggesting that this was the 'heavy instrument' which had made the three wounds on Mr. Rattenbury's head: which, in view of the human hairs and skin found upon it, it undoubtedly was. Mr. Croom-Johnson also quoted the various ' statements ' made by the accused and, concerning that made by Mrs. Rattenbury to Inspector Mills at 3.30 a.m., counsel commented :

> In the submission of the prosecution, if those words are right, blows were struck, according to this statement, by Mrs. Rattenbury, and the reason why they had not killed Mr. Rattenbury outright was that her physical strength was not sufficient.

It is a sign of the fairness with which Mr. Croom-Johnson

conducted the prosecution, both in this speech and subsequently, that he should have qualified the submission of the prosecution so pointedly. It may also be a sign of Mr. Croom-Johnson's own opinion of the case which he had to present against the female prisoner.

Evidence was then called to prove the possession of the mallet by Stoner on the evening of March 24th. This mallet belonged to Stoner's uncle, and Stoner had borrowed it from his grand-parents' house in the early evening of March 24th. He said that he wanted to drive in some tent-pegs with it. (In the reports of the trial as published in the daily press, no question is recorded to elucidate whether or not any tent-pegs were to be driven in during the next day or two at the Villa Madeira, so that one cannot judge whether this was a genuine reason for borrowing the mallet or an excuse. If no such question was ever put, this would seem a curious omission on the part of the prosecution, for the importance of this point is obvious so far as the degree of premeditation is concerned.)

The first important witness was Miss Irene Riggs, whose evidence occupied all the rest of the day. It included, however, nothing of importance which has not already been stated in this narrative. Miss Riggs was in the box five hours, and everyone, including the judge, was kind to her. In reply to Mr. Justice Humphreys Miss Riggs said that she had never known Mrs. Rattenbury take drugs, such as cocaine, morphia, or heroin.

Mrs. Rattenbury and Stoner had listened to the hearing intently but with expressionless faces. They sat at opposite ends of the dock, and took no notice of each other, not even by a glance. Mrs. Rattenbury kept her eyes fixed most of the time on the judge. Stoner, a little pale, appeared almost indifferent. Mrs. Rattenbury was wearing blue.

At midnight the queue began to form for the next day's hearing.

Police and medical evidence occupied the second day. A hare had been started to the effect that Mrs. Rattenbury drugged, in consequence of the finding of the hypodermic syringe and needles in the bathroom cupboard, and some time was wasted in chasing it before the explanation was reached that the syringe had been used for injections into Mrs. Rattenbury's elder son two years earlier. It was therefore finally accepted that Mrs. Rattenbury did not drug.

Cross-examination by the defence showed that Mrs. Rattenbury's own doctor was definitely sympathetic. He had no exalted opinion of Mrs. Rattenbury, but succeeded in making it plain between the words that he did not consider her capable of committing or planning this very crude murder. Discussing Mrs. Rattenbury's peculiar temperament with the witness, Mr. O'Connor put one telling question which the judge disallowed on the grounds that it was a matter for the jury to decide. Mr. O'Connor had, however, made his point:

As her medical attendant, and one who had every opportunity for seeing her temperament at close quarters, do you think it would be possible for Mrs. Rattenbury to take part in a crime of this description and then act perfectly normally and peacefully with her maid?

The witness's negative reply must have sounded almost as emphatically as if he had actually made it.

In his cross-examination for Stoner Mr. Casswell put his foot well down on the cocaine pedal and kept it there till he had forced the witness to admit that he had believed Stoner to be taking cocaine; the inference, which Mr. Casswell was too wily to press, being that the doctor still believed that Stoner had been taking cocaine. Another point which Mr. Casswell brought out was that when driving the doctor back from the nursing-home on the night of March 24th, Stoner had not appeared at all agitated or apprehensive.

The surgeon who had made the post-mortem testified that the three blows must have been dealt with very considerable force.

Mr. O'Connor made another cunning point for Mrs. Rattenbury in his cross-examination of Inspector Mills:

Did you follow up her statement, "I will tell you in the morning where the mallet is"?—No, I did not question her.

Was not that because you did not think she was in a fit condition to give intelligent answers?—No.

Why not ask her where the mallet was?—I did not ask her.

MR. JUSTICE HUMPHREYS (*to* MR. O'CONNOR): Do you really suggest that in these circumstances the police-officer should have cross-examined her?

MR. O'CONNOR: I do not suggest that. I do not blame him for not having pursued the point.

The judge, of course, knew perfectly well what Mr. O'Connor was really suggesting: that if Mrs. Rattenbury, having shown willingness to hand over the mallet, had at that point been pressed to do so, she would have been unable, because she did not know where it was—*ergo* it was not she who had hidden it, *ergo* it was not she who had used it. One cannot, of course, blame the Inspector for not having pressed this inquiry when Mrs. Rattenbury was in such a condition; nevertheless it is a pity that, fairly or unfairly, he did not do so. The result would at least have been interesting. It might even have settled definitely the question of Mrs. Rattenbury's complicity, for or against.

On the third day it was first the turn of the experts.

Dr. Roche Lynch gave the weight of the mallet as 2 lb. 7 oz., and stated a cautious opinion that the hairs on it "in all probability" came from the head of the deceased. In cross-examination, Mr. Casswell tried hard to persuade him to admit that a person who had shown such characteristics as Stoner had, together with such symptoms as counsel was apparently inferring Stoner had felt, though no very satisfactory evidence was ever called to prove them, must be a cocaine addict. Mr. Casswell put his questions in such a way that Dr. Roche Lynch could not help replying to many of them in the affirmative; but Mr. Croom-Johnson destroyed, in re-examination, much more than Mr. Casswell had gained, by two or three simple questions, eliciting the facts that anyone who had taken two eggspoonfuls of cocaine would, even if a mild addict, become desperately ill and would certainly not be able to drive a car within a few hours.

It seems to have been in Brixton Prison, whither he was transferred from Dorchester on May 14th, that Stoner began to develop this drug-fiend defence; possibly as a result of a certain successful interview which he had had at Dorchester. The senior medical officer of the former prison, Dr. Grierson, deposed that Stoner had told him that he used to take cocaine between slices of bread, and that at about 4.30 p.m. on March 24th he had scoffed two eggspoonfuls of it. If so, he must have been almost more than habituated; yet on May 14th he was rational in behaviour and conversation, and since then had eaten and slept normally and gained 8 lb. in weight. Mr. Casswell, with his usual ingenuity, got round all these difficulties by suggesting that the interval at Dorchester Prison had been enough to wean Stoner from his craving and restore him to physical normality, and that cocaine is usually sold illegally in a much diluted form, so that it would be quite possible to take as much as two eggspoonfuls of a sufficiently diluted mixture. With this evident fact Dr. Grierson had to agree. Once more, however, Mr. Croom-Johnson spiked his opponent's gun. Eliciting from the witness that Stoner had confided to him that cocaine always made him excited, causing him to curse and swear, Mr. Croom-Johnson asked simply: " Is that the usual effect of taking cocaine? " The witness replied that it was not; the usual effect of cocaine was to make people feel happy and contented. But the most unfortunate item for Mr. Casswell in this witness's evidence was the fact that Stoner had described cocaine to Dr. Grierson as " a brown powder with black spots in it ". There was no way of getting round this howler.

The medical officer of Dorchester Prison then deposed that during the time Stoner was under his care he showed none of the usual signs of a cocaine addict deprived of his drug; he seemed perfectly healthy and normal. Mr. Casswell prudently did not cross-examine this witness.

The case for the prosecution ended with witnesses to the stay of Mrs. Rattenbury and Stoner in London on March 19th and the purchases made for Stoner. Mr. O'Connor then at once called Mrs. Rattenbury.

For the third day in succession no recognition had passed between the prisoners. Mrs. Rattenbury now seemed tired, though she declined an offer of a chair in the witness-box, and a doctor was with her in the dock all day, as well as a wardress. Her evidence lasted three hours; and for those to whom a precedent may be welcome, it may be added that she wore "a smart blue dress and fur cape, with elbow-length blue gloves".

As has been said, Mrs. Rattenbury made a very favourable impression in the witness-box. She answered naturally, often using gesture to help out her meaning, and with composure; only when she was telling how she went downstairs and found her husband injured did she show emotion. She answered unpleasant questions with great frankness, and all those who heard her believed that what she said in the witness-box could really be relied on as the truth.

Nor did she try to gloss over or excuse her own conduct, as most witnesses do. In this connexion one passage during her cross-examination is peculiarly illuminating in more than one respect:

> Did you tell your husband that you were buying clothes for Stoner?—I never told him that I was buying clothes even for little John.
>
> You bought silk pyjamas at 60s. a suit?—That might seem absurd, but that is my disposition.
>
> You have told us that on the Sunday night Stoner came into your bedroom and got into bed with you. That was something which happened frequently?—Oh, always.
>
> Were you fond of your little boy John?—I love both my children.
>
> Were you fond of John?—Naturally.
>
> Did John sleep in the same room?—Yes, but in another bed on the other side of the room.
>
> Not a very large room?—No, but little John was always asleep.
>
> Are you suggesting to members of the jury that you, a mother, fond of her little boy of 6, was permitting this man to get into bed with you in the same room where your little innocent child was asleep?—I do not consider that that was frightful or dreadful.

The pluckiness no less than the honesty of that last answer is commendable. Mrs. Rattenbury did not, of course, consider her conduct frightful or dreadful, because it had been she who had ordered it, and she knew just how it had come about, how ordinary and inevitable it had been, how exceptional the circumstances were, and, therefore, how it had been anything but frightful or dreadful; though if she had been one of the ten million British wives and mothers who avidly read these words the next morning, and if the words and the circumstances had been somebody else's, Mrs. Rattenbury would doubtless have agreed with counsel for the prosecution that such a thing was both frightful and dreadful. (The more sophisticated readers would, perhaps, not mind the immorality so much as the bad taste.) As it was, however, the question (which we may hope was not intended as an incidental lesson in grammar) could only have been designed to show what a callous, inhuman, and abandoned fiend the prisoner must be; and Mrs. Rattenbury, instead of wriggling before this spear-thrust under her ribs, bravely accepted the challenge and replied, in effect, that counsel might think so but she did not.

With all the information which Mrs. Rattenbury's evidence afforded, we have already dealt; but there were one or two items not under this heading which may be quoted. It was plain that she had been thoroughly deceived by Stoner's drug-taking fantasy, and she denied with great emphasis that she had ever taken drugs herself. She showed considerable reluctance to speak of the wish her husband had expressed on the afternoon of March 24th to commit suicide. When counsel suggested that her feeling for Stoner was "just an infatuation", Mrs. Rattenbury replied: "I think it was more than that." "You fell in love with him?" asked counsel. "Absolutely," Mrs. Rattenbury answered. The word was her favourite one, and she used it often instead of a mere 'Yes'; a little character-pointer which is not without its interest.

Here is another instance of the witness's honesty under cross-examination, even when speaking the truth might harm her own case:

Were you fond of your husband?—I did not love him; no.

If he had wanted his rights as a husband would you have been ready to grant them to him in March 1935?—No.

If counsel had hoped to elicit some damaging admission upon the significance of which he could afterwards enlarge, he had it here handed to him on a plate, so openly that perhaps the gift embarrassed rather than helped him.

Mr. O'Connor's examination concluded with the usual meaningless question which defending counsel always put to their clients, as if the assumption was that anyone would rather confess to murder than commit perjury, and which the newspapers the next morning always call 'dramatic':

Did you yourself murder your husband?—Oh, no.

Did you take any part whatsoever in planning it?—No.

Did you know anything about it until Stoner spoke to you in your bed?—No. I would have prevented it had I known a half or a quarter of a minute before—naturally!

In this, as in the rest of her evidence, Mrs. Rattenbury no doubt spoke the truth. In fact the only statements of hers which seem open to any doubt are those in which she denied any memory at all of everything that happened after she was sick on the whisky she had drunk soon after finding her husband wounded; and one would not be sceptical here were the maxim not so well known that ignorance is the best defence. Even so, Mrs. Rattenbury almost carries conviction:

I can remember a few things, like an awful nightmare. I remember rubbing his hands because they were cold, and I wanted to get his teeth in for him to tell me what had happened. And little John standing in the doorway with his little face—I remember that. I remember getting into the car, but I don't know what car.

Finally, the judge himself put a few questions to Mrs. Rattenbury on this point, making clear to the jury her contention that she remembered perfectly what Stoner had said to her in bed, even down to the detail of hiding the mallet; it was only later that her memory failed.

"But you remember every word by Stoner just before?" persisted the judge.

"Yes, naturally," Mrs. Rattenbury replied. "I hadn't had that dreadful shock then. I was quite happy. Life was different."

Mr. Casswell was in a difficult position when he rose to open the case for Stoner, and he made no secret of his difficulties to the jury. He began with a reference to the case of Thompson and Bywaters, and warned the jury not to look on that case as a precedent for this one, for in that there was indisputable evidence that both the accused were present when the fatal blow was struck.

Mr. Casswell pointed out that the case for the Crown was one of conspiracy: two people were in the dock, and the prosecution averred that each was equally guilty with the other. Yet:

> Can you imagine any crime which bears less evidence of having been the result of two people working it out beforehand? It was the result of a sudden impulse—the mad act of one only.

> This is the position [pointed out counsel, as well he might]. The Crown accusing two people, and each one trying to take the blame on him—or herself: and one of them a cocaine addict whose statements cannot be relied upon. You can imagine that the defence of Stoner has been a very anxious task. You can imagine that few stones have been left unturned to find out what is the truth. Because if this had not been a joint trial—if I could have been in the happy position of representing Stoner and Stoner alone, I could have said boldly that the prosecution have not proved their case: the evidence against this boy is practically nothing. But how can I do that when there is someone else in the dock?

That counsel for Stoner intended to be very careful for that other person in the dock he showed at once. Referring further to the Thompson-Bywaters case, he said:

> Many doubts have been expressed as to whether one of those persons was rightly convicted. That is the sort of thing you will

be particularly careful to see does not happen here. There must be no mistake.

This was tantamount to an admission from Stoner's counsel that Mrs. Rattenbury was innocent. The admission that Stoner alone was responsible was a necessary corollary. Having committed himself so far on his journey between Scylla and Charybdis, Mr. Casswell then indicated what, in these peculiar and perhaps unique circumstances, his defence was to be. Suggesting that a possible verdict in the case of Stoner was 'guilty, but insane', counsel offered them what amounted to his own way out of the difficulty: that the confusion in Stoner's mind was such, and the toxic effect of the cocaine was such, that he was not capable of forming the necessary intent to make the crime of murder. In other words, he gave them the alternative of manslaughter.

> I ask you [pleaded Mr. Casswell], when you have heard the evidence, that in view of the facts of this case and incidents of the crime, it is impossible to say anybody did it in his normal mind.

(Even at the risk of breaking the narrative one must pause here to wonder whether advocates really do use in their speeches such peculiar grammar, or whether this is always a fault in the reporting.)

This was about the best defence Stoner could make. It eliminated Mrs. Rattenbury from the crime and so might prevent a repetition of the Thompson-Bywaters blunder; and this altruism might not be without its own reward in the favourable impression it would make on the jury. Moreover, the elimination of Mrs. Rattenbury would have another good result for Stoner in removing the conspiracy to murder, which intensifies the degree of this crime so definitely. By saying, "Yes, he did it, the poor lad, maddened by jealousy and dulled by drugs, in a single mad moment," counsel was making the murder of Mr. Rattenbury a much more excusable act than the prosecution's version of an abandoned woman who would stick at nothing to obtain her sexual gratification, plotting with her brutal young lover to batter in a helpless old man's head. And in any case, to attempt to make Stoner out completely innocent would, in the face of Miss Riggs's evidence alone, have been hopeless.

The trial was adjourned in the middle of counsel's address, and on the next day, the fourth, Mr. Casswell proceeded to develop his plea by citing the recent successful appeal which he himself had made to the House of Lords in a case of murder, when the Lord Chancellor laid it down that when dealing with a murder case the Crown must prove: (a) death as the result of a voluntary act of the accused, and (b) malice on the part of the accused. In commenting on and explaining this dictum, Mr. Casswell stated the law on this point so clearly and interestingly as to deserve quotation in full:

> If the defence either from evidence given by the prosecution or from evidence called for the defence shows an explanation which, if true, would amount to a good defence, the onus of proof is still upon the prosecution to show that the defence is not true. But there is one exception, and it was clearly pointed out in the recent decision in the House of Lords. If the accused's defence is, " I did the act, but I had not sufficient intent, owing to a disease of the mind, or to drunkenness, or to the taking of drugs, which rendered me in such a state that I was incapable of forming that design," it is for the accused to prove that.

This, then, was the defence made on behalf of Stoner, and to maintain it counsel had to prove that Stoner was a drug-addict; a contention with which he had not had very much success so far. Mr. Casswell went on:

> You have heard the evidence of Mrs. Rattenbury, and on Stoner's behalf I accept and endorse the whole of her explanation of the matters which led up to the day of March 24th, and what happened on that day. It necessarily follows that she, in my submission, did not commit this act, and had nothing to do with it. The prisoner Stoner does not deny—in fact, admits—that it was his hand that struck the blow.

This was very fair. Indeed, the judge seemed to think that it

264

was too fair, and that counsel had gone beyond propriety in making this admission. The newspapers naturally seized upon it, and quite properly. We, the public, who were trying this man and woman, of course were anxious to know where the truth lay, so that we might be satisfied that the condemnation or leniency as it might be of our representatives, the jury, had been properly applied; and our only way of learning such things is through the newspapers. To castigate these, as the learned judge did the next day, for giving prominence to such a crux in the case, on the grounds that they " seem to regard this sort of terrible tragedy as a godsend to them ", was not only giving one half of the picture and that the smaller, but is an indication of a rather unfortunate attitude of mind not uncommon among our higher judiciary officials, that what goes on in their courts concerns only those people actually taking part in the proceedings and not at all the public in whose name all trials are held, who appoint the officials to conduct them, and who in the persons of their representatives, the jury, decide the issue.

Mr. Casswell then concluded his very able speech by repeating the alternatives which he had suggested to the jury of 'guilty, but insane' or manslaughter, with the reasons why they might arrive at either.

The Stoner parents were Mr. Casswell's first witnesses. Mr. Stoner testified to his son's weak physical condition, fainting fits, and general backwardness as a child, and Mrs. Stoner said that when he visited her early in the afternoon of March 24th, Stoner appeared quite normal. (Mr. Casswell later contrasted this normality with the scene Stoner made over the visit to Bridport.)

Counsel then got down to the real job, and called his two experts who were to prove that Stoner was a drug-addict.

The first was Dr. L. A. Weatherley, a mental expert and the president of the Society of Mental and Nervous Diseases. He had visited Stoner in Dorchester Prison, and though not prepared to say that Stoner was mentally deficient he was convinced that Stoner was a cocaine-addict. His conclusion was based on

Stoner's description of the cocaine-addict's hallucination of touch, as being like a rash moving about under his skin. Dr. Weatherley, having made up his mind on the main point, naturally found that everything else fitted in, particularly the violent jealousy. Even the fact that Stoner possessed a small dagger was regarded by Dr. Weatherley as a symptom of addiction to cocaine, who also unspiked the gun disabled by Dr. Grierson by stating that after the exaltation of cocaine passed off it was followed by a feeling of great mental irritability.

All the incidents on Stoner's part after 4.30 on March 24th were put down by Dr. Weatherley to cocaine, particularly the threats and violence over the Bridport visit and the accusation of 'relationship' (counsel's excellent word) by Mrs. Rattenbury with her husband when the bedroom door was closed in the afternoon, which the witness considered "entirely an hallucination of hearing arising out of cocainism".

The judge, who appears to have become a little restive under this sweeping positivism, then asked the witness whether all these incidents might also be consistent "with his not having taken a dose of cocaine, but being very angry and jealous with his mistress", to which Dr. Weatherley, sticking manfully by his artillery, replied, "I doubt it."

Mr. Casswell, indeed, must have deplored this continued scepticism on the part of the judge, for after further references to cocaine-induced jealousy we have the latter asking again: "Do you know after sixty-two years as a medical man that some people get very jealous without cocaine or drink having anything to do with it?" This time the witness had to cede a little ground and admit that he had heard of such disappointing cases.

As may be expected, Mr. Croom-Johnson got very little change out of this veteran in cross-examination, Dr. Weatherley definitely refusing to agree that cocaine-addicts get irritable and upset when deprived of the drug; morphia-addicts, heroin-addicts, any other addicts you like, yes, but cocaine-addicts, just as it happens, no.

Dr. Gillespie followed Dr. Weatherley into the witness-box.

Dr. Gillespie, the physician for psychological medicine at Guy's Hospital, explained the usual symptoms of the cocaine-addict, laying stress on the 'morbid jealousy', under the domination of which a person is extremely likely to misinterpret all the goings-on around him.

Here the judge interposed, "Is that not true of all jealousy?"

Dr. Gillespie, who does not seem to have displayed the true British doggedness of Dr. Weatherley, hedged a little. "Yes, my lord, but I should have thought it more likely to happen in a diseased jealousy."

"Have you ever read the play of *Othello*?" asked the judge.

Dr. Gillespie hedged again. He had read it—but a long time ago.

This exchange seems to have thrown counsel as well as witness a little off his balance, for a few moments later Mr. Casswell asked what must be one of the most difficult questions ever put to a witness:

Is a person at the moment of committing that act of violence likely to think much beforehand of the consequences?

Nevertheless, Dr. Gillespie was equal to this, and replied, in effect, that he did not believe that such a person would think much beforehand while in the act of committing violence; wherein the doctor was undoubtedly right.

A little later, when the possible regeneration of cocaine-addicts was under discussion, the judge took the business in hand again and, thrusting a pin through all the verbiage, pricked Mr. Casswell's pretty balloon with this unkind but pertinent question to the witness:

Do you know in your experience any such case as this—a cocaine-addict suddenly cut off from any supply, given no drugs of any sort or kind to take the place of cocaine, and from the day that the supply is cut off, for a period of two months, being a person who could probably be described as rational, sleeping well, taking his food well, and being perfectly healthy?

267

Dr. Gillespie then had to admit that, on the whole, and perhaps with qualifications, he would be surprised to meet such a case.

That ended the expert evidence for the defence.

Those who expected Stoner to take his turn next in the box were disappointed. Mr. Casswell, rising to make his final address, explained that to put Stoner in the box could not help the jury at all, since he was under the influence of a drug at the time, and what he could say would be of little consequence. Nor had Mr. Casswell much new to say. He summed up the evidence he had called, and asked the jury to say that, from the time he threatened Mrs. Rattenbury at the telephone with a revolver, Stoner's acts were "not those of a normal boy, but the acts of somebody under the influence of insane hallucination". As for the contention of the prosecution that the murder had been planned and committed to get Mr. Rattenbury out of the way, "Whose way was he in?" asked Mr. Casswell.

One striking passage in Mr. Casswell's speech sums up nearly everything that we feel to be strange, and therefore wrong, about this case:

> In my submission the only motive that can be assigned was entirely unsufficient for this crime. It was simply the motive to prevent the trip to Bridport.
>
> You get this clumsy crime, committed in this clumsy manner, with no chance of an alibi, no attempt at escape, no chance of the defence of accident, no chance of pleading that it was suicide.
>
> By all these considerations you are driven, and inevitably driven, to the conclusion that this was an act of impulse, the act of somebody who had not planned it beforehand, who acted under an impulse—as I suggest, an uncontrollable impulse.

Much of this is true. The crime was certainly one of the most stupid murders ever committed. Yet it is possible to believe that Mr. Casswell's 'inevitable conclusion' contains only half the truth.

Repeating his offer of guilty but insane or manslaughter, Mr. Casswell sat down.

Mr. Croom-Johnson summed up the case for the prosecution very temperately. He suggested that the key to the solution of the problem was that "Stoner throughout this unhappy story was dominated by Mrs. Rattenbury", and asked whether it was possible to believe the word of a woman "who, upon her own statement, has for some years been engaged in lying to her husband about money matters". He cast doubt on Mrs. Rattenbury's assertion that her mind went blank, and said that it was his duty, on behalf of the prosecution, to suggest to the jury that the statements in which Mrs. Rattenbury had incriminated herself were the truth. Mr. Croom-Johnson also laid stress on the exchange between Mrs. Rattenbury and Stoner as the former was leaving the house under arrest; he described this evidence as "of the greatest significance in the case", and asked the jury whether it did not indicate to them that the two prisoners had had a common object that night.

Mr. Croom-Johnson was dealing with Mr. Casswell's suggestion of a verdict of guilty but insane, when the judge intervened to say that he intended to tell the jury not only that such a verdict would not be justified, but that they must put out of their minds Mr. Casswell's admission that it had been Stoner who struck the blows. "They must decide the case on the evidence and not on any quasi-admission his counsel may make. Stoner has not said so," remarked the judge.

Mr. Croom-Johnson concluded his speech with a remarkable sentence, in which he deliberately allowed the human being to show through the mask of duty:

> But if, and perhaps mercifully in pursuance of your oath, you can still bring yourselves to the view that you are not satisfied that a case has been made out to your satisfaction, then it will be your duty—and, possibly, a pleasure to us all—for you to say, not being satisfied, that your verdict is a verdict for the defence.

This was the clearest possible hint to the jury that the prosecution, though dutifully putting forward such evidence as there was against Mrs. Rattenbury, were not really pressing the case against her—and might even be grateful for an acquittal.

Mr. O'Connor began his address for Mrs. Rattenbury with a tribute to the fairness with which the prosecution had been conducted, as well he might. Counsel did not spare the moral character of his client, but warned the jury that this must not mean "that justice is to be prostituted because you have been misled, because of your hatred of the life she has been leading"; and he pointed out, rightly, that without her own statements there was no evidence against Mrs. Rattenbury at all. "Fragments snatched from the disordered mind of a woman sodden with drink and hysteria," was Mr. Connor's unflattering but graphic description of his client's confession.

Counsel for the defence came perhaps nearer the mark than counsel for the prosecution when he spoke of Mrs. Rattenbury as a woman "who, by her own acts and folly, had erected in the boy a Frankenstein of jealousy which she could not control". Disregarding the incorrectness of the literary allusion, this is more like the truth than that the key to the solution of the problem was Mrs. Rattenbury's domination of Stoner. One does not dominate what one cannot control, and there is plenty of indication in the evidence that Mrs. Rattenbury could not by any means control Stoner. A woman of that type, too, revels in being dominated.

Mr. O'Connor made this handsome reference to Stoner:

> Stoner has played a gentleman's part. You may possibly think that he has atoned for a great deal by refusing to commit the supreme crime of seeing his mistress go to her doom for a crime which he knows he committed.

It may, indeed, have been this plea, even more than anything Stoner's own counsel said, which influenced the jury's verdict.

With the end of Mr. O'Connor's speech the proceedings of the fourth day concluded.

On the Friday morning Mr. Justice Humphreys began his summing-up.

Beginning in the usual way by explaining the law as it bears upon two persons agreeing together to commit a felony, the judge remarked that his five days' experience of the case had satisfied him that he had been right in deciding that the two defendants should be tried together. Then, having dealt with such facts as were common to both prisoners, he proceeded to consider the case of Mrs. Rattenbury.

In view of the fact that upon many important matters Mrs. Rattenbury was the only person to have given evidence (said the judge), it was essential for the jury to make up their minds whether they believed her evidence or not; and that would depend to some extent on the kind of woman they considered her to be. This is much the same as Mr. Justice Shearman said in his summing-up in the Thompson case, and is a proper use of evidence concerning character. But whereas the judge in the Thompson-Bywaters case allowed the jury to gather that in his opinion a woman who could be guilty of adultery could just as well be guilty of murder—that the step, in fact, from adultery to murder was only a small one—Mr. Justice Humphreys was evidently not going to have any share' for his own part in yet another British condemnation for adultery on a charge of murder. Let us salute the first British judge who has definitely warned a jury against our own particular national injustice (does it arise out of priggishness, sadism, or womanly influence?) in these plain words:

Having heard your own counsel with regard to the facts of this case, it may be you will say that you cannot possibly feel any sympathy with this woman. You cannot possibly have any feeling except of disgust for her. But let me say this: that should not make you more ready to convict her of this crime. It should, if anything, make you less ready to accept evidence against her, if you think there can be any explanation consistent with her innocence. But I know you will not let it prejudice you against her. So far as it is material evidence in this case, you must use it. If you think it shows the sort of woman who might have the motive to do this thing, then you must use it because it is admissible evidence. But beware that you do not convict her of this crime because she is an adulteress—and an adulteress, you may think, of the most unpleasant type.

This is very fair; very fair indeed. One may, perhaps, have all sorts of feelings for Mrs. Rattenbury besides disgust, but still —Mrs. Maybrick had been convicted of murder upon a single instance of adultery and a suspicion; Mrs. Thompson had been executed for adultery. Mr. Justice Humphreys, at any rate, did not intend to add to the list of these victims of the British Courts of Morals.

This was an innovation indeed. So far from safeguarding justice as the written law defines it, most judges in the past have gone out of the way to inflame the jury to condemn on the moral issue instead of the legal one. Contrast, for instance, the more reasonable of Mr. Justice Humphreys' words with a passage from the summing-up against Mrs. Thompson (the preposition is used advisedly):

> Just at the end of a letter I shall have to allude to again, comes this: "He has the right by law to all that you have the right to by nature and love." Gentlemen, if that nonsense means anything it means that the love of a husband for his wife is something improper because marriage is acknowledged by the law, and that the love of a woman for her lover, illicit and clandestine, is something great and noble. I am certain that you, like any other right-minded persons, will be filled with disgust at such a notion.

Alas, that is more like the attitude of our national judiciary which, set to try human beings who have lived and loved as their natures dictated and not with their noses in the statute-books, are either utterly ignorant of human nature or else deliberately disregard it. Could not every judge, before he is allowed to take his seat on the bench, be put through a short course, followed by an examination in psychology, love and plain ordinary cussed human nature? Then, perhaps, they might not make such egregious observations.

Although he was careful to add the rider of warning, Mr. Justice Humphreys showed that he fully shared this conventional legal attitude both in his unchristian reference to disgust for the woman caught out in adultery, and in pronouncing that adulterous relations "lack the one thing that makes for ordinary peaceable happiness between married couples, and that is respect". To say that respect cannot exist between a man and woman whose relations are legally improper is just as silly as to say that respect invariably exists between married couples. Marriage does not make for the one nor adultery for the other, which may be legally and even socially regrettable, but is true.

As to Stoner, the judge pointed out that the jury

> had no more right to give effect to evidence in his case from motives of pity than you have the right to refuse to give effect to evidence in her case which may be in her favour, because you thoroughly despise her. It is a pitiable thing that you should have been brought to this pass, and I do not think I am putting it unfairly even against her when I say that, whatever your verdict may be in the case, his position is due to the domination of this woman.

This, whether fair or not, is certainly arguable.

The judge then tried hard to persuade the jury that counsel for Stoner had not said what he did say, or, if he had said it, had not meant it.

> A little mistake was made by those who thought that Mr. Casswell intended to say that his client admitted striking the blow. It would have been quite improper for counsel who was not going to call evidence, to say anything of the sort, and it is not what Mr. Casswell meant at all. All he meant was that its being the case of the prosecution that they had to prove that it was Stoner who struck the blow, he was in the position, or at all events did not intend, to call evidence to contradict, and therefore did not propose to address you on that part of the case. He had therefore to leave it there. That is all he meant.
>
> As I rather expected, I noticed those newspapers which seem to regard this sort of terrible tragedy as a godsend to them, have found one thing and one thing only to put on their posters, and that was " Stoner's counsel said he committed the crime."

As, however, Mr. Casswell's exact words, as reported, were "Stoner does not deny—in fact, admits—that his hand struck the blow," the newspapers apparently were right and the learned judge wrong. The parenthesis may have been unfortunate, but there it was; and a million British homes were quite rightly relieved to know the truth.

Mr. Justice Humphreys was on more fertile ground when he passed on to Stoner's alleged drug-taking. Without precisely ridiculing it, and indeed treating it quite fairly, he gave the jury plainly to understand his opinion that this was all bunkum. He pointed out the absence in prison of all the symptoms usual to drug-addicts; he made a very reasonable point in reminding the jury that Mrs. Rattenbury had said nothing of Stoner appearing abnormal or under the influence of a drug when he told her in bed what he had done, and he put forward for their consideration this significant suggestion:

> Now here I am bound to point out to you something which you may think is the most important fact about this matter, and perhaps is conclusive. There is one human being who knows whether Stoner was in the habit of taking cocaine or whether he was not, or whether he took it that afternoon. That person is Stoner himself. He is an admissible and available witness, and if he wishes, or those who defend him wish, to prove that he is or was addicted to drugs, had taken cocaine or was under the influence of cocaine, is there any witness on earth who could do it as well as Stoner? It seems to me, in the circumstances of this case, a fact of most profound significance that Stoner prefers not to give evidence.

This was a legitimate comment on the part of the judge, and is true enough, though it might be that Stoner, who, if he went into the witness-box to prove himself a cocaine-addict, would lay himself open to all sorts of other questions too, had further awkward secrets to keep hidden.

As to the plea of guilty but insane, the judge would have none of it; there was no evidence to justify it, and without such evidence the issue could not be left to the jury at all.

Lastly, Mr. Justice Humphreys commented on the 'statement' made by Mrs. Rattenbury in the morning, while she was still muddled by morphia. Saying that he had no power to withdraw this statement from the evidence, the judge hinted very strongly to the jury to take no notice of it. "It seems to me to be . . . not quite acting with the fairness which, I suppose, one may say is characteristic of our criminal courts," he remarked, with a kind of suave bluntness.

The judge then went through certain portions of the evidence in detail, and concluded after speaking for three and a half hours. His summing-up was not only absolutely fair throughout, but in places masterly; and one hopes that other judges will profit by it.

The jury were absent for about an hour. The verdicts were: Mrs. Rattenbury not guilty, Stoner guilty, with a recommendation to mercy. The recommendation in Stoner's case was presumably due to his youth and to the jury's belief, following the expressed opinions of the judge and counsel for the prosecution that he had been under the domination of Mrs. Rattenbury.

When asked if he had anything to say before sentence of death was passed, Stoner stood firmly erect and replied, in a low but steady voice: "Nothing at all."

Mr. Justice Humphreys then passed sentence, saying that the jury's recommendation would be forwarded to the proper quarter, and Stoner was taken back to prison.

Mrs. Rattenbury, who had been waiting, still in custody, in the corridor below while Stoner was being sentenced, was then called back to the court. As the wardress was helping her towards the short flight of stone stairs which leads to the dock, she met Stoner face to face as he was hurried past. They exchanged a silent look. Did each of them know it was the last?

Mrs. Rattenbury was kept standing in the dock for a few minutes while the officials discussed whether or not to proceed with a second indictment charging her with being an accessory after the fact, knowing that Stoner "had wounded with intent to murder". Mrs Rattenbury now looked tired and worn. Finally, it was announced that the prosecution would offer no evidence, and Mrs. Rattenbury was formally discharged.

The trial had been followed with great interest by the population as a whole, and the verdicts were received with relief. In the minds of most citizens the injustice done to Mrs. Thompson remained as a little lump of uneasiness, and there was a general feeling, which the judge and counsel for the prosecution interpreted, that a similar injustice must not be allowed to occur in the case of Mrs. Rattenbury.

It was this feeling which added the extra sharpness to the popular interest in the trial, but even without it there was plenty of reason for interest. Superior persons deprecate this interest in murder trials as morbid, or sensation-seeking; judges openly resent it; yet if one faces the corollary, it is difficult to see how any normal person can remain indifferent to a trial such as this, and its result. One might go so far as to throw the challenge to the superior persons that actually it is the interest which is normal and indifference abnormal.

For quite apart from the responsibility which, in a take-it-for-granted, undefined, perhaps unrecognized way, we, the people, feel as any democracy should feel concerning those who are being tried in our name and by our chosen representatives (so that any mishap to justice is not a thing apart from us, but brings shame on each individual man or woman among us), there is the common humanity which draws each of us towards another human being in prolonged peril of life. Here the popular interest in a murder trial is akin to that with which the account is followed of a disabled ship floundering in a distant sea. Will it keep afloat till the rescuers reach it, or will it sink? We know nothing of the men on board; we do not even know their names; but—will they live or die? This, too, explains why the interest aroused by a trial for murder is so much greater than that aroused by the most notorious of crooked financiers; and not only greater, but different, for it exists on a higher plane in the human mentality.

That it can exist simultaneously on a lower plane is not to be disputed, for we must admit that, spicing this interest in a rescue at sea no less than in a trial for murder, there is a minute pinch of sadism: nothing abnormal and only in proportion to the minute pinch of sadism which is common to nearly all of us, but there it is. It is, however, only when this pinch becomes a handful, so that there is positive gloating over the agonies which the accused must be enduring, that interest in a murder trial can be called morbid, which means diseased, or even sensation-mongering; and that surely can only happen in very few instances.

Then there is what, for want of a more precise term, may be called 'scientific' interest. This is the appeal exercised by the detective-story, in distinction to the thriller, the appeal of the puzzle, the wish to know the truth.

"Why," I asked myself when I began to write this account, "does this case interest you so much? Why do so many murder-cases interest you so much? Why do others not interest you at all? Are you morbid?"

"No," I replied indignantly to myself, "I am not morbid, and if you'll let me think a minute I'll answer you. Yes, I am interested on two main counts; as a student of character I am interested in the minds which, whether through attributes or deficiencies as the case may show, can first envisage murder as a practical solution of their difficulties and then, which is much rarer, turn this vision into action—in other words, I suppose, since most interests have an egotistical basis, as a psychological mechanic, if I may so describe myself to you, I am interested to compare these engines of the human chassis with my own, so like and yet, I sincerely hope, so unlike; and secondly, I have a sneaking passion for the truth, and when A says one thing and B another and the fact that C seems to prove both of them wrong, I will hunt the real truth through acres of examination, cross-examination, advocacy, summing-up, and other rough country, till I can feel satisfied that I have made my kill. Those are my two chief reasons, and as a minor one I can cite the interest I feel in the lives of other people and how they are lived, and nothing outside fiction so effectually knocks down the front wall of a house and exposes its occupants in the details of their strange lives as does a trial for murder."

Those who, as spectators, follow a murder trial, not in the

newspapers but in court, have recorded not without surprise that they found themselves paying very little attention to the prisoners in the dock. The fact that a life is dependent on the way the game is played, and the winning of it, is lost in the game itself. The efforts to dig out the truth, the efforts sometimes to conceal it, the vast attention paid to the rules under which the truth is to be sought as if the rules were more important than the truth itself, the manœuvring and counter-manœuvring inside those rules, the bull-fighters with their red flags and their higher intelligences cajoling, goading, or tricking the unwitting bulls of witnesses into the required position until zip! goes the sword, and the witness is pinned to the arena with an admission or a contradiction; these things hold the attention of the onlooker. Is it the interest of technique, and in court it seems to be paramount.

Political responsibility, common humanity, a pinch of sadism, desire to know the truth, psychology, life as it is lived by others, the technique of justice, and lastly, the determination of organized society to exact retribution for wrong-doing, these are the seven chief heads of the complicated, instinctive, popular interest in a trial for murder, and not one of them is abnormal. With the possible exception of the third, not one of them is even morbid.

Stoner had passed through his ordeal apparently unmoved. Through the whole five days of the trial he had shown no emotion, just as he had shown none after the murder. His face a little pale, his manner stolid, with a faintly sullen set to his mouth, he allowed no one to guess whether it was indifference, courage, resignation, or sheer inability to feel as other people do, that was holding him up. Mrs. Rattenbury had been slowly disintegrating under the eyes of the jury. During the long summing-up she had sat for the most part without moving a muscle; when she took up a glass of water it was with the mechanical action of a marionette.

Mrs. Rattenbury was not to profit by having been tried by a sensible judge and an intelligent jury. The ordeal had been too much for her certainly unbalanced temperament. On the third day after the acquittal she entered a London nursing-home for rest and treatment. At about 3.30 the next afternoon, of Tuesday June 4th, she borrowed £2 from one of the officials of the home and went out, after telling the matron that she would be back by nine o'clock. She appeared to the matron to be in a normal state of bodily health, and since the doctor had said she could go out neither the matron nor anyone else had the power to detain her.

From 3.30 p.m. there is a five-hours' blank. Then, at 8.30 p.m. on the same day a labourer, walking through a meadow near Christchurch, Bournemouth, saw a woman sitting on the opposite bank of a stream, a backwater of the Avon, near the place where a railway arch passed over it. She was alone, and was smoking a cigarette. The labourer noticed next, as he walked on, that there was a knife in the woman's hand, and as he looked at her he saw her tumble forward into the water. The man had to run up the bank on his own side of the stream, over the bridge, and down the other side. When he reached her, the woman was lying face upwards in the water a few feet from the bank. The labourer, who could not swim, waded out as far as he dared, but could not reach her, so snatched up her fur coat, which was lying on the bank and threw the end of it towards her, but the woman made no attempt to catch it. The man then saw that there was blood in the water, and as he could do no more for her he ran to a cottage near by for help. It was now about 8.40 p.m.

Collecting a second man, and a pole, the rescuer hurried back, but the pole was too short and they could do nothing. The first man then went to notify the police, while the second went back to his cottage for a longer pole. With this he was able to pull the body ashore, and when a policeman arrived at 9 p.m. he found it lying on the bank. A few yards away was a handbag, containing a number of letters, and a paper bag in which was a dagger-sheath. The body was identified later as that of Mrs. Rattenbury.

Examined by a doctor the next morning, the body showed six

stab-wounds in the chest, five large and one small. Five of the wounds were in the left breast, all passing downwards and inwards, and of these no less than three had penetrated the heart, one of them making a large cut through which the instrument had apparently passed more than once. The doctor considered that death must have been almost instantaneous and that Mrs. Rattenbury would have been dead before she reached the water.

At the inquest which was held on the following Friday, June 6th, at Christchurch, extracts were read from the letters Mrs. Rattenbury had left. The first was from a letter dated June 4th:

> I want to make it perfectly clear that no one is responsible for what action I may take regarding my life. I quite made up my mind at Holloway to finish things should Stoner . . . and it would only be a matter of time and opportunity. Every night and minute is only prolonging the appalling agony of my mind.

At this point the coroner broke off, saying: "Then this goes into quite a lot of neurotic statements." One would have thought that these neurotic statements would have been valuable evidence as to the deceased's state of mind, but nothing more from this letter was read.

The next extract came from a letter addressed to "The Governor of His Majesty's Prison, Pentonville," and ran:

> If I only thought it would help Stoner I would stay on, but it has been pointed out to me all too vividly I cannot help him. That is my death sentence.

Another passage had been written on the back of an old envelope:

> Eight o'clock. After so much walking I have got here. Oh, to see the swans and spring flowers, and just smell them. And how singular I should have chosen the spot Stoner said he nearly jumped out of the train once at.
>
> It was not intentional my coming here. I tossed a coin like Stoner always did, and it came down Christchurch. It is beautiful here. What a lovely world we are in. It must be easier to be hanged than to have to do the job oneself, especially in these circumstances of being watched all the while.

Pray God nothing stops me to-night. Am within five minutes of Christchurch now. God bless my children and look after them.

Another extract, written the same evening, read:

I tried this morning to throw myself under a train at Oxford Circus. Too many people about. Then a 'bus. Still too many people about. One must be bold to do a thing like this. It is beautiful here and I am alone. Thank God for peace at last.

For once there was justification for that stereotyped verdict, suicide during temporary insanity, designed in true British compromise to get round an obsolete law and so save anyone the bother of repealing it. By this time Mrs. Rattenbury, if still not legally insane, was for all practical considerations so. The egomania of the neurotic pushed aside even her children's claims upon her life. She could not await the result of Stoner's appeal. Since *she* could not save him, she would die; whether anyone else might save him, seems hardly to have interested her. It was not Stoner, it was herself whom she was concerned about, to the end. She probably never wondered whether her death could be the least use to anyone, even to herself; it was the grand, the final gesture, and if there was a touch of exhibitionism and more than a touch of melodrama about it, well, that was only in character. The method she chose, surely unique in the annals of feminine suicide, not only shows the determination which her mania had lent her, but seems to convey a masochistic hint; and that, too, would only be in character.

So ended Mrs. Rattenbury, who had done a great deal of harm in her forty years of life, performed an unnecessary number of foolish actions, and been a great nuisance to many people; an anti-social creature, incapable of seeing any point of view but her own, and hag-ridden by her own lusts; but, nevertheless, a woman more deserving of pity than of the easy contempt she was forced to receive, and to be admired insofar as that, within the limits of the nature which she hardly tried to control, she was capable of the generous gesture and even of a certain nobility. Of many women who have never caused a murder, less could be said.

On June 25th Stoner's appeal was dismissed, the Lord Chief Justice calling it a waste of time.

> The fact [he said], if it be a fact, that a lad of good character has been corrupted by an abandoned woman old enough to be his mother, raises no question of law such as can be employed as a ground of appeal in this court.

The appeal had been made on the technical ground that there should have been separate trials, and that a joint trial involved the risk of a serious miscarriage of justice. There are sound arguments for this, but as a ground of appeal it was hopeless, both precedent and the law leaving no loophole for argument, however reasonable. As a secondary consideration, it was suggested that not enough importance had been attached by Mr. Justice Humphreys to "the defence of cocaine" ("Cocaine is not a defence," interrupted Lord Hewart. "It is a substance.") and that Stoner should now be heard as a witness on his own behalf.

Not unnaturally the Lord Chief Justice would have none of this. He described it as a cynical request, and said, rightly enough, that "there are no such exceptional circumstances here as would justify this court in permitting Stoner now, upon further consideration, to offer himself as a witness". Lord Hewart did not add, though he may have had the thought in mind, "Now that he has had time to receive a little coaching to the effect that cocaine is not a brown powder with black spots." He did add, however, that "if there is any observation to be made of the summing-up on this point, it is that Mr. Justice Humphreys treated with almost excessive respect the suggestion put to the jury". In other words the Court of Appeal no more believed that Stoner had been taking cocaine than did the judge in the court below: and, one must add, than any reasonable person could.

That the appeal would be dismissed must have seemed to Stoner's advisers inevitable. However, another string was being pulled at the same time, and shortly before the appeal was heard, a petition for Stoner's reprieve containing (it was said) 320,000 signatures, had been presented to the Home Secretary. There was considerable feeling in favour of a reprieve, and in this case the petition was not, as these petitions often are, at variance with public opinion. An important London newspaper voiced its own views—which means that it hoped it was voicing the views of its readers—in a leading article thus:

> We do not think it is putting it too high to say that public opinion is shocked at the idea that the ghastly drama in which this wretched boy has been involved must be rounded off by his death. We hope the Home Secretary will make a merciful decision without delay.

It is perhaps a little euphemistic to describe the bashing of a defenceless, drunken old man's head in with a mallet, apparently borrowed for the purpose, as a ghastly drama "in which this wretched boy has been involved", but this was an accurate interpretation of the public's opinion of the case at that time. Mrs. Rattenbury was the villain of it, not Stoner.

However that may be, the Home Secretary, Sir John Simon, who, being a really clever man, no doubt had his ear to the ground as every politician should and so few have, complied with the public's demand, and within twenty-four hours of the dismissal of his appeal, issued Stoner's reprieve, commuting his sentence to that of penal servitude for life. This means that Stoner, if his conduct is good, will be back among us in about fifteen years.

How does murder come about? How does it happen that an apparently decent, even lovable youth, can take a mallet and bang a defenceless, drunken old man on the head with it, intending that he shall die?

Before we can answer this question we have to determine so far as we can whether Stoner did intend that Mr. Rattenbury should die: and if he did so intend, over how long a period this intention had existed prior to the striking of the blows. On this vital matter there is very little evidence.

Perhaps the most helpful pointer is Stoner's statement to Miss Riggs when asked if his finger-prints would be found on the mallet: "No, I wore gloves." If it is true that Stoner had worn gloves and did not say this merely to impress Miss Riggs with his cleverness, in accordance with the vanity usual in criminals, this statement is surely decisive: it can only mean that Stoner did intend to kill Mr. Rattenbury, and was not merely trying to give him a painful tap or two to stop him from going to Bridport the next day and either saw red or underestimated his own strength, for we have evidence that the blows were delivered with considerable violence.

It is true that no finger-prints were found on the mallet, though it is equally true that the surface of the handle was not suitable for them; and there seems no reason to disbelieve this remark of Stoner's. Assuming then that he did wear gloves, this proves premeditation and malice extending at least over several minutes; and once premeditation is proved at all, the possibilities are open to any extension of the period. As evidence here, we have the borrowing of the mallet.

The mallet seems to have been borrowed round about eight o'clock on the evening of the murder. Stoner gave as his excuse that he wanted to drive in some tent-pegs in the garden. The validity or not of this pretext is crucial, and one can only repeat that it is surprising not to be able to find, in the reports of the trial, a single question put to Miss Riggs on this point. It seems, however, to have been assumed by all sides that the excuse was not a genuine one, and if we make the same assumption we get the premeditation-period put back at any rate to somewhere near the time of the upset over the journey to Bridport, which seems to have occurred round about six o'clock.

Is this, then, the end of the hunt? Was it the insane jealousy that Stoner showed over this trivial matter which, kept at white heat for nearly four hours, caused him to murder Mr. Rattenbury that same evening, with the full knowledge of what he was doing and the full intention to do it? This was Stoner's own counsel's submission, and it may be true. It may, on the other hand, be only part of the truth.

There is this at any rate to be said for it. The crime was an almost unbelievably stupid one, and unless Stoner was simply half-witted he must have known that he had no chance at all of escape. The only sane way of explaining such an imbecile action is that it must have been committed on the impulse of the moment, without time for reflection. Yet we seem to have proved that the crime was not committed on the impulse of the moment, but after premeditation, extending over at least four hours, which is a long time. Have we then to reconcile two irreconcilables before we can suggest any explanation of how Mr. Rattenbury's death came about?

I think we have not. We have been considering single-track reasons, and human motives are seldom so simple and uncomplicated as the courts have to pretend. Stoner did not quite act on impulse, nor yet did he carry out what was a cold-blooded, fully premeditated murder; and to understand what really was in his mind, we must pay some attention to the unwitting inspiration of his crime, Mrs. Rattenbury.

We have seen that Mrs. Rattenbury was a temperamental lady; we have been told on the highest authority that she was a wicked one. But for a proper estimate of her it cannot be too much emphasized that, if she was a wicked woman, she was an unconsciously wicked one: and we will leave it to the ethicists to determine whether actual wickedness can be anything but conscious. In any case Mrs. Rattenbury certainly would never have thought of herself as a bad woman, or as leading an immoral life, or indeed as anything that she ought not to have been. These things are so different when it is we ourselves who are the centre of the picture, and not some stranger. A faculty for detached self-analysis is rare, and quite a high degree of it is required before a woman can rise, scantily clad, from a lover's lap, a glass in one hand and a cigarette in the other, and remark: "Well, well, I suppose this is an orgy, and I am an improper person to be taking part in it."

The excuses—more, the very excellent reasons, which come rushing at once in support of our behaviour do not merely cloud such clear-sightedness: they forestall it. That these excuses do not hold good for other people in quite the same way, is merely natural. We should be poor creatures if we did not each one of us consider ourselves thoroughly and peculiarly different from the mass of other people.

Just as Mrs. Rattenbury would never have thought of herself as a bad woman, so she would never have looked on herself as an ordinary person. She would have recognised with pride how much more sensitive, more highly strung, more finely balanced she was than anyone else. And therefore she would take it for granted that the rules of conduct which apply to other and ordinary people, did not apply to her: a trait which the neurotics and the egocentrical hysterics share with the true criminal type. Not indeed that Mrs. Rattenbury would ever have reasoned the thing out, even in this simple way. She would have just taken it for granted that she was an exceptional, but certainly not an immoral woman.

Nor would it have occurred to her that she might be doing Stoner any *harm*. We may give her the benefit of the doubt and believe her that she was deceived at first in Stoner's age. When she learned how young he was, she tried to break things off: not because of any harm to Stoner, but probably for the sake of her own pride. Stoner, however, would not let her, and perhaps she did not try very hard. Afterwards she fell in love with him, and believed him to be in love with her: and how (she would think) can anything be wrong, or harmful, between two people who love? Nevertheless, it is my reading of Mrs. Rattenbury that, if anyone could have convinced her during this period that she really was doing Stoner harm, and that his association with herself was the worst possible thing for him, she would have given him up at once—if Stoner would have allowed himself to be given up.

As for the academic question of whether the association of a young man with a woman considerably older than himself is to be regarded always as harmful to the young man, that is debatable. The issue is usually confused, because so often the woman is married, but the court seemed to take it for granted that any such association is a terrible thing in itself, quite irrespective of what is to come out of it owing to the abnormality of one or other, or both, of the parties: and not only the association of a middle-aged married woman with a young man, but that between a young man and any 'woman old enough to be his mother'.

There is a case against the former, of course, because adultery is involved, and adultery, if not a legal crime, is a sin; so that any such relationship must be sinful, and therefore the parties to it must be guilt-conscious. In that, and in the lesson to disregard the marriage-bond, is where the harm lies for the younger delinquent. The flaw in this argument is that the parties never are guilt-conscious; and if there is no consciousness of guilt, we have to rule out the adjective invariably applied in court to a love-story of this kind, 'sordid'. We have to go further, too, and recognize that many of these extra-marital love affairs between middle-aged wives and young men are, at any rate so far as the young men are concerned, of an idealism rarely reached in plain, hum-drum, legal marriage. And without necessarily defending the women in such cases, only too often they have, or think that they have, plenty of justification, just as Mrs. Rattenbury herself had on more count than one. In any case to label these affairs as 'nonsense' and 'disgusting' is to shirk the problem; but judges and juries seem to enclose themselves in a little moral world of their own, to which the difficulties and complexities of real life are simply not admitted. No doubt they have to do so.

This, however, is not a discussion on the ethics of adulterous relations between a young man and a middle-aged wife, but on the much simpler question of whether an association with an older woman does a young man any actual harm. It is an important question in this case, for it was the only thing of which Mrs. Rattenbury was found guilty; indeed one might even say that it was the only charge seriously brought against her. It is no less important outside this case, for though judges and juries may throw up official hands of horror when an instance is brought under their noses, many of them must be guiltily conscious of very similar episodes in their own pasts. For the fact is that such an affair is by no means a rarity; it is, on the other hand, quite common, and there are few men who have not had some experience of it. Just as there are plenty of men who try to seduce girls, so there are plenty of women who are ready to initiate youths. The sexes are more on a par than is usually pretended.

And the harm to the youth? The current cant, of course, is to talk about the woman 'leading the young man astray'. That seems to suppose that, but for this woman, the young man would have no experience at all before marriage. Yet of how many men can this be said? And if he is to have experience, which initiation is the less harmful, at the hands of a woman like this or from a harlot? Provided the young man keeps his head, the question answers itself; and since the thing is going on now, this minute, in thousands of cases, one may assume that on the whole the young men do keep their heads. Even though adultery is involved, there is a certain idealism which is infinitely better than the sordidness inseparable from the harlot; and one may even say that nearly every young man who is given his initiation in this way is a victim saved from the harlots later, for having found what sexual experience combined with idealism can be, he is not likely ever to be satisfied with the one without the latter. To this extent, therefore, one may say that the association with an older woman, so far from doing the young man any 'harm', does him a great deal of good.

If then the situation as between Mrs. Rattenbury and Stoner was, in its essentials, not at all an uncommon one, how was it that in this particular instance it led to murder?

The answer is, as in every equation in which human beings and not algebraic symbols are involved, the characters of the two parties.

In Mrs. Rattenbury there was no malice, but there was a great deal of foolishness. Unfortunately foolishness can often do more harm than malice itself.

If it is the foolish driver or pedestrian who is responsible for 90 per cent. of the road accidents, it is the foolish woman who must be blamed ultimately for most murders. Often she gets murdered herself, and usually she well deserves it. In other cases she is the incitement, often unconscious but none the less deadly. Even in cases of murder for gain a silly woman is generally mixed up in it somewhere: as extravagant wife, as greedy mistress, as accomplice, instigator, or victim. Outside fiction it is comparatively rare to find man murdering man for cold-blooded gain, as Palmer murdered Cook, or Lamson his nephew, without an unbalanced woman somewhere in the background to add a tinge of warmth to the affair.

It was the foolishness of Mrs. Rattenbury which led directly to Stoner's murder of her husband. One may wonder indeed that this particular situation, when a foolish woman is involved, does not lead to murder more often, with impressionable lads taking every silly word she says as angel's truth and looking on the unfortunate husband as a devil not fit to be alive. Apparently our youths are able to keep their heads even under the provocation of a Mrs. Rattenbury. And as for Mrs. Rattenbury, she would be alive to-day if the youth of her choice had not been a Stoner.

For Mrs. Rattenbury's type, though it may not be common, is unfortunately not rare enough. Most of us have met it at one time or another; and those who have, will not find it difficult to imagine something of what must have been going on at the Vilila Madeira during January and February 1935. (The reconstruction would, actually, be easier if Stoner had been of the Bywaters type, idealistic, warm-hearted, and impulsive. The probability that Stoner killed, in the end, more from a selfish than altruistic motive, complicates the emotional atmosphere.)

In assessing any type of woman, one must consider her under four heads: first, the self she shows to the world; second, the self she shows to her lover; third, the self which she either foists upon or exposes to herself according whether she is honest or dishonest, clear-sighted or myopic with herself; and fourthly, the true self that she really is. Sometimes two of these selves coincide, perhaps in the rarest cases of utter honesty three, but no one except a saint can show the world the true self as one honestly knows it to be.

Of these four selves the one which causes the trouble with the Alma-Rattenbury type is the third. Such women see themselves as unique, important, misunderstood, and, generally, ill-used; and they are obsessed with themselves and their own peculiar agonies. Indeed, to a woman of this kind, herself is the only subject of any real importance. Their intimate talk tends entirely to their own self-glorification, and much of it is devoted to the exceptional sufferings they have undergone; and the more their listeners appear impressed, the more they pile on the agony.

So wrapped up in their pet subject are they, that to a lover they come perilously near exposing their true selves, vain, self-centred, shallow, full of distortions, and with the self-chosen, masochistic squirmings of the pseudo-martyr, though, of course, to the lover they show themselves in addition as brave in adversity, uncomplaining in spite of endless complaints, and true-blue martyrs. The lover in any case has no eyes to see what is being displayed to him under this very thin veil, so all is well.

For such women the younger the lover is the better, because the less unsophisticated, and therefore the less likely to see through the veil. The choice is instinctive to them, just as all their actions and decisions are instinctive; for, deceiving herself just as thoroughly as she deceives her lover, a woman of this type has no idea that she has anything to hide, or why unsophistication better suits her book, or indeed that she is not everything she pretends to be.

She lives in a world of pretence. Even her inflammation of the young lover is academic. Such women lack a sense of reality. Exact details of truth do not matter to them so long as the effect produced is what they feel to be the right one. It would never have occurred to Mrs. Rattenbury, just as it probably never occurred to Mrs. Thompson, that with the less complex-minded young male, feelings are the precursors of action. That a young man should be afire to avenge her and her wrongs upon the cruel, drunken dummy of a husband which she has set up, gives this kind of woman a supreme delight. The idea that he might actually do so in bloody fact would fill her with genuine horror. This specimen of feminine psychology at its most incomprehensible to the masculine mind, has never been estimated by a British court of law at its true value. The French, of course, understand it thoroughly.

We may be certain, then, that just like an idiot child playing with fire, Mrs. Rattenbury deliberately inflamed Stoner's already considerable jealousy, still only with the idea in her foolish mind of increasing his affection for herself; for it is an axiom with such women that the greater the jealousy the greater the love. With the devilish instinct of her type, she would have showered attentions on her husband in the presence of her lover: attentions which she would not have bestowed on him had the lover been absent. If Stoner were not there, she would say a careless good-night to Mr. Rattenbury as he sat in a drunken semi-coma. If she knew Stoner was watching through the window she would kiss her hardly-conscious husband, ruffle his hair affectionately, address him by pet-names, and all the rest of it.

There seem to be two or three unconscious causes for this instinct. Such women delight in taunting their lovers, not by word but by action, with the unofficial nature of their position, and therefore with its precariousness. They delight in inflicting the pain of seeing the attentions which the lover covets for himself alone, bestowed elsewhere. They delight in reminding the lover that they are tied and bound, the helpless possessions of their husbands, that their horrid situation requires certain duties of them, and that repugnant as those duties may be, as honourable women they are determined to carry them out, at the cost of anybody else's feelings; and finally, with a truly damnable perversity they delight in showing their lovers that they are jolly well fond of this dear old gross brute of a husband of theirs, and the lover can lump it or leave it—in other words, they are not completely won yet.

Of course these women do not consciously realize why they do all this, or even why it delights them. They seldom act consciously at all. And though their minds are concerned almost exclusively with themselves and their own affairs (even their generosity, when they are generous, is often only another cause for self-glorification and praise), they are quite incapable of seeing through the fog of their own spreading to the real, selfish, petty core within.

This is exactly the way in which Mrs. Thompson behaved towards Bywaters, and a French judge and jury would have understood at their real value, which was nil, such absurd statements in her letters as that she had been feeding large pieces of glass to her husband in his food and it had done him no harm at all. To take them as literal fact was a piece of stupidity just as crass as that of Mrs. Thompson in making them.

We are justified, therefore, in assuming that this is the treatment which Mrs. Rattenbury accorded to Stoner, but in Mrs. Rattenbury's case there was another factor of the first importance, and that was the greater discrepancy in age. Any woman in Mrs. Rattenbury's situation must remain only too conscious of the difference in age between herself and a lad literally young enough to be her son; and she will be impelled to counter it by making herself more interesting and still more interesting to her lover. With a normal woman these efforts take the natural and harmless forms of affection and passion, intelligence, physical endurance, and the like. In the case of a woman of the neurotic, ego-centrical type, already bent on making herself important, the appeal will be made for pity. She is in any case full of self-pity already, so the material is all ready to hand.

Now pity carries with it the corollary of resentment. To pity the individual we must resent either circumstances or another person who had brought the victim into such a plight. Mrs. Rattenbury, then, like any other wife of this type, could only rouse pity for herself by causing resentment against her husband. That she had cause for resentment, Stoner could see with his own eyes. Mr. Rattenbury was a drunkard; he was mean when sober; he had actually used physical violence on his wife. His only virtues were his impotence and his complacence as regards Stoner, neither of which was admirable. So much Stoner could see, and we may be sure that Mrs. Rattenbury added detail after detail of a highly intimate nature, such as Stoner could by no means have known for himself, with the appalling lack of reticence which is a sign of her type.

The result is easy to imagine. As Mrs. Rattenbury poured out, in a wistfully brave voice, this and that grievous tale of her married life, instinctively exaggerating and even inventing in order to rouse her unsophisticated young lover to still more fervid heights of pity and love, Stoner, if he had any decency at all (and his later conduct shows that he had), must often have boiled over with rage at the thought of this exquisite, this altogether exceptional woman tied to such a gross brute. It is a situation, we may repeat, that arises often enough in each generation, but it seldom leads to murder. Mrs. Thompson was hanged for her share in the ancient game because, being a genuinely and not a pseudo-exceptional woman, she played it too well and really did drive her lover to the extreme step. She was no loss to the world, for all women of this type are a pest and a nuisance to society; but the law being what it is, her condemnation was as improper as that of Mrs. Rattenbury would have been. (But were the women of England, with their feminine contempt for letter and precedent, right, then, after all?)

So, during January and February 1935, though we know there was never any conscious incitement on Mrs. Rattenbury's part to Stoner to do bodily harm to her husband, we do get a great deal of unconscious incitement, quite apart from that form of incitement which lay in rousing Stoner's own greed and ambitions; so that whatever motives of his own Stoner may have had in wishing Mr. Rattenbury dead, he must have thought that he had plenty on Mrs. Rattenbury's behalf too.

There is no reason to deny Stoner some share of the higher qualities. We may assume, on the evidence of his jealousy alone, that his feelings for Mrs. Rattenbury, if not particularly noble—certainly nowhere near the plane of Crippen's for Ethel le Neve—were at any rate genuine; and we may believe that if he struck two blows for himself he may yet have thought that he was striking the third for her.

To admit that there was unconscious incitement of Stoner by Mrs. Rattenbury is not, however, the same as to assume that if Mrs. Rattenbury had not been a neurotic type Stoner would never have murdered her husband once he realized that she had fallen desperately in love with him. All we can say is that Mrs. Rattenbury's character probably hurried the tragedy on. But murder comes from within. If it did not, the husbands of all hysterical, feather-brained, self-pitying wives would come to violent ends. Murder depends entirely upon the mentality of the possible assailant: no amount of incitement will produce murder in one case, while in another case half the amount of provocation will bring a Stoner into the dock on the capital charge.

What was there in Stoner, then, that caused him to murder? He was sitting very pretty, with a complacent husband, a wealthy and generous mistress, and none of the material difficulties which usually accompany adultery; he had, for instance, neither the difficulty of access nor the financial problem with which Bywaters had to contend. Why, then, gild the lily with that ha'p'oth of gold-paint which was all that Mr. Rattenbury's death could offer?

It is difficult to find any other answer than that Stoner was a born bad hat. If Mrs. Rattenbury had not fallen in love with him probably the murder would never have taken place. As it was, we may see Stoner during these early months of 1935 with a mind divided: half raging with resentment against Mr. Rattenbury on his mistress's behalf, and half wondering what there might be in it for himself if only Mr. Rattenbury were out of the way. In all likelihood the visit to London in March made up his mind for him. He had not enough ballast to stand up under the temptation of so much unaccustomed luxury, which might be his ever afterwards if only two conditions could be fulfilled. Stoner returned from London to Bournemouth loaded with gifts, and with the knowledge that luxury like this was at Mrs. Rattenbury's command, that Mrs. Rattenbury was generous, and that Mrs. Rattenbury loved him to distraction— him, George Stoner, the bricklayer's son. Is it too much to believe that he returned, too, with the determination, wavering before but now firm, to secure his future while the pot was still on the boil?

This, at any rate, seems best to explain the various circumstances of this very stupid murder, and to reconcile those which appear opposed. That the murder was the result of a plan made between Mrs. Rattenbury and Stoner, which was the theory of the prosecution, can no longer be maintained; that it was committed in a fit of blind fury and jealousy, as a retort to the proposed visit to Bridport, which was the suggestion put forward by Stoner's defence, seems equally untenable in view both of the evidence of premeditation and the time which elapsed between the provocation and the deed. But if Stoner had been toying in his mind for weeks with the notion of how advantageous it would be to himself if only Mrs. Rattenbury were a widow; if he had progressed by an easy stage to the more or less nebulous wish to kill Mr. Rattenbury if the old man could not hurry up and die; and if he had come back from London with the decision fully formed to kill Mr. Rattenbury on the first opportunity that offered—then the pattern begins to take form.

Stoner wanted to marry Mrs. Rattenbury. That, I think, is the king-post of the structure. Stoner had assessed Mrs. Rattenbury's devotion to himself, and he was sure that, if she were free, she would marry him. His nest would then be nicely feathered, and he would have to fear neither woman's whims nor any other agency which might plunge him back into poverty again as easily and as swiftly as he had been lifted out of it. He would be secure. He would be rich. He would have, with all this wealth, a woman of whom he was exceedingly fond. And, to differentiate him from all the other youths who in similar circumstances would never have dreamed of murder, the inhibition which ought to have been there to restrain him was lacking: he simply did not shudder at the idea of murder. (Stoner's calm behaviour and dozing in the car during the early hours of the morning after the murder had been committed, is clear proof that he lacked the normal civilized person's horror of bloodshed and violent death.)

If this is the truth, the interval between the quarrel with Mrs. Rattenbury and the time of the murder becomes significant. Stoner would have spent it not in calming down, as might have been expected, but in working himself up. " This is my chance ! " one can imagine him muttering to himself. " He's asked for it now, and he's going to get it. I *will* do it this time—by God I will ! " And the borrowing of the mallet, the donning of gloves, and all the rest of it, just fall into line. Indeed the only thing that remains unexplained is the stupidity which apparently left no possible loophole of escape. But who can say what might not have been in a mind like Stoner's? It is quite on the cards that he really believed that, if a murderer wore gloves and left no finger-prints, he could never be caught. That, or some equally foolish notion, must have been in his thoughts.

It will be noticed that this theory cuts across the general belief that Stoner was dominated by Mrs. Rattenbury, as was taken for granted in court. I do not believe that Stoner was dominated by Mrs. Rattenbury for a moment. In matters of social behaviour and so on, of course, Mrs. Rattenbury had her influence, but when it came to action, Stoner was the predominant partner each time. There is evidence of it. Mrs. Rattenbury tried hard to prevent Stoner from going up to London, ostensibly to buy drugs. She had no success. Over the Bridport incident Stoner was not pleading; he was issuing orders.

Besides, a woman of Mrs. Rattenbury's type does not want to dominate, except in the mild way of influence: both morally and physically she loves to be dominated. It gives her a thrill. No doubt Mrs. Rattenbury taught and encouraged Stoner to dominate her. The only mistake both of them made was that she was not under his domination so much as they supposed. If Stoner was sure that Mrs. Rattenbury would marry him if he could set her free, Mrs. Rattenbury certainly did not want to do anything of the sort. She was quite satisfied with things as they were. But even so, if Stoner could have executed his plan without ending up in the dock, probably he would have got Mrs. Rattenbury to the altar quickly enough. As against all this, the only reason which seems to be offered for the assumption that Mrs. Rattenbury was the dominant one of the two, is that she was so much older, which, as many young men and older women could have told the court, is absurd.

How does murder come about? How does it happen that an apparently decent, even lovable youth can take a mallet and bang a defenceless, drunken old man on the head with it, intending that he shall die?

Well, that is how it comes about. And a community determined upon absolute justice would no doubt make foolishness a crime and, if it hanged the youth who struck the blows, hang equally the foolish woman who made the murder possible. But even there difficulties will arise. What if the youth is a criminal born, who would have gone wrong sooner or later in any case? Is the woman to be expected to discern this? And if she does not do so, is she to be just as culpable for his going wrong sooner instead of later as if she had corrupted with her stupidity a pure white soul?

Perhaps the statute-book is best after all. But what, in that case, is one to make of the condemnation of Mrs. Thompson? We should really make up our minds which variety of justice it is that we are going to administer.

POSTSCRIPTUM

Since the preceding was written, there has been published a full transcript of the trial of Mrs. Rattenbury and Stoner, edited by Miss Tennyson Jesse,[1] in the *Notable British Trials* series. When I undertook to write this account, I understood that this book would be published before the semi-official volume, but owing to certain delays that was not possible, and I am therefore taking the opportunity to add this postscript.

I feel it the more advisable to emphasize that this story of the case was written before Miss Tennyson Jesse's volume appeared, since I find to my mingled pleasure and dismay that in her brilliant introduction not only has Miss Jesse arrived at certain conclusions which are the same as my own and laid emphasis on identical points, but that we seem sometimes to have hit upon identical phrases for doing so. (For instance, we both remark on Mrs. Rattenbury's 'bad taste' in receiving her lover in a room where her small son was sleeping.) So, as the second arrival on the scene, I must defend myself against any possible suspicion of too obvious an inspiration.

It would be as well perhaps to explain at the same time that my account of the case was based entirely on the newspaper reports, which, of course, are not full, and was written without reference to any of those who played a part in the proceedings. Miss Tennyson Jesse, on the other hand, has consulted and talked with many of those who were called as witnesses, and she has therefore a great deal more information than ever appeared in the newspapers. Some of this information that she publishes clears up certain questions which were bothering me.

After consideration I have decided to leave my account of the case exactly as I wrote it, and just deal here with a few of the doubtful points.

For instance, with the full report of the trial before me I see that certain questions were asked about the possible erection of

[1] *The Trial of Alma Victoria Rattenbury and George Percy Stoner.* Edited by F. Tennyson Jesse. Wm. Hodge and Co., Ltd. 10s. 6d.

a tent or shelter in the garden for which Stoner might have wished to use a mallet, but the main conclusion is not altered, for it was made obvious that no such tent or shelter was to have been put up. The period of premeditation is therefore only confirmed.

From Miss Tennyson Jesse's inquiries certain interesting items emerge. Mrs. Rattenbury, for example, was the daughter of a printer living, in a poor way, in British Columbia. Mr. Rattenbury was married when he first met her, and she was cited in a divorce case which his wife brought against him. He was then sixty years old and Mrs. Rattenbury thirty-one. It was owing to this scandal that they left Canada for England when they married.

The occasion on which Mr. Rattenbury gave his wife the famous black eye was the only time they had a serious quarrel, and when he left the house Mrs. Rattenbury really feared that he had gone out to kill himself, which was largely why she sent for her doctor. It was the opinion of Miss Riggs and others that Mr. Rattenbury really did not know that Stoner was his wife's lover, although she believed that she had told him so more or less straightly; but Miss Jesse, after seeing the Villa Madeira itself, finds this hard to credit.

Stoner always told his counsel that it was he who had killed Mr. Rattenbury, but for weeks after her arrest Mrs. Rattenbury was anxious to take the full blame, in spite of the urgings of her solicitor and counsel. It was only when her elder son was sent expressly to beg her to tell the truth in court that she agreed to do so. Miss Tennyson Jesse makes the interesting point that this is perhaps the only occasion, when two persons were tried together for one murder, that "neither of the accused have abandoned the other in a scramble for safety."

I was not surprised to see that Miss Jesse makes hay of the ridiculous assumption, made by the judge and both counsel at the trial, that because of her greater age Mrs. Rattenbury dominated her young lover. And she quotes a most interesting and unexpectedly up-to-date letter written by Benjamin Franklin to show that in such cases enlightened opinion will be more ready to believe that it is the young man who dominates the older woman. She makes the further point that it is absurd to pretend, as a court of law always does in this sort of case, that sexual relations are actually physically harmful to a lad of eighteen. Anyone who has been a lad of eighteen once, as presumably even learned judges themselves have, know that this ingenuous theory bears no relation to fact. (The passages concerning this point were not reported in the newspapers.)

Another small point which was not clear to me was that the Central Police Station in Bournemouth took no less than half an hour to send a police-officer after the doctors had reported foul play, which is certainly very different from what we are led to believe in detective stories. Also the situation which seemed so dramatic of Miss Riggs and Stoner left alone together at the Villa Madeira after Mrs. Rattenbury's arrest, was actually made a good deal more prosaic by the presence of Miss Riggs' mother and brother, who moved in to stay with her there on the day of Mrs. Rattenbury's arrest until after that of Stoner. Miss Jesse also clears up the rather confused account of the events which led up to Stoner's arrest. Miss Riggs, it seems, had a talk with the doctor, in which she averred that, although Stoner had confessed his guilt to her, she could not bring herself to divulge to the officials the secret of Mrs. Rattenbury's liaison with Stoner. The doctor, however, persuaded her that, when a life is at stake, a matter of moral reputation is rather small beer, and Miss Riggs thereupon consented to make her statement to the police during the afternoon while Stoner was in London. Stoner was then arrested on his return to Bournemouth the same evening.

Miss Jesse animadverts, as any humane person must, upon the dreadful smugness with which an adulterous woman is always treated in an Anglo-Saxon court, and I notice that we picked out the same sentence of the judge's for comment. As she very truly says, "There are some of us . . . who are so constituted that we cannot see a fellow-human in the extreme of remorse, shame and despair, without feeling pity as well as disgust." One cannot emphasize this too much. As I ventured to hint myself, there was One who did not feel even disgust. As for what Mr. Justice Humphreys said of this wretched, silly woman, "more," comments Miss Jesse drily, "could hardly be said of George Joseph Smith, or of a systematic poisoner, or a baby-farmer." This is sadly true, but our judges must, presumably, suit their official remarks to the public, and it is the public who must take the blame. As Mrs. Rattenbury's own counsel repeated: "Let him that is without sin cast the first stone." And yet there are many, many who have that stone in their hands, ready for casting. Ready? Who have already cast it! One envies them their self-satisfied rectitude.

Are they perhaps those same persons on whose behalf the gentlemen of the Press are forced to go to such repulsive lengths? Was it to satisfy the beastly curiosity of these very stone-throwers, wallowing in the slough of their own smugness, that Mrs. Rattenbury was, to all practical purposes, hounded to her death by reporters? Every decent citizen should be grateful to Miss Jesse for printing the story. It cannot be repeated too often, so that the readers of the lower Press may learn what is being done, advisedly or not, on their behalf.

After her acquittal these carrion-crows gave Mrs. Rattenbury no quarter. They besieged the flat where she was trying to hide. When she was taken to a nursing-home by a doctor they pursued her, shouting, "If you take her to Bournemouth, we'll follow you." There can be little doubt that they finally unhinged an already loosened mind. In the pathetic fragments of notes that she left behind her, Mrs. Rattenbury referred to their persecution of her. And if this persecution had been questioned, the reply would have been: "Our readers demand it." One day, perhaps, a reporter of the gutter-Press, in a fit of decent feeling will murder the proprietor who gives him his orders, and then we shall have a trial worth hearing.

On one point only, I think, do I find myself at variance with Miss Jesse. She plainly finds it difficult to account for

Stoner's crime, and possibly she avoids the issue when she sets it down to " infantilism . . . an adolescent urge to heroics . . a gesture conceived in an unreal world ". It may be true that " our prisons are full of sufferers from infantilism, and what goes on in their heads bears no relation at all to real life", but I cannot feel that Stoner's action is to be explained quite so easily. Where personal advantage looms so large if a certain person can only be knocked out of the path, the consequent knocking-out bears a very solid relation to real life.

Those who wish to study this extremely interesting case at first hand and form their own opinions thereon, will be well advised to peruse the trial itself. It makes absorbing reading, and it is not too much to say that Miss Tennyson Jesse's penetrating and succinct essay which prefaces it may well become a criminological classic.

F.I.

PART VII

A NEW ZEALAND TRAGEDY

by Freeman Wills Crofts

A NEW ZEALAND TRAGEDY

TO all students of criminology the Lakey Murder Case in the North Island of New Zealand must ever remain one of the most notable on record. It had all the qualities to make it so. A brutal double murder by a clever but callous criminal; a plausible theory set forth by the murderer to account naturally for the facts and so avoid the arousing of suspicion; detective work of an extremely high order, involving persevering research, precise observation and deduction, magnificent team work and the use of the latest scientific methods; and finally a trial at which an overwhelming case was presented, though with the utmost fairness to the accused.

Ruawaro, the region in which took place this terrible crime, is situated some 75 miles south of Auckland and 14 from Huntly. It is in the base of that long peninsula which stretches from the square block of the island for some 250 miles towards the north-west. It is a remote area of rolling hills and valleys, of ridges and gulleys, and of lakes and swamps. Farming is the only industry, though there are allied factories, such as creameries. Life as judged by English standards is hard and somewhat primitive, but the settlers are gradually improving their holdings and making them more comfortable and homelike.

Previous to the tragedy relations between the various inhabitants were on the whole excellent, though there naturally occurred those occasional bickerings inevitable in all such small communities.

Samuel Pender Lakey and his wife, Christobel Lakey, the victims of this abominable murder, were a middle-aged couple living alone and supporting themselves by running a small dairy farm. This meant grinding hard work and but little profit, but the Lakeys made the best of things and were a happy and con-

305

tented couple. They were good neighbours and were generally liked and respected in the district. It is true they had had some disagreements with their neighbour, William Alfred Bayly, but these were of a minor type and there seemed nothing to suggest that the peace of the neighbourhood was about to be broken.

Events, however, proved that this was a superficial view. Though to all outward observation everything was moving normally, beneath the surface evil passions were alive. These grew till they blossomed into action. On Sunday, October 15, 1933, occurred the horrible crime which became known as the Lakey Murder Case.

In order better to understand what took place, it may be well to consider certain aspects of the work of a normal day in the Lakey household. As has been said, the couple lived alone and did all the work of their farm themselves.

They owned some thirty cows, and the first job in the morning was their milking. This began at five or earlier, and occupied about three hours. During the morning, also, cream from the previous milking, which had been separated overnight, was filled into cream cans and taken by Lakey on a horse-sledge down to the road at the bottom of his ground, where it was called for by the dairy factory lorry. A point which became of importance later was the position in which Lakey left his cans. He always placed them on the edge of the bank at the side of the road, so that the lorry driver by drawing close in could swing them aboard without climbing down off the lorry.

The day was spent in work of various kinds until the afternoon. The couple then had tea and Mrs. Lakey prepared supper, the heavy meal of the twenty-four hours. Between tea and supper came the evening milking. The cows were brought in again to the shed by Lakey, while his wife got ready the various tins and pails required. Both the Lakeys milked, and when the work was done Mrs. Lakey returned to the house with some of the milk. Lakey then turned the cows out into a paddock and followed his wife to the house with the remainder of the milk. They then had supper.

Such was the Lakeys' routine, and on that dreadful Sunday of the tragedy they carried it out normally until the afternoon. What then took place was only gradually learnt as a result of the police inquiry.

About 4.15 on that afternoon Mrs. Stevens, a neighbour of the Lakeys, noticed the husband and wife driving their cows towards their cowshed for milking, as they always did at that hour. She did not of course see the actual milking, but looking out again later she realized that it must have been completed, as the cows were then in the paddock in which they were usually kept during the night.

It was the Stevens' as well as the Lakeys' custom to milk their cows again in the early morning, and at about five o'clock, as Mr. and Mrs. Stevens milked theirs, they noticed that the Lakey cows were still in the paddock. The Stevens were surprised at this, as the Lakeys always carried out their work punctually. However, they supposed some trifling delay had taken place, and thought no more of the matter.

About 8.15 Mr. Stevens happened to look out again and saw the cows were still there. It was at once evident to him that something was wrong, so he called another neighbour, a Mr. Wright, and suggested going over to the Lakeys' to investigate.

When the two men reached the house they shouted in through the door to know if anyone were there. Receiving no answer, they went on to the cowshed, where they supposed the Lakeys had gone about the milking. But this place also was deserted. It was obvious from the condition of the shed and cows that the milking on the previous evening had been completed normally, but that no milking had been done that morning.

Now really uneasy, Stevens and Wright returned to the house and entered. They found no trace of the Lakeys. They had evidently not been there since the previous evening as the bed had not been slept in and the fire had not been lighted. Afternoon tea had obviously been their last meal, as the remains of it still stood on the table, but they had not had supper, the food for which was standing in saucepans on the cold stove.

That something serious had taken place could no longer be doubted, and Wright went to the nearest telephone and reported the circumstances to the police at Huntly. He then returned to the Lakeys' and began with Stevens to milk the cows.

In one way or another the tidings spread, and soon some half-dozen neighbours had assembled at the Lakeys' and had started a search for the missing couple.

They were presently joined by two constables. When the details had been told to these officers a more systematic examination of the premises was undertaken. But nowhere was there a trace of either of the Lakeys.

Matters were in this state when there came a shout from another of the searchers, a man named Slater. Not far from the house was a duck-pond, and it was from there that Slater called. The others hurried down.

At the edge of the pond and protruding a short distance into the water was a heap of old manure bags or sacks. Slater had lifted one of these and beneath it had found a dead body.

The remaining sacks were quickly removed and it was seen that the body was that of Mrs. Lakey. She was lying face downwards with her head in the water and her legs on the bank. The sacks had evidently been arranged to hide the remains.

The body was lifted out. It immediately became clear that the unhappy woman had been dead for some time as the frame was stiff.

Here at last was justification of the neighbours' fears. The arrangement of the sacks precluded the possibility of accident or suicide. With a case of murder to be dealt with the constables at once took more energetic measures. The body was carried into the house and a doctor and a force of detectives were sent for.

An examination of the remains revealed cuts on the chin, above the left eye and on the right elbow. Further medical investigation showed that death had occurred from drowning. The immediate suggestion was that Mrs. Lakey had been struck on the chin and knocked senseless, that her body had then been laid in the duck-pond with the face below the water, and that she had there died.

So much seemed clear, but it left the affair as a whole a greater mystery than ever. There remained the question of the whereabouts of Lakey, as well as the apparently insoluble problems of who had killed Mrs. Lakey and with what motive.

In the afternoon of that day Detectives Allsopp and Snedden arrived from Auckland and took charge of the investigation.

This was conducted on three main lines. First there was the search for Lakey, alive or dead; second, the taking of innumerable statements from neighbours and others who might have come in contact with the couple; and third, a detailed search of the premises and surroundings for physical clues.

In the first of these efforts, the hunt for Lakey, the neighbours turned out in strength to assist the police. The country was difficult. Surrounding the little settlement were lakes and swamps in which a body might lie hidden almost indefinitely. In circles of ever-growing radii, with the Lakey home as centre, the search proceeded.

The only place which was not thoroughly examined was the adjoining lake, and that because of the difficulty. It was large in size, and as the bottom was covered with weed, dragging on any scale would have been out of the question. The edge, however, was minutely inspected and no trace was discovered of anything having been thrown in.

On this day the first coherent theory of what might have taken place was put up by the neighbour already mentioned, William Alfred Bayly. He suggested that when walking close to the duck-pond Mrs. Lakey had had a fit and fallen into the pond, injuring her chin and eyebrow, and that Lakey had then found her and been terrified lest he should be suspected of her murder. So frightened had he been that he had lost his head and made a bolt for safety, covering the body with the sacks to postpone discovery and so give him as long a start as possible.

The police had already had this theory in their minds, as well as the more obvious one that Lakey had murdered his wife and fled. They had therefore arranged for the search for the missing man to be carried on throughout the entire country.

At the same time one fact had come to light which suggested to them that the truth might be something different from either of these theories. In searching the house it had been discovered that a brown suit of Lakey's and a pair of boots were missing. The suit was one of Lakey's best, and so far the disappearance of these articles lent colour to the idea of a voluntary departure. But further inquiry revealed an interesting point. The boots were not Lakey's boots at all.

It seemed that a Mr. Gilmour, a friend of the Lakeys, whose farm was approached by means of an unmade clay road, had formed the habit of leaving a pair of his boots at the Lakeys' house, so that when going into Huntly he could travel clean shod. He wore an old pair down his own muddy road, changed them at the Lakeys', and changed back to the muddy ones on his return. It was these boots of Gilmour's which had disappeared.

The police argued that if Lakey had gone off voluntarily he would have worn a pair of his own boots. It seemed to them that the fact that Gilmour's had been taken might indicate that a plant had been staged by someone who did not know of Gilmour's practice. If this were true it would probably mean that Lakey had been murdered, presumably by Mrs. Lakey's assailant. While, therefore, all inquiries as to the man's whereabouts were pushed on, an open mind was retained as to what had really happened.

The second line of inquiry, the taking of statements from the neighbours, produced a considerable amount of information. Little of it was, however, at first recognized as relevant, though afterwards the importance of a good deal was realized. It may be more convenient to summarize this information here, rather than give the items in the disjointed sequence in which they were learnt by the police.

There was, first of all, the matter of the cream cans.

It should be understood that the various farmers left their separated cream on the side of the road opposite their farms for collection by the factory lorry, and that Lakey always placed his near enough the edge of the bank to enable the lorryman to swing the cans aboard without leaving the vehicle. But on the fatal morning, while Lakey's cans were there as usual, they were placed a little farther back, with the result that the lorryman had to get off the van and climb up on the bank to bring them forward.

This again suggested foul play to the detectives. It looked as if the cans had been placed on the bank by someone other than Lakey, someone who knew his habits in general, but not in complete detail.

A second fact which became revealed was that the unpleasantness between the Lakeys and Bayly had been more serious than was at first realized. It will be remembered that Bayly was the man who put forward the theory that Mrs. Lakey had had a fit at the duck-pond and that Lakey had left the district lest he should be accused of her murder.

All the same the friction did not seem of great importance to the police, particularly as Bayly made no attempt to hide it. In fact he mentioned it to one of the constables, saying, "I suppose you already know that we were not on friendly terms."

The first dispute was about meat. Some sheep of Bayly's were not thriving on his own land. He obtained permission from Lakey to graze them on the latter's ground on condition that in return Bayly should supply him with a certain quantity of meat. They quarrelled about the carrying out of this bargain.

Apparently there were other causes of disagreement. One day a visitor to the Lakeys named Baldick overheard the two men threatening each other. "If you come on to this farm," said Bayly, "I'll attack you." On another occasion Bayly said of Lakey in the presence of a farmer named Stent, "I would shoot him if he came down here." On still another occasion Stent remarked to Bayly that he was not too friendly with the Lakeys, and Bayly answered, "Yes, I wish I could cause a row with all the neighbours and get them out of it."

A more serious dispute occurred about a road which Bayly

wished to make to his farm. This would have involved cutting an opening through Lakey's boundary fence. Bayly asked Stent to go with him when he approached Lakey on the matter so that he might have a witness of the interview. On hearing the request Lakey refused to allow his fence to be cut. High words ensued, and in the presence of three independent witnesses Mrs. Lakey cursed and swore at Bayly, ending up by calling out: "Your bloody guilty conscience is pricking you. You murdered Elsie Walker and we expect the same!" To this Bayly replied, "You won't see the next season out, Lakey!"

The reference made by Mrs. Lakey was to a case which had taken place some five years earlier. A girl, Elsie Walker, had been found murdered. Bayly was undoubtedly acquainted with her and her people, but there was no evidence whatever that he was guilty of the crime. The murderer, in fact, was never found.

In these disputes, none of which appeared very serious, there was no doubt that the bad feeling was mutual.

Another fact which came out as a result of the detectives' inquiries was related by a Miss Kenn, a visitor to the Lakeys. She said that as a Christmas present she had given her host a cigarette lighter. When its original wick was used up Lakey had replaced it with a home-made one of white wool, which he had obtained from his wife's work-basket. Here again it was not till later that the importance of the matter was realized.

There was next the question of firearms. Most of the farmers kept firearms which they used to shoot the wild fowl that abounded in the swamps, as well as rabbits and other game. From various witnesses it was learnt that Lakey had no less than four guns in his house. Of these, one double-barrelled shotgun and a pea-rifle had disappeared at the time of the tragedy.

There was, in addition, a considerable amount of testimony on various other matters relevant and irrelevant which need not be mentioned in this brief summary of the case.

While the search for Lakey was going on and statements were being taken from neighbours, an examination of the site for physical clues was not being overlooked.

In the Lakeys' house nothing of further interest was discovered. Nor was anything more found at the duck-pond. The entire ground surrounding it had been trampled by so many people since the discovery of the body that no individual footprints could be identified.

The search passed from Lakey's ground to that of his neighbour, Bayly, and there some traces of the recent passage of a sledge were observed.

These traces were followed as far as they could be seen. They were found to come from the private road to Bayly's house, go down close to a certain telephone-pole in the boundary fence separating Bayly's and Lakey's properties, turn there in a semi-circle and return to the private road. The suggestion was that something had been carried from Bayly's house to the boundary fence or *vice versa*. The gauge or width between the traces was carefully measured and the trace was pegged off for future reference.

On the following morning the first real clue to what had taken place was discovered.

A large wattle tree stood on Lakey's ground close to the same boundary fence between his ground and Bayly's which has just been referred to. It was opposite and close to the telephone-pole near which the traces of the sledge had been found. Beneath this wattle tree stood a pair of old cartwheels with part of the decaying frame of the cart still attached. In the ordinary course of the examination these cartwheels came in for close inspection.

At once it was noticed that portions of the surface of the woodwork had been sliced or pared away, apparently recently. Near these cuts or scrapings some dark marks attracted the detectives' attention, and with suddenly increased interest they saw that they were bloodstains. A number of drops of congealed blood were found on the centre and side of the frame and on the axle.

Some excellent detective work followed. The stains were first protected to preserve them for later examination and a meticulous inspection of the wheels was made.

It was then noticed that they bore marks of fresh poultry droppings.

Now there were no poultry near the wattle tree, Lakey's hens keeping up close to his house. The question therefore arose as to whether or not the wheels had recently been moved to where they were now lying.

The officers raised the wheels and at once saw that they had. The grass on which they were standing was fresh and green.

The next step was obvious : Could they find out where they had come from ?

Their efforts on this point were successful. They were able to find the traces the wheels had made in passing over the grass. These traces were the only ones in the paddock and they ran back from near the boundary fence and telephone-pole to a point close to Lakey's house. Where they had passed over cow droppings they were clearly visible. The tracks were pegged for reference and the cow droppings removed and packed so as to be available as exhibits at a future trial should such materialize.

Verbal inquiries were at once instituted into the points raised by this discovery and it was found possible to settle within limits the time at which the wheels had been moved.

There was plenty of evidence that they had lain for years close to the fence immediately surrounding Lakey's house and had been part of an old cart which had gradually decayed away till only these wheels and axle and centre bar were left. There was definite testimony that they had been in this position on October 11th, that is, four days before the crime. On the morning after the crime they were seen to be under the wattle tree.

The wheels, the sacks which had covered Mrs. Lakey's body, the marked cow droppings, and several other objects were then packed and sent to Auckland for more detailed examination.

That the police were on the track of a premeditated double murder now seemed certain, as owing to the boundary fence being in a different direction, the wheels obviously had not been used to convey Mrs. Lakey's body to the duck-pond. The suggestion that they had carried her husband was strong, but in this theory there was a rather overwhelming difficulty If it were true, where was the body? There seemed to be no possible place about Bayly's farm in which it could have been hidden.

But the fact that the trail of the wheels from Lakey's approached the boundary fence on Lakey's side close to where that of the sledge had gone on Bayly's ground was, however, so suggestive that the detectives decided that a special search of Bayly's farm was called for. They therefore obtained a search warrant and went over. They met Bayly outside his car shed.

Without producing the warrant they asked him if anyone had been near his boundary with a sledge. Bayly at first said no, but afterwards added that when he was returning from taking his cream cans down to the road for collection on the Monday morning, which he did on his sledge, he had noticed the telephone-pole on the boundary fence was leaning over and he had driven up to it to see if it were broken. This, if true, would have accounted for the tracks found. But doubt was thrown on the statement by the fact that when the detectives later examined the pole they could find nothing whatever wrong with it.

Bayly then asked the police if they would care to have a look into his car shed. They did so, but without finding anything of interest. Chief Detective Sweeny, who had been sent for on the discovery of the blood marks on the wheels, then produced his warrant. The search at once began, Bayly raising no objection.

In due course the officers came to examine Bayly's sledge. They measured it and found that its runners corresponded to the trail which had been found, though since Bayly's statement there had been little doubt that it had made the marks. But they found something less expected and more sinister. On some of the top boards were bloodstains. They asked Bayly if they might take three of these boards for examination, and again he raised no objection.

But this was not the only discovery of importance made that day. While Chief Detective Sweeny and his staff were at Bayly's, another constable was searching Lakey's implement shed. There, on a billet of wood he found traces of recent blood.

At once a more detailed search of the shed was undertaken and certain very significant indications were come on.

In front of the shed, which here formed part of the fence surrounding the house, was a kerosene case. When this was moved more bloodstains were found. They were on the wooden rail and battens of the wall, as well as on the grass and an adjoining stone.

Here a similar attempt to hide the stains had been made as in the case of the cartwheels. The surface of the wood had been shaved away. But this time it had been done with less care. Some of the bloodstained shavings were still lying on the ground beneath the kerosene case.

The amount of blood on these various objects was considerable. On some of the battens actual streams had run down. The surface which had been shaved seemed to have been covered with blood, as besides showing on the shavings, smears and spots were visible all round the area.

The rail, battens, shavings, certain blades of grass, and the stone—everything which bore traces of the blood—were removed by the police and sent into Auckland. There they were examined by Dr. Gilmour, pathologist at the Auckland Hospital, as well as by other medical men. They found that all the stains were of human blood.

The indications of what had taken place were growing in number and definition. There was human blood in considerable quantity in the implement shed near Lakey's house, there was human blood on the cartwheels which had recently passed from close to the implement shed to Bayly's boundary fence, and there was human blood on Bayly's sledge, which had recently passed from the same point on Bayly's side of the boundary fence towards Bayly's house. The detectives began dimly to visualize the murder of Lakey in his shed and the transit of the body to Bayly's. There was still, however, the overwhelming difficulty of what had been done with the body.

The search of Bayly's premises was resumed with greater vigour than ever. While it was in progress Detective Allsopp noticed that Bayly was wearing a belt to which was attached a sheath. The handle of the knife in this sheath had been damaged some time previously and looked curious to Allsopp. He asked Bayly if it was a file he had in his sheath. Bayly answered that it was a knife, and pulled it out and passed it over. Allsopp saw that it was ground to a razor edge, except near the shaft, where the edge had been slightly turned.

The search in Bayly's house was continued on the following day with further startling results. In the bathroom was found bloodstained clothing of Bayly's, a shirt with marks on the front and a coat stained on the sleeves. These were taken possession of.

Bayly was asked if he could account for the blood. He said he had cut his finger a few days previously, which might explain it. Also that he had been at a recent calving and might have got spattered.

His hands were then examined and two small cuts were found on one finger. These, however, seemed too old to fit in with his statement, though of this the detectives could not be certain.

In the bathroom were also found Bayly's belt, sheath and pouch. The knife was missing and Bayly was asked where it was. For answer he went to the kitchen and produced it from a cupboard. He raised no objection to handing these articles over, and all four of them—knife, belt, sheath and pouch—were added by the officers to their collection.

In the wash-house were two pairs of dungaree trousers, and Bayly was asked which pair he was wearing on the day of the murder. He replied that it was one of those pairs, though he could not say which. On one of them there were dark stains which looked like blood. Both pairs were also taken by the detectives.

While the trousers were being examined an empty pea-rifle cartridge fell from one of the pockets. Bayly was questioned about this also. He said that he had been shooting on the previous Friday and Saturday and must have dropped the shell into his pocket. "Where is your rifle?" he was next asked. He led the detectives to the separator-room in his cowshed, where the rifle was standing. There were marks like bloodstains on the barrel. These Bayly attributed to a hare which he said he had shot.

In due course all the bloodstained articles were examined by Dr. Gilmour in Auckland. He found that there were several spots of human blood on the trousers. On the rifle there was blood, but it could not be identified as human. There was no blood on the belt, sheath or pouch. But, perhaps the most significant of all the finds, in the thumb hollow on the blade of the knife there was human blood.

In the meantime the general search for Lakey was being pushed on with great energy. For miles in every direction rivers, lakes and swamps were inspected and were dragged in likely places. Over fifty police were engaged at one time, as well as numbers of adjoining residents. As a result of a suggestion that the body might have been burnt in a heap of burning slack at the Renown mill, a squad of constables shovelled over the entire glowing mass. Railways, ports, and shipping were watched in the whole of the two islands. Hospitals and mental homes were visited. Finally, a reward of £100 was offered for information which would lead to the man's discovery, alive or dead.

Then a statement of Bayly's introduced a fresh complication into the affair.

One evening he called on the detectives, who had made Lakey's house their headquarters, to say that a man and dog had been trespassing on his ground shortly before. He had surprised them about his car shed. The man had taken to his heels and had got away, but Bayly's dog had caught and held the other dog.

Bayly then declared that the dog belonged to his neighbour, Mr. Wright. To the police he said he did not know who the man was, though afterwards he hinted that it must have been Wright.

The detectives made inquiries and satisfied themselves that it could not have been Wright, as he was able to prove he was at home at the hour in question. They could not discover the identity of the man, or indeed whether any man had been there at all.

Some days later Detective Allsopp commenced a more detailed and systematic search of the swamps and waterholes on Lakey's and Bayly's farms. They had been inspected already, but not in his opinion with sufficient care. These waterholes were full of soft black mud, covered with slime and water. The new method of search was to probe them inch by inch with spades and spears.

By that Monday afternoon the searchers had reached a hole some 140 yards from Bayly's house, not far from where the cart-wheels and sledge traces had been found. There a constable's spear struck metal.

He reached down beneath the water and drew the object out. It proved to be the barrels of a double-barrelled shotgun, and was bright and free from rust. Close by in the same waterhole was the fore end of a shotgun. In another hole at a little distance was the stock of a pea-rifle.

The officers replaced these objects in the swamp, noting their positions. Then they brought Bayly down. When he saw the spot to which he was being taken, he showed considerable surprise. The detectives pulled out the articles one by one and asked Bayly if they were his. He replied that they were not, that he did not hide them and that he had no idea how they came to be there.

Search in the swamp continued, and later in the day the barrel of a pea-rifle was discovered. This fitted the stock previously found. The stock of the double-barrelled shotgun, however, was still missing, when owing to the dusk the officers had to knock off work.

That night a watch was put on the swamp lest an attempt to remove further hidden articles should be made.

About ten o'clock the two constables in charge saw Bayly leave his house and approach down the hill. They lay down silently and watched. They were satisfied that they could not be seen as they were dressed in dark clothes and were hidden in an old pit. Bayly came close to the swamp, then stopped and looked cautiously round in every direction. Then he moved silently on towards where the guns had been found.

When he reached the edge of the water the constables called out to him. Bayly looked round and said that it was all right and that he had seen them. This, however, the constables were satisfied was false. Bayly then returned to his house.

Next day the searchers came on the missing shotgun stock belonging to the double barrels already found. These discoveries now made up two complete weapons, a double-barrelled shotgun and a pea-rifle.

It will be remembered that a double-barrelled shotgun and a pea-rifle were missing from the Lakeys' house. It was natural to suppose that these were the same. The police therefore examined the gun licences in question and found that they were.

The evidence which was slowly being amassed was pointing more and more definitely in one direction. But there was still nothing of certainty in it. Now, however, a fresh discovery was made, which though it scarcely provided sufficient proof for court, banished all doubts as to the author of the crime from the minds of the investigators. This discovery was made at headquarters and was an outstanding triumph for use of scientific methods in detection.

Sergeant Dinnie, of the Criminal Registration Department at Wellington, was a finger-print expert and an adept at photographic work of all kinds. He was sent to Auckland to examine the exhibits and see whether he could suggest any development from the use of his speciality. He thought he could, and determined to try some experiments.

First he took one of the pieces of timber from Lakey's implement shed which had been pared or shaved, and of it made an enlarged photograph, using a magnification of eight and a half diameters. It showed fine ridges or scrapes due to irregularities in the edge of the knife. He cut the photo across in the centre at right angles to the direction of these ridges.

Then he took Bayly's knife and made a similar enlargement of its edge. This had to be done in nine sections, and when the sections were joined it made a strip some four feet long. The edge showed irregularities of the same type as those on the wood.

An interesting operation followed. The sergeant placed the two photographs together so that that of the wood scrapes was applied to that of the edge of the knife. Slowly he moved the former along the latter. And then suddenly he was rewarded for his trouble. At one point ridges and furrows exactly coincided!

Further examination and photographs of wood and knife were made under a magnification of ten diameters. These were checked by Dr. Dennis Brown of Auckland University College. He also carried out independent tests of a similar kind and these fully confirmed Dinnie's conclusions.

No doubt that Bayly had murdered Lakey now remained in the minds of the detectives, but the evidence against him was still far from complete. In the case of Lakey, failure to produce the body would make a charge of murder impossible, while there was no proof whatever that Bayly was concerned in Mrs. Lakey's death. Further investigation was required.

Under these circumstances it was decided to search Bayly's homestead once again. And this time discoveries were made which at last gave a clue to the ghastly truth and led to an overwhelming case being presented at the trial.

When examining Bayly's cowshed some days before this, the detectives had noticed a shovel bearing some deposit that looked like ash. They asked Bayly what this was and he said he did not know. The officers then said they would take the shovel for examination. Bayly, however, objected on the ground that he required it to carry on his work. The officers agreed to leave it, but they scraped off the deposit and sent it to Auckland with their other exhibits. It had there been examined and was found to be bone ash, charcoal and burned sacking.

This was a fact heavy with dreadful suggestion. It brought to the detectives' minds certain testimony they had received at the beginning of the inquiry, testimony which they now began to think had not been given sufficient attention. One item was detailed by a neighbouring farmer named Herbert, the second had been mentioned by many witnesses and indeed was within the observation of the detectives themselves.

Mr. Herbert had stated that towards dusk on the Sunday evening of the crime, he had looked across from his own farm to that of Bayly. From Bayly's cowshed was pouring a great volume of smoke. He had never seen anything like it before, and so impressed was he that he called another man named Brooker, and they watched it together. At times they could scarcely see the shed for the smoke. Off and on Herbert looked at it until he went to bed some three-quarters of an hour later. During the whole of that period the smoke had continued to pour out.

The second item was that on the following day and for two or three days after, Bayly's eyes were red and sore-looking, just as might have been expected had he been for any time in a smoky atmosphere.

The efforts of the officers were now concentrated on a new line of inquiry: a search for evidence of fires and burnings. It was not long before they found it.

On the ground not far from the cowshed they noticed the bottom half of a 40-gallon benzine drum. It had obviously been used as a stove, both because of its discoloration and because a square fire hole was cut out of the side. Asked to account for it, Bayly said he had cut the drum in two because it was old and useless and because he wanted the lower half to make a fire in. This fire was for the purpose of warming an iron, and he produced an old axe which showed signs of heat. He said that the upper half of the drum was in the orchard. The detectives took charge of both halves.

It was obvious that Bayly had cut the drum in two recently, for among the original statements which had been made was one concerning it. Different neighbours had mentioned that Bayly had a large copper which he used for boiling water for cleaning and scalding pigs. This until lately had been supported by means of steel slips on the drum. All testified to the fierce heat which could be generated in the contrivance.

The half drum was standing bottom upwards, and the searchers turned it over. On the bottom was a deposit of ash which looked identical with that found on the shovel. This was collected and placed in envelopes. On the floor of the separator-room of the cowshed were suspicious-looking stains, and from these samples were also taken.

Beside the separator-room there was a vessel containing sheep dip. The officers asked if they might empty this vessel, but Bayly objected. "If you empty it," he said, "you will have to take full responsibility if any of the cattle are poisoned." The dip was accordingly left untouched for the time being.

A few minutes later another discovery was made. In a small paddock not far from the house were a number of bones. Bayly was asked what he did with these. "I smash them up and put them in the garden," he answered. "Do you burn them?" the officers asked. Bayly said that he did not.

These investigations could have left no doubt in Bayly's mind as to the direction the inquiry was now taking. The heavy pall of smoke which had hung over the cowshed on the night of the murder was no doubt in his mind as it was in the officers', and it was evident that the cause of this smoke would be investigated with the utmost energy.

Whether or not these considerations weighed with Bayly is a matter of surmise. But he now took a step which immediately changed the character of the investigation, bringing matters at once to a head.

Bayly disappeared.

On the morning of December 1st the officers had occasion to call once again at his house, and it was then that they found he was missing. How in that district filled with police the man had been able to slip away, they didn't know, but all they learnt was that he had been gone several hours before they became aware of the fact.

Mrs. Bayly was questioned and she produced a letter from her husband. It was dated for the previous day and read:

30/11/33.

MY DARLING PHYLLY,

Yesterday in Auckland I received definite information that the police were going to try and put the blame of Mrs. Lakey's death

323

and Lakey's disappearance on to me. They have to vindicate themselves somehow—after the blunders they have been making in the search for Lakey, and think I will be the easiest one to catch. As you know, I was with you that night; but I do not intend to let them put their dirty tricks on me. I have picked out a nice spot to rest in, so love to you and the kids. The farm will bring you in a bit.

BILL

Then ensued a hue and cry! Immediately a warrant was issued for Bayly's arrest, and police circles in the entire island hummed with excitement and activity.

Detective Allsopp was early able to prove that the letter had not been received through the post, but had been written by Bayly before leaving home. He found a pad of similar sheets of which the top one bore the impress of the writing. It seemed probable, therefore, that the letter had been intended for the police rather than the wife, and it was suggested that its object was to convey the idea that Bayly was about to commit suicide.

Whether Bayly had really intended to give the authorities the slip is, however, doubtful, for two days later the police were informed that he was with his solicitor, Mr. Lusk, in a house near Auckland. There they found him and there he was arrested. He was taken to Auckland and lodged in the Central Police Station.

In the meantime the search on his farm was prosecuted with greater intensity than ever. Now attention was turned to the ground itself. Detective Allsopp remembered that on his first arrival he had noticed that a certain area near the house had been freshly dug. As nothing had since been planted at the place, the motive of the digging seemed obscure. It was therefore decided to dig over the ground again to make sure that nothing had been buried.

The officers set to work. Scarcely, however, had they gone a yard when they made a discovery which they believed would at long last solve their problem.

Coming up with the earth were bits of charcoal, pieces of burnt bone and grass. It looked as if the bones and charcoal had been emptied on the grass and then been dug in. Immediately the men stopped their rough digging and began to remove the earth with meticulous care, sifting every particle before throwing it aside. Their trouble was rewarded.

Besides many fragments of bone, they came on a clip and stud from a pair of braces, several pieces of cloth, a number of small nails such as are used in bootmaking, and two artificial teeth. All these articles were more or less burnt.

The area of search was then extended. The ground around the cowshed was opened and more pieces of burnt bone were dug up. Burnt bone was also found in the grass in various places. In a toolshed part of the case of a watch bearing a number was come on, and among some old bolts were a few small screws and springs which the searchers thought had come from a cigarette lighter. Different parts of what appeared to be the same watch, damaged as if the watch had been cut in two, were unearthed from various places. The charred stem of a cherry-wood pipe was also found and it was similar to one known to have been in Lakey's possession. From the grass of the orchard near the main house were picked up more burnt bones and rags, the toe-plate of a boot, part of a dental plate bearing a tooth, a trousers button, pieces of material such as is used for men's underpants, and part of a pocket of a pair of trousers.

The vessel of sheep dip was emptied and at the bottom were found more burnt bones and charcoal, the case of a cigarette lighter, and a tuft of hair.

It will give some idea of the amazing comprehensiveness of the search when it is mentioned that *several hundred* pieces of bone were found, and of the meticulous care with which the work was carried out by instancing the discovery of such tiny objects as single artificial teeth in the rough grass of a paddock.

All this vast array of 'exhibits' was turned over to the scientists at Auckland, and their work was characterized by equal comprehensiveness and care. The bones were classified into (*a*) those which were too small to be identified, (*b*) those which might be human, but could not be proved to be so, and (*c*) those which were definitely human. Of the latter, pieces of ribs, vertebrae, skull, thigh bone, and others were identified. No less than fifty-five fragments had come from the skull alone.

An attempt was made to reconstruct the frame from which these bones had come. This could not be done in its entirety, but certain conclusions were drawn.

There was no absolute evidence that the deceased had been a man, but the size of the bones and the muscular attachments which were found indicated a strength and build which was probably male. There was, however, no definite proof that the remains were those of a person of middle age. The deduction from the tuft of hair was more convincing. It was found to be human hair, two and a half inches long, coarse, and of a greyish-brown colour. This was almost certainly male, and corresponded exactly to Lakey's hair, both in colour and length.

An important point brought out by the scientists was that the bones had only lately been burnt. This was proved, not only by their freedom from dirt, but from the fact that some of them still bore charred flesh.

The finds other than human were also tested and certain extremely interesting conclusions were reached. Of these, perhaps, the most striking were in connexion with the cigarette-lighter and watch.

The small screws and springs picked out from among some old bolts were found to fit the lighter case taken from the vessel of sheep dip. The case was similar to Lakey's. But there was more. In the case was a home-made wick consisting of wool. It will be remembered that when the original wick was used up, Lakey had put in a new wick from his wife's work-basket. The wool in the lighter and that from Mrs. Lakey's basket were compared and were found to be identical.

The watch which had been cut in two was also shown to be Lakey's. Apart from its general appearance, its number was in the records of a Huntly watchmaker. He had sold it to Lakey. Moreover, the implement with which it had been cut in half was found. In Bayly's shed was a pair of strong shears, on the blades of which were traces of two of the metals of which the watch was made.

The various buttons, clips, artificial teeth, pieces of cloth and of rubber which were found and examined need scarcely be enumerated. It is sufficient to say that all of these were consistent with the theory that it was Lakey's body which had been burnt.

One very suggestive fact may however be mentioned. In or among the human remains were found no less than twenty-one grains of lead. Where had this come from? The detectives had little doubt. They believed it was from a bullet or bullets, and that its presence proved that Lakey had been shot. The assumption certainly worked in with their theory. If the deceased had been shot in his implement shed it would account for the quantity of blood on the wall and floor.

During the general inquiry a detailed investigation was made into the firearms and shells which had figured in the affair. These consisted of two shotguns and two pea-rifles in all, one of each type which were missing from Lakey's and which were found in the swamp on Bayly's farm, and the others which were in Bayly's possession. There was also the empty pea-rifle shell which had dropped from the pocket of Bayly's dungaree trousers.

Careful experiments by Dr. Dennis Brown and Sergeant Dinnie brought out a very convincing piece of evidence. They showed that this shell from Bayly's pocket had been fired from Lakey's pea-rifle. Dr. Brown fired seventeen shells from this rifle, and all of them had the same striker marking as the shell found on Bayly. Enlarged photographs, some to as much as sixty-eight diameters, demonstrated this clearly. However, to make the matter even more certain the police collected all the .22 calibre pea-rifles they could find in the district—no less than twenty-one. Shells were fired from all of these and in not one case did the striker mark resemble that of Lakey's.

The police case by this time had grown extremely convincing, but there was one point in it about which a considerable amount of controversy arose. It was argued in certain quarters that the theory must be incorrect for the simple reason that it would be impossible to burn a human body as it was assumed had been done to Lakey's. Authorities on the subject were consulted and were found—as is usually the case—to differ.

As this was fundamental to the case for the prosecution, a definite conclusion had to be reached. It could only be done in one way. Certain rather ghastly experiments were therefore carried out.

A 40-gallon drum, similar to that believed to have been used by Bayly, was obtained and a fire opening was made low down in the side, exactly as in the other. This was arranged as Bayly's was understood to have been, and a fire of wood was lighted. An old ewe weighing over eleven stone was shot and was placed head downwards in the drum, together with a pair of gumboots. The fire was stoked up with wood for an hour and a half and then left to burn itself out.

Next morning it was found that the body was entirely consumed, only burnt bone and charcoal remaining. These bones were similar in appearance to those which had been dug up.

Two other similar experiments were carried out when a large ram and a calf, both weighing about ten stone, were burnt. The calf was not shot, but was killed by chloroform. The results in all three cases were identical.

It was observed that during the experiments heavy black smoke was given out similar to that seen hanging over Bayly's cowshed on the night of the murder. This appeared to come, not from the bodies, but from the rubber boots.

Seldom, surely, has so great a mass of evidence been collected in the course of a single investigation as was here placed at the disposal of the Crown solicitors. Seldom, surely, has the guilt of the accused been so adequately established as was that of Bayly. It is suggested that there had been some dissatisfaction with the achievements of the police in previous cases and that they were here on their mettle. Be that as it may, no unbiassed person can consider their work without feelings of admiration.

At last the period of preparation came to an end and the test of the work came. Bayly was brought to trial.

The preliminary hearing before the Auckland magistrates began on January 16, 1934, amid scenes of great popular interest. There were sixty-four witnesses for the prosecution and two hundred exhibits, and the proceedings occupied ten days. The defence was reserved and the expected verdict was recorded. The accused was committed to the Supreme Court at Auckland for trial at the next session.

On Monday, May 21, 1934, opened under Mr. Justice Herdeman what must surely be one of the most notable trials which has ever taken place in any part of the world. Imagination staggers at its length and complexity. It lasted without a break from the 21st of May till the 23rd of June, twenty-nine days of hearing. There were 77 witnesses and 274 exhibits. To deal with the exhibits alone a highly elaborate cross-indexing system of reference had to be devised and carried out.

The morning of the first day was taken up in preliminaries, and in the afternoon the jurors visited Ruawaro, where they inspected the two holdings and the various sheds and fences about which they were going to hear. On the second day the proceedings proper opened with the address of Mr. V. R. Meredith, counsel for the prosecution.

Mr. Meredith spoke for the entire day. He began by reminding the jury that the responsibility they bore was the gravest that any citizen could be called upon to undertake, and warning them not to allow any preconceived opinions they might have formed from conversations or articles in the Press to operate on their judgment in this grave matter. Then he proceeded to outline the case in detail.

He described the Lakeys, their property, and the country in which they lived, mentioning the duck-pond, the pair of old cartwheels, the cowshed, and other objects. Then he detailed the daily routine of the Lakey's life, the clothes Lakey usually wore, his cherry-wood pipe, his cigarette lighter with the home-made wick, and the fact that he had a set of false teeth. The relations between the neighbours were then discussed and the history of the quarrel with Bayly given.

Turning then to the actual murder, Mr. Meredith told of the heavy smoke which had been seen over Bayly's cowshed on the Sunday evening, of the cows being noticed in the night paddock on the Monday morning, and the inquiries caused thereby, of the calling in of the police and the discovery of Mrs. Lakey's body in the duckpond.

The investigation of the police was then detailed: how they had found that Lakey's double-barrelled shotgun and the pea-rifle he had been lent were missing; how Bayly put up to them his suggestion that Mrs. Lakey had fallen into the duck-pond in a fit and that Lakey had fled lest he should be charged with murder; and how they came on their first real clue, the tracks of the sledge. The trail of human blood was mentioned; first, on the implement shed; second, on the wheels and frame taken from Lakey's house; third, on Bayly's sledge; fourth, on Bayly's trousers, and fifth, on the back of Bayly's knife. Then came the incident of the alleged trespasser and Bayly's suggestion that the man was Wright. With the theory of murder and suicide gone, Mr. Meredith contended, Bayly was attempting to fasten suspicion on Wright. But the attempt failed utterly.

The discovery that the deposit scraped off Bayly's shovel was burnt bone and charcoal, went on Mr. Meredith, was the first clue as to the disposal of Lakey's body. When, following this up, the police took possession of the cut petrol drum, Bayly grew alarmed. It was significant that next day he was missing and had left a letter containing a clear suggestion that he was about to commit suicide.

Mr. Meredith went on to describe the burnt bones, parts of underclothing, metal buttons, leather, boot nails, and other objects which were found.

" Whose remains are these? " he asked. " The evidence would indicate that no other inference could be drawn but that they are those of Samuel Lakey. If these are not the remains of Samuel Lakey, whose are they? "

A description of the method by which it was proved that the bloodstained wood had been shaved with Bayly's knife was also given, as well as the experiments with the guns and shells.

Finally Mr. Meredith summarized the theory of the prosecution concerning the affair. He said it was no part of the Crown's case to prove exactly how the murder was committed. The exact sequence of what happened that night on that lonely ridge would probably never be known. Two of the participants were dead and silent for ever, but there was the evidence to be put before the jury. For the Crown's purpose it was sufficient to establish that one or more murders had been committed, and that the accused was guilty of the commission.

Briefly, the theory of the Crown was that Bayly went to the Lakey's place just before the Lakeys completed milking and struck Mrs. Lakey on the jaw, knocking her out. When Lakey followed his wife up from the cowshed Bayly shot him, Lakey's blood spattering over the implement shed. It would appear that Lakey was attacked without warning, and that no struggle took place. Mrs. Lakey was dragged to the duck-pond by her assailant, and her head was submerged in the water until she expired.

Lakey's body was put on the wheels and frame and carted down to Bayly's boundary fence. The wheels could not be taken through the boundary fence, so the sledge was brought by Bayly from his own road to the same point to carry the body. From there it was removed to his cowshed, where it was promptly burnt in a drum. That this could be done there was no doubt. The drum Bayly subsequently cut in two and placed in different parts of the garden.

The smoke of the fire was witnessed by a neighbour, Herbert, and his workman across the lake, Mr. Meredith continued. The theory was that Bayly put the body in the drum and burned it, clothes, boots and all. That same night at some time he covered Mrs. Lakey's body with sacks in such a way as not to attract the attention of a passer-by; planted the guns in his own swamp for subsequent disposal; put Lakey's cream cans down by the road to prevent inquiry, and took Lakey's gun and clothes, with a view to setting up the murder and suicide theory, which he himself promulgated the next day.

If inquiry had been postponed until next day there would have been ample opportunity to have properly disposed of the guns and the residue of the burning. Detection would then have been impossible. One thing slipped, and that was that neighbours saw that Lakey's cows had not been milked. From 11 a.m. on the Monday onward Lakey's property and Bayly's were overrun with police and searching settlers. Bayly was compelled to get rid of what was yet unhidden at once, and necessarily in the neighbourhood of his own house.

With a peroration on the duty of the jurors a great speech ended.

For four weeks witnesses were called, examined, cross-examined and re-examined, and then Mr. Meredith made his concluding address to the jury. He submitted that the evidence proved conclusively that a body had been burnt at Bayly's farm, that there could be no doubt that this body was Lakey's because, first, several of the burnt objects found were Lakey's property; second, that there was a trail of blood from Lakey's shed to Bayly's, and third, that no one but Lakey was missing. Finally, he suggested that no one but Bayly could be guilty of the crime.

Bayly was defended by two extremely able counsel, Messrs. Northcroft and Leary, but from the first they had a hopeless task. Nevertheless they put up a brave fight. Their cross-examination of the witnesses was relentless, particularly of the scientific witnesses. They used maps, diagrams, blackboards, and photographs were thrown on a screen by a lantern.

By calling no witnesses they obtained the right to the final word with the jury. Their main line of defence was that the evidence brought forward by the Crown was entirely circumstantial. The position, Mr. Northcroft said, was like a chain whose links led to a certain conclusion. But the jury must remember that if one link in a chain broke, the whole of the remainder were absolutely valueless.

He suggested that several of the essential links put forward by the prosecution were faulty. The most important was that no real evidence of motive had been put forward at all. There was no evidence that Bayly had hated the Lakeys sufficiently to wish to murder them. Further, Bayly had been with a neighbour that Sunday afternoon. He was then in a perfectly normal frame of mind. Could it be supposed that he had suddenly risen up and behaved like a demon? Mr. Northcroft scoffed at the "almost superhuman confidence" of the experts in swearing that certain shells had or had not been fired from certain guns, and suggested that the prosecution had mixed the shells up. He argued that it would have been utterly impossible to have carried a body of the weight of Lakey's on the old cart frame and wheels, as the latter would have given way, and further, that Bayly could not have lifted such a weight across his boundary fence without leaving obvious traces: of which there were none. He declared that had Bayly done what he was accused of he would have been spattered with blood from head to foot. He called attention to the bearing of Bayly and insisted that at no time was it that of a guilty man. It was utterly impossible, he urged, that between 4 p.m. on the Sunday and the following morning Bayly could have performed all the actions with which he was credited. There was, moreover, no evidence of any kind that Bayly had even seen Mrs. Lakey on the Sunday afternoon. Her injuries might have been inflicted by accident. Finally, Mr. Northcroft put up the alternative theory that the crime might well have been committed by some third person, which theory would account for all the proven facts.

On Friday, June 22nd, the jury were again taken to Ruawaro so that they might once more inspect the various premises in the light of the evidence they had heard.

At last, on Saturday, came the final scenes. The judge's summing-up occupied some two hours. Immediately afterwards the jury retired. They were absent for 71 minutes and when they came back all saw that Bayly's fate was sealed. They brought in a verdict of Guilty, and sentence was at once passed.

William Alfred Bayly was executed at Mount Eden Goal,

Auckland, on July 20, 1934, a few days after his twenty-eighth birthday.

Thus ended one of the most remarkable criminal cases on record.

Leaving now the realms of fact for those of speculation, let us for a moment look at Bayly's plan. Considering it as we would the plot of a novel, and apart from all questions of morals or humanity, let us ask ourselves: How far, as a plan, was it deserving of success? Was it wrecked by accidents which could not have been foreseen or was it inherently defective? If Bayly had had more luck, or taken other precautions, would it have succeeded?

Its ingenuity cannot be denied. To make the murder of Mrs. Lakey and Lakey appear as the murder of Mrs. Lakey by Lakey was a scheme of a brilliancy approaching genius. In general the method by which Bayly tried to carry it out seems also flawless. Mrs. Lakey was murdered in the kind of way which Lakey might have probably enough employed, and no attempt was made to hide the crime. An attempt was admittedly made to delay its discovery, but this was strictly in accordance with what Lakey would have done were he guilty. Evidence that Lakey had left the district was supplied. He would never have done so in his working clothes. Therefore his good suit and boots were removed. The overwhelming argument for his having so left was not, however, one of clothes or boots. If he had not gone his body would remain. Therefore the body must be destroyed. Hiding it would not do; it might be found. It must be annihilated. And this to all intents and purposes was done.

That Bayly failed in his purpose was apparently not due to any defect in his plan. If its execution had been as good as its conception, he should certainly have succeeded. But its execution was faulty. He came down on details.

He made the mistake of taking Gilmour's boots instead of Lakey's. He made the mistake of leaving the cattle in their night paddock instead of getting them down to the shed. He went wrong in placing the cream cans too far back on the mound at the side of the road. He erred in taking his sledge on to soft ground near the boundary, instead of carrying the body to the road. He overlooked returning the wheels to their former resting-place. He failed to shave off all the bloodstains from the timber and to destroy the edge of his knife and resharpen it. He burnt the rubber boots, thus creating a black smoke. And so with several other small mistakes of detail.

It is interesting, if perhaps unprofitable, to ask whether he could have avoided these mistakes? In my opinion, for what it is worth, he could not. Or rather, if he had avoided these, he would have made others just as serious.

He obviously did not know about Gilmour's boots. He did not know, or had forgotten, about the placing of the cream cans. It is very unlikely that he would have had time to deal with the cows. Apart from this, an attempt to do so might have landed him into greater trouble. He might have been seen driving them down. If he hadn't milked them in the shed—which he could not possibly have done—they might have lowed and attracted attention. If he had carried the body to his road instead of putting it on his sledge, his clothes would probably have been much more stained with blood than they were. Perhaps a trail of blood would have been dropped on the ground. Probably, even if he had returned the wheels, the bloodstains on the wood and the tracks on the grass would still have been discovered.

Personally I do not believe it possible for anyone to carry through a complicated crime, as this was bound to be, without leaving traces which could be picked up by careful detectives. It is the simple crimes which are hard to detect. Bayly committed many errors. Probably any one of them alone would have hanged him.

It is interesting also to notice, in spite of what certain critics say, that real crimes do not make good detective stories. In this case the very first discovery of the detectives—the finding of the blood on the wheels and sledge—pointed clearly to the criminal. In a novel such an indication should involve someone other than the criminal, or if it indicated the criminal it should not be given until the last chapter. In real cases there can seldom be the 'twist' or surprise at the end so beloved of publishers, editors and readers.

Stories of real crimes move their readers because of the human element, which is usually much more predominant than in an invented puzzle. Conversely, as puzzles, real life stories are left far behind. And there is another difference. Real life stories have an atmosphere of sordidness and evil which is happily absent from almost all detective novels.

NOTE.—The Author acknowledges his indebtedness for information to the files of the *New Zealand Herald*, and to Mr. J. Halket Millar's admirable book *The Bayly Murder Case*, published by Messrs. Gordon & Gotch (Aust.) Ltd. The latter is recommended to those desiring a more complete description of the case.